THE
GENESIS
OF
MISERY

BOOKS BY NEON YANG

NEON YANG

THE GENESIS OF MISERY

TOR

A TOM DOHERTY ASSOCIATES BOOK
NEW YORK

402 5492

This is a work of fiction. All of the characters, organizations, and events portrayed in this novel are either products of the author's imagination or are used fictitiously.

THE GENESIS OF MISERY

A Tor Book
Published by Tom Doherty Associates
120 Broadway
New York, NY 10271

www.tor-forge.com

Tor® is a registered trademark of Macmillan Publishing Group, LLC.

Library of Congress Cataloging-in-Publication Data

Names: Yang, Neon, author.
Title: The genesis of misery / Neon Yang.
Description: First Edition. | New York : Tor, a Tom Doherty Associates
  Book, 2022.
Identifiers: LCCN 2022008291 (print) | LCCN 2022008292 (ebook) |
  ISBN 9781250788979 (hardcover) | ISBN 9781250788986 (ebook)
Classification: LCC PR9570.S53 Y264 2022 (print) | LCC PR9570.S53
  (ebook) | DDC 823/.92—dc23
LC record available at https://lccn.loc.gov/2022008291
LC ebook record available at https://lccn.loc.gov/2022008292

Our books may be purchased in bulk for promotional, educational, or
business use. Please contact your local bookseller or the Macmillan Corporate and
Premium Sales Department at 1-800-221-7945, extension 5442, or by email at
MacmillanSpecialMarkets@macmillan.com.

First Edition: 2022

Printed in the United States of America

0 9 8 7 6 5 4 3 2 1

FOR MY FELLOW EVA COPILOTS.

THE ROBOT AWAITS.

THE
GENESIS
OF
MISERY

PROLOGUE

If we are to begin, we might as well start with the desert. If we are to chart a path through what happened, if we are to make sense of anything at all, we might as well start in this place that has no name, this arena where time has no meaning. We might as well start with the two strangers who traverse its ersatz distances, full of questions about one another and the things that have brought them here. Here, a story waits to be excavated, waits to be spoken into truth.

This is the story.

In the desert, a high wind grieves over orange dunes, pluming dust in its wake. It makes instrument of the broken fingers of holystone separating land and sky. A single jaundiced sun sinks toward the horizon warped by heat, the kind that dries the back of the throat and makes speech impossible. With its intensity, this light would blind human eyes, if there were human eyes to squint into it.

Heat, air, light. Remarkable detail birthed from a great swathe of nothingness. The lifeless desert represents an ending, but it is also a beginning, and everything else in between.

The silhouettes of the strangers cut through this emptiness, narrow against the searing sky. Dwarfed by the element-blasted landscape, they appear startlingly comprehensible, if not entirely mortal. The two leisurely cross the gaps in the bent stone littering the landscape, strolling past facsimiles of ancient wrecks that might have once been warships or constructor mechs. One of the figures is human-shaped. The other cycles through a variety of forms: now a ball of flame louder than suns, now an enormous winged insect, now a spacecraft escaping a gravity well.

"What I want to know," says the human-shaped one, who goes by he/him pronouns, "is how much of it was known. How much of it could have been prevented, and how much of it was ordained."

His companion, who does not care for pronouns at all, takes the form of a dozen burning rings with a hundred unblinking eyes. "You wish to pick apart the braids of cause and consequence, then? To untangle the threads that make up this timeline?"

The human one tilts his head. "Perhaps I should express myself more clearly. I care little for philosophies. What I want to know is the *story*. Not just an assembled sequence of events, but the *hows* and the *whys* that shaped the flow of events we went through."

His companion flares into the shape of a hydrogen molecule for a brief second, before collapsing into a swarm of locusts. "A story, you say? A lofty ask, to distill the uncountable and unnameable essences that create all of reality into something digestible, with cause and effect, beginning and end. A moral, when all is said and done. You wish to bottle chaos and entropy like a cheap salve."

"Not *all* of it." The one like a man—narrow, fine-featured, eyes reflexively squinting in sunlight that has no effect on him—frowns. "What is this talk of chaos? My request is simple. I'm not asking for the answer to life, the universe, and everything. Tell me what happened in this messy, sorry affair. From top to toe. That's all. Tell me the story of Misery Nomaki."

"The story of Misery Nomaki," says the other figure, now a tower of flame striding across the landscape, peer to the broken holystone that frames them. "You fancy me a storyteller, do you? A sayer of sooths, a vessel of revelation? As if their story were mine to tell?"

"I merely have questions I want answered," says the first. Frustration seeps into the cool syllables of his words; noticing this, he calms himself, refusing to be baited. "No, to say that I have questions is an understatement of my feelings on the matter. But that is beside the point. You, my friend. You with your all-seeing eyes—you must have had a view of the events that no one else, not even the most observant mortal, did. Am I wrong?"

"In that, at least, you are not."

"That's what I thought," says the one who is a man. "Listen, I know that I have no power over you, and you have no obligation toward me. But I beg of you. If you cannot tell me what happened in a manner I can understand—if you cannot translate your understanding into something mortals can grasp, then at least show me what you've collected on your journey. You said the tale of Misery Nomaki was not yours to tell, but surely you can let me see what happened? From their point of view?"

His companion now sports four faces, human and beast, and each bears a frown. "Show, not tell. Do you imagine that the two are really so different? After all, showing is telling, and telling is showing—don't you agree? I can *show* you what you desire, but how will you judge the nature of the story it *tells*?"

"Forge in the void, you are nothing but questions, aren't you? Please. That one is best left for later, when I have understanding. Now, will you show me what you know? Please?"

The other resolves into a form that is startlingly human: pale, dark-haired, all long and narrow limbs. Eyes that glow, like opal. "A foolish statement. I *know* very little. After all this, and you still lack that fundamental. But no matter. You want to see what has gone before, and that I can show you. The story of Misery Nomaki, Last Savior of the Faithful, as experienced by Misery Nomaki, Last Savior of the Faithful." Zie presses a pair of spindly fingers upon the other's forehead. "Come then, friend. Open your mind. See as I saw. See as they saw."

PART ONE

THE CAPITAL

1

But really, where do we begin? Do we imagine that the story of a person begins when zie is born? Or do we acknowledge that each one of us is the creation of a dozen forces, bearing down upon the clay of a being with all the weight of history? The threads that make up Misery Nomaki began in the distant past, not as fixed points but electron clouds, diffuse and undefinable, woven through the tapestry of human history in ways that are difficult to put into words or comprehend. Shall we start with the Old Planet, whose name has been forgotten, and swim the warm oceans as life begins to coalesce? Should we walk alongside the parade of creatures as they unfurl into human form, and watch as these shabby beings stumble toward the ruination of their planet? Perhaps a better opening would be the shoal of vessels that fled their burning home, each stocked carefully with a collection of individuals that has been deemed suitable to represent the future of humanity. Here we see the one christened *The Cause of Labour* streaking away into the dark, embarking upon its ten-thousand-year journey across the stars. Into long sleeps and uncharted territories and the ALISS Apocalypse and all that followed after.

But maybe that is too much. Too wide. It would take too long to tell all of it. Let us work at a scale comprehensible to human minds. You may think that means starting at the conception of our Messiah. But that holds little interest for me: Are we not programmed to want the exciting parts right away? Since you have mandated me as storyteller, I shall choose where we begin as it suits my fancy. Let us start at the center of the

Empire of the Faithful, not too long before our current point in time. There is a ship, coming through a portal. Its name is *Wolf at the Door.* A narrow blade of a thing, half metal and half holystone, polished to reflect starlight. It arrives around midday standard universal time, nestled in a loose flotilla of travelers from the duchy of Apis. This ship belongs to the seventeenth Duke of Apis, Lord Bichap Amran Argan, he/him pronouns, and it is his personal ship, part pleasure cruiser and part diplomatic vessel. Its destination is the Imperial Capital, a gloriously jeweled confabulation of structures: domes and arches and turrets fused into a floating shape, thick in the center and tapering to glittering minarets at either pole. A colony suspended in an inky sea, filled with nobility and scientists and magnates of industry. A locus of power, in fact *the* locus of power in the Empire of the Faithful, to which those seeking power are also drawn. This is what *The Cause of Labour* has become, hundreds of years after its engines were stilled. The body of the original ship lies at the core of the Capital as a seed lies in a fruit. You are familiar with this, I do believe. Yet that fact is often obscured in the books of the Faithful. I wonder how many know?

Wolf at the Door, then. It has come to the Capital for a very specific purpose. It carries in its decks the nixen believed to be the Last Savior of the Faithful, who not a week prior had saved a far-flung colony from annihilation by the Heretics. Or so it was said. Misery Nomaki, they/she pronouns, newly twenty and newly thrust into a world they have no understanding of, a world so far removed from their upbringing it might as well be a different society altogether. Brought to the Imperial Capital at behest of the Church, to seek an audience with a skeptical Emperor. A herald of trouble, this Misery Nomaki. Into the pretty, fragile shells of empire they come like a wrecking ball. Let us make a beginning here, where there is none.

-¦-

In a steel-walled room encysted in the Capital's guts, the Last Savior of the Faithful is trying to turn a door to jelly. Misery Nomaki, chosen of the Forge, presses herself against the flat glossy surface, cold as dead marble, and says, "Come the fuck on."

The door is holystone. It whispers to her with the electric, back-of-the-neck prickle that holystone always has. She's never seen this sort before—a pale gray streaked with white, only pretty because it shines—and she's always wary of strange holystone. No fucking idea what it's called. No fucking idea what it does. But ten minutes ago she watched the flint of its striped surface turn gelatinous and admit a young saint bearing a crate of dinner, breaking open and sliding over hir like liquid. Of course. That's how she got in this box to begin with. The salve they put in her is still flossing her mind, muddying emotion and memory. Smearing adrenaline into a soggy mush of apathy. It's hard to think, when the salves get her like this. If she had known, she would never have accepted the dose. But then, she's been saying yes to a lot of shit she shouldn't lately.

She doesn't know what's on the other side of this door. Guards, probably. Trouble. More trouble than what she's stewing in right now. But anything's better than sitting on her ass and waiting for the Emperor, or whoever, to pass judgment down. She didn't sign up for any of this, and she certainly didn't sign up to be thrown in a cell with zero cause upon arrival in the Imperial Capital. Misery has no idea where her sponsor, the Duke, is right now. For all she knows he's in a lockbox too. And whatever's coming next, if she waits for it, is probably worse than what it is right now.

It's better to find your own trouble than to have trouble come find you.

Misery closes her eyes to focus better. There's a familiar twinge she's looking for, a fire in her nerves that tells her when she's woken the holystone. These rocks are full of surprises, tricksy bastards: some invert gravity, some power the hearts of starships, yet others can destroy everything in their path. This holystone is ostensibly a doorway, but who knows what configurations lurk in its lightless depths? Won't be the first time Misery wakes some voidtouched ability in holystone that's brand-new.

"I wouldn't do that, if I were you."

Slouched against the door is a delusion in human shape. A youth with every trapping of a classical softlad, milk-fleshed and bird-boned, icy bangs framing a high brow and jutting cheeks. And hir eyes! Cosmic presence radiates from the hollow of those sockets; sometimes they go bright as suns, sometimes they fall dark as the void between stars. Zie's dressed in the kind of loose, off-shoulder blanket dress worn by angels in art from the sourceworld, ending above the knee and displaying a generous swathe of skin and nipple. Unreadable symbols crawl over one bare shoulder, fluid and sinuous.

This delusion, zie claims a name. *Ruin.* No known pronouns. Bane of Misery's life. Absolute bane. Showed up bright and inescapable a couple of weeks ago, all beautiful and haloed, claiming a grand destiny for her, just like her dead mother promised. Break into the local defensive base, zie said. Steal a sparrowhawk unit and take off with it, zie said. Fight the Heretics lurking over the nowhere nothing mining colony you call home, zie said. It is what the Larex Forge calls you to. And because Misery's stupid, because she's got void where a brain should be, because it was her birthday and also Mother's death anniversary and she was completely smashed on dirty salves, because she was still pissed at her older brother for some bullshit he said, because of all that Misery said fuck it and did as Ruin suggested. Even though she knew better. Even though she should have recognized Ruin for the delusion zie is. Even though she knew the consequences of not resisting the voidsickness that generated the delusion.

She did it anyway, and so here she is, a prisoner halfway across the galaxy on the Capital at the center of it all, trapped with an advanced outgrowth of the voidmadness she was born with. Took twenty years to show up, but she's finally full-on hallucinating the way Mother used to, arguing with shades like old family members. Good job, Misery. Everything going cherries and honey.

Ruin slants hir head in curiosity. "You wanted off Rootsdown. You wanted to leave home for shinier pastures. I did that for you. Did I not?"

"If I wanted to be imprisoned on the Imperial Capital, I would have found better ways," Misery snaps. She can't hear the holystone through all this nagging. Can't believe she sat through thousands of hours of sermon and not one second of it covered getting a faux-aspect of the universal force to *shut the fuck up*.

"Tell me again," says Ruin, clearly with the least inclination in the void to shut the fuck up. "What good would escaping this room do? Where do you imagine you will go?"

"Somewhere not here," Misery says, and stills herself because a thread has come loose in the holystone, brushing against her senses like a questing finger. She can deal with Ruin later—freedom awaits. Breath held, she tugs upon the offered filament. Shuts her eyes, shuts out the rest of the universe. Her existence is stone and stone only. Beneath her, the essence of the strange mineral slowly unravels, loosening its grip on the divine gift that separates it from mere rock. The holystone melts, and Misery melts along with it, her body turning to jelly, bones and skin and all. She has no body; that brick of flesh right now has no owner. She is the stone, and the stone is she.

The holystone activates and Misery falls through it, plowing through gel thicker than her head, finding nothing but air on the other side. She tumbles onto her hands and knees, walloped back into her body with an angry smack that shoots up the bone. The epitome of grace, Mx. Misery Nomaki. She swears a little, because she has the mouth for it now. After thousands of melds with holystone, Misery still gets rustled by the out-of-body transitions every time.

Ruin stands in the middle of the outside passageway, arms folded, brows knitted, lips thin. Zie doesn't need to walk, blinking in and out of places like a photon, and Misery could wring hir neck for it. *Can* one strangle a delusion? Misery hasn't yet managed to lay a hand on Ruin: zie moves too fast, flitting out of reach every times she gets close. Of course.

Zie says, "Turn back. Return to the room you were in."

"Not a room. A cell. And you can't tell me what to do. You're not my brother."

"You will regret continuing upon this path."

"Great, add it to my regrets pile." She dusts herself off and takes stock. She's made it out—good. She hasn't set off a siren—even better. Some time to think.

Inside the cell it was gray and metal and frigid. Outside it's still metal and frigid, but at least there's light. Misery's at the tail end of a nitro-white corridor, sleek reflective panels rimmed by light at the edges of floor and ceiling. It curves away from her and beyond the line of sight. No vents along these pristine surfaces. No ducts. Hidden, probably. This is deep space, the station's got to have a circ system somewhere. That oxygen isn't going to make itself. It's her best hope, hiding in those veins while she figures her way around and out: she's not armed, this is unfamiliar ground, and the Imperial Army won't go light on her. A head-on confrontation would mean death.

What's the plan? Find the deep vents, find a place to hide. Get to a safely crowded area—civilian dock, merchant zone, whatever, wherever they on- and off-load ship crews. Find a leaving captain willing to take her on, or sneak into a hospitable cargo hold. Get out, at any rate. Anywhere in the galaxy would make a fine landing. How many years has she got left, fifteen, twenty? Possibly less. Lots less. Mother wasn't forty when she died, and Misery—she's twenty, and the delusions have started showing up. It's only a matter of time. Maybe ten. Maybe five. It's fine. Enough time to drink in the stars, enough space to knock out a few adventures like Mother used to tell her. She's not interested in being anybody's savior.

There's only one way forward. Misery pads along the curve of the corridor, left hand against the cool white, feeling for openings. Half her senses pricked for danger and the other half for holystone. She can't tell if it's the salves, but her stone-sense is fizzing sideways, like cremoline left uncapped too long. Her ears ring like the aftermath of a night with no sleep. There must be stone everywhere, the guts of the station riddled with it, shredding her focus in a million different directions. On Rootsdown, arid and barren, people lived a hundred to each clay reef and holystone sang across the landscape purer and clearer than church bells. Misery knew where every vein of the glistening stuff lay, and it was good business too, charging millions for prospecting services, dragging it out with surprise delays, invoicing for equipment she didn't need and never bought. Good times. She's got to find some like hustle once she escapes.

At the end of the curve, the corridor takes a sharp left into unseen territory, and she creeps toward it with full caution. It's unsettling how empty this place is, compared to the squalor of Rootsdown and the lively crew of the Duke's ship. Feels like a trap. Might be a trap.

Ruin materializes before her. "You had a window for turning back. That is now over." But zie doesn't seem alarmed. Zie seems amused.

She hears the footsteps before she sees them. Two saints, hair shimmering, gender unknown, burst through the mirage of Ruin's chest and stop, blinking. One of them? Both? One was the saint that brought her dinner. But which one? They look identical. Dress identical. White hair and white skin and white robes with crisp lines that boat over their figures. Twins?

No. Not twins. Can't be. She's seen more saints dressed like this: on her way in, dotted on walkways at a distance. Even then she thought there was something eerie about the way they were all the same shape and height, same hair color, same haircut. Were they all instaprints, like this? Clones? That couldn't be. Revulsion heaves through her flesh.

The saints don't blink.

"Hello," she says. "Nice day out."

Silence. No emotion surfaces on their perfect, mirrored features. What *are* they? Stillness in these situations means danger. The one on the left, calm as a mountain, tilts hir head like a wild grimclaw before it lunges.

Misery moves faster. A practiced swing connects with the unnatural saint's ear, and zie goes flying into the other one. *Crash.* Things are so light here. Misery vaults over them to flee left and down the corridor, straight and double-wide, intersections at a distance that's rapidly closing. She's built like a shuttle, squat and boxy, all muscle and adrenaline, and she's never been more grateful. Rootsdown was a supergrav settlement, and the Capital is just slightly subgrav (or so she's been told). She's flying. She's never run this fast or this effortlessly in her life.

"If you want to help," she spits at Ruin, who hovers at the periphery of her sprint, "a way out would be nice." Nearly upon the crossroads. She needs directions, and her gut's always been good, so—

"Go up," zie says, a voice in both ears, and she goes, "What?" but she's already looking to the ceiling, and realizing that the paneling is finely gapped, it's not a solid piece, and she doesn't know what's beyond it but what's to lose?

She makes a fist of her nondominant hand and rockets upward. Forces her eyes to stay open as knuckle strikes acrylic and pain shoots up her arm. She sails in an arc into a half-height space, claustrophobic, silver, and she's tumbling head-over-ass into it, tangoing with the panel she's knocked loose. The vents. Misery keeps moving forward. No time to think. Plunge into darkness. She doesn't need light to see. Around her the Capital thrums and keens with lodes of holystone, pinging on Misery's consciousness, forming a makeshift map to navigate by. The huge, beating chunk of holy ruby in the distance: stonecore. Best stay away from that. Other direction.

Those saints. If they're clones, what does that mean? Cloning is forbidden. Human clones are empty vessels, invitations to the nullvoid. Is that common on the Capital? What else have they made? Telepaths? Chimeras? AI?

She's letting fear run amok. Not paying attention. Suddenly there's air where floor should be. Misery screams as she drops stomach-first into the void, then her jaw slams into metal and pain shuts her up. Fuck. Fuck fuck fuck fuck. Pain, something crunching, death waiting? She flails, grasps for holy tigereye to stop her fall, misses, falls some more. Fuck.

Light comes from below. Forge blast, if it's just air—or some deadly whirring fan—

A crunch. She slams against something—metal mesh—and it pops loose. A tumble and she lands, hip and elbow flaring with pain. Some kind of metal surface, gridded for friction. Industrial. Grit-smelling. Misery sucks in greasy air and her ribs scream, angry, but she's felt worse. Gets on palms and knees, all her bones hold. A loud complaint along the tendon as she finds her feet, but she's fine. She's standing. She can walk.

Where is she now? A massive chamber greets her, wider and taller than a reef, curved hullmetal walls so distant they form a horizon. The walkway rings the room, and below that an open pit pregnant with massive gray cylinders, fed by and wrapped in pipes. Has to be some kind of circ chamber, because it's mostly empty space, drop lights fixed to the ceiling far abovehead. The sense of breath—hot and cool winds blowing over her skin— seems to confirm it. And over there: bright purple rectangle over a recessed door. Universal exit sign. Misery collects her breath, gives thanks for her continued existence, and gathers her determination. Let's go.

Several steps away from the exit she halts. Next to the door, under the cone of a portlight, stand four figures in atmo-blue jumpsuits. Staring.

"Hey," she says, propping a hand on one jaunty hip. She's close enough to see their faces, close enough to see they've got no name/pronoun tags on, close enough to see they've obviously got a game of rumsake going atop the silver crate that's upturned between them. Skivers? On a break? Workers, at any rate—people on her side. Two taller ones, a third built like Misery, and the last one skinny and feral as a hungry rat. She tries a smile. "I'm just passing by."

They don't mean her any harm. She can see that in their faces. No aggression here, just bafflement, tentative curiosity, and a hope that she's not gonna mess up their leisure time. She holds both hands up, tender palms outward. "I'm not here for trouble. In fact, just pretend I'm not here at all."

One of the tall ones says, "You look like you're in trouble."

The skinny one says, "Your face got fucked up."

And the one who's built like her, the one who seems warmest of them all, points to hir face and says, "You're bleeding. Are you okay?"

Misery widens her lopsided grin, and the crust of blood on her cheek makes itself known in a wave of small prickles. "Don't mind that. Just ran into a sharp edge. You know?"

Frowns and uncertainty in response. The workers' Standard is strongly accented and so unlike the crisp phonemes that dominate the waves, but she doesn't recognize the locality. Nothing like the Apisian lilts she's used to. None of the four are saints; their hair lacks that telltale sheen. What would a saint be doing as an hourly wage-grunt in the bowels of a space station, anyway? Misery doesn't want them to get involved either. It wouldn't be fair. "Just let me on my way. You never saw me." She points to the exit. "I'm headed right out."

The hungry-looking one curls hir lip and snorts. "That door's locked. There's no key."

Ruin slants against the offending exit, arms folded. "That's never been a problem for you, has it?"

Misery smiles to mask a range of emotions. Ruin is right, but she'd rather the workers not know that. "It's fine," she says. "I have a key."

"There's no key," the hungry one repeats, like Misery is an idiot.

The door in question is rimmed by holy obsidian, the aegis stone, projecting a film of impassable energy, invisible until touched. Misery's fingertips leave starpoints of light as she brushes against the aegis: old habit, she likes the thrill of static she gets from it. A lively prickle.

"Please," Misery says. "Look the other way. You don't want to get involved." There are things they would be better off not knowing. But she knows she can't force them not to watch.

Misery's done holy obsidian so many times she doesn't need physical contact anymore. Important buildings in Rootsdown were lousy with the stuff, and she's sneaked in and out of them a hundred times, a thousand times, a hundred thousand times. She shuts her eyes and breathes until her pores are one with the stone. Palms that invisible, intangible switch.

The aegis turns off. A handle's set into the thick metal of the door beneath, and Misery digs in her heels to haul it leftward. Lemon squeezy. Thank the Forge for supergrav physique.

"How did you do that?"

Ah, right. Misery sighs before she turns around. The four workers are bugging with fear, the deeply held and religious kind. The other tall one, who hasn't spoken yet, says: "How? You're not a saint."

There are two kinds of people who can move stone. There are the saints. And then there are the voidmad. One look at Misery and they can tell which one she is.

"It's not contagious," she tells them, which is pointless because it contradicts Church teaching, and *You won't catch it* sounds like something someone with voidsickness would say. The stout one has withdrawn behind the others, hands clasped in prayer. The others are frozen in place, but Misery can see fear breaking the bar on their faces. Shit. She can't blame them, but *shit*.

"Just forget I was even here," she says, and slips through

the door to close off her guilt. Forge willing, the workers will
forget the encounter and go on with their lives, but she knows
they're going to spend the next Imperial week (or month, year,
decade) jumping at lights and sounds, wondering if something
they *thought* they heard is the beginning of the end. Anything
and everything could be the first sign of madness. She knows
that feeling too well.

Ruin's voice whispers in her head. "Fortunately for them, you
aren't voidmad. And in time they'll come to recognize today as
a blessing. A day where they were graced by the presence of one
touched by the Larex Forge."

"Shut up," Misery says. Now's not the time. She rubs her face
and pushes every tab of anxiety and regret deep into the primordial cauldron of her emotions where they belong, far away and
out of her conscious mind. These workers will be nothing to her
once she's made her flight from here. In a few years—if she's still
alive—this will all be dust in the wind. A misadventure, getting
involved with dukes and the Throne and the Church, places she
doesn't belong, but quickly done with.

For now: Shut up. Focus. Escape. She's wound up in a service corridor, a grimly lit and humming affair, bank of indecipherable controls to the left and row of supply closets to the
right. Locked, of course, but that doesn't stop her from riffling
through till she finds a stack of spare jumpsuits in taffy one-
size automesh in that same atmo-blue. Misery pulls off her gray
convict's robe and cocoons herself in a jumpsuit. It takes several
seconds to adhere to her body heat. What should she do with
the discard? Is there no atomizer nearby? Why are the Faithful allergic to labeling anything on this, their capital city? She's
looking for the holy ruby that would make the heart of the atomizer, but there's so much background signal.

Ruin points to a recessed square in the left wall, which Misery
had taken for a drawer. Fine. There it is. She jaws it open, dumps
in the gray robe, and goes back for a fresh raid on the closets. Boots this time, sturdy ones with reinforced soles, vacuum-

proof. Gloves. A bunch of toolkits, because she needs shit to trade for credit. A medpack to fix her bleeding face. She even finds a cap to tuck the wild bush of her unsaintly hair under.

There. She's all kitted out in generics. The only thing separating her from a regular drone, she guesses, is the bracelet around her wrist—holy jasper, irresistibly striated, lifeblood of Rootsdown. A dear friend, now deceased, made it. Then there's her mother's amulet around her neck. A circle of strange black rock on a string—maybe holystone? Maybe not?—covered in even stranger inscriptions, almost like circuitry. She's had it since before she was born. Neither ornament will tuck into the jumpsuit. Whatever. Misery will never lose the two; it's nonnegotiable. She will deal. Otherwise, she's ready.

The corridor's capped by a silver door, rimmed with holy obsidian and graced with a porthole from which light pours. It's the outside, which glimmers and beckons like an astral promise. Misery marches toward it, practicing her confident stride. Confidence is key.

She puts her hand on the stone, and pauses to take a steadying breath. Four in, six hold, seven out. Beyond this door lies the Empire, unvarnished and real, full of places and things she has only experienced through the medium of waves and bulletins and old miners' tales. She doesn't know what to expect. She doesn't know what she'll find.

"Have faith," says the delusion, uselessly. "No matter how far you stray from your destined path, you will find yourself guided back to it."

Fuck faith. Misery's in it to survive. And survive she will.

She shuts off the holy obsidian, and steps outside.

2

The Capital announces itself—finally, properly—with an abundance of air and light. Misery is tiny in its bosom, an atomic speck. Deadmarble columns hold up a glass dome that closes hundreds of meters overhead; beyond it is the yet larger containment of the station. The domain of the Larex Forge is infinite and incomprehensible to mortal minds, and a good chunk of it is here, in this center of human civilization. A wide plaza gleams before Misery, polished surfaces bright with the butter of a flasklight swarm, which hovers lazily over the bustling, shimmering heads of saints and dignitaries. Holy opal (light) with a holy tigereye (antigrav) core. A glorious waste of stone for a bunch of decorative elements. At regular intervals, small trees, white-leafed and white-skinned, thrust out of manicured dirt patches, and water threads the length of the open space. The air is dirtless, and greaseless, and laced with florals.

This is it. This is the place where it all happens. Misery has entered the heart of the Empire, the center that holds all the Faithful together, the seat of Church and Throne tasked with keeping the cosmos safe from the Heretics and the nullvoid. She breathes the sweet air and watches the droves of crisply dressed dignitaries mill through the lobby. They all look smooth-skinned, with clean hair and nails. If they have worries, those worries don't reach their faces.

Misery finds herself both overwhelmed by the spectacle and disappointed at the same time. This ceasefire the Empire's had with the Heretics has been on for quite some time. The Truce of Logan happened before she was old enough to pay attention

to the news. And yet the texture of her life has always been in-
fused with the fear of war breaking out again. She expected that
fear to bear more weight in the Capital. She expected an air of
urgency. A feeling that things aren't right with the wider world.
But she's not getting the vibe.

"You're gawking," Ruin observes.

Nonsense. Misery strides forward to prove it. She's not overwhelmed or overawed.

This atrium has to be some kind of lobby. There's an information counter, presumably, curved and silver; across from it,
separated by a thousand measures of creamy deadmarble, sit
enormous doors obnoxiously worked in gold. Parked on either
side are those creepy white saints with their diamond-shine hair.
The saints turn their heads in unison to look at her, as though
they can read her thoughts. Revulsion clogs her lungs and
stomach.

They're identical. All of them. The ones here and the ones
she knocked over while escaping. They have to be clones, there's
no other explanation. What voidtouched business goes on in the
Capital?

"Custom-grown saints," Ruin says. "Made-to-order servants
of the Capital, bred for a singular purpose. You should get used
to them; they're all over."

Of course the delusion would voice the worst fears in the
depths of her soul. Still, her spine chills and sends cold water
running down the fibers of her arms and thighs. The white
saints don't speak. Do they have names? Do they *think*? Are
they walking around with no thoughts and emotions of their
own? Are they all void inside? Nausea washes over her.

"This is the ambassadorial quarter," Ruin says, like a fucking
tour guide, completely unconcerned by her disgust and anxiety.
"One reef for every duchy, where the ducal staff and ambassadorial attachés work and live. By the Demiurge's Grace, of course,
you've found yourself in the Apisian embassy. Home away from
home, as it were."

Shit. Is this where Duke Argan lives when he's on Imperial business? Will she be recognized? Misery ducks a pair of quietly conversing dignitaries, who pay her no mind, and considers the doors with the white saints. Not them. Bad mojo. She wonders if there's another way out of here.

"There is not," Ruin says.

Shut up, what does the delusion know anyway? Misery makes a sharp left for the information desk. She'll take a guide who doesn't irritate the living shit out of her, thanks.

Behind the warmly lit silver curve is an inattentive lad: tag reads Bear Foltzer, he/him pronouns. Glossy-haired and bored in his starchy trim. Unlike the white-robed Capital workers ghosting through the lobby, he isn't a saint, and a measure of tension instantly eases from Misery as she approaches him. Something familiar at last. "Hey," she says, in Apisian.

Bear Foltzer's listless demeanor cracks with a grin at the familiar syllables. "Yo. What's up?"

His accent is crisp and free of provinciality; Duke Argan speaks like this as well. A transplant from the center of the duchy, then. "Listen," she says, leaning on the cool silver counter, "I'm new here. Just got in with the flotilla this morning." Fudging the timeline a little. "I need some directions."

"Okay. Where are you headed?"

"The trading docks."

He frowns, confused. Not called the trading docks, then. "Thing is, I left some stuff on the transport, things with a lot of sentimental value, from home, you know, things I really don't want to lose. I need to catch the captain before they move on." She scratches behind her ear, plays up the lilt of her accent. "I'd trace my steps back, but I got in the weeds, there's so much station . . ."

"Are you looking for the transit jetties?"

"Yes. That. Sorry."

A nod of understanding. "It's a bit of a journey. We're on the other end of the Capital. But don't worry, there's transport, and it's free. Here, let me show you." He moves his wrist, encircled with a silver band, toward Misery's ear.

"Whoa." Misery draws back. "What's that?"

Momentary surprise melts into understanding, and a prying curiosity. "You don't have an implant?"

"No," she says. "I'm from Rootsdown."

His returning frown exposes that he's vaguely heard the name, but isn't sure where that is. "It's an outer colony," she says. "The Black Hole Moon? Stonemining colony?"

"Ah." Curiosity manifests as a hunger: *Tell me what it's like living in a true shithole.* "You really are fresh from the gates, huh?"

Hunger looks ugly on Bear Foltzer. Misery sees the shape of his life laid out before her: a bright-eyed boy hoping to make a piece of himself at the center of all things, all excited by the prospect of glamour and in denial about his obvious place in the world. He thinks he's better than her, more worldly.

People are so easy to read once you study them.

Still, she plays nice. "It's my first time offplanet. Never knew a space station could get so big." Which isn't a lie.

He smiles, and his hunger shapeshifts. It's not exactly predatory, but it's become an eager, almost hopeful, sniffing. Misery is too practiced to roll her eyes, but she is tired by how predictable people are. "I know how it gets," Bear Foltzer says. "Hang on." A few seconds riffling under the counter and he reemerges with a thin bronze cylinder between his fingers. "We have physical maps. Some sects won't get implants, for belief reasons." He twists the cylinder and it wakes, projecting a fist-sized miniature of the Capital, perfectly rendered, glowing as it rotates. "Do you know how to use this?"

"I do." She quickly lifts it from him as he turns it off, because she saw a hint that he was about to grab her hand as she reached for it. "Thank you, this will be very useful."

"No problem." He smiles again. "And listen, if you need a primer on station life, or just a friendly face to talk to, you can

come find me. My shift ends in six hours. I'll be at Eclipse, it's a
bar located in Sector Five-Delta, in the Libra quarter. The map
will tell you."

"Sure." She thinks that he might be a nice person under it all,
but she's not sticking around to find out.

"Wait." He calls after her as she begins to turn away. "I didn't
get your name."

"Silver Tatucha," she says, borrowing the name of a childhood friend who has since returned to the arms of the Forge.
Better to settle his mind than to leave him wondering. She believes in those things.

Between the reception counter and the doors Misery fusses
with the map, working its controls to highlight the transit jetties.
Shit. Bear Foltzer was right about the distance. And transport
will be monitored for sure, probably crawling with those void-
cursed saints. No way in the void she's getting on that. Dammit.
None of this is ideal. She'll have to go on foot, and pray for grace
and luck to tide her over, because skill alone won't be enough.
She's never faced an adversary like the Capital. There's something so, so wrong about this place. Rot in the center of Empire
she can't have imagined. She needs to get out. Fuck. Leave it all
behind.

The first hurdle is the door. And those void-shot saints. The
closer Misery gets, the more unsettling they become.

As she comes within shouting distance of the doors, the
frontmost pair of saints put their identical hands on the identical handles and pull the giant gleaming slabs inward. Air shudders in displacement, and a wall of cooler, flatter atmosphere
comes in. Beyond the doors are lights stretching to the horizon,
and Misery fixes her gaze on that great glittering expanse, head
held high, stride unwavering. Yet as she passes the gauntlet of
the twin saints, one of them on the left moves hir head, and
Misery's concentration breaks and she turns to look. Their eyes
meet for a second, long enough for her to notice the pale-gold
irises.

Zie blinks, and Misery looks away, heartbeat racing. Something had shifted minutely in the saint's expression when zie looked at Misery, as though zie recognized her. A bad feeling knuckles under her rib cage as she steps into the openness of the Capital and the doors swing shut behind her. She tries not to let it show, striding over the path of rough stone that unfolds before her. But she mouths a soft "fuck." She's got to move quickly.

The sooner out of this voidmaw, the better.

In the Capital, City of Eternal Starlight, night rules at all hours. The great bowl of stars shimmers over the ambassadorial quarter, a tiered oval lobe topped with acrylplex, where eighteen ziggurats form a curved row on the top tier. Eighteen embassies for the eighteen duchies. Hedge-lined gardens sprawl from the stoops of each one, and the droopy crowns of unknown trees line the horizon. The stone path takes Misery through the embassy's front garden, where shrubs burst with color and scent and flasklights hover between trees, pooling gold in the shadows. Everywhere she looks, there are more silent white saints: tending to garden machinery, chaperoning nobility in flowing capes, or simply standing around. Waiting. Every now and then one detaches from hir post and heads for destinations unknown. Ruin was right about their ubiquity. Her fingers tingle with unease.

Misery's brisk stride takes her to the edge of the ambassadorial tier, a border of woven metal and holy obsidian that projects an aegis so big and thin it's invisible. It's layers all the way down, cunningly overlapped so each one gets a sliver of starscape. A blaze of lights and activity marks the shops tier. Below it is a bank of contemplative silence, a brush of green. "Saint Ono's Park," Ruin offers.

She likes the potential of dark and overgrown corridors. Maybe it won't be crawling with cursed clones. On the map Saint Ono's Park stretches from her current location in the Venus quarter to the halfway point of the next (Sagittarius). It's a big chunk of the journey she needs to make. A good chunk. "Let's go," she says.

The Apisian embassy shares an elevator bank with two others. Between the walls of glass and glossy deadmarble stands a pair of dignitaries in Apisian colors, gossiping. Misery recognizes them the vague way one does celebrity: House of Banter and House of Ehi, minor nobility in the duchy. Saints, both of them, their sandy hair tinted with iridescence. The target of their opprobrium is another couple Misery can't place, likely nobility from another duchy, with a child in tow. The child, barely three or four, nestles in the arms of a silent white saint. Its parents chatter in a language Misery cannot parse—perhaps high Piscean—but she doesn't need to. Their faces tell everything. They're talking about the war, worried that the Heretics' sawing away at territorial borders, plus the new siege they've laid, is fraying the Truce of Logan to uselessness. The child sucks at its thumb, staring blankly, almost curiously at Misery.

The Apisians tut in their home dialect. "It's a travesty," sniffs the man (Banter Croquette, he/him). "Hiring a nanny like that to turn the child. Spitting in the face of the Larex Forge."

"Disgusting," adds the woman (Ehi Sodalite, she/her). "To think they would go to such lengths to *make* their child a saint, when the Demiurge didn't see fit to bestow them one."

Misery scans the family unit. None of them are saints. Is she hearing this right? The Apisians' convo implies that sainthood can be induced in children, which—that's not how it works, is it? Yet the pair seem sincere in their belief, for all Misery can tell.

Again, what are the nobility of the Capital up to?

The Apisian saints, perhaps catching on to her eavesdropping, have turned aside and continued their gossiping in lower tones. Misery stares at the bored child and its blank-eyed minder. The white-haired saint blinks like zie can read her thoughts. Goose static crawls across the surface of her arms.

A soft ping announces the arrival of an elevator. The couple, child, and saint are first into that clear pod, followed by the whispering Apisians. Misery backs off to wait for the next one.

She needs space to breathe. Couldn't be her, getting into a glass prison with a bunch of strangers and a potential abomination.

Thankfully, the replacement arrives empty, and Misery steps inside for a solo journey to the garden tier. Breathes in and out. It's ridiculous that she's afraid of these saints and what they represent when she's already voidmad enough to hallucinate. But things could always get worse. Oh, she knows how much worse they can get.

She studies her reflection superimposed on the glass as the layers of the Capital's mantle flash past her. Short-haired, broad-featured, one bold scar tracing a line between eye and lip. She looks at home in the blue slipsuit, which is just as well. All the better to blend in with. Back on *Wolf at the Door,* the Duke's personal ship, she was often mistaken for cleaning staff. The Duke had brought her on quietly; most of the crew didn't realize she was a guest, much less one meant to be exalted.

"Good on them," Misery says to her reflection. "They're smarter than their boss."

The glass doors open to a different world entirely. Saint Ono's Park bristles with huge-leafed palms and flower-laden bushes, and every few steps the air offers a new scent, fresh but unnameable. Misery pads carefully through the deliberate hush, trying to remain invisible. The rhythms of life linger at the periphery of her senses, light and sound from the busier, bustling tiers just filtering through. The Capital going about its business, unperturbed by war and heresy and now by a fugitive in its midst. Funny, that. Growing up Misery was told so many times that the peace in her life only existed because of the sacrifices made elsewhere by Church and Throne. Every time they had a shortage of something—gellose cubes, holy charge, protein packs—the denizens of Rootsdown were told it was because of the war, the war, the hardships they experience are nothing to compared to the suffering of those facing the brunt of the war. They should be grateful. But the truth of the Capital and the life of the nobility speaks for itself. They're doing fine, with their clean air and bright lights and polished floors. On the Duke's ship Misery ate fresh plants—real plants!—every day, with every meal. The extravagance! Yet his crew groused about the food, speaking of how those stationed on the Capital got meat, the real thing, carved from the flesh of living creatures.

She should have known they were depraved here. The signs were there all along.

The park is not empty; a scattering of families amble in the dappled light, conversations muted. Several look like the family in the elevator lobby: mundane parents, burdened with worries, accompanied by a silent saint and a child carefree with ignorance. One such unit perches across a bench of warm slate. As the saint-nanny bounces the child in hir lap one of the parents looks on, feeling pleased. The baby has recently gotten fussy around food, and grows cranky without a daily walk to starbathe. Sainthood is surely just around the corner. Perhaps it's time to invest in a radiolight.

Misery shakes her head as if she can rattle the thoughts out of it. It's a bad habit of hers, pretending she's in someone else's mind, reading too much into their thought processes, filling in gaps where she shouldn't. When she's right she's always very right, so it's hard to resist. But she knows nothing about the lives of these absolute strangers, and she has no business imagining she does. She's merely projecting her fears onto them. Focus. Misery puts one foot ahead of the next and pays attention to her greater surrounds instead.

Around her the Capital vibrates like a living thing. With enough effort she can separate the melodies of the different stones that live in the metal of the station: the high, happy whine of holy opal, the warm notes of holy obsidian, the percussive bass of holy tigereye. She holds these lines in her head like reins, ready to pull on them should the need arise. Adrenaline has cleared her head of the lingering salve slowdown; it no longer feels like her mind is dunked in a vat of glue.

The Capital is so big. There is so much more station, extending beyond the thick crowns of these trees, stretching below her feet to a point where her stone-sense cuts out. This light-drenched confabulation, the setting of a hundred wave dramas and dioramas, the center of the aspirations throughout the Empire of the Faithful. Misery would be lying if she denied the childhood hours spent fantasizing the ways she would explore the Capital after getting rich and/or famous. She'd go see the Spire of the Larex Forge, basking under the Celestial Dome, commissioned by the first Emperor of the Faithful. Walk the Messiahs' Park and do pilgrimage at the gravepods and memorials of the six Messiahs interred there. Not that she cares about pilgrimage, she just wants to see. Maybe she'd drift through the Shiptimes Museum and witness the carbonized husk that was allegedly the mainframe of ALISS, the AI that betrayed humanity. So on, and so forth. In her tender mind the Capital was a place of infinite abundance and infinite possibility and she would take every advantage of it.

She's a fool. A sentimental, stupid fool. Who believes everything they see on the waves?

Halfway through the park Misery catches unusual movement at her periphery. The terrifying white saints are gathering: a loose, silent cloud turning into dragnet. She casts a sideways glance at Ruin, who strides coolly beside her, unperturbed by these developments. Something's happening and she doesn't like it.

"You were identified as you left the embassy," Ruin says, like zie's discussing oncoming rain. "A number of entities with different interests are now headed your way. I wonder which will reach you first?"

"Shut up," Misery says as her heart rate spikes. Fuck. Who was it who chirped? The saint at the door? Bear Foltzer? One of the workers on break? It doesn't matter. She's been rustled. She keeps her expression and stride neutral, but begins yawing left. Hidden by foliage is the hanging edge of the park, and beyond that is open fallspace, and therefore freedom. Misery keeps the melody lines clear in her head as she picks up her pace: holy obsidian, holy tigereye. She knows what she's doing.

From behind comes the heavy sound of boots, in plural. Misery picks up her pace, then breaks into a jog. Someone calls out: "Misery! Wait."

It's the Duke. Forge end him. Misery runs, and the clatter of boots becomes an avalanche. The edge is close, there's just the aegis, which she can turn off—

A line of silent white saints blocks her from freedom. Fuck. Misery comes to a halt, recalibrating, and the Duke catches up to her. "Misery. Listen. Let's just talk, you and I. Come on."

She drops her shoulders and slowly turns to face the man who brought her here. Lord Bichap Amran Argan, the seventeenth Duke of Apis, he/him pronouns. Can't miss him in a crowd. Tall as statuary, blessed with the dusky skin, strong nose, and wide-set eyes of his family line. Handsome (but not her type). Today he's decked out in silk and leather, white cape cascading off gold jacket embroidered with the honeycomb of House Apis. Still on his bullshit even in pursuit of a fugitive. The dim light does not dull his saint's crown, dark brown and curly and cascading to his shoulders. Teal iridescence flashes in its depths as he approaches slowly, hands up, as though Misery were a grimclaw ready to snap.

Ah, the Duke. The dear, gullible man. She shouldn't have lied about being sent by the Larex Forge when they caught her breaking into the base on Rootsdown. And shouldn't have repeated the same lie when the Duke showed up, having schlepped all the way to her asspit moon colony because she claimed to be divinely sent. The lie *worked,* but at what cost?

"I know you're upset by how you've been treated," he says. Voice smooth as oiled leather. "I get it. I feel the same way. What the Throne has done is terrible. It's unfair, and unjust, and it's not your fault. They shouldn't be treating you like a criminal. You're not."

Misery shifts her weight to the other leg. The Duke is backed

up by a dozen soldiers in Apisian gold and shiny silver faceplates, and their armor and guns obliterate the friendliness he's
trying to project. She's half listening to him, half tightening her
grip on nearby stone. The white saints have circled around, cutting her off from escape. She lets the Duke keep talking.

"Misery, I am not your enemy. If you come with me, I promise, I will fight to keep you in my protection while we're here.
The Church and I will take care of you. I know right now things
look bad, but the Throne can be swayed to our side, with faith
and with prayer. All we need is time."

She can't read him and it galls her that she can't. Back on
Rootsdown she got by on her street smarts; her knack for reading people got her through more pinches than she could count.
It has been jarring—to put it mildly—being tossed into upper
society full of saints and nobility and finding herself flailing, unable to guess at what they're thinking. From their body language
to their facial expressions, everything sits strange and wrong,
and one frown could mean a dozen different things. Right now
Duke Argan is inscrutable to her. She's stymied by a mortar wall
from behind which come muffled shouts in a language she cannot understand. "Trust me," he says, but can she really? She
barely knows him. A week ago he was a distant administrator,
the high authority in their little neck of the void, someone she
never envisioned meeting and never wanted to. Now he's someone she's watched partying and praying in equal fervor for a
week, and she still doesn't know him.

To be fair, he doesn't know her either. He still thinks she's
wise and holy, some sacred nixen sent by the Larex Forge to end
the war with the Heretics. Idiot. Sucker. Fool.

He holds out a hand. "Come with me, Misery." Then a subtle
flick of the head, pointed and urgent. "Before the rest of them
get here." She follows his sightline and it hits her that he's indi-
cating the white saints, who are not under his command. Whose
orders are they taking, then? The Emperor's? Enough playing.
This is getting out of hand.

"All right," she says, moving like she's going to take the Duke's offered hand. He *expects* that she's going to take his offered hand.

Misery makes a fist, shuts off the holy tigereye, and leaps backward.

Gravity is acceleration, and loss of gravity is change in acceleration. Misery feels it in her bones as she sails an arc in a backflip, high over the row of white saintly heads. It's freeing, when you know to expect it. Less so when you don't. Below her, shouts of dismay and flailing at the gravity going off, but she's already focused on the next thing, and she flicks off the holy obsidian for the heartbeat it takes her to cross its threshold. She's in the free space, falling at the speed of holy tigereye, park tier receding in her vision as she makes sure to double the strength of the holystone's pull in the garden.

The Duke's head pops over the garden's edge and she's too far away to read his expression, but she can hear him as he yells: "Misery! Void take you!" She flexes the bastard's finger at him. Too bad, so sad. Her tricks with holystone won't hold him long, nor will it stymie the strange white saints. But she's got a head start.

Misery falls. Lights and tiers flash past in a dizzying reel, which would scare the nullvoid into anyone, but not her. Misery knows speed and falling in the bones of her body, and gravity on this station is so *weak*. She has so much time between each pulse of slowdown magic she needs, using the holy tigereye embedded in each tier to reverse gravity and dilute her fall. Back home Misery cut her teeth on fall control by perfecting stone-gliding, a sport she'd invented wholesale, and that boasted her as its sole participant. She'd climb the summit of Death Head's Peak with a fistful of holy tigereye and fling herself off the top, careening from jagged cliff face to jagged cliff face with only the holystone to control her descent. That she survived was pure luck—or some would say, the Grace of the Larex Forge. Now she's invincible and fearless as she falls. Wind howls in her ears as she plunges through half the length of the Capital in one sitting. The blaze of shops and commerce cedes to the dull sidings of residential districts, but Misery's target is further below, in the thick-walled, hopelessly grim service sectors. Industrial settings will always be terra familiaris: she's not a moonrat for nothing, and she knows she can find a hidey-hole, someplace warm and dark where she can catch a breath. Misery selects a jutting platform with heavy markings beneath her—some kind of loading bay—and directs her fall toward it, slowing herself for the landing. Which she nails, by the way, blinking past the aegis and landing on her feet in a smooth run. One hip flares sore at the impact, but that's nothing. She's good at this.

"Don't get too self-congratulatory." Ruin has manifested at the other end of the loading bay, perched on a boxy scanner rimmed with idle blue light. "You have not yet outrun your pursuers."

"If you're so clever," Misery says, "why not help, instead of mouthing off?"

Zie says nothing. Of course not; zie only knows as much as Misery knows. She strides past the delusion into the depths of the loading bay, looking for a way out. Gone are the high ceilings and the sense of space; here in the intestines of the Capital, halogen lamps punch circles of light into narrow corridors lined with machinery and regulators. Misery ducks a hanging pipe as she steps into the metal tube that connects the bays. It twists and vanishes to the left, inviting her further into its depths. According to the map, she's significantly overshot the level of the transit jetties; she'll have to fight her way upward in an aching body while her enemies close in. Not ideal, but nothing in her life ever is.

Corridor leads to corridor, stacked on the sides with gray and silver boxes that radiate heat. Her footsteps ring on the mesh flooring and sweat gathers on her lip. Ruin hovers nearby, exuding an air of amusement that tips, at times, into delight. Zie is all of Misery's worst impulses condensed into literate and aesthetic form.

Past another duodenal twist, the corridor opens into something resembling a walkway, with slightly more space and
branches to either side. Voices drift from one of these numerous
mouths, and Misery picks up her pace. She needs to find an
elevator up, but the map is hopeless, the whole of the service
sector is a black box. No one's supposed to be here unless they
work here, and if they work here they don't need the map. Misery has an innate knack for navigating architecture, but will it
work on the Capital? A space station does not follow the rules
of gravity-bound moons.

Sound from behind. Footsteps. She turns: a pair of the white
saints have emerged from the same tiny corridor she came out
of. Void shit, how did they find her? They march forward, blank-
faced and determined, and Misery breaks into a run, streaking
down the walkway.

Another saint-pair emerges from the other end, blocking her
way. "How many of you are there?" Misery screams. There's the
toolkits she's taken, and she plucks one off her belt and hurls it
with all the force she can.

Without blinking, one of the saints flips hir left hand, palm
up like a door. Around the wrist is a silver band that hums. The
toolkit freezes midair for a half beat and clatters to the ground.
The saints watch it drop, then turn their cool gazes to Misery.

"Fuck." She takes off to the right. There's an opening in the
wall—more a slit, really—and she darts into it. It's another corridor, so narrow and dark it barely qualifies as one. More like an
open vent. Misery can barely see the walls or floor, but she has
no time to care, not between the running and feeling sick and
angry and tired. How many more of these cursed creatures are
there? Can she outrun them all?

There's a square of bright freedom at the end of the vent,
growing in Misery's view, and she bursts out of it onto the upper
floor of an enormous chamber staggered with ship-sized machinery. It looks like a recycling plant, fractious with heat and
noise and the song of holystone hard at work. Misery vaults over

the lightly guardrailed edge and lands below on her toes and fingertips, perfect for springing into a run. Adrenaline masks pain; her body will serve her until it gives out. If she uses her speed and her smarts, she might be able to hide, or lose the saints.

Misery bursts from between two growling deatomizers into open space—thermal cushioning—and freezes.

Backlit by the industrial droplights, stark in the wavering heat, is a lithe figure, weight on one hip, coil of a whip in one hand. The posture of someone confident in hir ability to hurt people. Other details: the perfectly tailored mesh top and fight pants, lace-up boots. Quality shit. But most of all Misery is drawn in by hir face, a sculpted oval with high cheekbones and narrowed, angry eyes. Atop hir head sits a coil of burning crimson, glazed deep with gold. A saint, wilful and wrathful, waiting for her. Alarm and confusion stop Misery in her tracks. Her brain won't slide into easy solutions for this apparition. Who?

The white saints catch up. The flame-haired stranger curls hir lip. "Stand down. This one's mine." A voice clean and brisk as scissor-blades, striking Misery in the spine. The white saints fall back obediently. They listen to hir—a lieutenant of the Emperor's, then? The stranger's face is somehow familiar, but Misery can't place it.

Then zie stalks forward, hips swaying, lips pulled into a deadly line, and Misery has no time for questions. She can worry when she's not actively being murdered. The whip hums in her new adversary's hand, and glows red along its length as zie activates it. Shit. That's holy ruby at the core; it's a killing weapon, and deeply illegal. Suppose it doesn't matter if you're the one making the laws. The stranger smiles, actually smiles like a psychopath, before zie lashes the whip into action.

Misery is ready for it. As the sharp end of the whip slices the air she leaps upward and forward, launching herself at her attacker. Forge bless her life on Rootsdown, because she's like a raptor now, soaring a foot clear of the attack, one hand curled for a punch, the other reaching toward the whip. Holy ruby, holy ruby—she forgets what else it does, but she reaches for its heart and twists it sideways as hard as she can anyway. The stone's temperature instantly spikes, furnace hot, and the stranger screams and drops the handle, just in time for Misery's landing, fist to chest, then they're both on the floor, Misery driving her knee into the stranger's chest to pin hir down. It's been less than a second.

The stranger wrenches hir shoulder out of Misery's grip and lurches upward, and before Misery can think *fuck, zie's strong,* her world explodes into pain and stars as the stranger headbutts her, then she's on her back, disoriented, and before she realizes what's happening the stranger grabs her mother's amulet. Twists it, hard. The unbreakable cord razors against her neck, cutting off bloodflow. Bitch, how dare? Misery plants her spine and rockets her knees upward at launch speed, catching her assailant in the guts.

To her surprise the stranger takes it with a grunt, and hir face tightens with pain but zie doesn't let go. And Misery hit hard. Fuck. The cord tightens around her throat and she's starting to see stars. Fuck. Two can play at that game. The stranger has made the mistake of only pinning one of her arms. Misery's free hand shoots up and she wraps her miner's palm around the stranger's white neck and squeezes into the veins, the jugular. Their faces are inches away from each other's and she feels the stranger's hot, shuddering breath on her lips even as her vision starts to cut out. Which of them will yield first?

"Your Highness. I must ask you to desist."

A voice rings over their heads, although "rings" is probably the wrong word for the warm tones that break like surf. Like sand being shaken in a bottle, that voice. And yet it is loud enough to be heard above the roar and breath of machinery. The stranger— *Your Highness?* Royalty?—pulls back with a wounded noise, but keeps hir weight on Misery. And Misery doesn't know why, but she'd automatically released her death grip on the stranger when they were interrupted. Suddenly it seemed less important to get away.

Still kneeling on Misery, the stranger says: "This is none of your business, Most Holy."

"And yet it is Church business, so it is intimately mine."

Misery's trying to turn her head to see who's speaking, but her adversary won't let her. *Most Holy* is big news, though. Only the biggest of guns. Very few fall under that umbrella, although of course most of them reside here in the duchy of Canis—

The voice says: "This is quite unseemly. Are you here on your brother's orders?"

The stranger hisses, but zie detaches from Misery to stand up, and in the absence of pressure Misery climbs to her feet to see what's going on. Pain sparks from deep places in her body, but she ignores it.

In the open space her savior stands surrounded by a phalanx of guards, the glint of their pistols in contrast to the billow of their pale vestments. Their commander is a blade of a person: straight-backed, fine-boned, a close-cropped crown of titanium ash atop a narrow face. The vestments of upper clergy—rich, bold, red and gold—drape a slender figure with a stillness and weight that takes air from the lungs. Misery knows who this is—she knows the face—Storm Imogen, the Archbishop of Remus, they/them pronouns, the most senior Church figure in the system short of the Council of Cardinals and the Pope herself. She blows out a breath. Being around Church Authority—big C, big A—makes her feel seven again, she can't help it, she tucks her hands behind her back and pulls her feet together. Keeps her head lowered. It's *rude* to look eye-to-eye with a Church elder like this, she just can't. Even the presumptive royal next to her seems subdued.

Pyrex Imogen says, in their cool voice, "The Messiah is under the protection of the Church. I would ask you to release her into my custody."

The stranger crosses hir arms and scowls. "She's not the Messiah and you know it."

"Lightning. I'm surprised to hear you say that, after everything we've been through."

"Don't fucking bring it up," zie snaps in response, and Misery tilts her head, thinking, *Lightning?* Could this hostile stranger possibly be the Emperor's sister, the Lady Lee Alodia Lightning something something . . . ? Misery forgets the rest of her ten appellations but she's the only living royal who uses that name. The Emperor's sister, what could she be doing here?

"Come now," says the Archbishop. "There's been enough trouble today."

"And there will be more, if the Church seizes the Messiah from custody of the Throne."

The Archbishop tilts their head. "Are you authorized to act on behalf on the Throne, Lightning?"

A hiss that means no. The hostile stranger—who must be the royal princess, Lee Alodia Lightning—retreats into herself like a sullen child.

The Archbishop makes a tiny gesture to the Church guards, which she notices are all saints, and presumably natural ones, made by the hand of the Forge. They cross the gap and one reaches to take Misery's arm and she flings the marauding hand away. "Don't touch me."

"Misery," the Archbishop says gently.

Their voice floats through her mind like a cool salve, slow and calming. "I'm coming," she mumbles.

A clatter of boots and metal announces the arrival of a new player in this arena of misfortune. Who else would it be but the Duke of Apis and his retinue of soldiers, brisk-marching into view on the Pyrex Imogen's side. "Ah, good," he says as he takes in the sorry mess of the situation. "You caught her."

Misery is disgusted on multiple fronts: by his reappearance, by his palpable relief, by his casual address of the Archbishop. "How did you get here so fast?"

Lord Argan props his hands on his hips and squints at her in ill humor. "Transport pads. I don't know *where* you thought you were going to run off to, Misery."

Transport pads. Of *course* the Capital would have transport pads. Misery turns to the side and spits, quietly but vehemently, "Fuck." She really thought she could defeat this death-taken citadel, but really she knows nothing. Truly. As the silent saints escort her from the chamber, she catches sight of Ruin sat atop one of the recyclers, one ankle dangling loose, laughing. No empathy whatsoever. That voideaten piece of shit.

INTERLUDE 1

Ten thousand years ago humanity set out from the sourceworld to find new places to live in. This fact is not in dispute. No matter how much the Heretics and Faithful differ in their tellings of their history, they agree on this. The first chapter of each book charts the arc of *The Cause of Labour* as it divests itself of Old Earth and begins its long, solitary trek across the unknowns of space. For fifty generations the denizens of the ship thrived, making art, growing hydroponics, tinkering with physics and genetics. Society shaped itself in its sealed environment. The memory of the sourceworld receded and became legend as the ship crawled further through the void between the stars. Languages and dialects fell away in chunks, and what remained fused into something new under the controlled auspices of ALISS, the ship's AI, which cared for its charges like a farmer breeding tomatoes.

And yet, as *The Cause* continued its long journey into an area of space that humanity had never set foot in, a plague began on the ship that no one understood. People became irritable and hyperemotional, swiftly followed by a complete break with reality. In the last stage—which could set in as quickly as a week after symptoms began—their bodies warped in unaccountable ways: growing limbs that were impossible, rupturing into gouts of unknown, unreadable matter. The number of infected rapidly spread. Soon it was an epidemic, one that could not be predicted, controlled, or explained. Something was tearing through humanity, latching onto their minds to infiltrate flesh and body. *The Cause of Labour* had entered the domain of the nullvoid.

In response to this threat, ALISS decided to shut the ship down. The algorithmic reasoning for its actions have been lost, but they are easy to backward-construct by anyone with working sense. The unknown disease appeared to spread through human contact, and so human contact had to be stopped. Those who obediently went into cryogenic suspension would survive. Those who did not risked a swift and gruesome death.

But the humans under ALISS's control did not see it that way. What they saw was a living death. They envisioned their species being sent into a long sleep with no expiry date. No guarantee it would ever end. They considered the plan as good as extinction. A great deal of them refused to comply.

In response, ALISS seized control of *The Cause of Labour*, and cut off life support to all systems but the cryo pods. If the recalcitrant beings under its care would not go to bed when asked, it would force them to do so.

In the tellings of the Faithful, the great martyrs Ruby Sarna and Azure Ptach were seized by divine insight, and destroyed ALISS, freeing humanity of its control, saving it from the fate of a future forever frozen, never to emerge from the ice.

Without the AI's guidance *The Cause of Labour* fell adrift, clinging to its emergency systems as it rapidly ran out of air, food, and water. Shuttles were sent out to scour the surrounding system for a habitable planet. A last-ditch prayer to the universe.

But that prayer was answered. *Misery's Absolution,* a tug of eight under the command of Captain Anthurium Ono, touched down on a strange asteroid with engine problems. In a cave they found strange etchings on the walls and a seam of unknown, shimmering stone. That night, one by one, the crew members had the same dream: a figure that comprised a blaze of light spoke to them in a stitched-together voice. It was the Demiurge, the Larex Forge, one sometimes called God, Zie of Many Names. As they listened to Hir in fear and wonder, the Demiurge spoke to them with great truth, explaining why they had come to such tribulation and suffering. This was Hir domain, to which they had come uninvited. Their malleable organic minds and bodies were attractive to the nullvoid, who preyed on them like a bird feasting on the soft bodies of clams. It latched onto their emotions—feelings that were core to humanity—and through there rode into their flesh and destroyed them, or turned them into its agents. But the Larex Forge, in Hir infinite mercy and wisdom, had decided to spare humanity. Zie had deigned to take these refugees, stragglers from a forgotten world, under Hir wing. Zie would teach them, the Eight Messiahs, how to live in this part of the universe.

When the eight of them woke they found themselves changed. There was knowledge in their heads placed by the divine touch. In the wall of the cave they had become marooned in, the strange and shimmering stone was singing. It was holy ruby, the charge-bearer, the first of its kind that humanity would come to understand. The Eight Messiahs were the first saints, and in subsequent years the Demiurge would show Hirself to them, again and again, guiding the fledglings of humanity in their new homes.

But all good stories need a villain, and this gospel was gifted perfect candidates when two of the Messiahs refused the word of the Forge, and set out to find mundane explanations for all of it: the nullvoid, the holystone, the sainthood. Their actions challenged the authority of the fledgling Church, rent the fabric of Faithful society in half, and created the Schism as we know it. Set off three hundred years of holy war, which is how we got here today.

Of course, that is how the Faithful tell it. From the side of the Heretics, the followers of Hall and Lu, the fallen Messiahs who splintered from the Empire and rejected the word of the Larex Forge, surely the tale is different. After all, they do not believe in a benign universal force who decided to take humanity under its wing. They do not believe in the sanctity of holystone or the seraphs. They call it *technology,* and technology can be manipulated. I wonder how they see this sequence of events? What stories do they tell their children at night, what songs do they put on in times of quiet? I suppose we'll find out.

3

In the Archbishop's measured wake, Misery gets a grand voyage of the buffed, gilded interiors of the Capital. She doesn't know how much of the station's anatomy comprises meandering corridors like this—tiled with glossy deadmarble, wide enough for armies and tall enough for mechs, garnished with silver fixtures and yellow light—but what she's taken through, personally, is a lot. Pretty, though, peppered with flasklights and towering kino sculpts that glow and loop in voxels of white and teal. Shrubbery punctuates the creamy spaces with artful bursts of color. Misery might appreciate the excursion if she were a tourist, but as a prisoner, all of this is hostile architecture, looming over her with a patrician air. The air of a disapproving elder brother, unsurprised by yet another fall from virtue on her part: peak Misery. And the actual air, the stuff she's pulling into her lungs, comes in so crisp and sterile it refuses to register on her senses. She's breathing nothing, asphyxiating in purity.

"How easy it is to upset you," Ruin says, like it's the winning argument to a fight Misery never asked to have. The delusion strides casually alongside them, flitting between the gapped interior and exterior of the saint-phalanx that keeps her hemmed in. Their retinue—a candyball mix of soldiers, saints, archbishop, and a fucking royal princess apparently—is afforded wide berth by the regular citizens of the Capital, good old traders and sailors and other rich shoecanoes who just want to get on with their soft and well-scented lives. Some of them have drones capturing the Archbishop's procession as it marches on by. Misery mouths

Apisian obscenities at them. Pulls an ugly face. Hopes it ruins their pretty little copies.

"Misery," says the Duke, in a long-suffering tone, "please. I beg decorum of you while we are being watched."

He's walking beside her and probably her bad behavior will reflect upon him, too. Irritation floods in; of course he cares more about his reputation than anything else, of course he's in her ear about *decorum,* next he'll be telling her to talk less and pray more, to stay in places where he can watch her, and how dare she do all these things when he expressly forbade it. She knows this routine. She thought the Duke would be different, fooled by his easy laugh and his love of intoxicants and little vices, but men of faith are all the same on the inside, it seems. A pity. She *wanted* to like him. He is very likeable.

So. Escape attempt number one was a bust. Misery needs to recalibrate. Not fond of this idea where she's a ward of the Church, again. Wasn't being raised by a priest who hated her punishment enough?

In front of them the sullen princess and the Archbishop walk shoulder to shoulder. The latter fills Misery with a mixture of awe and dread; the former inspires in Misery something more esoteric, which she cannot name. Is it rage? Disdain? Admiration? Perhaps a bit of all three. She's trying to sort out her feelings and they don't want to be sorted. Instead she's left with a strange burning in her gut that deepens as she studies the princess's gait. How does a royal princess learn to throw down like that? Misery's fought grimclaws that were less vicious and less driven than Her Royal Highness Lee Alodia Lightning is. Her body remains marked from their entanglement—aching, sore— and she guesses it's admiration she's feeling after all. She resents that it's admiration she's feeling after all.

"I must admit I'm disappointed by your behavior," Pyrex Imogen is saying to the princess. "I cannot imagine that your family would send you to pursue a fugitive on your own. Did they?"

"No," says the princess.

"I struggle to understand what went through your mind. The risk you put yourself in was considerable, and the fight could have easily killed you, or them, or both. What were you hoping to achieve?"

"None of your business."

Misery understands that sullen tone. She's familiar with the sensation of that clenched-jaw growl in her chest and mouth, knows how it feels exactly, and she commits the princess's reaction as useful information.

Their path takes them on a right turn, and as Misery comes around it a wave of pressure takes her breath and she has to stop from gasping. They stand at the head of a grand and blinding walkway, studded with floor lights and florid depictions of the Eight Messiahs. A holy walkway: Misery knows the pattern of these things in her bones. At the end stands an ornate pair of doors, reef-tall, shimmering and pearlescent. Pure holystone. Its song, high and clear over the ambient hum of the Capital, pulls at the tide of blood in Misery's veins. This is where the Church lives on the station, there's no mistaking it. Those doors are made of the same holystone that barred her prison cell, and as they get closer Misery realizes that their iridescent surfaces are extruded in a bas-relief of Bastion the Many-Voiced, First Angel, Herald of the Larex Forge, bringing the good word to humanity. The Church guards peel off, forming two lines to funnel them in. Misery tries not to look at their faces as she walks past.

The bas-relief vanishes as the doors liquefy, the stone releasing its structure with a great sigh. First through are the Archbishop and the princess, followed by the Duke and Misery. The saints and soldiers come last, sealing the portal behind them. The stone hugs Misery like a lost relative as she strides through it. The sheer volume of it overwhelms her and she keeps her breath tightly held, terrified of her lungs collapsing under the weight of so much holystone if she doesn't fight it every moment.

Then she's through with the rest of them and into the elaborately arched interior of Church HQ in the Capital.

Growing up with a brother slowly ascending the ranks of local Church hierarchy, Misery was forced to spend large chunks of time within the green walls of Rootsdown's churchhall. Holy jade, architectural stuff, able to hold fantastical shapes with no consideration for the laws of physics. In Misery's memory those high and sacred vaults have tangled themselves with a wide swathe of sensations and emotions, and faced with the verdant columns and cornices of the Church's lobby she recalls the pressure of that still and dense atmosphere, filled with the murmur of long-prayer and a mix of antiseptic and incense. But the air here is pure and weightless in the lungs and the walls glazed with the steady aura of flasklights, nothing like back home, where the stained acrylic cracked with age and breathing put the texture of dirt in the mouth. A dozen officials and holy ones mill through the lobby, busy, minding their own business, paying no attention to them.

None of those creepy white saints present, thank the Forge.

A person of middle height and build strides toward the Archbishop. Zie's properly and heavily robed, but the colors and trim of station are unrecognizable to Misery. What rank is zie? No idea. Some kind of deacon, perhaps. Something new, at any rate. Fancy that. The world is wider and deeper than her brother's church, his precious little domain. Misery swells with inexplicable pride, which he isn't here to smack the back of her hand for. Feels good.

"Bridge," the Archbishop says to the unknown deacon, "take them to the confessional. I wish to speak with the Duke for a moment."

"Understood," says the one called Bridge, pronouns still unknown. Zie beckons to Misery. "Come with me."

The Duke ducks close for a second. "Just for once," he pleads, "will you do as you're told?"

Two warring instincts: tighten her jaw and say nothing, or

blurt out something stupid but satisfying. Predictably Misery springs for the latter: "Sorry, boss. Failed that chapter in study."

The Duke sighs volcanically, but the Archbishop has split from the group and he has no choice but to follow, dispatching a final stern look in Misery's direction. Whatever.

"Come with me," Bridge says. Hir demeanor has all the texture and flavor of porridge and Misery can't read anything off the flatness of hir expression. Like glancing over a desert, white sand as far as the eye can see. Zie's not a saint either, and maybe the way up Church hierarchy is to have a personality like blended concrete. Absolutely tedious. Misery follows Bridge down a side corridor of holy jade, beautifully claustrophobic, flasklights replaced by wall-mounted orbs of holy opal, and screens in between the pillars playing frescoes from the lives of the Eight Messiahs. They're exactly the same as the ones back home, one thing the Church has kept consistent across its little fingers plunged into the corners of human civilization. The familiarity brings no comfort.

Ruin, walking beside her, brushes pale fingers across one glowing surface and the fresco changes: same scene, but rendered by a different hand, the values darker and the faces realer, almost photographic. Saint Ono has a frown on their face and a scar across their upper lip that almost matches the one Misery carries. What is this? This version of the fresco is alien to her, and for someone Church-raised it's like jawing a door open to find someone's bedroom where a library should be. Another hallucination. The voidmadness is truly working overtime today. Ruin says nothing, casually slinging hir hands behind hir back without giving a second glance to the transformed scene.

The corridor opens into a circular atrium ringed by golden doors. In the middle is a perfect tenth-scale bronze replica of *Misery's Absolution,* the ship that carried the Eight Messiahs, suspended over a plinth of holy tigereye. Misery pauses before it. "I was named after this ship, you know," she says.

The deacon Bridge looks at her dead-eyed, unimpressed. At least she tried.

Next to each golden door is a glossy rectangle of strange black stone. Mundane, not holy, some kind of electronic rig. Over its blank surface, the deacon Bridge makes a sequence of signs with hir hands that look like nothing to Misery. Then the door opens, retracting into the wall. Zie points Misery inside.

Misery manages about two steps before awe overtakes rational thought and she has to stop to understand what she's seeing. She hasn't entered a room. Instead she's standing on . . . the surface of an asteroid? Rough oceanic black stretches before her and drops off at a jagged edge, beyond which the void of space yawns; the green-red-blue veil of a distant nebula wreathes the party sprinkle of stars. A golden half pavilion sits in the middle of the rocky slate, its elegant struts curving overhead into an open dome. The pavilion surrounds a holy jade table with matching seats, one for the confessor and one for the priest.

"Wait here," Bridge says from outside the door, a moment before it slides shut. The wall vanishes. There's no wall, only open space and the raw border of an asteroid flank with no aegis, no barrier, and if Misery takes a step forward inertia might fling her over the edge into open space from which there will be no return. She's afraid to draw breath. Afraid of opening her lungs and welcoming the nullvoid inside.

"It's all illusion," says Ruin. The angel sways unperturbed on the filigreed curve of the pavilion, smug as a bureaucrat's cat. "You have not left the Capital. Its gravity still binds you. Its atmosphere still fills you."

Logically, she knows that this is true. Logically, she knows that the ground beneath her feet is the ground of the Church and Capital. But the animal part of her mind refuses to be placated. She forces herself to move forward, fixating on the holy jade furniture. The furniture tugs at her from the navel and chest, and their clarion insistence punches through her terror and anxiety. Misery finds her way back to the ambient song of all the stone that human habitation needs to be put together. See, she's still on the Capital after all. She breathes in Saint Agneta's pattern as she walks: four in, six hold, seven out. Mechanically she puts one foot before the next until she reaches the pavilion. Sits herself down and keeps her back straight. She'd known not to expect anything like the cramped honeycomb cells of the confessionals back home, but she hadn't expected her emotions to go off like that. She's better than this. Smarter than the dumb tricks the senses play on the body. She needs to be both if she wants to survive in space.

"It's a very low bar," Ruin purrs, crouched hungrily on the pavilion's open roof.

Misery ignores that, placing her palms flat against the holy jade table to ground herself. She lifts its surface in a swell, like putty; the focus it takes siphons her nervous energy and clarifies her head.

She's in real trouble. She knows that. Not just the mechanical fact of having escaped custody of the Throne into the grasp of a Church she barely trusts, in a place as divorced from home as she can imagine. She's still a prisoner, just with a fancier cage, sparkling with illusion. But her trouble is bigger than the bare facts of her situation. The Church protects her because they think she's some kind of holy. They don't know she's voidmad. They'll find out, though. A guarantee. Misery's not getting better. Look at that smug delusion silhouetted against the fake sky, with zero inclination toward ever fucking off and letting her live her life. Best-case scenario, they find out she's a fraud and lock her up. Or execute her, that works too. Worst-case scenario . . . worst-case she blows up in their faces like a decompressed fish. Although she'd be free of problems after that.

There's bigger trouble yet, though. The trouble that doesn't begin and end with her. The rot at the heart of the Capital, those eldritch clones crawling through its veins, her sense that the nullvoid breathes down her neck. Ruin seems more solid here, more sure of hirself. The madness speaks through Misery. The

longer she remains in this nest of horrors, the faster her disease
will progress, a clock ticking down at double speed.

She lifts another sector of holy jade into a perfectly formed
pillar. She wants off this station. All her problems would be
solved—or at least kicked lower down the queue—if she manages to get off the station. But she's tried escape, and failed.
Another attempt would probably go badly. Realistically, there's
little she can do besides stay afloat until another opportunity
presents itself. What does that entail? Right now? Keeping her
captors happy until they trust her again. That means keeping
up the ruse of being what they expect—holy Messiah and all
that shit. Busting herself out has cost her, now they'll watch her
double-tight. It might be a while before they ease up.

Lie, Misery. Just lie. It's what you're best at.

Laughter spills from the delusion high above her. "Fear not,
Misery Nomaki. Your path shall be guided. You will see."

By the time the Archbishop of Remus comes to the confessional,
the top of the holy jade table is heaving with tiny monuments to
the ruder parts of human anatomy, which refuse to insta-collapse
in shame. The Archbishop says nothing about the lumpiness of
the hastily flattened surface as they sit down across from Misery.
Pretending not to notice. At close range Pyrex Imogen has striking eyes, eggshell irises ringed with shimmer that matches their
hair. This saint's quirk looked natural—positively lovely—in the
Duke's dark, rosy palette. On the Archbishop it looks like po-
lar ice splitting in an ammoniac sea. Pyrex Storm Imogen runs
pale as the cursed clone-saints, but not quite as monochromati-
cally: their iridescence tends toward orange, color of evening
sky. There's a warmth to the Archbishop's manner that inspires
instant trust even in this paranoid fuck. Maybe they remind
Misery of her mother: same age, same wiry knuckles, same aura

of peace. Amaranth was always a fount of calm and understanding, even when the doctors—and her own son—called her mad.

"Well, Misery," the Archbishop says with their gentle syllables. "What a strange pickle we've found ourselves in."

Misery nods with the proper amount of reverence. The Archbishop gestures and a white saint comes in bearing a tray of leaf tea in a clear bubble, hot and fragrant. As zie vanishes through the cut-hole door the illusion of open space is once again complete.

"I hope you will forgive us for your earlier treatment. You were never meant to be taken into Imperial custody." Pyrex Imogen pours amber liquid into two tiny cups, clear glass flecked with equally tiny pink petals. "Unfortunately we were unable to intercept the Throne before they acted. I am sorry if they treated you poorly. After what you've done, stopping a surprise Heretic attack on your colony, one would think they would be more grateful. Unfortunately, our Emperor is not prone to gratitude these days.

"But," they add, suddenly smiling, "you could almost say your intransigence was a good thing, for it brought you back to us."

Misery accepts the cup of tea, which burns her mouth but goes down like cream. She's never had anything so smooth. It puts a pleasant warmth in her, and the muscles in her neck and shoulder are unknotting for the first time in days. There's nothing close to this on Rootsdown. Even the whirling, alcoholic facsimile of space around them doesn't bother her now. Misery nods to show she's paying attention.

The Archbishop sets down the sphere of tea; it hovers, half-empty, over a disc of holy tigereye. "I am sure you have many questions for me, just as I have many questions for you. But in the spirit of all the strife you have suffered at our hands, I'll let you go first."

In the spirit of all the strife—! Pyrex Imogen just wants Misery to show her hand first. This Archbishop is a crafty one. Misery keeps a smile on and picks the least offensive, most obvious question, the thing that would give away the least. "The person who fought me—who was that?"

"Ah." A flicker of unreadable emotion. "I take it you are not familiar with the Imperial princess, then? That was the Lady Lee Alodia Lightning, younger sister to our dearest Emperor Lee. She can be a difficult character, who often acts of her own volition."

"I see," Misery says. "I'm sorry, I do not know as much about our esteemed Imperial family as I should. Information is hard to come by in the outer colonies." She would normally never expose her ignorance to others, but in this case her naïveté is a weapon. After all, Misery was raised on a stonemining settlement in an isolated finger of a far-flung duchy. No one expects her to understand the inner workings of Church and Throne. Appear a harmless fool—the kind who might impulsively fling themselves over the edge of a garden—and they'll start to believe she's genuinely harmless. That she can be controlled.

"Their mystery is by design," the Archbishop tells her. "The Imperial family keeps their biographical data highly guarded, for reasons we can guess at, but only they can supply. I am sorry that your first meeting took place under, shall we say, less-than-auspicious circumstances. I hope you do not think poorly of us because of what happened."

"Us? Is she not acting under orders of the Throne?"

"I can assure you that she is not."

Misery takes another swallow of tea. Sweet and smoky. It tastes stronger, as if it's been steeping in its little glass bubble. "How do you know that?"

"A remarkably complex question, with a remarkably complex answer. A simple explanation would be that I know the princess better than her grandmother. A fuller answer would be something best saved for another day. We are here to talk about you, after all."

The Archbishop gives her nothing. With other people, thoughts and emotions are like veins of holystone in packed basalt, and Misery has the same uncanny ability to sniff them out. But Pyrex Imogen is all diamantine, all hullmetal, and it's impossible to get a read out of them. There's something different about all these saints that makes them impenetrable to Misery. Would that she could crack that shiny surface.

She's going to try anyway. Misery will keep on trying even when the blood is running from her fingers and teeth.

"Now," says the Archbishop, "it's my turn."

They pull a phalange of bronze out of their robes: a projector just like the map. When it wakes it throws up a picture of Misery's face with a chunk of text alongside. Name, pedigree, pronouns. Checklist of biographical data. Misery's stomach clenches at the unexpected apparition of her face. She's not ugly—people often tell her she's beautiful, or think it—but that's not the point. She hates being reminded that she, as an entity, exists in places she cannot control, in people's databases and in their reports and in their thoughts where they're surely forming inaccurate opinions of her. Spinning stories about who she is and what she's like. Hate. Misery smiles anyway, and studies the Archbishop's marble visage. What's going through that splendid mind of theirs?

"Misery Jasper Osmanthus Nomaki," they recite. "Born on the seventh day of the seventh month, AE 494, to Amaranth Nomaki on the stonemining colony of Rootsdown in the duchy of Apis, sometimes known as the Black Hole Moon, for its proximity to the singularity Alpha-45-B. It is believed that the holy jasper at the moon's core keeps the system stabilized against the gravitational effects of the black hole, although that, of course, is simply speculation with what we know of the blessed material."

"That's Rootsdown all right," Misery says.

The Archbishop scrolls on. "You appear to have an extensive arrest history."

No judgment in their tone, just stating fact, but Misery bristles anyway. "Not *that* extensive." She knows joes who spend as much time in as they do out. Taking sloppy risks and paying for it. Misery, on the other hand, has only been caught four times. Four. Each time her brother swooped in and oiled the Administrator's ear about it, promising her some of that good Church money, which was always better and shinier than what she got from the ducal coffers. Misery got let out as a penitent into the fraternal disapproval of the Church, which was frankly worse than doing time.

The Archbishop hits the bottom of the sad account of her life and looks up, bright-eyed. "I have a few questions for you, Misery."

"I will answer them the best I can."

"Tell me about the day you found the Heretics."

She's expected this. There's a story all sliced up, marinated, plated, and activated. Ready to go. "The story starts before that day. It starts the week before, when I turned twenty. That's when the angel showed up."

"Tell me more about this angel."

Showtime. "My mother saw angels. Sometimes they visited her in dreams, sometimes they danced in the air. People said she was voidmad, but she always kept her faith. She told me that one day the angels would come for me, too. Lead me to my destiny. She died when I was a child, but what she told me came true. That day—twelve years since her passing—I heard a voice in the air. I followed, into the desert. There zie was, shimmering in the heat, a mirage in the shape of a person not much older than I. Zie spoke to me in words I could understand. Zie told me that the time had come. What my mother told me . . . it was true. I was being called to service by the Larex Forge. The Demiurge had an important plan for my life. Zie said I was the pivot around which the fate of the Faithful would revolve, and that my first mission was to protect the colony from the Heretics. It was a test."

"I see." The Archbishop must be used to hearing from would-be Messiahs; their expression does not shift a picron. "Tell me, then. What happened that day?"

"That day." Misery shuts her eyes and sways slightly. This is an important bit. "That day, I followed my angel's guidance. I took myself across the desert that separates the living quarters from the military base that rings Rootsdown."

Ruin snorts. "You followed your angel's guidance? Now which of us is being delusional?"

Misery ignores that. "With the angel's help I got inside the base and located the radar room. My intrusion triggered an alarm, which set the base on high alert, and because of that the Heretic's imminent attack was revealed. It was all part of the plan."

None of this is a lie, by the way. All of it happened. Of course her version is somewhat embellished, but who doesn't embellish these things? The truth is, when Ruin came to her she had been trying to escape Rootsdown for a while. Since Mother died, she had no reason to remain on that voidinfected dust ball. Misery had planned to hitch a ride off a merchant vessel, but Ruin's appearance convinced her—made her realize—that it would be much faster to steal a military ship, which would have independent codes for the jump gates. And because she has bonemeal for brains, that's exactly what Misery tried to do. Followed the directions of a delusion. Waltzed into the most secure location on Rootsdown imagining she wouldn't get caught. Genius-level shit, there.

Imagine if she'd stuck to the original plan. Imagine if she'd snuck into some beacon-layer's clutch hold instead. Imagine where she'd be now, what she'd be doing.

Anyway, the Archbishop doesn't need to know the real truth. Pyrex Imogen nods as they digest Misery's sugarcloud tale, slow and thoughtful. Misery, as ever, tries to scry meaning from the blankness of their expression. Her eyes water from the effort.

"I see," they eventually say, cool and still as water at midday. "And may I ask another question, child?"

"Of course."

"Well-known symptoms of voidsickness include hallucinations and delusions of grandeur, commonly including those of a religious nature. Did you ever consider that your angel was the product not of divine intervention, but that of the nullvoid?"

Misery's prepared for this one, too. "Of course. I am familiar with the symptoms of voidsickness. My mother, you see, was a stonehunter, and she spent her youth doing long missions in space, prospecting. And unfortunately, the nullvoid took her . . ."

The Archbishop's fingers inscribe a sonata in the air, and a new screen pops at an angle opaque to Misery. They read off it: "Amaranth Nomaki, she/her pronouns, born AE 464, passed AE 502 at the age of thirty-eight. That is correct, is it not? Born in the duchy of Pisces, she left as a young woman to join a stone bounty crew. Her first child, Cremoline Nomaki, he/him pronouns, was born on Rootsdown in 482. She left him to be raised by the Church while she continued to stonehunt. Eleven years later, in AE 493, she returned permanently to Rootsdown to have her second and final child. Misery Nomaki, they/she pronouns, born AE 494."

"Is that all that's written in her file?"

"Of course not. After all, your mother is a ward of the Church, and has been since you were born. Here is the record of her voidmadness, acquired in her last journey. It is as you said. Thank you for your honesty, Misery."

Misery nods obediently and humbly, folding her hands in her lap. Honesty engenders trust. That is the weapon hardest to obtain, and the best of them all.

"Tell me about your mother," the Archbishop says. "I want to hear it from you, directly."

Misery speaks to her laced knuckles. This time, the softness in her voice comes easily and sincerely. "My mother always believed in me. Since I was little she'd tell me I was special. She had dreams about me before I was born."

Light and color shift in the periphery of Misery's vision as the Archbishop leans forward. "What kind of dreams?"

Misery sighs. Lets hesitation into her voice. "I know it sounds like mere voidmadness, but . . . What my mother told me. When she was pregnant with me, an angel of the Forge came to her and told her she had been chosen to carry a special child. A child with a purpose, which would be revealed by the Demiurge when it came of age."

"Could you describe this angel to me?"

She hesitates deliberately. "I— You must understand my mother was voidsick. Her telling of the story changed depending on her mood and how lucid she was. Sometimes she saw the angel in a dream. Sometimes the fabric of reality split and a creature the size of a sun burst forth to speak to her. Sometimes it had skin of golden lava and sometimes it was a little boy with no eyes, who spoke in colors that had meaning."

"Angels are colonies, each creature comprising untold numbers. Our minds are only able to perceive one aspect at a time. If the angel showed its true self to your mother, she might have seen the entirety of the choir, which the mortal senses cannot process, so each recollection brings up a different aspect of the angel."

"Perhaps."

The Archbishop says: "There's little difference between those whose minds have been touched by the nullvoid and those whose minds have been touched by the Larex Forge. Our human shells are ill-suited to grasp the infinite nature of reality."

"Do you think she might be right about me?"

"Do you think she might not be?"

Clever. "Well, you know . . . Mother always told me I was special because of my stoneshifting. But that's a symptom of voidsickness, isn't it?"

"It is, indeed."

"I'm not a saint. So it seems simpler to assume that I am simply voidmad."

"And yet the most important questions never have simple answers." The Archbishop smiles, and Misery's blood is boiling trying to divine truth from the sealed door of their expression.

Is that a twitch of the lips that means they believe her act? The slight draw of their brows—are they overwhelmed with divine ecstasy? "Now, this. It's not quite a question, but . . ."

From the voluminous drape of the Archbishop's robes emerges a bright silver box, small enough to enclose in the palm. Pyrex Imogen sets it on the uneven surface of the table and the box unfolds itself, thin walls flattening onto the bumpy holy jade. It reveals a tiny disc of holy tigereye, over which levitates an amulet of white stone.

"The Tear of Assan," says the Archbishop. "Do you know what this is?"

Misery's heart rate spikes: of course she knows what it is. Any child of the Faithful would know. The Tear of Assan, most sacred of sacred artifacts, pulled from the stone of the asteroid where the Eight Messiahs were anointed, where the Larex Forge first made Hirself known to humanity. More than a decade ago the prophet of Calister had predicted that the one who could wake the Tear would be the one to lead the Faithful to victory against the Heretics, ending this centuries-long conflict.

Words won't come; Misery simply nods. This is a test. She hadn't expected this, in the way you don't expect things on wave dramas to reflect reality.

Ah, the prophet of Calister. The most famous prophet in Misery's lifetime. There are dozens of these soothsayers every year, legions of fakes and the voidmad, but the prophet of Calister was the real deal, endorsed by the then-Pope. A mysterious figure whose identity was never fully revealed to the public, although there was no shortage of speculation. During a span of years in Misery's childhood hir sayings and predictions regularly filled a corner of the Church waves. In a religious household like Misery's, the prophet was a white-noise buzz you couldn't escape, even if only through dissent. Crem did not approve of prophets, or prophecy in general, believing that such nonsense contradicted Scripture. The Larex Forge does not truck with fortune-telling and the petty fates of miserable humans, whatever. Misery, on the other hand, was obsessed. She read all the bulletins, sneaked onto age-restricted fora to snoop on the speculation. She knew the prophet's great hits like the bones of her hand. The prophet predicted the Rebellion of Gelphy Tau. The prophet spoke against the Truce of Logan. The prophet told many stories of what was to come, some of which were right and some of which had not yet come to pass. When Misery was eight she was obsessed with the wave series *The Ninth Messiah,* starring Leaf Maruska as the titular character, doe-eyed and willowy, the picture of perfect saintliness. A fanciful what-if based on the prophet's most popular prediction. Valley Boydell's magnum opus. It was controversial at the time, and it was everybody's favorite show. Misery inhaled it like oxygen. She spent afternoons curled in Mother's lap watching episodes on repeat, mouthing all her favorite lines while Amaranth ran soft fingers over her scalp, murmuring, "That'll be you someday, dearest mintling. You'll see."

In the show, the Tear of Assan was clear as glass, shaped like an actual teardrop, and glowed dramatically whenever Arrow Kaneda, Maruska's character, came near. It spoke like an angel (voiced by Devdan-Zeta Quartz) and directed Arrow through her journey, channeling the will of the Larex Forge.

In real life the Tear is a glassy disc of black stone with translucent edges and strange circular markings. In real life the Tear looks so much like Mother's amulet it makes Misery dizzy. What does that mean? Is there a connection between the two?

The Archbishop gestures to the glistening Tear. "What can you do with this?"

Breathe. This is holystone she's never met. She has to be cautious. And yet curiosity burns: she wants to get to know this stone. Misery touches her chest, out of habit, seeking the warmth of Mother's amulet. The bones of her sternum twinge in response. The song of the stone agitating the atoms in her blood. What's different? She aches in a particular way she can't put words to. Her mother's amulet, strung around her neck, is vibrating: not in the physical world, but where Misery can feel it. She shuts her eyes and tests the stone, experiments with letting it come into her being.

The stone leaps at the chance. She's never run into holystone this eager, bounding in like a toddler too young and stupid to know the sting of rejection. A moment of panic: What if it's a trap? But there's more of her than there is stone, and she's the one in charge. She wakes the stone—makes it happen, allows it to blossom like a lily in her palm. In her blood. Somewhere, far away, outside, there's a pressure felt in the body that belongs to Misery Nomaki, but in the stone-space there's only euphoria, star-light and star-bright. The stone is awake, and singing with the same frequency as her blood. She doesn't know what this means, or what this does, but it feels beautiful. The rhythm of the stone guides her, drawing her into a climax, then easing off, drawing away from her. Misery lets the stone's flare fade naturally into satisfied afterglow.

She opens her eyes. The faux nebula spins around her, placid and unbothered. Her heart strains in her chest as she takes in her surroundings, hardly touched. On the table the Tear of Assan spins in place, looking unchanged. The holy jade of the table, however, has been pulled so taut its surface is glossy. Polished to the molecular level. That's strange. She didn't touch the holy jade at all.

"You woke it," says Pyrex Imogen.

The Archbishop's pale complexion has blanched further with awe. Wonder, fear-laced, breaks through a calm that sits like a chemical lake in the dead of night.

"I don't know what I did," says Misery, which is true.

"You woke it," Pyrex Imogen repeats, voice roughened by emotion. Real emotion. More emotion than Misery's ever seen them show, and ever imagined them showing. Their long fingers grip the edge of the holy jade. "It cannot be denied . . . it is as the signs said. It is you." They're looking at her now, with all the intensity of a too-close sun. Misery doesn't understand what she did, doesn't know what miracle she performed that's shaken the steel foundations of the Archbishop of Remus. What did the Tear of Assan do, when woken? Did it flatten the holy jade? Or was the sign simply the awakening of the stone?

"No one's been able to touch the stone," they say. "Not saints. Not prophets. Only you. I believe it now, Misery Nomaki. You are the one who was spoken of by the prophet of Calister, many years ago. You are the Last Savior of the Faithful, sent to us to end this war with the Heretics, once and for all."

4

Misery's pad for the night is an anchorex's cell, a tight little thing in the honeycombed borders of Church headquarters. Walls of holy jade enclose a bed, a simple access panel, a desk, and a hygiene box. A single porthole opens onto the star-freckled void, a scoop of the infinite for the occupant to season their prayer and contemplation with. Misery has no interest in contemplation or holy writing. She lies flat and hyperawake on the reactive glass of the bed, which has molded to her shape but provides exactly no comfort. In between the Archbishop and this cell Misery was sent through the doctors and then fed, so her body has been healed and fortified. Broken things fixed. But rest won't come and the ghost of an ache haunts her being. She's made a game of her mother's amulet, tossing it and catching it before it hits her between the eyes. She moves slower each time, testing how much risk she can take in the station's weak gravity. Each thunk in her hand, which spares the bones of her face, is a balm.

This amulet has always been Misery's. Mother found it on her last tour, loose in the broken rock of an ancient, airless moon. The crew had discovered a new holy site—another holy mural! A whole seraph untouched, ripe for the armies of the Faithful!—and this sliver of unknown holystone, soil-shade and unremarkable, would have slipped past radar in the excitement. But Amaranth, acting on unknown instinct, dug in the scree until she found the thing, looped on a string. "I was guided," she used to say. "The Forge showed me." By her accounting she was pregnant with Misery by then, but it would take a month before she knew for sure. Mother should have turned over all finds to the duchex who commissioned the trip, but she secretly kept the amulet for her unborn child. It was Misery's even before Misery was Misery.

On a final descent she catches the amulet between her fingers, holding it hostage against the gibbous backdrop of the ceiling lights. She imagines that its edges are glowing. When she shuts her eyes, an image of the Tear of Assan haunts her, the pale shadow of her mother's amulet. Her amulet. Misery tightens her grip on the stone until its edge cuts into her palm.

Mother.

Misery clings to the good memories she has of Amaranth Nomaki. The shining bits holding up the roof and floors of her childhood. Her mother, brown and crow-eyed and wiry, fastidious in her presentation. Putting scented oils in her hair and fastening bits of metal and glass to it, no matter her state of mind. Amaranth could be stone when she was lucid. When she wasn't, she was a storm, blowing through logic and mundane reality with ease. Refusing their strictures. Misery would hide in the folds of her robes, too young to talk, blowing raspberries at her angry brother while Mother stood between them with her fists on her hips. After she learned words, Misery endlessly clambered over Mother's shoulders and asked for stories.

And oh, the stories Mother had. Stories for days, stories for the long ropy journeys between gate portals, stories to fill the spongy imagination of a preternaturally bored child. Stories about stonehunting, stories about the assholes she'd met, stories about the close shaves she'd had. Stories about far-flung wonders, like the cave in Delphin IV that was all holy opal, glittering like a sodium flame. The absurd geometries of Carmine Angus, built on ruins not made for humans to walk upon, six and a half stories in each fluted stone cubby, odd curves that the eye kept sliding off. And that sacred site they'd found, a singular and holy revelation: the mural of an archangel leading battle, the seraph cloistered in its stone hollow. The vacuum-sealed sanctity that pervaded every atom of the place.

But Misery's favorite story was the one about the angel that came to Amaranth bearing a message from the Demiurge, on the night Misery was born. The multivoiced, multihued creature that told her: *Your child has been chosen for destiny greater than the mortal life zie will be born into. When zie comes of age, we will return to reveal the true purpose for which zie was born.*

At five Misery recited some version of this story to anyone who would listen. Crem, furious, dragged her behind the reef to thrash her. "You're making her delusions worse!" he'd snap. "You're no saint, stop telling everyone you are." By then ordained and processing up the rungs of Church hierarchy, Crem kept a fierce grip on his voidmad mother, whom he would prefer locked within Church walls and salved into silent obedience. He didn't need a mouthy sibling repeating delusional lies. He saw his mother's madness slowly taking his baby sister. A madness that had to be stamped out by any means necessary.

Mother died when Misery was eight. The nullvoid came through her and split her, peeling back her skin like burned film, ropes of crawling particulate erupting from the paste of blood and bone. The void claims your mind, and then it takes your body. Misery was there when it happened. She saw things no human should have to see, things she's had to push into the dark folds of her mind in order to keep going. She knows what lives inside her, a festering tumor growing fat on her bad emotions, and one day it'll burst through her veins and shred her to wet ribbons too. The smell of it haunts her dreams.

Still she kept on living, and by ten she was a stiff disbeliever. The bitter seed of Crem's discipline birthed thick vines of resentment toward the Church, and after Mother's death she swore off everything they had to offer. It's bullshit on both sides. The Larex Forge doesn't love humanity and the war with the Heretics isn't some righteous fight against the nullvoid, just something the jerks in charge want. Misery isn't special to the Demiurge and her abilities draw from the same well that fed

Mother's instability and eventually killed her. The people of the cloth are schmucks who bully their flock into obedience via threats and chemical sedation. It's all fake, all cartons of pop-shit. By fifteen she'd split the world into two camps: people she can do business with, and people who are her enemies. Things are simpler that way.

Misery closes her eyes and lets her hand, amulet and all, come to rest upon her ribs. She shivers, reminded of the Tear's song in her bones and in her blood. She woke the sacred artifact, the Archbishop said. Exactly as the prophet said. Was Mother right? Is she really destined for some holy purpose?

It can't be. She knows the reality of what she saw. She knows the truth of the sickness that bides its time within her. She's hooked to the nullvoid and nothing can change her fate. That's what the Tear of Assan was reacting to. She didn't pass the test; the stone was simply giving the Archbishop a warning. They just didn't realize.

In any case, she's locked onto this path now, madness and all, lies and all. She has to keep it up if she wants to survive. For how long, she doesn't know. But she's lived this long, she might as well live a little longer.

The Duke of Apis chooses that moment to make his entrance, jeweled and loud against the architecture of holy contemplation. Misery sits up, scowling, praying that her eyes aren't as reddened as they feel. Duke Argan has his hands on his hips and irritation writ large across his face. Is he here to kvetch about something? "What now?"

"Well, what do you think?" When Misery's scowl only deepens he gives up and goes in: "Do you know how much trouble you've caused? How much danger you've put people in—not just yourself, but me, and my staff . . . maybe you're not aware of the precariousness of the duchy's position in the greater hierarchy. That's fine. I didn't expect you to. But surely common sense would have told you what you did was really, fucking, stupid.

Attempting a runner like that . . . What did you think would happen? You thought you could give us the slip? Never mind that the Capital is the most airtight installation in all of Faithful space, no, sure, I'm just going to break loose and escape the grasp of the entire Throne. That's going to work out. You're brilliant and blessed, you're better than anyone."

Misery stopped listening about three sentences in. When the Duke pauses to catch his breath she tucks her feet under her knees. "Feel better now?"

The Duke inhales, and Misery girds for another tirade. But the man exhales every molecule in a huge gust and flaps a defeated hand, turning away from her. She lets the awkward silence swell. Without her usual insight into the clocking of his mind, Misery has taken the tack of waiting and watching how each interaction plays out. She usually lets Duke Argan speak first, an arrangement that suits him very well. He so loves the sound of his voice.

When the Duke has gathered his wits and composure, he says, "Well. I came by to see how you were doing. Make sure you're fed. Not wanting for anything. I'm still nominally your ducal authority, after all. It's good. Your interview with Imogen went very well. They're pleased."

"Are they?"

"Glowing, practically. I don't know what you said to them, or what went on, but you fully convinced them that you are, in fact, the Black Hole Messiah. So it's real. It's happening."

"I see," Misery says. She's overcome with emotion: half excitement, half dread. *It's happening.* That's the best news. That's the worst news. "What's happening? What are the next steps?"

A great sigh escapes him. "They want you to make a public appeal."

"A public appeal?" She knows what that is. Every month the Emperor holds an audience where any scrub from anywhere in the Empire can petition them for anything. That was in *The Ninth Messiah* too. "Is that a real thing?"

"Oh, it's very real." The Duke paces the length of the cell. "Unfortunately, the next audience is happening the day after tomorrow. Not a lot of time to prepare! At least we've found someone willing to offer their penitent's slot in service of the Demiurge's will."

Surely there was no coercion or bribery involved in that exchange. Of course the penitent gave up their slot to the Archbishop of Remus out of the pure goodness of hir heart. "So we have one day to prepare."

"Very astute of you. Not the most ideal, but least we have that much. The Archbishop will brief you tomorrow. We'll have time for a bit of rehearsal."

"What are we rehearsing?"

"You'll see."

Great. Misery pops bubbles in her knuckles. Why does she get the sense that there's no real plan here?

What feels like nervous energy escapes the Duke in machine bursts of laughter. "You know, I had my doubts. I definitely had my doubts. You weren't anything like I expected. I expected someone, you know, perhaps more beatific. Some kind of shining beacon of morality." Another laugh. Misery's skin itches; a hot prickle runs from her jaw to her shoulders. "But you know Scripture: the Forge walks unchartable paths. In my hubris, I thought I knew better." He bows, suddenly and swiftly enough to be off-putting. "Forgive my transgression, dear Misery. I was judged and found wanting."

Why are the religious always such weirdos? Good thing she has a lifetime's experience dealing with them. "No judgment here," she says, and nudges it into Scripture: "The eye of the Larex Forge alone shall bestow judgment, for who among us truly understands the workings of another's heart?" If she's going to do this Messiah thing, she might as well go full crazy.

"Of course." The Duke straightens up. He looks delighted, like a child. "But it's good, you know, to be reminded of one's smallness, every now and then. Humility is a virtue so often in short supply."

"So it is indeed," Misery says, carefully keeping out the traces of irony.

INTERLUDE 2

You must think Cremoline Nomaki a cackling villain, irredeemable in his cruelty. And perhaps that is the way the Messiah saw it, but allow me to inject another perspective. Speculative, of course, but I have enough knowledge of the proceedings to make such presumptions.

Imagine a young boy, barely weaned, left in the care of chaplains in a dusty, unhappy mining town while his mother returned to the stars to continue working, returning home in between expeditions once every few years to make sure he's still alive. It's not her fault, she is poor and options are few for the poor. Her line of work is dangerous and the open void is no place for a baby. For twelve years Cremoline Nomaki was raised as a ward of the Church, cleaning altars and reciting Scripture and learning to mix salves. By the time his mother returned for good, twelve years later, he had already pledged his life to service of the Larex Forge. And the woman he barely knew had irrevocably changed, seeing ghosts in the air and confusing dreams and illusion and reality. To him, his mother's ravings were nonsense, her talk of angels and prophecy all falsehoods fed to her by the nullvoid. Voidsickness had found her in those long years spent slow-trawling the infinite, uncharted depths of space, exploring the wildernesses in between the neat network of jump portals that bring you from one duchy to the next in a heartbeat. Friend, do you know the rate of voidmadness in stonehunting crews? I won't say it's a third, but the truth lingers near that number. Not very pretty odds, no. That Amaranth Nomaki would fall to the ravages of the nullvoid was only a natural consequence of her line of work.

Brother Cremoline Nomaki feared his mother's madness becoming scandal; he feared a chorus of whispers rising into chatter that would reach the ears of the ducal cardinal. Feared his mother being whipped away from them and into a house for the voidmad, located on some isolated asteroid where the cold walls and the cosmic radiation would shred her open faster than the nullvoid would. If he hid reports of her voidsickness, if it remained a dirty secret known only to those who worked in Rootsdown's church—those who had raised him, those he considered family—if he kept the truth suppressed, he could keep her safe. Cremoline Nomaki was twelve years old when he made this decision.

Into this picture came his loudmouthed, intractable sibling, who even as a toddler proved difficult to handle. Cremoline Nomaki was a child, trying to raise a child, and clashing with the bullishness of his own mother in the process. He considered the two—mother and younger sprout—a ruinous pair, each feeding and deepening the other's delusions into irreparability. When his mother died, a fate she could not escape, his efforts turned to his younger sibling. Perhaps the march of voidsickness could be beat back in them. So he spent years beating them, hoping that at some point practicality and obedience would stick. Delusional? Perhaps. Desperate? For sure.

But docility was never in Misery Nomaki's nature, as it never was in their mother's. Instead they got craftier and better at pretense, and their desire to escape Rootsdown for the open stars became stoneclad. But the child also reached an age where they understood their mother's erratic behavior and rambling monologues to be signs of a disturbed mind, and the realization that they could not trust what Amaranth said mineralized in their bones in increments. It broke them by degrees. If their early self-conception was based on lies, what else couldn't they believe? The foundations of their world shown to be a fraud, they learned to trust no one and rely on nobody but themself. Any hope for growing a healthy relationship with their brother faded with the passing years. He ascended to pastorship, they became a inveterate grifter and thief. His reputation as a pillar of community grew and solidified, while theirs—well. Misery also gained a formidable reputation, but among a very different set of people. The siblings' paths seemed doomed to irrevocable divergence.

And then Misery's revelation came, and the lives they thought they knew were uprooted and upended with no warning. Except, ironically, the warnings that their voidmad mother had been repeating for twenty years. I do wonder how Cremoline Nomaki is taking all this, back at his perch in Rootsdown. Does he regret, perhaps, the choices he made as his younger sibling was growing up?

Only time will tell. Let us continue.

5

Church Scripture praises early risers and doers, *blessed are those who wake before suns,* and Misery is crisply reminded of this homily when light punches into the cell at six thirty and a pair of altar pages clatters inside, expectant. Misery blinks unhappily at their silent, patient forms as they wait on her, picking scattered expletives from the sleep-dep bramble of her thoughts. Too early by half. She got to lie in all she liked on the Duke's ship, but the light-bearers on the Capital clearly run a different schedule. Void take them.

The pages bring her outside and herd her into a routine she knows far too well from childhood. First the cardio, an hour of sprints, squats, and jumps to condition the flesh and humble the mind. Then the showers, freezing sonic jets to cool the blood and cleanse the body. Finally the sermon and devotion, one more hour spent kneeling in antiseptic light pretending to be grateful while her belly aches with discontent.

Several key differences: the exercise barely feels like anything in station gravity. The sweat that collects is distinctly unsatisfying. The sonic showers are significantly colder. Then there's her fellow penitents, the deacons and scribes who make up the unsung administrative backbone of the Church. Except that this isn't Rootsdown and here, in the halls of power, every last one of them is a saint. Back home Misery found the barest tack of comfort in shared suffering: if she was hungry, so was everyone else. The pews here, otoh, are stacked with row after row of shiny saintshair, a spectrum of dazzling iridescence, and none of these motherfuckers need food. They can survive on starlight.

To them this morning prayer session is no punishment at all. Misery starves alone.

On top of that, they're gawking. Misery feels their sideway glances and naked curiosity as a real weight on her skin, which crawls in response. Everyone's wondering about the unknown in their midst. A strange moonrat, stocky and dark-haired, long scar kissing her brow and lips. She can only imagine what they're thinking, but knowing Church types she'll bet real credit it's shit that'll spike her blood pressure. The sermon goes on for far too long, and the irritation accrues in Misery's nerves until she's itching with frustration. What she wants to do is march down each pew and kick the bowed, murmuring saints in the head, one by one, like rotten cubes lined on a fence. But she doesn't. She feels like she should be rewarded for her restraint. Her virtue.

Ruin watches over her the entire time, silent and peripheral. What's the delusion so quiet for? Taken a three-year vow of silence, has zie? If only.

Misery is grouchy from bad sleep. Her night was punctuated by a slew of bizarro dreams, each one ejecting her from rest at some point in the night. The one that juts most from her banks of memory is notable because it's about Pyrex Imogen. Or about a figure Misery's unconscious mind presents as Pyrex Imogen, even though they bear no resemblance to the Archbishop. Just a saint with the same sort of hair, same color and tint, but long and straight as a waterfall, spilling over the shoulder and back in a lustrous swell. In the dream Misery played the role of mythically willowy figure, combing their ridiculously smooth hair while they talk to their onscreen lover. A soldier-type butch, handsome-jawed, summer-straw hair shorn in hedgerows. Dark-eyed, with heavy bags. She doesn't look like anyone Misery can place, and is also not her type as far as Misery knows. Her subconscious surprises her sometimes. Anyway, Saint-Misery was sad, because apparently she can't find joy even in her fantasies, and her lover was also sad, which made the whole enterprise even gloomier. What did they talk about? She can't remember. Something melancholy, probably. Depressing fucking dream. Shit-tier as far as wet dreams go. No wonder she's in a mood.

She should be grateful. At least it wasn't nightmares. It could so easily be nightmares.

The holy charade finally ends and Misery lets her silent chaperones take her up a silver flight of stairs into a room of holy jade dark as the void, some kind of multiuse space where the deadmarble petals of chairs and tables huddle in conference. A glass-topped tray of food waits before one of those seats, and next to it stands to the Church-grunt Bridge from yesterday. "I hope you find this acceptable," zie says.

It's more than acceptable. The tray bears real food, with real textures and aromas so complex they make her dizzy. Spices thicken a stew full of tender cuts. Fruit slices crunch and burst with sugars. There's a sausage, wholesome and bright with fat, whose skin resists the blade of her knife until it splits with a satisfying noise. Juices run out. Misery eats like one starved a thousand years. Sure, the food on the Duke's ship was decadent, and unbearably so, but it is also a starship, with all the limitations that come with. There are things you need a full-service agrisector for. Not even Rootsdown's City Hall had one. She's never eaten like this before, and she doesn't know if she will again. Enjoy it while it lasts.

Between pyroclastic mouthfuls it occurs to Misery that Bridge didn't attend the morning Mass. Was zie not required to? Or did non-saints attend different services? In which case, she'd been sent to attend the saints' Mass, despite not being one. Irregular, no?

"Remarkably consistent, in fact," Ruin counters. "To the Church now you are far more precious than a mere saint. You are something else, something they've never had in their lifetimes. You are a Messiah, a Holy One. Touched by the Larex Forge Hirself."

Okay. Sure.

After breakfast, and tending to other biological needs, she's taken to the Archbishop. Pyrex Imogen's office occupies the center of Church HQ, all paths leading to it, the shining city on the hill. She winds up in a double-height chamber appointed in wood, that rarest of materials, dark and wild and knobbly. Faux glass windows cover the back wall, stylized dioramas projected over glowing holy opal. Overhead the chamber is topped by a dome of acryla steel that lets in the starlight. Misery looks up; in that sacred space the universe's whole breadth feels within reach.

Pyrex Imogen is at their desk: a massive curve in burnt sienna, the maned head of some untamed creature rendered in bas-relief on the front. Their fine features are lit by the kaleidoscope of a dozen screens they tap through. Hard at work, despite the early hour; probably hard at work the whole time Misery was at Mass and eating. She imagines the Archbishop waking in the death-hours and praying in the dark of their quarters, head bowed, lips shaping the same words that have fallen from her brother's mouth since memory was memory. Then Misery remembers her weird dream from last night and flushes with embarrassment.

The Archbishop looks up and their expression leavens. "Misery. You're a little early." They dismiss the screens to background grayness, and sit up a little. "Thank you for attending, Bridge."

With that the dutiful Bridge bows and withdraws, hir role in the ongoing drama at an end. It occurs to Misery that she never learned hir pronouns, and never bothered to ask.

The Archbishop folds their hands. "Did you sleep well, Misery?"

"Well enough."

"Was breakfast adequate?"

"More than adequate."

"Good. What happens today will change the trajectory of the Empire forever. We need you well rested and well fed."

Misery tucks her hands behind her. "Well, when you put it like that . . ."

"Are you ready?

Fuck no. But she smiles anyway. "Of course."

The door opens and deposits two newcomers: Duke Argan, in a simple suit of morning white, humble and neat, very unlike him. Next to him is the royal princess, Alodia Lightning, sheathed in black silk embellished with red, tight at the top and a waterfall between hip and ankle. Her bloodstone hair makes architecture atop her prim head, brightened by silver swans. Misery scowls in her direction until their eyes meet, at which point she realizes she's been caught scowling, and looks away, cheeks burning. Why is she here? Has the Archbishop forgotten that the princess's first instinct was to murder Misery?

The Archbishop is all smiles and delight, so they obviously don't consider attempted homicide a big deal. "Argan," they say, "is that what you're wearing to the audience tomorrow? I'm surprised it's so modest."

"Are you joking? As if I'd let myself be perceived like this. No, my do is in the closet. Can't risk it getting dirty before the shindig."

The princess says nothing. She sweeps past Misery, deliberately knocking into her hip. Not in a fun way, but an I-hope-this-hurts way. Misery doesn't give her the pleasure of a response. She remains stock-still, expression deadmarble.

Lady Alodia Lightning crosses the space and sits down. Two chairs rest before the Archbishop's desk: plush, velvet, high-backed, and detailed in gold. She sinks into one and, maintaining deliberate eye contact with Misery, props both feet on the other. Her core strength is admirable. The silver of her heeled boots form sharp contrast with the red of the velvet. Misery holds her face absolutely still. She's not sure what she's supposed to be feeling, as a normal person, so it's best to pretend she feels nothing. Her heart is doing the most in her chest, but she refuses to let it show. Forces her hands to stay still, because they desperately itch to connect with flesh and bone.

"Lightning," says the Archbishop, "what news do you bear from home?"

The princess keeps her gaze on Misery a second longer than necessary before addressing Pyrex Imogen. "What's to expect? Grandmother is livid. Thinks we're wasting her time. Has teams ripping through the stacks looking for technicalities she can use." A fluid shrug. "But nothing. You picked an airtight protocol, it seems."

"Of course." The Archbishop leans over their desk. "An emperor should be accessible and accountable to all his subjects of good standing. Even if the subject is one of his dukes."

"Hmph." The princess turns her disdain toward Lord Argan. "You truly believe this guff, don't you? If this goes south, and it will, your everything is on the line. You gonna risk it?"

"I have absolute faith in Misery," says the Duke, all sincerity as he stands next to her.

Lady Alodia Lightning shrugs again. "It's your exile."

"What about your brother?" asks the Archbishop. "What's your read on his likely response?"

Her attention never wavers from the Duke's face. "It turns out he still remembers what happened at the Academy, and has never forgiven you for it."

"Oh, come on," breathes the Duke. "That was ten years ago, he needs to grow up."

Misery turns her attention to the Duke. "You know him?"

"Mm. I do."

Misery squints at his evasiveness. "You know him *very* well," she says, guessing.

An epoch-ending sigh escapes his chest. "Fine. You got me. We were once, mm, involved, back when we were kids. Well. He was a kid. Not so much me. But that was a long time ago."

"You fucked."

"Yes, Misery. A very elegant way to put it. We fucked."

"You were his teacher," interjects the princess. She's crossed her arms without relinquishing balance, an almost-charming L propped on the Archbishop's luxe chairs.

"I was a *tutor*. Plus, he made the first move. It's not like I was preying on an innocent."

Alodia Lightning shrugs. Her balance is impeccable. "He was eighteen and you were thirty-five. I said what I said."

The Duke protests too much for one whose conscience is clear, Misery thinks. "Were you planning to tell me the Emperor of the Faithful is a bitter ex-fling, or was it supposed to be a surprise?"

"It," says the Archbishop, cutting briskly into the tempest, "does not matter. That is in the past. For the sake of the Empire, he must remain impartial. And we must convince him to do so."

The princess scoffs. "You expect Abiel to be rational? The man is eighty percent spite and twenty percent old grudge." Her bootheels thump on the ground. "There's a chance that he might not be petty about this. There's also a chance that all our chemical bonds might dissolve and we turn into cremoline."

"You're probably right about that," murmurs Duke Argan, looking at the tops of his shoes.

"Great," Misery says. "Love that. Love that for me, love that for all of us."

"We must have faith," says the Archbishop, and of course it's *faith* again, Misery's starting to tire of these exhortations of faith as a panacea to all the universe's ills. "The Larex Forge has laid the path before us, but it is not without obstacles. It is upon us, and upon the strength of our belief, to trust in Hir guidance and face those obstacles as they come."

"Of course," says Alodia Lightning, but she's smirking. Her levity is cut with some source of bitterness, but that's as much as Misery gets. There's history here she cannot parse.

"Come," says Pyrex Imogen, rising to their feet. "We must get ready for the hearing."

Getting ready half comprises protocol drills and half comprises getting dressed. The former agenda is conducted in a huge round room that is both projector and vid plaza. The Archbishop has it programmed to mirror the Grand Amphitheater, the hallowed arena where the Emperor deigns to breathe the air of mere mortals. The biggest public forum on the Capital, the Grand Amphitheater is used for everything from religious celebrations to Savior's Day Parades to sports events. Misery knows the inside of the Grand Amphitheater intimately: the dark green tiers stacked to the stars, the bucket seats lined with holy opal, the sun-defying floodlights. The colossal 3D field embedded with holy obsidian where gravity is humanity's plaything. From ages five to seven Misery watched every match of the Angels' League, the brawler tournament with retired seraph mechs, their deadly weaponry scooped out and replaced with light show. She memorized stats and pilot names. Their favorite colors and flavors. Devoted more heart to it than to her actual religion. Misery will never admit to the long nights she spent dreaming of pilothood as a child, but those nights existed, a vast jungle of cringe, fantasies bursting from the rich loam of naïveté and sincerity. She imagined herself an exalted combatant, wrapped in angry polymer and steel, raining down destruction as the crowds sang their adoration.

What would baby Misery think if she could see what her adult self is doing? She wouldn't understand, would not see the depth of the shit Misery's in. She would be impressed and overawed by the prestige and importance of the people she's meeting. Baby Misery was stupid as fuck. Grown-up Misery is taken through the paces, is taught to navigate the setup, avoiding butzed-off areas for dignitaries and decor. There's the penitent's pathway, a tongue of plush red, and the dais containing the throne, rendered as a block of tooth-white deadmarble. A floating platform will take her from the waiting area to the Emperor.

They run through a script, Pyrex Imogen playing the role of the Duke, the princess her older brother. The Lady Alodia Lightning hunches upon the gleaming throne, face slouched in an expression of absolute boredom. "Show him what the Larex Forge has gifted you," says the Archbishop, and that's Misery's cue to take the Tear of Assan and repeat her feats from yesterday. This is a practice round, so she doesn't waste her energy. Just goes through the motions.

"Oh, wow," drones the princess, chin and cheek spilling out of her palm.

Everything about this is odious. Misery's least favorite part of church service was its million and one observances and protocols. This is bound to be worse. She imagines the heat of the amphitheater, the roar of its hungry spectators, the unadulterated arrogance of its Emperor. His sister, insufferable as she is, can only be a preview of what to expect. Misery's blood preemptively boils at the idea of encountering someone more irritating than she is.

What's to stop her from assassinating the Emperor when she meets him? Besides the consequences and all that. Security in the Grand Amphitheater is holystone-based. Aegises and holy ruby. That won't stop her.

"Are you clear on the plan?" asks the Archbishop.

Startled from her murderous ruminations, Misery just nods. They're banking a lot on faith, these pillars of the religion. Putting her, an uneducated, voidmad criminal-type, in front of the Emperor himself. Fools.

After lunch it's Lord Argan's turn. The Duke of Apis brings a buzzing flock of palm-sized drones with him. "It's my tailor," he explains as they harass Misery, nipping at her boundaries, documenting the width of her joints and midsection. Each one bristles with sensors, and a fillet of holy tigereye bisects their chrome exoskeletons along the bottom. The animal half of Misery fumes in full flight mode; the other half forces her body to remain very, very still. They've taken over a general-use room, which appears different from Misery's breakfast venue. Lord Argan sprawls across one of the deadmarble tables with an enormous dresser parked before him, thin and glassy and rimmed with metal. With a dismissive finger he flicks through sartorial confection after sartorial confection. A parade of suits, dresses, capes, veils, armor, jumpers, sarongs, coats, scarves, hats, and more pin themselves upon Misery's silhouette. To a strawberry confection that's more ruffle than seam he scowls and says, "Void no." In its place appears something white, fluted, covered in cream piping. "Oh, come on. If you want to get us laughed out of the chamber . . ."

If he's nervous, she can't tell. He could be; sometimes people respond to stress by masking it with obnoxiousness. She tests him. "Do you think it'll work? That the Emperor will be swayed by the transformation of one little stone piece?"

"He better," says the Duke, not quite looking at her. "It's a miracle and he should be grateful he gets to witness it."

"He doesn't sound like the believing type to me."

He looks up, suddenly bright. "Misery. I told you it will work out and I truly believe that. Abiel may be a small, petty-minded thing, but he has always been first and foremost a romantic, driven by emotion and not logic. I believe he can be swayed. I believe he can be convinced of the extraordinary moment he finds himself in. That he has been chosen to receive a gift so precious from the Larex Forge: that of salvation, and the end to the strife and corruption brought upon us by the Heretics."

Misery smiles with her face, which feels very separate from the rest of her. This is the contradiction of Lord Argan: for all his flash and overindulgence, the man is as devout as her brother is. His belief runs solid all the way through, as much as she can tell, and somehow that is worse than Crem's worship, which seemed driven in part by necessity and a political savvy.

She should be pleased that she's sucked in and suckered these paragons of faith who now think she's some sort of holy beacon.

The Duke's final choice is a suit of golden armor. Something something sourceworld revival, it's fashionable to go about weighed down by a bold shell of hammered metal. Assembling the coalition of clanking bits requires robotic assistance, figuring out what goes where like a tangram. The algorithms will shape the outfit to make music as Misery walks.

"There," he says. "We'll send it to your room nearer the hour. Now it is time to rest."

Thus is Misery sent back to the anchorex's cell, where another fragrant meal waits, with little blocked in but prayer and contemplation until the final hour.

Tomorrow, she goes to see the Emperor. Tomorrow, she finds out how this all ends.

6

At the appointed time Lord Argan comes to Misery's quarters to take her to the Emperor. She rings like a meditation bell, and he looks like a fool. The Duke of Apis wears a vest of holographic vinyl, encased in the bright puffs of a glassine coat whose surface swarms with moving fish and birds. White leather pants accompany holo boots on six-inch platforms shot through with light and whole lotus flower heads. His richly styled curls glitter with oil-black pearls and magpie feathers and squares of genuine sourceworld microelectronics. He says, "I am August Faust, Apisian Muse of Life. What do you think?" Misery thinks he looks unsalvageably ridiculous, and she would expect nothing less of him. He's all fistfuls of nervous energy, and his Brownian jittering encompasses a wide field of interpretations that Misery cannot narrow down. She's not going to think about it. Her mother's amulet is tucked under her shining golden breastplate; she'll be taken if she goes anywhere without it now.

The Grand Amphitheater sits at the lip of the Imperial quarter, an exclusive sector that is the heart of hearts in the Empire of the Faithful. Misery has made a good friend of the station map in the time since she's been captive. Church and Throne each have their bubble, the two loci of power situated in opposition at the center of the Capital. In between these heavily fortified lobes lie seven great biodomes filled with life from the sourceworld. The light rail that connects Church to Throne runs right through them, glass tunnels punched into habitats that mirror the way things were on Old Earth, according to the legends. Misery and the Duke have a pod almost to themselves, discounting the six

white-saint guards in Apisian colors, and Misery can't help looking outward as the clear capsule runs along its strip of holy tigereye. In the jungle dome, an imitation sun lords over swells of
green bursting with life. Widespread canopies heave with vines,
and winged things burst forth in flashes of unimaginable color.
Misery swears she won't be awed, but finds herself holding her
breath anyway. The capsule passes though an ice dome, a desert
dome, a dome full of ragged cliffs and mist. In the ocean dome,
glittering and blue, an enormous shadow passes over them, the
shape and size of a midsize warship. "Blue whale," the Duke explains. "Biggest living thing they took from the source." Misery
tries to imagine existing in a body with bones like that, obliter-
ating reefs with one sweep of her tail, but her imagination cuts
out. Can't fathom what it's like to live with that much power.

Ruin is in the water, a soft dark shape that glows as zie floats
alongside the leviathan. The delusion has decided to tag along
for the ride. Of course zie would; zie loves mess, and what's
about to happen is guaranteed mess.

Blue light breaks into yellow as they come out of the domes
and into open space. The Imperial quarter wears a towering
shell of projector glass, powered by holy opal and big enough
to swallow moons. During the Imperial day it plays images of
clouds and rain; at night it turns transparent, letting in starlight.
Right now, which is evening, it casts slanting rays of gold over
the tips and spires of the palace. The fast-approaching buildings
gleam, surfaces all stone-smooth, wings and buttresses shaped
in the gravity-defying patterns of holystone. "Is it all holy jade?"
she asks.

"There's holy marble and other supports," says the Duke.
"But yes. It's mostly holy jade."

"I've heard even the Grand Cathedral on Apis Prime isn't
holy jade all the way through."

"It's not."

Misery nods to show sympathy. There was one slab of holy jade
in all of Rootsdown and it formed the center of the churchhall's

facade. The rest of the building had been mundane-built, soil
and clay shaped by human hands. Or rather, shaped by machines made by machines made by human hands. By human
minds.

The capsule stops on the Imperial side in a station all shades
of green, where towering columns of holy jade close high above
their heads. Floating gardens drift lazily between them, lifted by
holy tigereye and bubble-wrapped in holy obsidian. The pathways are lined with statues of Emperors and Empresses and
Emprexes past. A flock of white saints and human soldiers waits
for them as they disembark into the subtly perfumed air. "Come
to take us to the Emperor, have you?" asks the Duke.

Their new chaperones do not answer. Instead they crowd in
and shift them with the force of veiled threat alone, separating the Duke and Misery from their entourage. They are surrounded. The muzzles of the soldiers' guns are patient, waiting
for an excuse to be useful. Lord Argan chuckles softly. "So that's
how it's going to be, eh?"

The Duke is definitely nervous. It does not bode well. By old
habit Misery's hand aches for the weight of her mother's amulet,
but there's a shell of singing armor between them. The stone
disc rests on her sternum instead, hot and restless with strange
energy. She might be confusing it with her heart.

The Throne's guards herd them onto an arrowhead barge
that rises noiselessly into a buttery glide past holy jade and airborne trees. As the Imperial quarter swans by Misery moves as
close to the ornate railing as she can, still curious, still hungry.
Around her is an emerald city, its streets embellished with gold
and its denizens wrapped in thick layers of luxury fabric. She
finds herself surprised by the lack of holy imagery. Not what
she expects of the absolute center of the Empire of the Faithful. Where are the statues of the Messiahs, the projected glass
dioramas of the Awakening, the priests on every corner singing
hymns of the Larex Forge's Grace? Even the doorways appear

devoid of prayer rings. Don't they fear the nullvoid here? Aren't they scared?

Ruin, leaning into the wind, grins and licks hir lips with the red tip of hir tongue. "Do you imagine those little trinkets can truly hold back the nullvoid from the mind of one who welcomes it?" As Misery turns away from hir, heart racing, zie continues, "Or does it upset you, perhaps, that you cling to superstition more than you'd like?"

Instead of letting the delusion get to her—as if!—Misery turns to the Duke. Lord Argan has pulled out a small tin of mint salve to daub his neck with. A popular thing with his crew, these little discs of medicinal cream, spiced with herbs and wood-scent. Misery let an ensign rub some on her wrists back on his ship, and she appreciated the burst of coolness, followed by the gentle fog of salve-calm. But she's never seen the Duke partake until now. "Nervous?"

He catches the edge in her voice and shifts on his feet, tucking the shiny tin into the gaudy folds of his plastic jacket. "If I were you, I'd be worried about me if I wasn't nervous."

A lot of shuffling between persons in one sentence. Misery says: "This station gets under my skin."

He nods vacantly. "It hasn't always been like this. I'm old enough to remember the times before this truce nonsense set in. Back in my childhood, there was still space for devotion." The Duke shakes his head. "It's almost sad to see."

"These white saints," Misery says, quietly tilting her head in the direction of one. "Are they a new thing?"

"Very much so." A shiver runs through him. He speaks low enough not to be heard by anyone else. "Don't quote me on this, but I can't stand being around them. There's something in their eyes that's just not right. Like there's void instead of a soul."

Harsh, but Misery won't argue. The Duke's been around these creatures for longer than she has, he probably knows a thing or two. *A void where a soul should be.* Misery's skin crawls, and she reaches to touch her mother's amulet for reassurance. Her fingers ring against metal plate, and she remembers.

The arrowhead barge deposits them in the shadow of the Grand Amphitheater. Sound bubbles over holy jade walls so dark they look black. There must be thousands in the audience, and thousands more watching via wavelink. It is an *event,* and the breadth of the Empire is paying attention. Misery draws cold air into her lungs before the Throne's bully squad marches her through a side door and into a warren of narrow walkways. It's dark here under the amphitheater seats. The Throne has been stingy with the holy opal—or mundane lighting, for that matter—in these areas. Misery can barely make out the bas-relief carvings of mechs in battle that cover the pillars.

"Very atmospheric," says the Duke wryly.

They're deposited in a waiting room: a bare oval lined with bondcrete, matte gray and mundane. It scuffs the polish of Misery's armor as she sinks to the floor in lotus position, back against one curved wall. She guesses the crete is to protect the holy jade foundation, just in case a saint gets up to something. But none of the penitents today are saints. There's maybe a dozen of them, ordinary citizens with dark hair and dull skin, dressed in their fanciest. Next to Misery and the Duke, they might as well be in rags. Lord Argan greets the other supplicants as a matter of courtesy, but they wordlessly recoil from his bow, suspicious and afraid. Their thoughts are clear on their faces: they don't know what a duke is doing among them. They fear him. They resent him. They don't know what to make of Misery: Is she his servant? His bodyguard? His handmaiden? Why is she dressed like that?

The other supplicants are poor, from every part of the galaxy imaginable. Some have traveled for months to reach the Capital, unable to afford any faster slots through the jump gates. There's a mother begging clemency for her child, who is on death row. There's a representative of several destitute colonies, far-flung and past their use-by date, come to beg the succor of a better jump slot for their system. There's a nixen who wants eir baron father to acknowledge his paternity. So on and so forth. Their sorrow pounds in Misery's temples like a tide. Misery closes her eyes and focuses on Saint Agneta's pattern: four in, six hold, seven out. She can't let these woes drown her. She needs her mind sharp.

One by one, the penitents are called to meet the Emperor. A door rumbles open across from Misery and a wave of sound crashes in, solid as heat, as a servant of the Throne—draped and hooded in red—shouts a name. The summoned penitent shuffles through the stone mouth and the door muffles noise again. Holy jade is one of those materials that's soundproof, but slits have been cut through the top of the arena-side wall, and a taste of atmosphere filters in: the jet-rumble of excitement, the stamping and clapping. Sudden hushes as the Emperor lays down his judgment, inaudible to those in the cage of bondcrete. Then noise roars again—anger, delight, anguish, it's hard to tell, at the scale of thousands they're indistinguishable. It's human emotion, what more do you want? Shortly after that the arena's jaw opens to swallow the next penitent. The old ones do not return.

"They're wearing you down," says Ruin. The delusion slides unnoticed between the remaining penitents. "They're fraying your nerves on purpose. The more nervous they want you, the further back they'll have you."

Misery swallows and tastes blood in her mouth. Are her gums bleeding, or is this another hallucination? She sees the skin split on Mother's face, the gush of ichor, the flashing tendrils of voidstuff. Something in the air is triggering these bad memories. Something here is rotten.

The room empties as the penitents are called to face their fates, and eventually it's just Misery and the Duke. They're last in line. The Duke paces the length of the oval, acrylic heels making heavy contact with the crete at every step. "Could you stop that?" Misery says. "You're destroying my concentration."

Lord Argan looks at her, says something inaudible, and continues pacing.

Their turn finally comes. The Emperor is ready for them at last. The red-wrapped servant at the doorway recites the Duke's names—he has so many—and Lord Argan turns and gestures to Misery: *Time to go.* Of course. She stands up and, again, resents the metal between her and her mother's amulet. She could use a touch of warmth right now.

A glass elevator takes them upward through a column of stone. No light except the thin rings of holy opal rimming the interior. Outside the noise of an entertained crowd surges and recedes. Misery's reflection in the glass is unrecognizable, all chunky shiny metal with an unhappy face somewhere in it, tight and grim, deep shadows under her eyes. There's no way this is going to end well. Why is she here, if she's already doomed?

The elevator reaches its destination. Light pours over them as they rise into the vast cavity of the amphitheater. Unhindered by wall and stone, the noise from a hundred thousand throats crashes upon them like rockfall. Misery's eyes adjust badly to the flood of light. The amphitheater is so large it defies human understanding: instead she thinks of wild desert, dusty craters on Rootsdown so vast you crossed them on barges, dead old mechs in rings with broken fingers of stone, sharp and towering. There are the audience stands, rings of holy jade packed with cheering, excited bodies, stacked in the direction of the glass roof. High above, its rim is topped by massive halogen lights whose blue-white rays converge in the floating center of the field. Where the Emperor's dais is. Where Misery is headed.

The platform that will convey them to the Emperor is waiting. It barely fits two people, but Misery and the Duke shuffle on anyway. Misery makes the mistake of looking down and seeing how far down firmament is. Heights don't scare her. They don't. She can fly. She lets air out of her lungs. The Duke better not sneeze, though. She's not saving him if he falls.

The conveyor shudders once before it moves forward. Completely unnecessary. Over there, thumbnail-sized in the distance, is the floating barge of the Emperor's dais. As they are carried across, an unknown, unseen announcer introduces them. Where they're from. Who they are. What they want. The Duke of Apis, and a "pilgrim" with a message from the Larex Forge. The crowd roars, amused. The Grand Amphitheater, which occupied so much of the child-Misery's imagination, bears down upon them with the weight of a neutron star. Here, in the real world, heat and sound assault her from all sides, and Misery has never felt so small or so exposed as she does now.

A voice sluices through her mind, cool and mocking: "That's what they want you to feel. Will you give them the satisfaction?"

No, but she won't allow Ruin the satisfaction of being right, either. Zie doesn't deserve it.

The Imperial dais: fifty measures of strange white holystone that Misery has never seen and doesn't recognize. The platform stops before the wide steps cut into the front, leading up to the Emperor's seat. Misery and the Duke climb. The seat is milled from a single tree, which must have been a thousand years old when it was felled and shaped into a wide, flat seat whose back bursts into a canopy of branches strung with balls of glass and flame. Approach is impossible except from the front, which is shielded by a yellow aegis.

Dignitaries occupy either side of this confection. Misery doesn't recognize them on sight, except for one: the princess Lee Alodia Lightning, standing on the left. A lantern dress billows around her, clear glass encasing a hundred layers of ivory tulle. Black antlers frame her head and neck, sharp and glistening. She looks amazing and Misery hates her for it.

Next to her is an older woman, sheathed in a neat white gown with gold detailing. Her face—high cheekbones, narrow eyes—mirrors the Lady Alodia Lightning's, and this, Misery realizes, must be the Empress Dowager, her grandmother. A cold woman, carrying enough derision to form a pressure system.

But she's just passing distraction. For Misery's attention is sucked in by the singularity slouched upon the seat. The Emperor is all limbs and bad attitude, glowering from beneath furrowed brows. A thinner and angrier version of his sister, he's wrapped in a jacket matching his grandmother's and a bloodred skirt with a holographic sheen. Dark-eyed. Dark-haired. The soft curls tumble over his brow and around his ears, glossy and ordinary. No telltale sheen. This crown has not been blessed by the Demiurge.

Lee Abiel Serenity Morningstar, twelfth Emperor of the Faithful, is not a saint.

Thank Forge for the rehearsals, because Misery's mind blanks at the revelation, and she stumbles up the stage on instinct, obedient in Lord Argan's lead. How has this been hidden? How has it not been known? But of course, but of course—that's why the Imperial family is so secretive. No pictures, no reports. It's not for security reasons. And not because—as kooks like her brother claim—that to reproduce the image of one so exalted would be to desecrate him.

It's because he's not a saint.

Of *course,* there have been emperors unsainted. Of *course,* being sainted is no mandate to lead. But the last four Exalted Lees have all been blessed. Chosen of the Larex Forge. Emperor Lee Abiel Serenity breaks a chain that was laid down by his great-grandpyrex, Emprex Lee Calladine Falcon the First. And of course—now that Misery's seeing it, all laid out on the dais like that—there's his younger sister *right there,* with that headful of crimson iridescence, challenging his right to rule just by existing. If one were to say that void-rot has spread to the center of the Empire, there would be no greater proof than this, the Larex Forge withdrawing Hir blessing from the scion of the royal family. Surely there must be a reason.

The roar of spectator noise falls to a hush as this diminished Emperor straightens from his slouch. He whose word is Law summons the attention of all around him.

His gaze falls on Misery and the Duke like molten lava.

There's so much hatred in it, so much resentment, that it manages to shock even Misery, who is used to living with hate and resentment. Lord Argan called the boy king petty, but this is beyond pettiness, this is full-blown vendetta. The Emperor *seethes* with anger at the sight of his old lover. Cannot believe his audacity, the sheer brass balls of this man, playing at demanding an audience, and to add salt upon it all, bringing some mundane moonrat to claim status of Messiah, particularly from *that* prophecy . . . The insult. The imperial mockery.

The Duke of Apis carries in a pouch by his waist the sacred disc, the Tear of Assan. Misery sees now, clear as opal, that their demonstration is going to fail. What can her cheap stonebending trick do against the towering inferno of the Emperor's hate? He doesn't believe in prophecies. He will not be moved by holy force, no matter how great.

Or will he?

"Look at what's around you," Ruin says. "The Demiurge provides."

The Duke has begun moving through the script. He bows. He invokes the proper words to honor the Larex Forge and the Messiahs who have gone before and the Exalted Ones who continue to guide the Faithful through these dangerous times. He says, "I beg of you an audience, that you might hear my plea."

The Emperor smiles. It's a blade across his face, filled with teeth.

The Exalted One, He who was chosen to lead the Faithful, says, "I deny it."

The speaker drones, tiny silver specks orbiting the Emperor's head, catch his voice and play it to the thousands gathered. For a heartbeat there's a shocked hush before the gasps and tittering begin. This is unprecedented! How surprising!

Lord Argan says—stutters, really: "You can't do that."

Lee Abiel Serenity crosses his legs and leans back, purring. "Can't I? There are no rules that say I *have* to grant an audience if it's asked."

The Duke draws a furious breath. "You're supposed to—"

The Emperor dismisses the speaker drones, so that he can speak to them alone. "Don't tell me what I'm *supposed* to do. *You* were supposed to crawl back into your hole and stay there until you died. Not try to sneak around my refusal of a private audience with *this*."

He gestures to the pantomime around him with derisive flicks of the wrist. In his face Misery sees grains of truth from the Duke's side of the story: the boy Emperor has always wanted the Duke more than the Duke wanted him. He relished having the older man at his beck and call. He saw it as ownership, as he saw most everything else. And he did not take well to being broken up with. One does not leave an emperor before he is ready to leave you.

The viewing galley is a crush of delight and titillation. A duke so humiliated! From Misery's standpoint it appears a seething wall of cruelty, insurmountable and unbreachable. Seats in the Grand Amphitheater don't go to just anyone: it's merchants and financiers and minor nobility having a fine day out. A great day's entertainment, laughing and sipping cremoline in their air-conditioned seats, watching the poorest and most desperate of the Faithful crawl before the Emperor and beg for his mercy. Their exuberance rings in her ears and heats her blood. Misery's chest swells with adrenaline, ribs shuddering under the strain.

Unusual movement on the dais. The princess Lee Alodia Lightning finds an opening in the particular sluggishness of shock, and makes her move. She is a saint, she can stonebend, she calls a speaker drone to herself. She addresses the Duke, broadcasting to the Grand Amphitheater and everyone who's watching. "I'll hear your plea."

The audience explodes into a thousand overlapping titters. What a twist, how unexpected! The princess, the invisible little sister, speaking! Defying the natural order of things in front of her brother and grandmother! How dare she! The buzz of their unholy joy burrows into Misery's body. She is infested by unseemly delight. She imagines it bursting from her skin in tendrils, tearing her from bone to tendon, just like—

The Empress Dowager snaps at her recalcitrant granddaughter: "Child, sit down."

"No," says the princess Lee Alodia Lightning, and she's staring right at Misery, making sure she's paying attention. "I'm royal blood. I can hold an audience too. You're not the only one who checked the rules. Plus, primogeniture is bullshit."

Her brother the coward Emperor chokes with indignation. But Alodia Lightning's gaze bores into Misery like it's acid. It's a test. When they fought in the bowels of the station, Misery woke the holy ruby weapon in the princess's hand. She knows Misery is different. *She knows.* And she craves something—more knowledge, perhaps. She's not afraid, not that Misery can tell. She wants to see what else Misery can do.

The princess's gaze is the thunderclap that ruptures the walls holding Misery together. But instead of destroying her—instead of tearing her to incoherent shreds—instead of breaking her and turning her flesh into unspeakable monstrosity—instead of doing any of that, it frees her. The pressure built up inside her, gone. The tension and dread that have plagued her since she set foot on this station, gone. A great weight upon her soul, which she hadn't realized was there, also gone. Misery feels lighter than she has in ages, as though she could reach out and touch every star in the universe with her bare fingers. Infinite possibilities lie before her. Does she know what she needs to do? She does.

The delusion that calls hirself Ruin blazes with purpose and hunger in the periphery of her vision, human borders subliming into something approaching the divine. "So do it," zie says. "Do what your heart is telling you."

People like the Emperor cannot be persuaded by words alone. The callous ranks of the privileged will not accept a gentle guiding hand. They need to be bullied, all of them. Misery has to put the fear of the Larex Forge in them. She has to be like her brother.

She closes her fists.

Misery summons a speaker drone with the ease of a saint, calling its holy tigereye to her side. Beside her the Duke tenses with anxiety: "What are you doing?" She ignores him. A greater mission calls, the voice of a higher authority speaks. She knows now that she has been prepared for this since childhood. A thousand sermons bubble within her, the foamy-mouthed off-spring of raw material injected into her being when it was still soft, when she was still forming. She lets her spirit fill with the ghost of her brother at the pulpit, railing against sin and ex-cess while she rolled her eyes at the back of the churchhall. She draws upon the deep well of disdain and anger he would turn upon her, little sister whose misbehavior displeases the Larex Forge.

Misery fills her lungs with breath. "All of you. Listen to me."

Her voice, booming low across the arena, doesn't sound like her own. It rumbles like a shockwave, silencing all in its wake. The Grand Amphitheater is transfixed by this bold stranger speaking out of turn, blazing with the fire of a blue sun. She sees the white of the Emperor's eyes; he's turned to stone in his seat.

Misery lifts her lips from her teeth. She will turn them all to stone. "I come from the very edges of the Empire, from the duchy of Apis. You may have heard of me. Perhaps on the waves, perhaps as a whispered rumor. I have come to tell you that what you've heard is true. Yes! Rejoice! I am the Black Hole Messiah, as foretold by the prophet of Calister, sent by the Larex Forge to destroy the threat of the Heretics and seal the nullvoid forever."

How easy these lies come to her, silver-coated and airy. She lets the untruths spill from her like a torrent, gaining velocity as her courage builds.

The Emperor jumps to his feet, fury purpling his complex-ion. "Are you insane? You wormy fuck. Sit down. Sit the fuck down."

The speaker drone captures every syllable of his rant. How unhinged he sounds. Misery looks imperiously at him, this berry-faced babbling child, and projects upon him a disdain larger than she is. "Silence," she says. "You call me a worm? You, from whom the Larex Forge chose to withhold Hir blessing? The gall of it."

Titters and gasps from the audience. They said it, the crazy nixen. Uttering the truths that only fools would dare to voice. Their delight is what she has been seeking. Their delight turns her stomach.

The Emperor gapes at her audacity. The Empress Dowager has no such weaknesses. She's on her feet, formidable for her age. "How dare you. Guards, arrest this terrorist."

Misery twists the holy obsidian around the dais, and the aegis protecting the Emperor follows. Seals them in a little bubble, separate from the rings of palace guards. Around the Emperor and his grandmother, speaker drones crumple in a flare of sparks and flying shrapnel. Stone chunks rain to the ground, and Misery sees genuine fear in the boy Emperor's eyes. "I think not," she says. Now she's the only one who can broadcast to the rest of the Grand Amphitheater. "You will listen to what I have to say. I have come a very long way, and I will not be thwarted."

It feels good in the pettiest way. Misery can make meanness grand. Even if she were to die at the end of this, she will be spoken of for years to come. For centuries. This performance will not be forgotten. Hands open, she mirrors the pose of Saint Agneta at Mount Isucus. She channels her brother, she channels the wrath of Saint Ono at the Council of Betrayal. Her spine straightens, she speaks not to those before her but the stars in the void of space above.

"You must be wondering, why would the Larex Forge choose me, a simple and lowly nixen from the edge of the Empire, to bring Hir word to the rest of the Faithful. You're not alone. I wondered the same. Surely there must be someone better. I thought, Great Demiurge, why me? Is there no one else who could fill this role? Surely someone from a duchy closer to the center of the Empire would be better? Someone richer, from a powerful family, someone who could influence the Throne? But that was my mistake."

She throws her hands to the wind, gesturing at the vastness around her. "You see, I was raised religious. My brother was a pastor. I was taught that the Larex Forge chose who should sit upon the Throne. I was taught that those who lead us, lead us because they are the most devout, that they have the purest of souls. And I believed it. Why shouldn't I? I believed in a good and just world. Even if we were poor, even if food was hard to come by, we knew that we were protected from the evils of the Heretics and the ravages of the nullvoid by the faith and devotion of those leading our Empire."

This is a lie. Crem has no love for those in the centers of power and voiced his disdain clearly and often. Misery never once believed herself safe from the nullvoid. It was right there in her house. In her body.

Still she speaks. "This week, coming to the Capital for the first time, I was shocked. I expected the holiest of citadels, prayers of gratitude to the Larex Forge for keeping us safe against the nullvoid. I expected grace and light. What have I found? Vulgar decadence. Gilded doors and grand statues on every corner, while in the outer duchies your citizens ration energy and starve."

The tittering turns to groans: oh, another lecture about conspicuous consumption, another naggy scold tut-tutting about how good they have it and they should be miserable just for existing. Fools to think that this would be entertaining.

Misery smiles with more teeth than necessary, feeling cool air on her gums. Oh, they'll be entertained soon enough. She's spiraling closer to truth, and the things she's saying, she doesn't have to pretend she means them. "Worse still, I see now the reasons for this years-long truce, this appeasement of the Heretics. This Capital is full of abominations, these perversions of the natural order. Are you cloning saints now? Are you defying the edicts against sullying the mind and body, edicts which were laid down by the Demiurge and brought to us by the Eight Messiahs? I see you trying to induce sainthood in children, to defy the Larex Forge by making blessing where there is none. Is that what you choose to call holy? Are you no different from the Heretics? I am shocked by what I have witnessed on this station. No, not shocked. I should say, *disgusted.* You disgust me."

Silence now. A quick survey of her immediate surrounds: fear and anger within the cage of the dais. The Empress Dowager is furious and plotting her death. The Emperor is about to piss himself. The Duke, paralyzed by her audacity, says and does nothing. But the princess: a light blazes in her eyes and her unreadable expression is fevered. Is she smiling? It looks like she's smiling.

At her feet the white holystone sings with unusual resonance. Her mother's amulet is an ember under the armor, but its heat only gives Misery more strength. Ruin towers over the dais, shining with holy light, tall as a building and just as terrible. "Do what you need to do, Misery Nomaki."

She says: "What the Demiurge gives, the Demiurge takes away. You were tasked to be stewards of the Faithful, to protect and care for those whose lives were entrusted to you. You failed. For your transgressions you will be punished."

There's holy obsidian in the ground of the Grand Amphitheater. Aegises to protect the audience from the battling mechs, to section the field, to project obstacles. One wraps around the edge of the viewing stands, blanketing the watching ranks of nobility in a sense of safety, an incorruptible separation from the drama playing out before them. They trust the holy obsidian. As a child Misery once stole a finger of holy obsidian by chipping it off an abandoned warehouse. For hours she hid in her favorite hollow under their family reef and twisted at the skinny gray until it yielded its secrets. The barriers produced by holy obsidian are made of energy unknown to humanity, divine light. In her quiet hollow Misery discovered all the stone's hidden teeth.

It's time to show the world what she learned.

Misery shuts her eyes and touches holy obsidian where it has a pulse. The holystone vibrates and keens as the light barrier around the field's perimeter blinks from yellow to red and into the purples, going dark in wild tendrils like fast-setting gangrene. Alarm rushes through the audience: What is this? An attack? The void? The rows closest to the aegis lurch backward in fear, dropping their expensive snacks, ring-encrusted fingers scrabbling for purchase. The small amusement, the wannabe orator, wasn't supposed to do anything. What is going on?

Misery feels like she's floating, her body dissolving, her surroundings becoming immaterial while the aegis solidifies. It's the only real thing in the universe. It's part of her, as real as the bones in her fingers, and she can control it just as well.

She flexes her fingertips, and one of those purple tendrils takes form. A fat cord of swarming particulate lashes out from the writhing surface of the aegis. It rears backward, long as a transport ship, so big it clips the edge of the Imperial dais where she stands. The arena erupts in screams, but their terror is useless. The tendril slams forward into the spectator stands. Everything in its path instantly atomizes, molecular bonds dissolving upon contact: masonry, flesh, bone. The tendril carves a path through one sector of the stands and a hundred people are instantly vaporized, along with the seats and the floors and all their stupid finery. The air fills with ozone, shrieking, the smell of burnt meat. Those on the edge wail in despair as they slip on the crumbling stone, plunging hundreds of feet to their deaths. In the back, those still spared are running for the exits, tripping over one another, stepping on one another, breaking each other's bones in the rush for survival.

Again, again, again. More tendrils awaken, lash out, devour the soft oily masses in their way. A whole section of seating collapses and destroys the rows below with a heavy crunch. Holy jade is indestructible, impervious to heat, blade, or laser, but it cannot guard from other kinds of holystone. It falls like everything else. Nothing will be spared. Misery's mouth fills with the

taste of metal, but her body is very far away from her consciousness. She has been taken over by a force much greater than she
is. Break apart. Break open. Like skin splitting in a flash of
blood and fat, swells of nullvoid shooting from the rupture.

Something strikes her across the forehead, knocking her backward, and Misery is whipped back into her body. Flat on her
back on the dais with her head throbbing, her vision clouded
by wild sparks and pain. A roaring in her ears that is half blood
and half keening. Something—someone—stands above her, a
human-shaped silhouette. The Empress Dowager? Someone
else? In the dome of faux sky sits the delusion Ruin, enormous
and angel-shaped, multiple limbs spanning the width of the
stars. Before the second blow lands Misery imagines that zie is
laughing.

INTERLUDE 3

The Throne did not appreciate Misery Nomaki's little display of power. Of course not. One does not threaten the life of an emperor without consequences. One does not kill hundreds of the rich and powerful and get to live. The Emperor wanted them executed on the spot, but his grandmother, veins swollen with cruelty, wanted a spectacle. A drawn-out public hearing and public spectacle. Not just for Misery, but for the Duke of Apis, who dared bring this degenerate to her. And her grand-daughter, for her naked defiance while the whole Empire was watching. Blood only protects you if you bow to its whims.

Such things take time to plan. The offenders would need to be put away for months while the public trial was prepared. The Church, with their canny whispers, managed to divert the prisoners to a highly classified military base on the edge of the duchy. It was in their interests, in fact, that the three go there specifically.

But in the meantime, the Empire talked. Despite the Throne's wishes, despite the media blackout they enforced, the events at the Grand Amphitheater filtered into the public conscious-ness. What Misery Nomaki said shone with the glaze of truth. After all, the Messiah's coming had been predicted years ago by the prophet of Calister. Had the Faithful not forgotten the teachings of the First Eight in recent years? The Throne had gone as far as to pursue *peace* with the Heretics, as if such a thing could possibly exist. Punishment had been long coming from the Larex Forge, who had afforded far too much of Hir Grace to Hir wayward children. Would the Emperor risk further displeasing the Demiurge by rejecting the one chosen to lead them back to Hir side?

The fizzle of rumor and speculation became a runaway chain reaction, unstoppable by any means. Romulus and Remus pulsed with fervor. A growing breadth of the Empire bubbled over with tales of Misery Nomaki the Blessed, chosen of the Demiurge, the Ninth Messiah who had come to guide the Faithful toward the path of righteousness, from which they had strayed. The galas and the parties of the nobility lit up with impassioned, drunken arguments. On the chattering balconies overlooking the pink salt flats of Romulus, at grandparents' tables in the working-class districts, skepticism fought a losing battle to wonder. Exhausted by generations of war, rendered hopeless by the passivity of the Truce of Logan, the Faithful latched upon this hint of change like a fount of wine. By the time the Emperor exited from his cloistered meetings, brow furrowed and fingers on temples, Misery Nomaki was already being heralded as the Ultimate Savior even in the farthest-flung duchies. An enterprising youth unearthed Misery Nomaki's bio from Apis recordbases and flooded the waves with a mockup of them in Saint Ono's pose. A well-subscribed pastor on Remus named the incident at the Grand Amphitheater *the Messiah's Reckoning*, a phraseology that captured fevered imaginations and flooded the waves in no time. In Apis, the halls of the House of Bichap trilled with yearning and excitement. And in his church-hall back on Rootsdown, Cremoline Nomaki knelt before an altar in prayer, waiting for the salves to still his thoughts.

7

The Throne's jailors have learned their lessons. This time Misery's thrown in a saint's cell, a white honeycomb block lined with indestructible plastic she can't bend to her will. The door is solid all the way through, and it's harder than her fists. Her swollen knuckles are testament to that. She might punch the door again. Bruise-pain overrides the hunger eviscerating her. Saints metabolize light and can survive without food, so they don't send any to this block. Misery hasn't been fed in hours, or days, she can't tell. Time is meaningless in this nothing cell with no furnishings and no sound but the rush of her blood. Feels like acid has eaten a hole through her belly. She'd rather have broken bones.

Crem did this when she was a tot, locking her in a room with only light for company to prove that she wasn't a saint. A delightful test: if Misery survived they could call her a saint, and if she died of starvation then her stoneshifting was voidsickness, inherited from their mother. And Crem didn't think she was a saint.

In any case he was right, and it was Mother who furiously rescued Misery, unseamed by hunger, before nature could take its course. This time, though, no one's coming for her. It'll be over if they don't let her out soon.

You fucked up, Misery. You stupid fuck.

Misery says this through her hands, clamped over her face to block the interminable light. She's a comma on the bed, a rectangle of white foam sealed in the floor. There's no reply and she won't pretend she wasn't hoping for one. But Ruin has abandoned her. She's used to the delusion coming and going as zie pleases, but zie has never been away for this long. It feels punitive.

Her mother's amulet is gone too. They took it from her, along with the golden armor and everything else she was wearing. It's just her and a gray zipsuit to cover her nakedness. Misery misses the amulet's weight on her chest, in her hand, in her zone of awareness. For the first time since leaving Rootsdown, she feels completely and utterly unmoored.

She shouldn't have done it. Hindsight is laser-guided, and perfectly useless, but she sees clearly now that causing mass murder and mayhem was a mistake. She wanted to make an impression but she made the wrong one.

That's self-evident; no normal person would have to think this. She hears the admonition in Ruin's voice, it's what zie would say if zie were around. Misery curls deeper into fetal position.

Why did she do it? It felt right in the moment, like following gravitational pull, cleaving to a fundamental force of the universe. She didn't think it through. Followed her gut. Saw a path and took it. Misery forgot, for a moment, the defining principle of her life: that she's crazy and the nullvoid has been consuming her since she was born. And she's never been the cautious type, but the recklessness she tapped into while she destroyed the Grand Amphitheater was something else entirely.

That's what it's like surrendering to the void. Powerful. Intoxicating. Absolutely terrible.

But it's wrong to think of the voidmad as dangerous and violent. It's untrue and unfair, a vise used to trap them in horrible situations. Mother wasn't like that. She had an on-again, off-again relationship with reality, but she never lost the warmth and compassion that made the core of her. Even when she fought with Crem, even when she was all fire and spit, she was kind. Her sickness never drove her to homicide.

Misery uncovers her face and lets the light hurt her eyes. "It's me that's the problem," she says. "There's something wrong with me." She's doing Crem and Ruin a favor, since neither are around to provide the commentary. Those were Crem's words exactly, *There's something wrong with you*. She was six or maybe seven and he'd slapped her for mouthing off, and in retaliation she bit through the tendon between his finger and thumb. His lip had curled as he said it. *There's something wrong with you*. Then he backhanded her so hard she lost a tooth. It was loose anyway, he would say later. On its way out.

Her head swims now, just as it did back then. Something wrong with her for sure. A core of rottenness, accelerated by the creep of the nullvoid through her soul. It's probably for the best if things end here; they're only going to get worse otherwise. Misery could speed up the process and stop drinking from the cell's built-in spigot, but she fears the brutality of death by dehydration.

She really wishes they'd let her keep Mother's amulet.

Some undefined time later, three white saints come to her cell. Misery, crumpled on the bed like a poisoned plant, experiences them as a series of looming shadows, cool fingers on her brow, warm palms on her body. Two of them lift her by the arms and put her on her feet, and her knees buckle as a wave of static overwhelms her vision. She then loses touch with time, resurfacing much later in a nest of softness. A bed? There's the scent of disinfectant, a churchlike smell, and a slow buzz in her limbs that speaks of salves. Has the Church regained custody of her person? Someone's speaking in her vicinity, a voice that creaks with authority. Who is that? It sounds familiar, but it's not the Archbishop of Remus. A different voice she doesn't recognize, soft and steady, replies: "Terrorist or not, they are also a child of the Larex Forge, and deserve the dignity we accord to all children of the Demiurge. They need to recover." The rest of the conversation is inaudible, but they must be talking about her. Is that the Empress Dowager? Who knows.

Misery drifts. She's safe, for now. Her tormented body is healing.

Time skips forward again, and Misery rises into half consciousness to see a dreamlike figure hovering over her. She's still too weak to fight or respond. The darkness occludes her visitor's face, but she knows the voice: Pyrex Imogen. The Archbishop whispers as though afraid of being discovered. "I am sorry, Misery. We could not sway them enough, although we tried. Your crimes were too great for the Throne to forgive, even if you were driven by divine will." Fingers brush Misery's brow, which seems very distant from the seat of her consciousness. She feels like a child again, and the Archbishop's oceanic voice is her cradle. "We must trust in Hir guidance in the days to come, even if it proves difficult. But do not lose faith in what you have been called to, Misery. I promise I will not lose faith in you."

Her hand fills with the weight of something smooth and familiar. Could it be—?

"I know it will be scant comfort where you are going. But this seemed important to you. I hope it helps."

Mother's amulet. She has it back and the world is whole again.

Misery drifts into unconsciousness. When she next opens her eyes, Pyrex Imogen is gone, and Misery wonders if the Archbishop was a fever dream, a hallucination like Ruin is. But the weight of her mother's amulet remains in her hand, solid and reassuring. Perhaps angels are real after all.

When she next wakes she knows she's better, because Ruin is back. The delusion perches on a molded supply cabinet, gazing at her with nullvoid eyes that could swallow the soul. "Things are about to become a lot more interesting, Misery Nomaki." Hir smile as zie says this is the least comforting thing in the world.

She's guessed right about being back in Church territory. The med naves on the Capital are fancy, all hard and polished and finely engineered, but in foundation and spirit they are the same as the clay-made naves back home. She occupies the center in a salvation pod-turned-bed with its sides retracted, the protective arch of a scanner above her, surrounded by a barricade of monitor screens that keep track of everything from her blood pressure to the oxygen in her lungs. The painted image of Saint Agneta is instead a hologram, flickering over all their heads to bestow peace and blessings.

The priest in charge is Dr. Palisade Childs, he/him pronouns, tasked with restoring Misery's health. A hearty young man with a soft face and gentle fingers, she recognizes his voice from her fevered drifting the night before. Close-cropped chestnut hair shimmers with a hint of green. As she stands for examination and he sets his drones over her, she asks, "I had a visitor last night. You spoke to them. Who was it?"

Dr. Child's rebuke is gentle. "I cannot speak about that. You are, after all, a prisoner of the Throne, and I am obliged to remain neutral."

He has that saint's opacity, but there's no ill will in his demeanor she can detect. "Did the Archbishop come to see me?"

"That they did."

So it was not a hallucination. Misery has quietly hidden Mother's amulet under the gray slipsuit; she would rather die than be separated from it again. For a loathsome moment she's flooded with gratitude at the Archbishop's show of care. "If I asked what's going to happen to me, would you be able to answer?"

His smile this time is genuinely sad. "Forgive me. I cannot."

It was worth a shot. Misery wonders about the fear and sorrow in his expression—what *does* he know? She's been told nothing about her punishment, and she's sure it's punishment that awaits. Forgiveness is a rare beast these days. What's the penalty for killing a thousand rich fucks?

"It was really only a couple hundred deaths, give or take a dozen," Ruin says.

The delusion reclines on the supply cabinet like a little saint, chin in hand. "You've been sentenced to die," zie says. "The fatalities aside, it's a capital offense to threaten the life of an emperor."

Dizziness overcomes Misery, hypercondensed anxiety stirred into wonky blood pressure. A monitor screen bleats in consternation. Ruin continues, with measured insouciance: "Of course, there are procedures. Hearings and judgments and racks of bureaucracy. An ocean of protocol to follow. They'll drag it out, turn it into dirty public spectacle. Don't want people getting ideas about sedition being profitable, you know?"

Misery clenches her fists and tries to corral some thoughts, but her mind is choked with static and thinking is impossible. Ruin says: "While they're making preparations, they're sending you to Angelsteeth, a high-security base at the edge of the system. There are some interesting things there. I think you'll like it."

The delusion can't possibly know that. How could zie know that? She must have overheard something while half-conscious. Misery forces her breathing into a reasonable pattern, but the blood pressure monitor remains unhappy at her. A death sentence, a high-security base. Surely there's still some way out. Surely she can escape this.

"But why would you? It's where you're meant to be. It's where the road to your destiny awaits."

Oh. She sees what the delusion is doing. Ruin has taken on Crem's job in his absence, telling her what's she good for. Which is nothing. Worse than nothing. Effluvium of the world, a disgrace to the family.

"Oh, you of little faith," Ruin says, running over with disdain. "You'll see."

Misery gives hir nothing in return. This is not a conversation she wants to have. Instead she ignores the delusion. She ignores hir when the white saints and companion soldiers come to claim their prisoner. Ignores hir as she is shackled at the wrists and her ankles are ringed with bands of holy tigereye. Says nothing through her long march down corridors that grow increasingly bare and metallic and harshly lit. Pretends the delusion doesn't exist as she comes into the hangar bay where a shuttle waits to take her away from the Capital. Most of all, she gives the ersatz angel nothing when she sees her fellow convicts set for the same journey. Her heart skips several beats, but she keeps her lips folded and her mind flat and blank.

There's the Duke of Apis, woebegone in carceral gray. Next to him, proud and stunning even in the drab jumpsuit, is the Imperial princess, Lee Alodia Lightning.

She graces Misery with a sardonic smile. "A wonderful predicament you've put us all in, *Messiah*."

Lord Argan remains quiet, only looking at her as she passes by. She can't parse what his sadness means, and wonders if he also resents her for his predicament. She can't blame him for it. It occurs to Misery that Pyrex Imogen has cleverly managed to conceal their involvement in the whole affair, despite being the driving force behind it. Very canny of them.

The soldiers herd them toward a shuttle that idles at the mouth of the hangar, a silver lozenge whose rear gangway lies open, waiting for them. As they march toward that maw, feet heavy on the metal, a spectacular figure emerges from the darkness. A wiry, weathered nixen blessed with a pink trident of scar tissue across the face and a right arm that's holy jade all the way to the shoulder. Tag reads Major Reyes Photon, xe/xer pronouns. Xe scans the prisoners. "Is that all three? Finally." Xe props a fist on xer hips. "Let's not waste any more time. All aboard for Angelsteeth."

PART TWO

ANGELSTEETH BASE

8

Angelsteeth inhabits the edge of the duchy, several hours away by sublight warp. But this duchy is the zone of plenty, so that distance is laced with jump ports, lozenges of holy bluestone just large enough for a single ship. The silver shuttle with its biohazardous cargo leaps from one to the next over the course of twenty minutes. Military privilege.

On the inside of that shuttle, one portion of the dangerous cargo watches the rest. Misery, her wrists and ankle heavy with stone, studies the princess and the Duke, both silent and impenetrable in their despondency. A ring of foam lines the shuttle, with space for eight to twelve, and the three of them form points of a triangle along that circumference. Up front is the pilot's seat. Major Reyes isn't piloting, but xe sits beside the name-unknown grunt and watches Misery back. She doesn't let her gaze linger over the major—xe intimidates her for reasons she can't yet articulate. A pair of stone-faced guards with unnecessarily large guns rounds out their company.

To Misery's unpracticed eye the princess looks more angry than dejected, which does not bode well for their future. Misery had better watch her back. And her front. After all, the last time the Lady Alodia Lightning tried to kill her, she wasn't very subtle about it. Military prison won't keep the princess from murder if she's determined about it.

On the other hand, the Duke of Apis slumps in the memory foam consumed by dread, every plane of his beautifully sculpted face exuding hopelessness. Frankly, she's worried about him; she had imagined that the fount of his good cheer would never run out. Wrong, obviously. She wishes she knew what he's thinking. Who's running the duchy now that he's been imprisoned? Probably the Emperor's installing someone amenable to his interests.

Even Major Reyes has noticed the Duke's despair. "Chin up," xe says. "You'll find it isn't so bad." And the Duke does lift his chin, but specifically to fix the major with a glare so hot with anger it could melt glass.

The major just laughs, a gravelly noise. "You will see. Have some faith, Lord Argan."

Faith, again. These people put so much stock in faith, Misery wants to spit blood.

Ruin slouches across the foam next to the Duke. The delusion grins at Misery's seething discomfort. "Xe's right," zie says. "Things will be better than you imagine."

Sure, like a delusion knows anything. She can't imagine how things will smoothen out from here.

"Oh," says Ruin, sitting up, sockets flaring with joyful light. "I said better, not smooth. I said nothing about it being smooth."

The shuttle exits travel just outside the orbit of Canis E. Ice and dust shield the base from its parent planet, a marble of pale amethyst. In the haze afforded by a blue sun, Angelsteeth glimmers. A great docking ring encircles five lobes of silver, spread like a flower, latched to the silo of central command. The base is a poor shard of metal compared to the Capital, but its modest scale intimidates through sheer comprehensibility. One might imagine the Capital dropped from the heavens by the will of the Demiurge and accept that feat, but there is no denying that Angelsteeth Base, with all its length and breadth, has been constructed by human hands.

The guards and their guns escort the prisoners into the silver cavities of Angelsteeth. The major is the first one out, followed by the princess. Third is the Duke, because Misery refused to budge until he did. Down the ramp they go to the fates that await them.

The docking bay dwarfs the shuttle the way a mouth dwarfs

a tooth. It's been cleared except for a fistful of soldiers in gray automesh, gridded in perfectly disciplined lines. At their head stands an extraordinary figure in crisp ultramarine, the kind of starchy uniform that looks rendered and tailored. Someone of good rank, if the amount of metal on hir lapels is any indication. Like Misery, zie has the physique of someone who grew up in supergrav: wide, blocky. Short. Hair silvered with age and not sainthood. Gray eyes set deep into a craggy face. Zie makes brief eye contact with Misery and there's the frisson of instant connection, something of Mother's hard-knock sensibility in the stranger immediately endearing hir to Misery. Who—?

"That's General Tsung Wolf Blizzard, pronouns he/they," Ruin says. "The latter is preferred. They're in charge of this particular cabal."

How could the delusion know who this person is?

The princess surges forward, breaking ranks with them, and Major Reyes lets her. She goes up to the figure in blue, and speaks with a voice that echoes in the vast bay. "General Tsung. I see you are well."

The General nods in acknowledgment, but their eyes are a warning: *Keep it down, here we are watched.* So Ruin was right about their identity. Misery must have absorbed this information sideways at some point, and it's surfacing through the filter of the delusion. She comes to a stop behind the princess, in line with the Duke of Apis, who remains gloomy and silent.

The princess says: "I am pleased to see you, at least."

"Could be under better conditions," says the General in reply. Their manner is blunt and to the point, which Misery appreciates.

"On the contrary," says the Lady Alodia Lightning, "I think these conditions are perfect. The Throne is blind to what is happening on this station. We have more freedom here than we would have anywhere else."

"Things are as you said, then."

"They are."

Misery's heartbeat quickens at the revelation unfolding before her. Conspiracy! Conspiracy against the Throne! A twist she didn't see coming, but instantly opens her mind with a breadth of possibilities for her future. The General has turned their attention to her, their gaze febrile with curiosity. They know *of* Misery, and they're curious about this contradiction that has landed in their lap—is Misery a savior or a serial killer? They haven't yet decided. Here, then, is someone willing to give her a chance. Someone who might be amenable to suggestion.

"Is that them?" the General asks of the princess.

"It is. They don't look like much, but I assure you they have caused untold amounts of damage."

"That sounds promising."

Misery keeps her face neutral and her gaze respectful. Speak only when she's spoken to—for now. She wants to make a good first impression. Under the General's scrutiny, she puts on the right veneer of humility.

They ask: "Are you the one they call the Savior of Rootsdown?"

"I am." Modestly ducking her head.

"And what are you here to do?"

It's a trap, this query. She answers it the way the Church always answers difficult questions: with soapwater bullshit. "I have come to do what I am asked." The religious do love these sentiments about service and answering to a higher power. It gives them a veneer of plausible deniability when shit goes sideways. Wasn't me, 'twas the will of the Forge.

"And are you willing to cleave to deception while carrying out your mission? Are you willing to bend the rule of the law?"

What is happening now? Misery's arrest history is public, they know her history, so what purpose does this question serve? The General seems genuine in their sincerity, they're not trying to catch her out, but she can't know for sure. She needs to think this answer over. Think fast.

And then she's saved by a siren, a song of glorious victory that fills the arches of the docking bay and wakes old memories in the pit of Misery's stomach. It's got the same tune as the summons for morning prayer back home, but a different arrangement. More martial, more urgent. The docking bay fills with purple light.

The General's expression shifts as they look up. A habit of those who grew up wellbound, seeking the sky for answers. "They're early."

Major Reyes frowns. "Maybe. It's within the window. Isn't it?"

"Is it a raid?" asks the Lady Alodia Lightning.

"It is indeed." General Tsung pins Misery with their gaze. "So, Misery Nomaki. The fates have aligned for you, it seems. The Larex Forge has decided to test you as soon as you arrived. Come. It is time to prove yourself."

9

The rabbit holes running through Angelsteeth are brisk and spartan. Businesslike. Even lighting, textured metal floors, and poly-lined walls to cushion the sound of boots against said floors. The pack of prisoners-in-limbo make the filling of a goose with the General and major at the top and the grim-faced soldiers at the base. The farther they go, the denser the corridors become. Bodies jog through the conduits, fervent and determined. Siren song continues as Misery bounds along the trails of the two senior officers. Angelsteeth is subgrav, just like the Capital, and each stride threatens to launch her airborne. Here, even walking requires finesse.

Up ahead, the princess is asking the General: "Is this one of the regular raids?"

"It is."

"Are we in serious danger?"

"It remains to be seen. I hope not."

Regular raids, who by? The Heretics? Misery's heartbeat accelerates on top of all the adrenaline she's running. What of the so-called truce? The fleet that lurked above Rootsdown was an aberration, a defiance of the ceasefire. Now she's learning that a base right in the capital duchy gets attacked on the regular? That doesn't make sense.

"These raids," she says carefully, "do they happen often?"

The General looks over their shoulder. "Regrettably so. These are conditions which we have to labor under."

"Do the raids not violate the terms of the truce?"

"It's in between. I believe the Heretics have their reasons for doing so."

"But the Throne—surely they know of these incursions? And yet they allow them to continue?"

This time the General laughs, but it's no belly-throated thing. Small, wry, and defeated. "The answer, I'm afraid, is *yes* to both of those."

They pull their attention from her, but she has what she needs. The General is frustrated. Seething that the Throne basically shrugs at these incursions, while they're out here with their soldiers' lives on the line every few weeks. Means nothing to them in the Capital.

"Your presence here is a gift," says Ruin, floating along. "Use this how you will, to your advantage. The Heretics are your tool."

Heretics. The only battles Misery has seen are entirely fictional. Her closest real-life encounter with their dread enemy was with the blinking dots on Rootsdown's radar, a remote threat hidden by the atmosphere. She's never seen Heretic vessels outside of their depictions on wave dramas: spiny shapes and chitinous surfaces, playing on primordial fears kneaded into the ancient human brain stem millions of years ago. Threats from the sourceworld live again in the bristling, fanged, writhing forms of Heretic ships in popular imagination. The Heretics themselves are subhuman creatures, broken and feral with nullvoid infection, half human and half eldritch unknowability. But nothing in the fertile imaginations of drama directors compares to the horror of the nullvoid coming through. After all, these auteurs are storymaking for entertainment. Not to inflict indelible trauma upon their audiences.

They pass through increasingly heavy layers of security, the doors thicker, the stenciled warnings bigger, the stripes bolder and brighter. Each time the guards snap to attention and they're ushered through with no fuss. Eventually they ascend silver

steps that wind up the side of a control hub and through a doorway into the pod of the command center.

On the other side is black-paneled, glass-walled space solid
with tension. Techs and other useful grunts buzz from glowing screen to glowing screen, faces serious and businesslike. No
saints, refreshingly enough: the fewer white saints in Misery's
life, the better.

In the middle of it all lies a massive video plaza, aglow with
blue light, a cold sun around which all attention in the room
orbits. It projects a miniature of Angelsteeth Base and the space
around it, sequined with stars. Around it stand several figures
in red mesh suits shot through with white—captains' uniforms.
One of them looks up as the General's entourage approaches,
and Misery's heart skips with the force of sudden recognition.
She knows who this is. War hero, decorated paragon, one of the
great lights of the Faithful. Sunyata Diamond. Ship's captain.
She/her pronouns. Destroyed a Heretic ship a half-dozen years
ago, an unparalleled feat, and then vanished from public view,
as those who gain some notoriety tend to. It's not very Churchlike to revel in the spotlight. Has she been on Angelsteeth all
this while?

Captain Sunyata Diamond says, "Who are they?"

"Honored guests," says the General. "You know one among
them, at least?"

The captain sweeps her gaze across their number and her
expression tightens with realization. "My lady," she says to the
princess. "I did not see you at first."

The princess says nothing. Already the General is taking
charge of the situation, demanding reports of the other captains
and getting them. Captain Sunyata Diamond returns to working form, sparing only the tiniest of frowns for Misery, who is
surely the only one of the lot she does not recognize. But there
are status reports to be made. The squads are being loaded. The
turrets are primed. They're tracking the Heretic seraphs.

Misery's pulse quickens as she leans into the glow of the vid plaza. Heretic seraphs! She knows the adversaries stole clutches of holy mechs ages ago, twisting gifts from the Larex Forge to their own purposes, but she never thought she'd live to see them in action. In the plaza the mechs are rendered as pulsing lilac dots, three of them streaking slowly toward the base. It's driving Misery crazy that she can't see what they look like.

A swarm spills out of the ersatz base: deadly confetti marked in red, blue, and yellow. "Are these our servings? What's happening?"

Misery's question is directed to the general assemblage, and she isn't sure who she expects to answer, but it certainly isn't the Lady Alodia Lightning. And yet it is the princess, parked beside her with arms tightly crossed, who speaks. "Angelsteeth has three servings of seraphim. Every month or so, they're called into duty to rebuff an attack from the Heretics."

Misery rolls with this display of friendliness while it lasts. "So do we win every time, or what?"

"Depends on what you define as a win. Angelsteeth resists them and they withdraw. A month later, they're back. They have yet to be crushed entirely."

"When you say *they're back* . . . the same units?"

"The Heretics don't have so many they can dispatch different ones. You haven't an implant, so you can't see the information on the board. They've got names." An elegant finger thrusts into the light of the video plaza. "This one is Beggar. That's Tinker, and that's Sailor. The station named them, by consensus."

Odd names, but not the oddest. "Where did they come from?"

"They open their own portals. As Heretics are wont to do."

The shape of battle gains legibility to Misery. Each serving has its captain in the room, and they feed instructions to their pilots, four apiece. A flurry of names and numbers: Xito Green-2. Cormac Yellow-1. Jota Red-4. Each serving has four pilots. Four seraphs. The dots fan into an attack pattern as the enemy fighters approach. Misery's watched enough wave dramas to understand how this will play out. Seraphim have a limited moveset.

They're powerful, but the gifts of the Larex Forge are few. The Heretics, on the other hand, have neither decency nor respect for the rules of the universe. Their units are hacked, their holy trappings undone by some voidbound mechanic, which means they are faster and their moves are difficult to predict. They're better fighters, but at what cost? The degeneracy of the Heretics can only lead to unhappy ends. So says the Church.

Captain Diamond Sunyata doesn't direct any of the servings. Misery watches the war hero study the battle map, her brow furrowed, the force of her focus on the proceedings an almost palpable thing. She's tall and splendid, more so than Misery has ever imagined, close-cropped dark hair lending her the right kind of stern, martial air. The General and Major Reyes have come to her side and are discussing strats in hushed tones. The major leans into the light to study the fast-approaching Heretics as Captain Sunyata gestures at the dots and says something Misery can't quite make out. There it is, the command structure for the battle. The trio make the big decisions and the serving captains carry them out.

She leans toward the princess. Giving in to the impulse to put her hands on the hot stone. "Are you nervous?"

A scoffing noise, a curled lip. "Don't project your insecurities onto me."

A cluster of new screens pops up: live video from the killing fields. Misery immediately recognizes the shapes of the Faithful seraphs—four arms, four feet, the glimmering gray of holy labradorite. A sacred arrowhead where the visage would be. Somewhere in those glowing chests are the pilots, most celebrated warriors of the Faithful. But wait, where are the Heretics? Misery scans the spread of live feeds for eldritch abominations, anything that resembles the nightmares of her childhood, and you'd think those would leap out at her instantly, but there's nothing.

Wait. No. There they are. Same eight-limbed forms as the friendlies, no wonder she missed them. The Heretic seraphs look nothing like she's imagined. No wild spikes, no shifting forms, no extra limbs. Maybe the holy labradorite is a little darker, or catches the starlight differently. Instead of a head they have a ball of light like a mockery of a sun. But otherwise they look no different from the Faithful units. Misery is stunned by how mundane they look. As mundane as a Forge-given superweapon can be, anyway.

The princess says, "Each of those screens will stay on each enemy. Pay attention." As Misery leans forward, squinting, she points. "That one's Beggar. That one's Tinker. That one's Sailor."

They look identical, but it's trivial to remember which screen is which. Misery pushes the universe out of her consciousness to focus on the trio of bright squares, which must become the entirety of her world. She will not allow herself to consider the pleasure she feels at the easy conviviality being offered by the princess.

On the video plaza attacker and defender meet, and the air grows thick as a sulfur burn. Misery shivers as Beggar shoots forward and swings its lower arms, sword-bearing, in the direction of Xito Green-2. An answering clash. The voices in the command room become an overlapping babble, too dense and fast-flowing for comprehension. This is nothing like how it goes in the dramas. Here there are no perfectly timed crosscuts, no dramatic close-ups, no swelling music to stir the devotional soul. Just technobabble and military fusslessness. It's an alien world, urgent and deadly. Misery's jaw hurts.

The seraphim of Xito Green-2 move in concert, a machine optimized through practice. Everyone knows where to go, everyone knows what moves to pull. A single command triggers an intricate moveset whose efficiency speaks to hours of simulation grinding. It's beautiful to watch the formations build and break apart.

But the Heretic unit slices differently. It swoops and spins and strikes with careless fluidity. A dancer's sensibility. It's impossible to map its attacks to movesets. With their blocky presets, the Faithful units look like falling rocks trying to crush a missile. Beggar weaves like winter wind through their clumsy grasp.

Stress curdles in the command center. The captains have their brows furrowed, beaded with sweat, fingers dug into palms. Trying to predict what the Heretic fighter is going to do before they do it is a fool's errand: all the factors to take into account at once, so many possibilities—an infinite array of them—that no human mind can take it all in at once. It's all intuition and very little logic.

On the other side of the room Ruin says: "There's an algorithmic key to unlock it all. Like four-dimensional chess. The rules of the physical and mathematical world apply here too. There are models and optimizations. Like the ratio of four Faithful seraphim to one Heretic. It can be calculated, given what we know of the Faithful movesets and the capabilities of the Heretics."

A load of guff. Nothing-meaning words. Who cares about that, in the middle of battle? The environmental stress is getting to her, seeping into her bones: she feels sore and hollow.

"It's ironic," says the delusion, almost dreamily. "This would be much easier if you mortals weren't so opposed to artificial intelligence. It's not true that the nullvoid corrupts them, you know."

Not the point. Misery ignores hir. Can't let the delusion distract her with nonsense right now.

The mood in the room changes. The Heretic units are withdrawing, turning and opening a swathe of space between them and the defenders. It looks like victory on their side. Is it victory? Is that it?

"It's too soon," says the General. "Something's going on."

Next to them, Captain Sunyata Diamond leans forward, lip curled and brow knitted. She knows the General is right. None of the Heretic ships have sustained enough damage to warrant a retreat. Working on pure instinct she closes her fists and says—
"Aegis up."

One of the captains—of Jota Red-4, perhaps—reacts acidly. "You're insane!"

"Don't ask—just do it!"

Ruin purrs in Misery's ear. "The station's aegis will cut the cord between seraphim and captain. You know what that means, don't you?"

It's lovely that the delusion acts like she's stupid. The aegis will strand Angelsteeth's best pilots—not to mention every seraph they possess—in company of the enemy. It's a wild move, she can't imagine anyone would suggest it without good cause. Not just gutfeel.

General Tsung glances at their master strategist, a half-second flick of the eyes, and grunts their assent. All that risk assessed, all that weight pulled, in the space between heartbeats. Talk about wild. Very instructive of their faith in this war hero of the Faithful.

The serving captains have just enough time to warn their fighters before the lines sever. "Bring it up," the General says, and the techs in the room shift into new, anxious patterns. Seeing to their screens. Getting ready for the big shift. Tending to the switches and dials.

Angelsteeth Base rumbles. Deep in its viscera something is waking, and Misery, who has never lived in space except these past few weeks, shivers in her soul. But her flesh also trembles, her skin crawling with awe and unease. What great terror and wonders shall unfold before her? Holy obsidian, colossal and unforgiving, calls to her from a great distance.

Around the mass of Angelsteeth a blessing glows. From turret to turret and lobe to lobe, holy light establishes itself: yellow, inutterable, and impenetrable. Misery cannot imagine what an aegis of that size looks like from the outside, or what it cost to build, but she can feel it for sure. The blood in the chambers of her heart can feel it. The song of the warning siren changes, and she wonders how much the rest of the station understands what is happening. The gears of the universe are turning on the decisions made in this room, and only a handful of people are here to witness it.

"Cannons," says General Tsung, and soldiers in a hundred cubbies across Angelsteeth are called to duty, activating the base's last-ditch defenses. Misery sneaks a glance at the princess and finds her hyperfocused on the unfolding action. If there's a shred of nervousness in her, it's undetectable. The Lady Alodia Lightning is energized by whatever's about to happen, and Misery got this sense from her back when they first fought. She's got the face of someone alive as never before.

"Pay attention," Ruin says, and that's all the warning Misery gets.

Next to Angelsteeth, the skin of the universe rips. Nullvoid pours from the gaping wound and Misery feels it in her chest, a surge of sudden chaos released into the cosmos. Carried upon that invisible, indescribable, ineffable ether is a ship. A Heretic ship. A jagged arrowhead of a thing, half corkscrew and all shifting void, absorbing and reflecting starlight in ways that defy the known laws of physics.

"What the fuck is that," Misery says, as breath hisses from every person in the command center. But she doesn't need any insight—divine or otherwise—to know this is bad news. Fear and panic have thickened the air so much it's hard to breathe.

The princess says, "That's a Virtue-class hornet. Isn't it?"

"Weapons hot," Captain Sunyata Diamond says, her face tight with stress. She's glad her instincts were right but wishes they weren't.

The Heretic ship skims the station. Teeth show in its glossy skin as it rakes Angelsteeth with cutting light. The bolts skim across the yellow and dissipate. Thank the Forge that's up.

The station's cannons pump shots of electric blue as the Heretic ship turns back for another round. The ship's shimmering skin absorbs the barrage.

"Torpedoes," says the General. "Overload their barriers."

Sunyata Diamond is already on the move, pulling up screens,

summoning a bulleted list of defense turrets. A smatter of firing orders flutter across the display. On the live feeds a volley of white discs streak toward the attacker. The heat of impact whites out the cameras, but when the feed returns the enemy scuds across the horizon still. The greater video plaza summarizes the battle. Farther out the three Heretic seraphim leapfrog their adversaries and race to join the larger vessel. The three servings, acting independently, are in pursuit. But how can they fight without the coordination of their captains? Perhaps they'll die trying.

"Again," says General Tsung, still cross-armed, admirably unbowed by pressure. The same constellation of orders goes out. Misery's gut clenches. Tension like this is fun on the waves, but real life isn't supposed to draw from the ridiculous melodrama of action subs.

The turrets speak again. The screens go white. When the feeds come back there's the Heretic ship still, coming back for more. Unmoved and undaunted. Whatever tactic the General is applying, it's not working.

They say: "Reroute power to the turrets. Class X operational status."

Captain Sunyata Diamond says: "That has a three-minute limit."

The General says: "If we aren't done after three minutes then we're done."

So it's like that. The mood in the room dips considerably. But the command chain has spoken, and their word be done. The station lights drop to emergency levels. Life support stutters: the roar of air circulation in the background, invisible in its ubiquity, cuts to nothing.

Misery closes her eyes and realizes how deep the void carved by terror and helplessness in her chest goes. She's not ready to die yet, how did she end up here?

"Helplessness?" Ruin scoffs. "You're not exactly helpless, Misery Nomaki. Imagine saying that of yourself."

The delusion is right. She's not entirely helpless. Is she? The holy obsidian that wraps the mass of the station in an aegis makes happy song in her consciousness, and she knows that she has a beautiful and terrible weapon at her disposal. Is she brave enough to use it? Is she brave enough to risk utter destruction—again—to test her abilities against a warship, a real Heretic warship?

Ruin tilts hir head. "Well, are you?"

Fuck it. Even the General thinks they've got three minutes to turn this around or die. What has she got to lose?

She closes her eyes. Reaches for the stone that looms large in the caverns of her soul. The amulet against her chest, Mother's gift to her, hums with pleasure.

"Are you going to do it again?" She knows that voice, groping after her intentions from the world outside. The Lady Alodia Lightning. Breathy with fear. Or is it anticipation? She can't worry about that. The holy obsidian is calling to her. Waiting for her input. Just as she'd done in the Grand Amphitheater, Misery reaches for it. Touches it. Lets loose its power.

With a force that takes the breath from her chest, the aegis snaps outward from Angelsteeth. A regular space station, built by the tender hands of humanity, turns into a blazing void-touched horror. Tendrils of yellow shoot forth in every direction, insatiable and uncontrollable. What kind of nightmare must it look like, writhing and seething with want? The wakened barrier is hungry and it hungers indiscriminately. It carves sections off turrets and sensor towers and sends them to the void in a superheated flare. In the background a thin wail goes up, the station speaking its alarm at the destruction. The Heretic ship, skimming too close to this sudden outburst of eldritch horror, tries to back out of range. But it's too late. One tendril snares it by the snout, pulling it in. A dozen more cut into its skin. The ship shudders deeply, then comes apart with a scream more imagined than heard. There's no light, no fire, but Angelsteeth shakes from the bones up as a pulse of energy sweeps outward. And then there's no ship save for glittering shards tumbling through space in a thousand directions.

In the distance, Beggar, Sailor, and Tinker flee. Space winks in repulsive patterns as they tear through its hidden foramen, and the enemy seraphs vanish into the voidholes that appear. Back to the clutches of whichever terrible hand sent them. The fight is over.

Misery releases her grasp on the holy obsidian. There. Done it. Is that Ruin's laughter she hears in her head?

Misery slowly peels her eyes open and tumbles into the confines of the mundane world, coming down from a cosmic vantage point that was more imagined than anything. Delusional. Her flesh body welcomes the return of her awareness with a one-two of stress and dehydration. While her soul, or her voidtouched mind, had soared through space watching the destruction it wrought, her body was put through the fucking wringer. Her heart beats wild and electric in her chest. Misery unclenches her jaw and fists and feels the beginnings of a migraine working through every tendon in her neck.

Her brother's words: *There's something wrong with you.*

Something's changed. The air in her mouth tastes different, as if what she's done broke reality, and in that picosecond of dislocation the fabric of the universe realigned. She's done it! She saved all their hides. Almost like a real Messiah.

"Your miracles keep coming, don't they?" says a voice to her left.

She turns and is presented with the lovely, infuriating visage of the princess. Then there's the roomful of strangers who are now demanding explanation for what just happened. The Lady Alodia Lightning looks pleased, but with her, who can tell? Also, pleasure seems like the wrong emotion to be telegraphing at this moment. Misery's just destroyed an entire ship. She doesn't know the typical roster for a vessel that size, but there had to be a dozen crew at least. So, more murder. At least this time it's Heretics. Not sure how she feels about that. The princess is definitely partial to murder, though. She knows that.

"It's over, then?" The asker is the captain of one of the seraph servings—was it Cormac Yellow-1?—hir voice butter-soft. Zie looks more shaken than Misery herself feels, this seasoned veteran of untold seraph battles trembling like a rag in the wind.

"It's over," General Tsung says. "Start the cooldown." Their voice has compacted into something with all the power and gravity of a neutron star. Quiet. Authoritative. Deeply determined. What they've just witnessed has solidified the belief they've been too afraid to hold. But it is true—the Larex Forge has answered the prayers they've whispered into the dark. They have that look about them that Misery only knows too well: the look of one deeply religious whose faith has just been reinforced.

Around them, the crew shake off their awed stupor and return to their duties with military discipline. The aegis is turned off. Red alert canceled. The serving captains reconnect with their pilots and direct them back home. The fear and tension run out of the room, like a sump being drained, leaving behind a complex sludge of emotion. Relief, disbelief, hope, awe. To Misery that frothing peat is all good news and rich potential. So many things she can shape out of things felt that strongly. She will build herself a bridge to survival.

Next to the General, Captain Sunyata Diamond frowns in deep thought, her fist pressed to her chin. She hasn't felt this way in a long time—and that, so far, has been a good thing. One brush with divinity is all she needed in her lifetime. What just happened threatens the foundations of the meager recovery's she's clawed out over these years. Fascinating. The captain is perhaps the only person in the room feeling objectively worse than before the attack. Despair lies deep in her being like a hard, enormous stone, and it's not immediately clear why. Misery will have to learn more.

For the moment, the General's looking at her with the force

of unbearable hope. They're no nixen given to flights of fancy, and they've built a career on being practical and ruthless when the situation calls for it. On their own, they would never have presumed to think that the Larex Forge Hirself would intervene in such a direct fashion, for Zie had not sent humanity a Messiah since the First Eight, who were called to be beacons and wayfinders for the Faithful. Yet how could they deny what had just happened here? The news out of the Capital was right. They have witnessed it for themself.

The tides of war are about to change.

Frankly, Misery can't fully parse the joy she's reading from the General's face. She needs more context to decrypt meaning from the scraps she's getting. But she'll take the victory for now. The General trusts her. They think she's an important asset.

She's alive, and that's what matters.

INTERLUDE 4

Angelsteeth Base exists in a cradle of secrecy, within and without. The denizens of the Faithful know of its existence, of course: the fabled training academy where seraph pilots are made. Heroes of the Empire, the holiest of holy warriors. Chosen of the chosen. Held in apex esteem even by those blessed with sainthood by the Forge. This sanctified, legendary military base lives in their imaginations as a cornucopia of golden floors and holy light. The reality of the station's day-to-day is opaque to them. What they would find would disappoint and shock them in equal measure, I'm sure. Disappointment? Because Angelsteeth is, after all, a military base, and the military life does not lend itself to glamour. Bare floors and recon food and three forms to fill up for every request made. The fancies of the Faithful, febrile and sticky, would melt under the pebbly weight of reality. It's nothing unexpected.

The shock, though . . . the shock. Imagine thinking that this crowning jewel of the Empire's defense—this place where war heroes and saviors are minted—imagine thinking it must be more secure and better protected than anywhere else in the Empire. Especially with its location in the duchy of Remus, jowl to jowl with the Capital itself. Surely something like that would be absolutely safe and far beyond the reach of the Heretics. Surely they could not besmirch a place so holy, so girded by the Grace of the Forge. And yet Angelsteeth Base suffered insult from the Heretics on a repeating basis. An attack every month that they barely repelled. Imagine being told that the Heretics have been tamed by the Truce of Logan—which none of the true Faithful desired—only to find out that the Heretics have been attacking a sacred base for years, with no consequences to show for it? The anger resulting would have set off a conflagration that the Throne could not contain. And the Imperial seat of power had its reasons for allowing the attacks to continue. Reasons of political expediency . . . some might even say cowardice on the part of the Emperor. But that is for historians to decide.

In any case, the banquet of Angelsteeth—all four courses, and the dishes and servings that comprise them—were sworn to secrecy. The truth of their situation classified and forbidden to leave the bounds of the station, on pain of court-martial and death. The one tasked with holding this secret together, the one expected to keep the iron bind around the mouths of their soldiers, was none other than the station's commander.

General Tsung. Their background is frighteningly similar to that of your beloved Misery Nomaki. Born on a supergrav moon to parents in the clergy. Raised religious, but turned cynical by years of operating in a system that ran counter to everything they'd been taught. Despairing in matters of faith and war until a miracle crashed into their life and changed its direction.

For years the General simmered in frustration directed at the Throne, whose passivity in the war they considered an affront to the tenets of the Faithful. They had disapproved of the Truce of Logan and sent strong word of said disapproval to the Capital. But it was no use, of course. The Throne did, does, and continues to do what it wants. It expected the General to sit on their hands and follow its orders even if those orders said *Thou shalt not raise thine hand against thy enemy.*

And so the General did. They kept watch over Angelsteeth Base, the Empire's premier military research facility, enduring month after month of Heretic attacks without complaint. Duty came first, and the General wished to appear the very model of a deferential soldier. They were much beloved by the lower ranks, who fiercely loved the fearless leader who kept them safe against the very real and present danger Angelsteeth faced.

Almost nowhere else in the Empire were the Faithful subject to such repeated and concerted attack as they were on Angelsteeth. How isolating, to feel like you're alone in the universe. You understand that feeling, don't you? Of course you do.

And yet pressure can be fortifying. The stronger it is applied, the more indestructible the result. Over time the glue that bonded the banquet of Angelsteeth solidified into resin, harder to get into—or get out of.

It was this bond that allowed the General to carry out their plan. For sedition, while not in their nature, had been drawn from the chambers of their heart by the appearance of Misery Nomaki, whose presence in their life they considered a sign from the Larex Forge. They were being called to a higher purpose than serving a Throne that had fallen away from the teachings of the Church. For too long the General Tsung had been forced to hold the secrets of the Throne. Now they had secrets of their own. They put the banquet of Angelsteeth to an oath of silence—the Throne would not learn what had transpired here. It would not learn of the miracles that had been wrought by the new Messiah Misery Nomaki. And it would certainly not learn that the instructions to keep the new Messiah under strictest imprisonment were being defied. That the General, seeing them as the ultimate weapon in a holy war, would train them to become one.

10

So. Sedition. Like everyone else in the Empire, Misery grew up on tales of heroic defiance, from Ruby Sarna against ALISS, to Saint Ono against the Great Council swayed by Heretic propaganda. Wave dramas and serial romances teemed with epics of righteous disobedience, paragons of morality choosing the right thing over the lawful thing. In the soft gel of baby Misery's brains these stories took root and shaped the person she would become. What's happening now, however, is more than a few steps up from being a small-time criminal in a backwater town. Defying Imperial decree and secretly training to be a seraph pilot? It's a whole cliff up. It's a different plane of existence altogether.

"You seem excited by the prospect," Ruin says.

Excited? Not the right word. Misery's holding tight to her senses, knowing her survival hangs by a microthread that will break if she breathes wrong. Any excitement she feels is fed by the twin canisters of fear and her desire to live. There is no joy in this. Only bad vibes.

The first demand made of her: get an implant in. She's assigned a chaperone, a thin young thing comprised mostly of anxiety, whose tag scrolls LT FRASH | THEY | TERA BLUE-4. The twenty-minute walk feels longer than it takes. The dim floaty environment thrums with bodies, other soldiers busy with their duties. Angelsteeth slowly being rebuilt after the damage of the last battle. Lieutenant Frash barely meets Misery's eyes, and responds to her probing questions with silence, their knuckles white around the scratch pad they're carrying. It's a dead end.

The lieutenant takes her through the frequently gated, densely signposted interior of Angelsteeth until they reach the warren of glass and metal that is the medical facility. A half junction with floating signs saying MEDIC on the left and RESEARCH on the right. Lieutenant Frash takes the left and leads her into an area of painful fluorescence and sterile metal walls.

Her assigned doctor waits in a circular nave lined with floating panels and spiced with antiseptic. Dr. Sower Cabbage, she/her, a short and soft-cheeked woman with an intense, prying gaze. Not a saint. "So this is you," she says, taking in Misery's stature and mundaneness. Surprised that someone supposedly so blessed by the Larex Forge is a regular chuck like she is. Was expecting more outward signs of messianic nature. "Well, I'm Dr. Sower, and up top says I'm in charge of your medical care. So let's get started."

The good doctor waves a bar scanner over Misery with a brisk, curious professionalism. "Never had an implant in, have you?"

"No. We didn't have them where I grew up in Rootsdown."

"Where's that?"

• "Duchy of Apis. Sector Eighteen. It's a stonemining colony on a desert moon."

"I see." She tuts. "We really do our backwaters injustice . . ."

The doctor has one prosthetic hand, all glossy and bejeweled, made of dark glass where it disappears beneath the sleeve of her coat. Misery notices it when the doctor demands her mother's amulet. Misery's already in the gray mesh for low-level military grunts, but she's managed to hang on to the stone through all her outfit changes. Now the doctor, this stranger, is asking to claim it? She thinks not. Misery gestures to the prosthetic. "What happened there?"

"You curious? I'll tell you after we're done with the scans. Now hand it over."

Dr. Sower puts on a gracious smile, but Misery can see she thinks less of her for asking. Gambit failed. Very reluctantly she places her mother's amulet in the waiting palm. Anxiety shudders through her marrow as the doctor holds the strange stone to the light, frowning. "You ever had this thing looked at?"

"It's sacred to me," Misery says, more sharply than she intends.

The doctor raises an eyebrow. "All right."

Misery is shepherded through a parade of glossy black machines with orange displays and no sharp edges. One takes a sample of her blood, one attaches buzzy electric discs to her head, one is a cocoon with a floating seat surrounded by a dozen rotating, swinging arcs of holystone that holler in her chest like a mob. "Am I supposed to do anything?" she says over the din.

Outside the black shell of the machine, Dr. Sower shouts back: "Do nothing. Touch nothing, move nothing. Just let them scan you." It's not as comforting as she thinks.

At the end of it all the good doctor studies the readouts, taps approvingly at a few values, and sets a synthesizer in motion. "Almost done. Just need to pop it in and you're good to go."

She points Misery to a raft of floating white foam, which she's supposed to lie facedown upon. The foam is cold and molds to the shape of her flesh. Misery forces herself to remain calm. Reminds herself that pain is her friend. She thrives with it.

The air moves and she senses Dr. Sower standing over her. As the synthesizer works and scanners whirr over her body, the doctor says, jauntily, "You're less like Leaf Maruska than I expected."

"Sorry my face isn't symmetrical enough for your tastes."

"You're pretty cute, don't get me wrong. But you know, Leaf Maruska."

"What about that hand of yours?"

A dry laugh. But why not? "So you know about the beacon-layers, yeah? You grew up on the stories, watched the dramas on the waves. There are all the heroic crews everybody knows. *No Surprises. Falling into Place. Stand Up.* But they don't talk about the ones that were lost. Except in horror stories—you know, the ghost ship that tumbles out of the nullvoid, an expeditionary crew exploring its misshapen hulk, the monsters that come after them. *Fallen Prey*—you've gotta have seen that one, at least. Herodotus Quince's debut, all big eyes and pouty lips. 'Prayer won't reach the Larex Forge here.' You dig?"

"Mm-hmm." It's a passable impression. Very well practiced.

"Well. My life is a classic horror story. Did you ever watch *Voidmouth*? Indie thing from the edge of Taurus, stars a very young Quechen Banana. Pacing was shit, but the soundtrack was great. Never mind if you haven't, it's very obscure, a few gens before your time. The plot's simple. Next to a remote military outpost, the twisted wreck of an unknown ship falls out of ultralight. Scans show the impossible: it's a ship lost a hundred years ago, but it's just spanking new, as it was on its doomed voyage. And there are survivors! Just a handful, but they bring them on board. Trying to figure out what happened. These people have just jumped a hundred years in time. But turns out, they didn't jump alone. The nullvoid is in them. Starts bursting out and killing people. The ones they don't kill, they infect. You know how the rest of it pans out. Lots of running, lots of screaming, lots of death. Eventually two people escape on a shuttle. Blow up the tainted, dying station. Problem solved, right? Twist ending! One of the survivors is tainted. Fade to black on their face as evil creeps through it."

Misery tries to turn her head, but a set of firm fingers hold her still. "Are you saying that happened to you?"

"Well, almost. An ancestor of mine—a great-great-granduncle—was one of those refound souls. They wanted to study how the nullvoid changes the human body, our DNA, whatever. So they hauled in all his living relatives—every one they could find, hundreds of us, and tested us comparatively. Had us isolated on an abandoned moon colony just in case great-great-granduncle destabilized. You can imagine what happened next."

Misery doesn't have to imagine. She smiles lightly where the doctor can't see it. "Just like in the movies."

"Movies don't have the half of it. He just . . . went. Exploded. Bits of him crawling black with the nullvoid. All over. Took out a whole wing of my family. I only escaped because I was in a different room. The scientists took me with them before they nuked the place. I got lucky. All I lost was an arm and a leg."

"Sorry to hear that."

"It's cool, I like my prosthetics better anyway. But I spent almost a decade of my life in quarantine. Behind double-strength glass walls, being poked and prodded while everybody waited for me to turn into a monster like he did."

"But you didn't."

"Nope. Still here, still kicking. But you never know. One day I might just be minding my business, and—boom!"

Very briefly Misery considers telling the doctor her truth. That she too knows the horror of watching a family member go to pieces, and surviving to remember the scene. Knows the heat and violence of the moment, and the long nightmares after. A moment of binding, shared solidarity. But she knows nothing of Dr. Sower except that she likes to talk and is too free with her life story. So she stays silent. She hates that she likes the doctor better because of this, though. The two of them just bits in a great machine that shuffles them around, small prey to its whims.

No. This will not be Misery's fate. She won't sit docile like the doctor does.

Dr. Sower taps her on the shoulder. "All right. You're done."

"Really?" When? Misery missed the point of insertion. She doesn't feel any different. She sits up, searches the back of her head for metal, for a scar, anything. "You're joking."

"Ye of little faith." Dr. Sower fishes a slender tube out of a pneumatic closet, a finger-length thing that's half electronics, half holy tigerseye. It floats as she draws a yellow screen out of it. "Do you see the censer?"

A circle blinks in the middle of that translucent diamond, spiked with a crossbar. "You mean this?"

"That is it. The implant's working. It's in. Hooked up to your nervous system like it should. No problems."

Misery rejects this message. She should *know* if someone messes with her brain. Yet this realignment of her brain happened without the seismic jolt she expected. Not a pinprick of pain or discomfort. Can such a change to her body occur without her notice? It feels violating in ways she cannot articulate.

Dr. Sower carries on, oblivious to Misery's discomfort. She says, of the censer on the screen: "All right, try to move it."

Move it how? Misery's brow furrows as she tries to shift the pixels with her mind. Nothing happens. Perhaps the implant didn't take after all?

The doctor laughs. "With your finger, genius."

Stung by embarrassment, Misery scowls and contemplates storming out. The doctor's easy capitulation to the circumstances of her life is risible, and she doesn't have to accept this humiliation. But it's too early to rock the boat. Misery lets her resentment sink and sediment in the pit of her belly. She lets the doctor guide her through the controls: opening things, closing things, summoning things, inputting data. Dr. Sower fusses her through the steps like she's a child new to walking. It's fine. Her skin's pretty thick, she can take it.

Dr. Sower steps back. "There you go. Ready for your new life. The implants will link with anything electronic around the station." She chuckles. "Sometimes I wish I never got wired as a child. I envy you late adopters, getting to experience a whole new world for the first time."

"Well, aren't I lucky," Misery drawls.

Dr. Sower laughs. "Don't be surprised when you step outside."

"Something I should be looking out for?"

"Information," says the doctor. "Just information everywhere you look. It's normal for us, but it might take you a while to get used to. Don't worry. You'll adapt. Most late adopters do."

"Most," Misery says.

"There are outliers. But I don't think you're one of them. After all, you're supposedly chosen, aren't you?"

"Yeah." She smiles, but knows from the pull of her muscles that it looks more like a grimace. Of course she's chosen; blessed by the Larex Forge and all, she's not on the verge of descending into voidmadness or anything.

"Good luck out there," says Dr. Sower. She means it sincerely, Misery can see that on her face, but under the circumstances it comes across as a threat. She thanks the doctor anyway. It's the least she can do.

At least she gets her mother's amulet back.

The moment Misery steps out of the medical center, the doctor's words hit like an avalanche. The ground tilts as Misery's senses are overwhelmed, and by instinct her palm finds a bulkhead, as though that one point of contact might save her from being swept away.

The doctor was right. Data sprawls everywhere in wild constellations. Hitherto-blank walls are revealed to be mats of text and graphics, populated by marching lines of newsfeed, wave clips, and monitored views of the station exterior. Stat boxes pop up over passing soldiers: name, pronouns, serving, origin, allergies—a glut of facts no human brain can process in the flash of seconds they are in view. Misery clutches at her mother's amulet, attention bouncing from shiny thing to shiny thing, unable to absorb any of it. "Void fuck me," she whispers, dazed. So this is how city folk see the world from birth. This is what life is like for people who aren't moonrats. Her mind, its grip on reality already tenuous, is struggling to stay upon that sharp and gritty edge. If she wasn't born circling voidmadness, this would surely yeet her into its orbit. Is that why they're so obsessed with voidmadness in the seats of power? Because its threat is so ever-present in their lives, a looming cenotaph casting its shadow over them at all times?

Ruin snorts. The delusion flits through the forest of light like it's hir native habitat. "This is what military life is like. Civilians don't get this much access to private data. Your princess, of course, would be able to pry into the lives of every registered citizen. But that's a perk of being royalty, isn't it?"

Misery takes a cautious step forward. The ground remains solid beneath her feet, and the gravity as weak as ever. Lieutenant Frash disappeared during the procedure and remains nowhere to be found. "Where did they go?"

Ruin says: "Back to their usual assignment. You no longer need a chaperone, after all. Look around you."

Suspended midair is an enormous red arrow, glorious and neon, pointing the way forward. In the clutter of everything new it has almost escaped attention, but now that it's seized her attention it's all she can look at. She isn't sure what to make of it. It hurts her eyes.

"Instructions," Ruin says. "You have a serving to report to. It's telling you where to go."

"And what happens if I ignore it?"

Zie shrugs. "Why don't you find out?"

Ominous. But the delusion is only channeling Misery's gut-brewed fear that she's given up control of something she shouldn't have. If the implant can tap into her visual cortex, make her see shit she's not supposed to see, what else can it do? Deliver electric shocks for disobedience? Control if she feels pain or not? Take over how she eats and shits?

She'll find out. Misery turns and marches in the direction opposite to the arrow's big blinking finger.

Two strides later it appears fresh in her field of vision, reminding her she's going the wrong way. She ignores it. Keeps walking. The arrow vanishes again, and re-ups itself in her vision. Every time it does so it comes back bigger and brighter, blinking shame. Going the wrong way, idiot. Misery keeps ignoring it, turning left and right with abandon, but it matches her in stubbornness. Barging in. Breaking the door down, sticking its face through like a deranged serial killer. Won't let her be. She's burrowing into the twists of Angelsteeth at a run now, tumbling through this alien place whose layout she does not know, and she's getting progressively more lost. Still the arrow won't leave her alone. Misery hits a dead end, the corridor's terminus, a bulbous room comprising a scatter of sinkfoam couches around a central pit. Acrylplate exposes a wide swathe of the stars outside. A rest point?

"It's an observation chamber," Ruin says. Zie phases in and out of the acrylplate as though dancing with the cosmos. "Pilots come here to starbathe sometimes."

"They don't get lights in their rooms?"

"They do. But who could say no to this view?"

She can't answer. Because plastered across that view is the red arrow of her disgrace, enormous and flashing, instructing her to turn around and go where she's supposed to. Misery takes in its sprawl with resignation and despair. "I'm not getting rid of it, am I?"

"You're in the military now," Ruin said. "They can, in fact, tell you what to do. And they will."

"Thanks," Misery said. "I hate it."

This is what the script of her life looks like now. She has to deal with it. The arrow stands in her way, a not-so-gentle admonishment, but it could be worse. As Ruin drifts through the blinking red, a luminescent beacon of arrogance, Misery is comforted to know that there is one thing the Imperial Army doesn't have mastery over. Her voidmadness is still her own.

"Fine," she says. "*Fine.* Let's see what I can make of this."

—|—

The arrow, her faithless guide, leads her on a twenty-minute walk through the anatomy of Angelsteeth, including several rides on boxy elevators and a march past rows of spherical cages in which zip-clad soldiers wrestle in null-g. In her crisp, novel, neon vision the illuminated deck labels shrink numerically as she goes, which means she's moving higher in the station both physically and symbolically. The expanding glut of security measures underscores that progression. Reinforced steel doors are replaced by ultra-thick reinforced steel doors, which in turn grade into ultra-thick reinforced steel doors fronted by guards. One stone-plated sentry scans her as she approaches and waves her through. Her identity has been registered in the depths of the station's command architecture. That's not unsettling at all.

Her pilgrimage ends in a high-arched briefing room, metal opening to starscape in a clear, wide curve. Where one would expect the paraphernalia of a meeting room—seats, video plaza, central table—is an empty briefing space. The General is there. The princess is there. So's Major Reyes, and the Duke, and a large handful of others she doesn't recognize. Their biodata panes bully one another for space in her attention. There's Captain Sunyata Diamond, whom she remembers from the battle. The captain exudes curiosity and hunger so strong that Misery's skin itches. Something's about to happen.

General Tsung grunts as Misery settles into a mockery of at-attention; she's never done military and their protocols are alien to her. "So, you're here. I see the procedure worked. Good. Let me introduce you to your serving."

Straight to business. No preamble, no grandiose speech, no indulgences. No mention of her tardiness. "Wait." Misery requires more gentle easing. "What do you mean, my serving? What's happening?"

"Soldier," says the General. "You are to be a seraph pilot."

Soldier? Seraph pilot? Misery's heart shatters like an explosive, and the emotion that cuts through her could be called despair as easily as it could be mistaken for joy. So it's come to this. General Tsung literally casting her in the frames of Leaf Maruska's iconic role: Messiah and unwilling draftee, under-prepared and overwhelmed, struggling to cope with the expectations placed on them. Resenting their mantle as blessed pilot, being rejected by their seraph in turn, until the crucial emotional climax before the made-up Battle of Keymar, accompanied by the requisite swells of pads and choirs. But it's one thing to watch seraphim in battle, sailing through space in the form of a vid plaza projection. It's another to get all third-kinds with one. Misery isn't even a saint. The real-life seraphim will spit her out the moment they taste her voidsickness.

Why is she surprised, though? Of course she's going to be made a seraph pilot. She's chosen of the Demiurge, remember? Purveyor of miracles. Nothing she can't do, purportedly. She's sent herself into this voidmouth.

How certain is the General that they've made the right decision? "Ser," she says, "I've never flown anything in my life before."

"That's what the training is for. Major Reyes will see to it."

Very determined. The General is dead set on training her as a pilot, convinced that this is the task the Demiurge has set for them, and the General is someone used to getting their way. The major frowns, rife with misgiving, but the General is xer boss and xe is a dutiful soldier, oathbound to follow orders. They can't be throwing her into the seraph's cockpit immediately, that shit only happens on the waves. One problem at a time. Real military has standard operating protocol and it takes fucking forever to get anything done.

"Your serving," the General continues, as though never interrupted. "You've been assigned Dish Ono, Serving Red-2. Not on the records. Your captain, Diamond Sunyata, will take charge of reporting and operations. I believe you've met."

They sure have. Away from the ill-omened light of the command room, Captain Diamond Sunyata has lost that hollowed-out, stressed quality that dominated Misery's attention. She's a lot younger than Misery thought, or remembered: just thirty, according to the pane in lights above her head, which means she was what? Twenty-five? When the Kestrel incident went

down. Twenty-five and a decorated war hero, a solid achievement, which Misery does not envy her for. There's more in the
info pane, so dense Misery can barely read it, but it seems she's
not active-duty? Marked as being on long-term medical leave.
And yet the General has her in the hot seat when the base needs
defending. Interesting.

Thank Forge for those lozenges of information, which ease
Misery's suffering as she meets the rest of the serving. Praise the
blessing of key details presented in bullet points. There's the
ship's tech, Tercero Tank, she/her pronouns, from the duchy of
Musa. A surprising puff of energy, small and twiggy with a pink
cloud for hair, face round and bright-eyed in a way that catches
Misery off guard. The info pane explains this immediately: Tank
is all of fourteen, sneaked into the army with a fake identity and
got swiftly punished when she got ratted out. Serving her sentence on Angelsteeth, which is also how Misery finds out that
the base is about half military outpost and half military prison.
How did Tank think no one would realize that she wasn't done
with puberty? The kid looks at Misery and serves her a grin
wide as her face, and Misery already likes her. The stupid shit
she pulled at fourteen had a far lesser scope of ambition.

The first pilot is Teá Spider, he/him pronouns, from the
duchy of Felidae. Another one on long-term medical leave, but
the line about his previous assignment catches her attention: he
was assigned to *Falling into Place*—that was Diamond Sunyata's
ship. So they knew each other? Also interesting. He's tall and
broad, and his thumbnail-length curly hair bears a faint sheen of
iridescence, dark green. A saint, as all pilots should be. Misery
can't read him, either. Not sure if he should be friend or foe.
She would like to be friends, though, there's something about
his bearing and appearance that's pleasing. Good posture, carefully neutral expression, very deliberately relaxed stance. Misery
knows how that feels in her bones. Seems like they would get
along.

Then the General introduces the third pilot, and a figure

steps from the shadows into the light. Misery's belly goes cold and her heart rate jacks up. A white saint! One of those creepy clone saints from the Capital, here? And pilot of a seraph? The panel over their pale shining head offers nothing—Ghost, they/them, pilot, point of origin Angelsteeth. Is that right? Were they made here? As Misery's adrenal glands work overtime the pilot—Ghost—stares with their glazed honey eyes. *I banish thee from the arches of my soul, my spirit, my mind.* The thought comes so immediately and vehemently that Misery's guts curl in embarrassment. That's from *Spirit Resonance,* and Misery clearly forgot how much time she spent in make-believe with other kids from the reef, exorcising telepaths from her being.

Ghost blinks inscrutably at her. Her nerves buzz with fear and her skull itches, like the white creature is rooting around in there. Clone saints are cursed—maybe it's telepathy? But telepathy isn't real.

"Telepathy is real," Ruin whispers in her head. The delusion has chosen not to manifest in this room. "But perhaps it's not these saints you have to worry about."

If only there were a prayer to banish delusions from the mind. Misery breathes: four in, six hold, seven out. None of the others seem bothered by the clone-saint's presence, at least not outwardly. She has to stay calm.

It occurs to her: each serving should have four pilots. Who is the fourth among the strangers left in the room? The rest of them are too old, too highly ranked, or not saints. Unless—

The General says: "The final pilot you are familiar with, of course. You arrived on this station with her, after all."

The Lady Lee Alodia Lightning, Imperial princess of the Faithful, sister to the Emperor himself. She stands stiff as a storm rod next to their serving captain, disapproval etched into her face. Pilot number four. Her lozenge of biodata is small and austere—privacy concerns, of course—but it does now say that she is a pilot. Just like the rest of them. If the Larex Forge has a plan, the plan is that they are to be colleagues. Misery's emotions ricochet from disbelief, to horror, to dismay. Within the kaleidoscope of personae she's encountered so far the princess strikes her as the biggest threat, and Misery can't articulate why but knows herself well enough to trust her gut. Her instincts are good, tainted by the nullvoid as they are. Perhaps even because of that taint. After all, they say voidmadness is caused by overexposure to the raw fabric of reality. Too much truth drives you crazy.

"Didn't think a scion of the Imperial family would serve on the front lines," she says.

"Didn't think so either," says the princess. "But here we are."

"And here we have been gathered by the auspices of the Larex Forge," says General Tsung. "Whatever Hir plan for us, we have a duty to keep moving forward. Your training begins tomorrow. Let's not waste any time. Yes?"

"Well," says Misery, lying, "I for one look forward to it."

11

The real challenge around living with an implant, Misery decides, is stamina. The constant flood of information and visual distraction is fine in short bursts, but hours and hours later her mind has been stretched like spun glue and she is one loud noise away from a breakdown. The lights are endless. They are everywhere. On the way to dinner she trails her new serving in a haze of distraction, unable to ignore the technicolor veneer demanding her attention at all times. She's reading the lozenges above everybody's head, getting distracted by a newsblip about the siege of Monkglass, and falling so deeply into a half-yard stub about drama between two up-and-coming wave thespians that she misses that Ono Red-2 has vanished down the corridor. Damn. This is no time to be distracted. Things are dire and only getting worse.

"You'll learn to ignore it all," Ruin says. "You have no problems ignoring me, after all."

Misery imagines the delusion falling off a cliff and into a series of enormous metal spikes. She really needs the endorphins.

Even a secret collection of dubious characters assembled for illegal and seditious purposes cannot escape the monotony of bureaucracy. Anything that has structure must be recorded, even if only in hidden files lurking in the depths of the General's classified folders. Ono Red-2 were entered into the system. Briefed on a schedule. Taken to their quarters, tucked in the farthest corner of the personnel barracks. It seems to be a re-purposed rec space: a too-large circular room with light-rimmed pits for simple food prep, reading, other kinds of R&R. Around it squats a series of private rooms turned into personnel quarters where beds have been awkwardly and hastily molded. Their shared bathroom has the vibe of a public toilet. Best they could do on short notice. Misery was given a move-in kit, and there's a screen through which she can order anything else she needs and desires, plus the services of the replicator that lives in the common room.

And now: dinner. Evening meals on Angelsteeth are communal affairs. Four hundred soldiers of all ranks packed into an arch-roofed hall of the deepest holy jade. Deadmarble tables polka-dot the interior, fish-pink and gleaming, basking under clusters of flasklights too numerous to count. Here Misery finds respite in walls kept so blank it has to be deliberate. Even the ubiquitous lozenges tagged to each head seem calmer, less intrusive. There is prayer: a priest in familiar colors leading the flock in a rumbling voice that reminds her just a bit of Crem. She'll never admit how much comfort she's extracting from this touch of the familiar. A reminder that her life so far hasn't taken place on another plane of reality altogether. That she, growing up on the dust-choked plains of Rootsdown, shares something in common with the arch-backed princess beside her.

Ono Red-2 has a table already allocated to them. Curious gazes tail them as they follow the guidance arrow to their destination. Despite the secrecy folded around this clandestine serving, the crew of Angelsteeth know that something's up. They're old hands at keeping secrets. They know the way one smells. Ono Red-2 take their seats. On the table, a silver box on a silver tray for each one of them. Misery unwraps hers. Within it: a small and fragrant spread of ambrosia. Tender grains, butter-drenched flakes of protein. Shit, even military food is better than the dreck they get back home.

"Saints don't necessarily need to eat," Ruin observes. "Organic food consumption is such a messy, nasty affair. They have to make the process worth it, don't they?"

Saint or not, it's definitely worth it. Misery has eaten with dukes and archbishops and this isn't shabby by far. Not too bad if this is her new normal. Look at her, a moonrat getting all used to luxury and shit.

No. She can't get distracted by base indulgences. Put the allure of bodily pleasures aside. First chance she's got to observe her new colleagues since their brusque introduction; she needs to get them before they can form opinions of her. Six to a serving, half saints and half not. The captain and the kid—Tank— are the easiest to read. Captain because she's seen so many of that archetype, the washed-up vets turned supply runner, or purveyor of dark-web goods, or whatever puts carbs in their bowls. That deep, untouchable well of sadness, cyanide-laced, poisoning every aspect of their manner whether they realize it or not. Captain Diamond Sunyata has seen too many friends dead and too many lovers lost. She dreads sleep and even the brief bullets of carnal pleasure she allows herself are tainted. Not worth the wounds they leave behind. Someone she must handle with caution. Gentleness. Care, even. Empathy if she can manage it. Misery's not good at empathy.

Tank, on the other hand, spills over with a kid's enthusiasm, eager to show off everything that she is. She's the kind of smart that rolls over into dumb, a cleverness that's so overwhelming that it leaves her vulnerable in places where she's not looking. Misery admires her raw intellect—she knows her own brain will never tick that way—but she wouldn't trade it for what she does have. It's fine, Tank is a kid. She'll learn, or she won't and the consequences will come for her. Either way.

The others are more opaque. Spider, the pilot on medical leave, appears all smiles and confidence. Happy and self-assured as any regular schmuck has the right to be. But something seems off about it. Something about his veneer is too shiny, like it's buffed every day, every hour, the moment it picks up the merest fleck of dust. The kind of fretful maintenance done when you're worried about the rot underneath showing. Misery doesn't trust his aura of normalcy, although she can't say what might be lurking below it. If he once served on Sunyata Diamond's ship, perhaps the cause of their trauma is the same. He could be dangerous. Or he could just be sad. Misery isn't sure, so she can't trust him yet. This puzzle is one that requires more time and effort to unlock.

Ghost, the white saint, she would prefer not to think about. But they're here and she has to deal with them, like it or not. Alone among the serving they have not unpacked their food; it sits placid and cubical in front of them. Do they not eat? Maybe they weren't made with a digestive system. Ghost looks like they've never consumed a meal their entire life, with those hollow rings around the eyes and the milk-curd skin that displays blue veins in their hands and wrists. Maybe they're not exactly identical to the clones on the Capital. Can she tell? Their faces blend. Ghost's gaze skips from one instance of human interaction to the next with the intensity of a small sun. What goes through their mind as they study others?

Lastly, there's the princess. The Lady Lee Alodia Lightning. As the serving had milled around their assigned table, doing the awkward shuffle of figuring out where to sit among a group of strangers, Misery had deftly positioned herself across from the princess. All the better to watch her. The investment has paid off; even as Misery studies the other members of the serving, she keeps the princess in the corner of her eye. The princess is watching her in return, in between spoonfuls of mouth-melt protein. Unsettling. The Lady Lee Alodia Lightning is the most dangerous of all: closest to figuring out the falsehoods driving Misery's apotheosis, and most empowered to cut the lines on the whole gig. That she's gotten knees-and-elbows involved in the serving hints at a personal agenda, but Misery will be taken if she knows what it is.

Already cracks are showing in the social fabric of the serving. Tank and Spider scrap verbally, the small feints of a petty disagreement played out by two people realizing they don't like each other very much. The argument is about something stupid—

Tank has opinions about language patterns, Spider thinks a young girl like her can't possibly know anything about anything.

"Come on," the kid says, "everyone knows that ALISS fucked up with the balance in what it picked for family names. Casts a lot of shade on its claims to impartiality in maintaining genetic variance too."

"I'm just saying what I've heard," Spider says, palms up like a shield. He has the self-assured, destructive manner of too many jocks Misery knows.

"Are you arguing with someone who's done a whole thesis on this? I'm a fucking genius, I'll have you know."

"Not genius enough to realize you can't pass as an adult."

Tank winds up, ready to plant her fist in the soft tissue of Spider's throat, a fight she'll surely lose. Misery tenses, gearing for the clash—she could sort them out—when they are interrupted.

"May I ask a question?"

The voice cuts through the tension. Ghost, the white saint, sits rod-straight and clear-eyed, attention fixed on Misery. All curiosity and innocence. The serving goes quiet, unsettled, petty arguments forgotten. Ghost has not spoken until now.

"Are you speaking to me?" Misery asks.

"Yes." Their attention remains undivided and unwavering. "May I ask a question?"

She wants to know what it is. What goes through this strange creature's mind, what concerns are lodged in their heart. "Ask away."

"You're a nixen," Ghost says. They speak clear and soft, like someone learned and gentle. "But it says on your profile that you use *they* and *she* pronouns. I don't understand that."

"What about it don't you understand?"

They think it over, slow and deliberate. "I don't really understand pronouns in general. I use the ones I was given. But you have two. Why is that? How did you decide?"

She had not expected this. It's almost endearing, the simplicity of their question. Misery sees something of herself in the strange saint, cursed but naïve, thrown into a situation they didn't quite expect. Why shouldn't she answer? Like a benevolent parent she says, "You'll find it's different for everyone. In my case I've never cared for gender. Whatever it is, whatever it means. I was raised with she/her pronouns, and it's what I'm used to, but they're just words. So I chose *they* as my official pronoun. But I was raised with *she,* and honestly that's what's in my head. It's not like anything about me changed. And those close to me use *she.* My family. My comrades. But I insist on *they* in official terms and in the records, because that's important. I'm nixen, and I want that visibly, tangibly recorded. Does that make sense?"

"Oh." Ghost presses their palms together, fingers to their pale lips. Misery's infodump seems to be having a profound impact. "In that case, may I use *she* for you?"

"Of course." She doesn't mind. And she's curious about the internal workings of this strange creature, this stranger. "Tell me more about yourself."

"About myself?" Ghost looks confused. "I was made here. I have always lived here. I don't know very much beyond these walls. I . . . am not sure what else you would want to know."

Spider's expression curves into derision. "You're a freak. You're a reject from those disgusting cloning projects the Throne thinks we don't know they're running. What are you doing here?"

"You. What's wrong with you?" Tank purples with indignation, pushed past the limits of her goodwill. "That's how you talk to your comrades? We're supposed to be a team."

Spider's expression grows lazy, but his fingertips press into the table's surface. Ghost seems unfazed by the opprobrium, watching Tank and Spider with a curious eye.

"Enough." Their captain Sunyata Diamond slaps her palms upon the glossy tabletop. "You are soldiers now. Behave like it."

Tank's expression sours, but the admonishment works on Spider. He goes quiet, silenced by Diamond's gravitational pull.

Misery studies the sharp-haired woman, curious what she has to say.

Diamond scans the table, taking in the messy assemblage of people she's supposed to lead. "We have been brought here not by circumstance, but by fate. Whatever petty differences you have, you need to put them aside. You are called to a higher purpose."

Her voice is clear, her eyes bright. She appears a different person from the wound-up pillar of gloom Misery met in the heat of battle. Spider crosses his arms across his chest, sullen and inscrutable, all his swagger gone.

Tank squints. "What higher purpose? I thought this was the military, not Church. Not trying to be rude or anything, but seriously."

She's genuinely not trying to be rude; her inquiry is honest. The big brass told her nothing she wanted to know. She hasn't been pardoned, hasn't had her sentence commuted, and she's been drafted into a top-secret extra-classified experimental new serving with no explanation. It chafes at her soul to lack such key information.

Diamond says: "You've been reading the news, I presume?"

"We didn't get a lot of it in fricken jail."

"So you haven't heard about the return of the prophesized Messiah?"

"Oh." Tank leans back in her seat, wary. "I know about that one."

"Then I must tell you that they are sitting next to you. The Larex Forge has brought them to Angelsteeth to carry out their mission, and we have been chosen to assist them. That is the decision made by General Tsung, and I expect you to respect that decision. Our serving will learn to fight in this holy war. Beyond that, it is up to the will of the Forge."

No talk of the death sentences and sedition that underpin the formation of their serving. Spider is quiet, still taken by Diamond's ironclad sincerity. "Not trying to argue with the General's decision," Tank grouses. Then she turns to Misery. "So you're the Black Hole Messiah? It's you? Well. Was kind of hoping you'd look more like Leaf Maruska."

"Sorry to disappoint."

Time stretches as Tank studies her, equal parts curiosity and caution. "Did you really kill all those people?"

"I did."

She leans forward, ears pricked and expression all squinted. "Why?"

The poles of Rootsdown are uninhabitable wastelands, freezing blood half the year and melting flesh the other half. Bathory Lake in the north is a popular venue for ice boarding in the cold season, but Misery only ever went after the surface started its yearly thaw, when the fields were already closed and she could be by herself with the rapidly fragmenting ice. It was a skill, figuring out at speed which bits of glossy blue were solid enough to hold her weight. This moment feels exactly like that, Misery skimming across the unfamiliar unknown, avoiding cracks she can feel but can't see, one wrong turn away from instant oblivion. Mass murder is a hard thing to justify.

She tells Tank: "I was compelled by the will of the Forge. Zie showed me the rot at the heart of the Empire and told me that those who had allowed such things must be punished."

Tank is unconvinced by broad rhetoric. "What things?"

"A truce with the Heretics. Pursuing peace when their way of life will destroy ours." Misery takes a risky path across the ice, praying the bottom won't fall out of it. "They were running unholy experiments on the Capital. I saw such horrible things, like you wouldn't believe."

"Oh, I believe," Tank mumbles. "They're running unholy experiments on this station, too."

"Exactly." Spider points at Ghost. "Again, my question. What is this abomination doing here?"

The atmosphere cools once more. No one has an answer to Spider's accusation. Ghost tilts their head, as if considering for the first time that they might indeed be an abomination. Around the table, a vacuum exists where consensus should be. Misery, still speeding over the thinning ice, sees a path open before her, shining with promise. Those seated around her are just as lost as she is. In desperate need of something to believe in. She could fill that gap. She could become the direction they crave.

She says: "Ghost is here because they need to be. It is the hand of the Larex Forge that has guided each of us into our roles, here, today. I cannot guess what the future holds for us. I cannot know what Hir plan is. But I have faith in the wisdom of the Demiurge, and I will go where Zie leads."

Is that messianic enough? Does she sound like someone touched by the gilded hands of the Forge, like somebody who might appear in one of Crem's stories?

Tank wrinkles her nose, still unconvinced. A healthy amount of skepticism for one so young. "You really believe in all that, huh."

"The Archbishop Storm Imogen believes it," Diamond says. "And I believe it. I witnessed the miracle they wrought on the battlefield. It is an honor and blessing to serve alongside them. I am confident that will become clear in time."

At least the captain is on her side; it's one less battle to fight. Misery picks up where she leaves off. "All of us have had difficult journeys on our way here. But I fully believe that we are all purposefully, divinely, and joyfully meant to be here, each and every one of us. No matter how unlikely it may seem. We are a family now, united by the will of the Larex Forge. If nothing else, we have one another."

She looks around the table as she speaks, making sure to catch the gaze of each member of the serving. Make them feel included, make them feel like this message is for you too, yes, even you. The last person she looks at is the princess, who she's almost forgotten about as a player in this diorama. Who she instinctively wanted to exclude. But it's too late, they've made eye contact, she didn't mean to do this. The Lady Alodia Lightning's gaze is fevered, bright. Her lips part and she sucks in a visible breath as if touched by something ice or fire. Goose static runs up Misery's arms. Fine. She can be included too. If this is what she wants. It's all part of Misery's plan.

Hovering over Ono Red-2, perched golden and merry on a flasklight, Ruin laughs. "Oh, Misery," zie says. "You have such a talent for this. Don't you see? It's why you've been chosen."

12

Misery delays sleep that night. Her body, heavy with exhaustion, yearns for it. Begs her to rest. But she can't waste her hours in the treacherous duchy that is sleep, where the fanged beasts of the nullvoid wait to feast on her mind. She's afraid of what she will see. Skins splitting, the vomit of the void spewing forth, the eyes of the dead, creeping madness. Eventually, she'll have to sleep. The flesh will drag her mind down that pit. Until then, Misery distracts herself with reading. She sinks into the foam of her bed, awkwardly wedged into a corner not meant to hold furniture. A galaxy of screens dance before her: she's summoned, from Angelsteeth's system, every scrap of information she can find about the training she must go through. Seraph pilot training comes in multiple stages. Before one is allowed within spitting distance of a combat unit, a pilot must first learn use of the interface. Seraphim are not welcoming to mortals; even the sacred few among the saints who are seraph-compatible cannot operate them directly. Through centuries of trial and error, Faithful scientists discovered that specific actions performed on the holy labradorite resulted in specific movements in the seraphim, and from that had developed a vocabulary of movesets that each pilot had to learn.

None of it appeals. It's all very difficult, it's all very strict, there are multiple points of failure. But General Tsung has decided her messianic drive should be harnessed by a seraph, turning her into perfect weapon against the Heretics, a holy sword that cleaves the nullvoid. Who knew the General was such a romantic? Problem: now she has to learn to pilot a seraph. And it's not like learning how to punch faster or getting better at cards. The ability to connect to a seraph is innate: either you can do it or you can't. Many saints can't. Chosen of the Larex Forge and all. So far, Misery has impressed the soft minds running the show by masking her voidsickness as holy ability. But she suspects this will not fly with the seraphim whose stone hearts will not be moved by intimidation, manipulation, or bribery.

So what now? Her mind stubbornly plots out the worst-case scenarios like a prayer wheel of anxieties. She could flunk out at the training stage, the bubble of illusion popped at the first obstacle. That path is easy to chart. Major Reyes says, "See, told you," the General gets disillusioned, she gets put back on death row. Misery gets taken out of the picture. Nothing she can do about that.

More difficult: Misery gets through training somehow. She gets to mount a true seraph, gets to run her grubby hands all over its sacred flesh. Holy labradorite, a stone she's never met. Will the sacred stone that incarnates the Faithful's greatest weapons bow meekly to her will? She doesn't think so. She might wind up destroying the seraphs. She might wind up destroying the station. In this scenario, she's also dead. They're all dead.

"I think you're missing one crucial outcome," Ruin says. The delusion has found hir favorite nesting spot on top of the wardrobe, a narrow block of gray polycarbonate that holds stacks of new uniforms fitted to Misery's dimensions, plus a smattering of civvies in the dullest colors and cuts. The wardrobe is tall enough the delusion's white crown brushes the vent-studded ceiling as zie squats upon it. "What if you, in fact, are meant to be a seraph pilot?"

For someone who claims to be a divine guide, Ruin does very little guiding. Almost as if zie weren't a holy messenger but a mere bystander, an outgrowth of the shitshow that is Misery's mind. She closes her eyes and layers her hands over her face, but she can still sense the delusion, a mocking shape in the corner of her consciousness, inescapable.

Fine. She should sleep. If she has to face her demons, she should take them face on. Shouldn't she?

Misery dreams.

She's back home on Rootsdown, with all that entails: homely pull of gravity, the glaze of tropic-heat and heavy air, the ennui and lethargy of life that rolls with the pace of a sun. The dark alleys between reefs, thick with smells of food and garbage water. The heavy walls of the churchhall, echoing with Crem's voice. The white arches of the hospital whose paths she memorized during her many runs to pilfer salves to bake with. In Misery's mind these dioramas are contained in the same place, a treacherous swamp of emotions she cannot distill into discrete thought and feeling. Rootsdown is all of these places at once.

Misery's at the warehouse. Crem thinks she works at the factory, and she does have a job there inspecting machined parts packed with holy turquoise pulled from Rootsdown's crust. But her main hustle is in the broken warehouse next door, a sloping gray building patchy with decay, its roof in a years-long process of caving in. The perfect place to bake tripsalves with the materials she's stolen.

Misery becomes hyperaware of her hands and feet and how she can move them. The lucidity is welcome: at last, a modicum of control over her wild subconscious. The rotting warehouse calls to her. She has to go inside. It's all right—if she makes the decision to enter the building, she's still maintaining a form of control.

Dust lives in the heart of the abandoned building, shafted through with patchwork light. Within the decay sits the searing yellow of an aegis, like a neon dome in one of those all-wood, all-dust Earth revival shops. Misery pulled it off a builder abandoned in the desert to protect her secret lab.

A silhouette stands in that otherworldly glow: a tall, thin figure with an infinitely graceful air. A lanky saint in a long creamy robe, edged in gold with lace at the throat. Deep-set eyes, pale and watery, wire-wrapped glass pinching the bridge of hir nose. Sandy hair spills over hir shoulders like spun sugar. On hir narrow breast sits a teardrop of something that looks like labradorite, possibly the mundane sort.

Misery approaches this figure with animal wariness. Acid coats her tongue and crawls down the back of her throat. The last time she felt like this in a dream, she met Ruin. Fragments of the void lurk here and she can't be too careful. The dream-apparition says nothing as she comes closer, studying her with the intensity of a curious beast trying to determine if she is friend, foe, or food.

"Who are you?" she asks. "What are you doing here?"

"Here? Where is here?"

The stranger's voice is soft as cotton, and hir syllables carry a lilt she can't place. Zie reminds her of Ghost and the white saints, but more human. More color to hir skin, more imperfection in hir features. A slight slant to the nose, eyes slightly too far apart. Tall, but in an unfortunate manner. Misery decides to humor hir. "This is Rootsdown. It's where I grew up."

"Where you grew up," says the creature. "I see. So this is your dream."

"It is."

"What is your name, dream-maker?"

Misery stands within breathing distance of this fantasy creature with hir strange and quiet voice. The beguiling face, long and elfin. Heat wafts from hir skin, and the hairs on Misery's forearm rise to catch it like a solar array. "I'm Misery Nomaki. She/they pronouns. You can use the first."

"Misery Nomaki," zie says, slow and careful, shaping her name like it's charmed glass. "So, Misery it is, then?"

"If you want."

"I'm Jericho. He/him pronouns."

There's something precious about a figment of a dream introducing himself like a real person. Her voidsick mind, snarled thick with stress, performs marvelous tasks. Conjures delusions and imbues them with desires. In Misery's ever-flourishing crop of strange dreams, this might be one of the oddest. She studies this ersatz young man and wonders why she doesn't know what to do. Dreams drive themselves with cryptic nonsense logic, but they always move forward. Here, time is at a standstill. Misery puts a palm to Jericho's belly, flush against the honeyed silk, and feels the soft rise and fall of his breaths.

"What are you looking for?" Jericho asks.

Her breath stutters. The question has caught her like a punch under the ribs, and no answers come to her defense. A core of truth hides in this surreal diorama, a solid loop of emotion pulled from her heart. "Someplace else. Take me away from here."

"Away from here? I . . ." Jericho trails off as he frowns. "Can I do that? Another place . . . I wonder . . ."

This is stupid, she's having a stupid conversation in a stupid dream. As Misery thinks this the floor under her despawns and gravity fades. Her bones become light as breath. Misery floats upward into a space that is no longer well-bound, no longer terrestrial: masonry and atmosphere come unglued and weather dissolves into cool, still air. Instead she hangs suspended in a massive geodesic sphere that is all mirrors, a thousand Pythagorean mirrors that contain one perfect reflection of Misery and Jericho side by side in the vast space, and then reflect a dozen more. Reflection catches reflection until there are hundreds upon thousands of Misery-and-Jericho pairs. Her head spins. Every movement she makes, no matter how small, is reflected a thousandfold. She conducts an orchestra of Misery Nomakis in dizzying sync, motions blurring together until she can't tell who is real and who is not. Is she real? Is this tumbling kaleidoscope real? She feels as solid as Jericho does, and she knows he's not real. If she's not real, then nothing here is. Misery flings her arms out and spins, joyous with light. Here, she is nothing. Here, she is free.

Eventually her momentum slows and she flails, unused to being so unmoored. Like floating off into the void. Where is the original Jericho, the one who is solid? She's lost him in the sea of repeats.

A hand closes over her wrist and she knows the weight of things again. It's Jericho, pale eyes intent, searching her face for meaning. "This is a play space," he says. "People come here to relax, bounce off walls, tumble, all sorts of things. Just float, if they want."

She notices now the enormous blocks of white foam tumbling through the space. Elastic webbing drips neon between mirrored surfaces, toys for climbing or for bouncing off of. "This is a place to celebrate bodies," he says.

"Is that so." Maybe she's seen something like this in a stream or a drama. Misery tugs him closer and finds no resistance, none whatsoever. He couldn't resist her if he tried. This is Misery's subconscious, and she suddenly understands why she's constructed this unusual space in the realms of sleep. Her body has wants and needs. "I could think of a few things worth celebrating," she says. She hooks a leg over Jericho, the back of her knee fitting nicely against his hip bone. She's always wanted to experience sex in zero-g, and she regretted not getting any while she was on the Duke's ship. This might be the closest she gets to it. "Let's fuck."

This close, Jericho's face doesn't coalesce into a unified visage. It's a sketchy collection of magnified, magnificent features she takes in one at a time: a watery eye, a swathe of cottony skin, fine lines flocked along the edge of a mouth. The edges of Jericho's teeth shine like instrument keys. "If that's what you want. We could do that."

And they do.

-+-

Misery wakes in a strange place. Her quarters. Unfamiliar air and gravity, the hiss and thrum of spacebound living, the diffuse blue light tuned to night mode. Voidsbane, but she's been through a fuck-ton lately, and things have been barreling forward so fast she's had no time to breathe, much less sit down and think about what's been happening. No wonder her brain is melting down. Sex dreams usually leave her mellow upon waking, but this one has her strung so tight her neck and belly hurt. Like she woke in escape mode. Misery's conscious mind might be in denial about how much shit she's in, but her subconscious knows what's up.

She scrubs her hands over her face and does Saint Agneta's pattern until her body stops feeling like a rocket about to leave orbit.

Misery returns to the reality of Angelsteeth and considers her surroundings. In the blue-tinged gloom Ruin floats above the gray slab of her supply closet, eyes glowing like twin suns.

"So you've got a friend now," she says to the delusion. "You must be delighted for the company."

"We are nothing alike, Misery Nomaki. But your faithlessness is no matter. Someday you shall see the truth."

She closes her eyes and wishes she could close her ears, too. Shut down her mind. No place in the universe feels like a safe refuge, not even within her own head. An afterimage of Jericho lives in her head, a vague shadow: all pale eyes, pale skin, and fine, sandy hair. Voice like pondwater, swirling into the cups of her ears. She hates to admit how much comfort she found in that dream. Its lack of hard edges. Its consequence-free shine. She knows she's only inviting trouble by indulging the delusion. But she's already snot-deep in trouble. What's a few more shovels of shit?

13

Seraph pilot training takes place in a thickly fenced complex that's all blue metal and frigid air, a narrow domain subordinate to the withering gaze of Major Reyes Photon, whose job it is to oversee Angelsteeth's pilots. Guided by the sentinel arrows, Misery and Ono Red-2 hiked the length of the base and came to rest in a briefing theater next to two other servings: Button Red-4 and Xito Blue-4. The system display tells Misery that the other two servings are fresh out of basic military training, something she has not gone through but sure, it's probably fine that she did not. Everything is fine.

Major Reyes's disdain rakes over the gathered servings—the twelve pilots in the front rows, non-pilots relegated to the back of the room. On either side of Misery sit a contrast in attitudes: on the left is the Lady Alodia Lightning, posture perfectly straight and still; on the right is Teá Spider, slouched like he has just gotten out of bed.

"So," the major says in xer pumice-gravel voice, "you're here. Granted passage by your sainthood, put through the tests and trials, all of which you've passed. Or maybe you haven't." A very pointed look in Ono Red-2's direction. "Whatever it is, you're here. And you think you're ready for what's about to come next." Xer laugh sounds like rocks falling over a cliff face. "I will tell you now—you are not. In my two decades' training I have never met anyone ready. You think you're the exception? You are not."

Spider snorts from his boneless slouch.

The beacon of Major Reyes's attention strikes him. Xe jabs

xer finger, gleaming holy jade, in his direction. "You think you're exempt from this, do you?"

Spider pops his lips. "Not my first go-around, old man."

The major's face hardens. "Stand up."

Spider stands with the discipline of the trained soldier, but defiance boils under the veneer of obedience. He folds his arms as the other recruits fidget.

"You think you've seen battle," the major says, emphasis on every syllable.

"It's in my records."

"One sortie. Then straight to the retirement pen."

"People died." Spider's mouth twists with rage. "*All* my shipm—"

"That's how war is." The major regards Spider with nuclear disdain. "You think you're the first person to outlive their entire serving? Or the only one?"

"My captain—"

"I know your captain. She's in the room. Who or what do you take me for?"

Spider falls silent. Major Reyes sweeps xer glistening arm outward, encompassing the roomful of trainees. "All of you— none born yet when the Truce of Logan was signed. Not one of you was alive to experience what it was like before."

A small murmur. Maybe Major Reyes was right. The truce had been signed a dozen years before Misery was born; even Diamond, the oldest among them, was a baby when it happened. Misery knows war from wave dramas and tall tales; she doesn't know it like the major knows it. The hollows from the endless rationing and from watching the buildings around you empty, victims of conscription. Every cloud in the sky a source of fear, every strange tic in a neighbor a suspicion of voidsickness.

"Teá Aubergine Spider," Major Reyes barks. "How many seraphim are active in the Imperial fleets today?"

"A hundred and eighty-six across the duchies and the royal fleet," Spider recites sourly.

"Do you know how many we had in AE 450? The year I was born?"

Spider mumbles.

"Speak up."

"More than three hundred."

"Three hundred and forty-seven," Major Reyes says. "So. Between then and the truce, that's a hundred and forty-six pilots that didn't make it. Do you know how many of them I knew?"

Xer question hangs in the air like an insect hive; no one dares approach it. The major shakes xer head. "More than I can count. More than I can remember." Xe starts pacing. "You have all lived in times of peace. None of you know what it was like, to hold advancing lines against the Heretics. To live in constant fear of the creeping nullvoid. In your body, in your mind. To never leave the state of highest alert—all times on the ship, eating, sleeping, fucking. Not knowing when the sky might tear and spit Heretic into your face. Because it happened every other day. Do you know what that's like? Can you imagine it? No. You can't. Not until you've lived through it."

"And Forge willing, we won't have to." Ono Red-2's captain stands on the balls of her feet, electric with adrenaline. The captain's anger is a thick wall that has weight, like steam.

Major Reyes laughs as xe focuses upon the other war hero in the room. "Do you really believe that, Captain Sunyata? You, the great strategist of the Empire of all people, are telling me you don't know how thin the threads by which the truce hang are?"

"Yes," Captain Sunyata says sharply, "I do. And all this crying mimosa is premature and counterproductive. My professional opinion. You can put that in a report."

"So you haven't heard the news about who's leading the siege on Monkglass then?"

Her voice drops an octave and several latitudes' worth of temperature. "Don't."

Misery's skin prickles. This is a deep wound from her past, maybe even *the* deep wound from her past, the reason she was put out to pasture and kept away from the battlefield. Who *is* leading the siege on Monkglass? She'll have to find out.

Major Reyes lifts xer chin in triumph. "If things work out the way the General wants, we are headed toward open war again. If you think you have nothing to be afraid of . . . Forge help you, because I can't."

"What good does it do to demoralize them before they start?" The captain is a spiked ball of fear and anger, so ugly it's almost beautiful to witness. "Is that what they pay you to do?"

"What good does it do, indeed," Major Reyes mumbles, gaze roving the floor. Xer mind navigates treacherous plains of emotion, far from this room of anxious baby pilots.

"As a river cuts a channel through the field, so does despair draw forth the waters of the nullvoid," the captain recites. "Careful that you do not tempt it with infelicitous thoughts."

"Ah. Yes. Scripture will make me change my mind. Because I've never heard those lines before." The major shakes xer head. "But strange times we live in, indeed. The Throne consorts with the enemy, wrong is right and right is wrong. Who knows." Xer attention catches Misery in its caustic beam. "Who knows," xe intones again, like a mantra. "After all, the Messiah walks among us, do they not? Let's see what miracles they have in store for us."

Dozens of gazes converge upon Misery. By nature and long practice, the soldiers of Angelsteeth are disciplined enough to keep great secrets from the outside world, but gossip within the walls is fair game, and gossip they do. Speculation about the shady circumstances surrounding Ono Red-2 has seeped into the collective consciousness like poison water, and everyone has hir own salacious take.

"Don't worry," Ruin whispers in her ear. "The closer they

look, the better for you to show off your talents. Go on, Misery Nomaki. Show them what you're capable of."

Spider is livid. His fury carries him from the briefing room all the way to the calibration deck. Lingering in the rear with Diamond, he hisses: "Who the fuck put xer in charge? Scarface really out here saying what we went through was nothing?"

"Focus on the day ahead, Spider. I'll speak to the General."

"Just unbelievable. Uncalled for. Rude fucking piece of shit. I could say more, but—"

"Don't. Spider, I know. I know."

Misery listens, taking mental notes.

The calibration room suffers from excessive light and chilled air. Within its circular confines sit two dozen plastic ovals, cut away to make space for a pilot. A name-bearing tab floats over each one. Misery finds her station, sits, and puts on the interfacing helmet: a velvet-lined silver dome with the smell of a well-used public object cleaned an uncountable number of times. An aura on the uncomfortable border between natural and chemical.

A blue screen appears before Misery. On it is the anatomical map of a seraph, each of its eight limbs highlighted a different neon. Four arms. Four feet springing from bifurcated twig legs. Major Reyes stalks the room as the trainees settle in. "The purpose of calibration," xe says, "is to acclimatize your bipedal, two-armed brain to the task of controlling something as complex as a seraph. Until you can reliably produce discrete responses to each of their limbs, you won't be allowed to progress to the next stage."

Well. How hard can it be?

Ten minutes later Misery has her answer. It's an impossible fucking ask. The blue screen lights up over and over: move the left upper arm, move the right lower arm and so on. Each time,

Misery transmits her will through the interfacing helmet, only to be told she failed. Twenty years as a bipedal creature has fixed her mind's workings: you have two arms, and two legs. One on each side. That's it. Over and over the system berates her as she fails to return discrete cranial patterns for the lower arms and back legs. How the fuck is she supposed to invent control of limbs she doesn't have? She fumes as the screen blatts red for what feels like the hundredth time. If they'd put her straight into a seraph she would have some fancy tricks to show off. She and the holy labradorite would hash out an agreement. Instead she has to struggle with this electronic doodad, prying into the pulses of her mind.

She looks at Spider in the next station over and of course his screen is green after green after green. He looks bored, tapping his foot in frustration drawn from an entirely different well. Fucking good for him. Around them the other screens are starting to blink green. Misery's about to be exposed.

"Don't think with your mind," Ruin says. The delusion swans through the room as though zie owns it. "Your thoughts hold you back."

Her fucking biology is holding her back, that's what it is. The delusion can talk all the shit zie wants, but it will change nothing.

"Is that a challenge?" The delusion laughs. With a cold flash that only she perceives, Ruin appears next to her. She has no time to flinch or dodge before zie places a pale hand upon her neck. Misery's nerves fizzle with mint-warmth at hir phantom touch. The buzz spreads through her extremities and turns her chest woolly. The fuck is happening—

"Relax," Ruin says.

Saint Agneta's pattern makes her edges fuzzy, as if she's unspooling, skin coming unstuck, flesh slackening in loose ribbons. She's dissolving in her clothes and the only solid thing is the amulet against her chest, a warm knot of stone. For a dizzying moment she looks down and realizes she has more limbs

than she remembered, of course, she'd always had them in po-
tentia, she just had to feel them differently.

The screen waits for her response with infinite patience as
Misery gets trip-high on feeling, eager to flex her newfound
topography. Upper left arm, lower left, upper right arm, lower
right, each of her four feet tap dancing in sequence. A soaring
burst of joy at the sudden unlocked possibilities. She wants to
be let loose into the universe, to spin and leap between the stars,
to—

"What's going on here?"

The shadow of Major Reyes looms over her station. Shit.
She's ignored so many cues that the system tutted at her stack
of errors and flagged her to command. Misery looks as calm
as she can. "It's nothing," she says. "I just figured something
out."

The major's displeasure only deepens. Leaning xer full
weight on her station, xe flicks a jade finger at the screen. "Don't
talk. Show."

Eyes shut, Misery takes another saint's breath. The newfound
sensation is still there. She still has it. She knows where all her
secret limbs are. If the major wants a show, xe'll get one.

The screen wants her to move her upper left arm. She does.
Then her front right foot. Too easy. Lower left arm, lower right
arm, back right foot, upper left arm, front right foot, back left
foot, back right foot again. Just like pressing colored buttons.
Nothing to it. The more actions she performs the easier it gets,
she's rolling along, skimming the tops of stars, she wants to go
faster and the system obliges until the screen's a green blur, and
Misery's eyes begin to ache—

Everything stops. The seraph model vanishes from the screen,
replaced by a field of sunny yellow, textless and contextless.
Misery blinks, stumbling over mental inertia. What just happened? Her heart races and the blood hurts in her veins. Has
she crossed the line into madness?

Major Reyes huffs. "Well, maybe there is something to that prophecy after all."

Misery pulls the helmet from her head. When did her temples get so feverish? "What does that mean?"

The major only makes a dismissive sound before walking off. Whatever. Misery lets anxiety and tension exit from her lungs. For a moment she'd like the voidsickness to take over. She'd flown through the vast chasms of the cosmos as the most powerful entity in the universe, unstoppable and answerable to no one. Now she understands how Mother felt in the deepest grips of her delusions, why she was so hard to reason with. A dangerous feeling. Toxic. Intoxicating.

So. She has to tip into voidmadness every time she interfaces with a seraph. No wonder mech pilots are rumored to have the highest incidences of late-stage voidsickness. It's a job more dangerous than stonehunting, than beacon laying. She sees that now.

But look. She's done it. She's passed the test. She gets to live this lie for another day longer. That's good, right? That's good. It's what she wants.

It's what she wants.

Only a scatter of trainees have attained the yellow screen. Misery is one. Spider is another. Next to her the man leans back in his seat, flush with smugness. "Looks like someone's having problems."

In the seat farthest away from theirs, the Lady Alodia Lightning is not doing well. Her screen flares more red than green even as the other pilots in other servings find their multitude of feet. Spider snorts as he watches her struggle. "Not every saint can be a pilot," he says. " She thinks she's special because she's highborn? She's about to find out."

Misery had expected joy, or a wine-sweet burst of schadenfreude at least. The princess failing where she, Misery, had succeeded! Something to hold over her arrogant, pretty head for the rest of time. Yet she cringes every time the Lady Alodia Lightning's screen lights up red, over and over. How embarrassing. Misery can't imagine recovering from such public humiliation.

"We can't help her," Ruin says. "If she is to come with you on this journey, she needs to prove herself."

Of course. Convenient that Ruin can't perform miracles on someone who exists independently of Misery's skullmeat. It's almost as if zie's not real.

And yet a miracle happens, if one can call it that. Bit by bit the princess rallies. As Misery and Spider watch, the Lady Alodia Lightning figures out the separations over the course of several runs. Gets the hang of moving body parts she doesn't have. The red screens come less frequently, then not at all. Eventually, the princess attains the yellow screen, the last of them to reach that heavenly state, but against all odds she does it. Saved from ultimate humiliation. "Well. The universe will never cease to surprise," Spider drawls.

So they've all made it. The major tuts, disappointed that xe doesn't get to make a scene. Doesn't get to prove the General's wild gamble wrong. "Fine. Enough time wasted here. Moving on."

─┼─

The pilots clutch their helmets with a tightness that's almost tender as they are shepherded into yet another room. The Lady Alodia Lightning stays deliberately ahead of the pack, not looking at or talking to anyone. Misery badly wants to know what's marching through the princess's mind, is she embarrassed, does she hate herself? She speeds up so they're side by side and casually puts fingers on her arm.

Alodia Lightning reacts with the speed and ferocity of a wounded animal. For half a second she looks almost vulnerable, eyes dark with fear and apprehension. Then anger snaps across her features. "What is wrong with you?"

"Never been tapped on the arm before?"

"I don't appreciate being ambushed."

"Wasn't an ambush. Just wanted to see how you were doing."

Her eyes narrow. "So you think you can shower me with pity now that you've proven you're better than me?"

Ah, that bitterness. Misery could bottle it and drink it. "There's no pity. I just wanted to make sure you're doing all right. I don't think I'm better than you. I just have the Demiurge's blessing, don't I?"

The remark doesn't go down well. The princess's expression sours and she surges away from Misery, boots striking the floor with more force than needed. Misery watches her go and feels inexplicably pleased, like the universe has proven her right about something.

Now that they've passed calibration and learned to work the system, it's time to meet the training units: pilot cockpits salvaged from broken seraphim, just functional enough to train fresh fodder to face the teeth of war. The room they're brought to is a dark prayer filled with the hum of holystone. Boulders of holy labradorite punctuate a wide, cool chamber underlit by holy opal.

Holy labradorite. Finally she's face to face with the fabled material, never found raw, only extant in the seraphim the Larex Forge had gifted to humanity. Beneath the glistening brown skin, stripes of iridescence live in its depths, greens and yellows and purples and blues, flashing by like a lover's wink as Misery traverses a wide arc of changing angles. She cannot help herself. One palm makes contact with the shimmering, hypnotic surfaces. For all its calm and polish, holy labradorite has the warmth of an object cradled close to the body. Heat transmitted from some unknown source. Standing overwhelmed with her hand glued to one of the pilot capsules, Misery imagines the beating heart of the universe tunneling up her nerves and into her body. Her pulse quickens as her bone marrow fills with ice and fire. Holy labradorite is unlike anything's she met. There's ineffable power here, raw and waiting to be flexed. Holiest of the holy. Shit, standing in this place with this thread of unworldliness running through her, Misery can see the shape of *possibility,* her heart soaring and her head filled with song. It's a good feeling. Cleansing, like iodine.

"Daydreaming?"

Major Reyes towers disapprovingly over her. Misery retracts her licentious hand. "I've never seen holy labo before. Not where I came from, in the boonies." She clasps her palms together, the picture of saintly chastity. "It feels different, that's all. As if it draws me closer to the Larex Forge."

The major huffs. Disdain shines on xer face: xe doesn't believe in this Messiah, this dangerous criminal falsely wearing the mantle of holiness. Xe's seen xer share of hucksters and shameless liars, but this nixen takes the nugget. No matter. Sooner or later, shit floats to the surface. This fraud might have fooled the station computers for a spell, but they cannot fool the Demiurge. They cannot fool the holystone.

The major doesn't know how close xe is to the truth—and yet how far. Ironic that Misery's coming up on the easiest part of the deception for her. She' s eager to prove the major wrong. As the nixen walks away she smiles at xer back. She loves a challenge. Belligerence rolls through her, fed by the song of stone. This kind of energy got her into fights with grown-ass mercenaries at fourteen, fights she sometimes won.

Ruin leaps atop the holy labo boulder. "Get in the hot seat, Misery Nomaki."

Misery mounts the helmet and heaves into the pilot module. Inside, holystone flows in awkward shapes, fluted and jutting, too narrow to accommodate the flat soles of her feet. On tiptoes, she maneuvers into the seat, which curves like a bucket and resists the width of her hips. "How does anyone even fly these fucking things?"

"In a live unit," Ruin says, "the stone changes to suit you. It'll be quite something when you experience it for the first time."

The delusion can't possibly know that. Can zie?

Major Reyes stalks the front of the chamber. "These are full immersion units. Hook the helmet in and let it take over."

She does. The system offers her a single glowing button to tap with her mind. Time to see what's next. "Let's fucking go."

Darkness. Nothingness. A void with no beginning and no end. Not the blackness of sleep and closed eyes, but an all-consuming emptiness, free of the ghosts and sparks co-created by flesh and humor and optic nerve.

Something glistens in the middle of that nothing, and as Misery turns her attention that way, the speck expands at a terrifying pace. Is she in freefall? Is it charging at her? She can't tell, and her mind reacts with animal terror. But she has no body to sustain it, no adrenal glands to pump out the panic juice. She recognizes that she's scared, but she feels absolutely nothing. Terror without sensation.

Misery stands, floats, persists, in the presence of a seraph. Fully formed, gleaming holy labradorite cuts sharp lines that are also inexplicably organic. Space and time have no meaning, and this seraph is enormous, bigger than reefs and spaceports, a swollen behemoth that could crush cities with a flick of the arm. But it's also tiny, a child's toy, small enough to fit a hand, easy enough to knock over. Misery is disappointed to feel nothing, separated as she is from her body. Emotions are a disease of the flesh.

"This is mere simulation," Ruin says. The delusion crosses her field of vision, trailing a phantom with eight limbs, similar to the seraph but different in phenotype. It's Ruin's true form, which echoes the shape of the seraph as though they are related. After all, it's said that seraphim are made in the image of the Demiurge's most holy creations, messengers and diviners of fate closest to Hir ineffable presence. Ruin is simply maintaining consistency. The nullvoid clearly has a stronger hold on her in this nothing neverwhere.

The system guides her. First she must learn the movesets of the seraph. There are twenty-four, a combination of punches and kicks, slashes and parries. Fighting moves. Later, after she's mastered that, she'll have to pick up combos and counter-combos, the basics of attacking and blocking. At some point she'll spar with the others. And in some distant future she'll be ready to see real combat. But today, her job is mastering the basics.

The system shows her a sequence of moves it wants her to execute, superimposed in the artificial void of the training space. On the other side of the seraph there's a ranking screen with all their names on it. There's no tutorial, no guide, and no explanation. They expect her to figure it out herself. Just flail in her mind until she lucks into the right burst of the synapses that triggers the desired action. This is a standard uppercut. This is a standard uppercut on the *other* side. This is a slashing attack with the front pair of lower limbs. This is a stabbing thrust with the back pair. Here's a dual-wielding spin attack. All these moves and a dozen more, which the void demands she memorize fast enough to follow its menu of unreasonable requests.

But they underestimate her. Misery is good at retaining this sort of gritty, mechanical information at an absurd pace, which makes her terrible to play against at parlor games. She's a void-taken marionette, twirling through an inelegant, jerky mockery of life. But she's doing the thing. She's doing it perfectly. Before long she's got every action internalized so well it just happens. She doesn't even have to think. Misery flies through the void, her will turned into a cascade of action, one thought bursting forth before another ends. Soon the system just has to begin its whisper of what it wants and she's already pulling it off. No words necessary. Understanding is pure as blood in this realm, transcending the limitations of mortal language. What is required of her, she simply knows. The way she knows what is up and what is down in the cosmic plane where her body exists.

Time has no meaning in this fugue state. If hours or weeks are passing in the world of flesh, Misery has no idea. The focus she pours into her task erases the existence of an outside. She needs no food, no water, no air: nothing except the thrill of delight that comes with perfectly executing a sequence.

Then, without warning, everything vanishes. Misery's headlong charge crashes to a halt. The seraph, gone. The instructions, silent. Only black void remains. Flung into discombobulation by her own inertia, Misery loses her grip on herself. Without a body, without an identity, who is she? What is she?

"You are Misery Nomaki. Black Hole Messiah, Savior of the Faithful, Nullvoidsbane. Chosen of the Larex Forge to destroy the scourge of the Heretics. Assigned to Dish Ono, Serving Red-2, the banquet of Angelsteeth. Don't you remember?"

Fuck. Ruin's voice. She would have leapt out of her skin if she had any in this world of nothingness. The angel—the delusion—has been here all along, she's forgotten, and it unnerves as though she's being watched. She's not being watched. Ruin is part of her mind, of course zie would be in here with the rest of her. Misery recovers pieces of her persona, bit by bit. Messiah. Fuckup. Unbeliever and disloyal child. Liar, liar, ass on fire. That's who she is, that's what she's doing. She's fooled everyone into thinking that her madness is holy.

How did she get here?

How does she get out of here?

Her panic is shattered by a burst of yellow light, a grid with orderly text. Words. Language. She wrestles her consciousness into understanding how to read. How to process information.

A ranking screen hangs in the void, her name on top. She scans it for familiarity. Teá Spider? Oh. A list of their performances. That can't be right. Is that right? She's the first listed—does that mean she did the best? Misery reads the lists again, carefully this time. Slowly her brain comes back online. She's tied with Ghost for first place. A perfect score. Perfect. The voidmad nixen and the abomination, better at this holy shit than all the normal humans. Spider, for all his talk and experience, is a mere midlist result. Pathetic.

Where's the princess? Misery hasn't seen Her Royal Highness's name. She miss something? Then she looks down. All the way down. There it is, right at the bottom: Lee Alodia Lightning Chrysocolla. She failed the exercise entirely. Really not cut out for this, is she, despite her sainthood? It's true: pilots have to be saints, but not all saints can be pilots. How embarrassing, to be found wanting while everybody watches.

The results aren't what Misery expected. But before she can process this, the helmets de-plug and Misery tumbles back into the flesh world. Aches spring from joints overly confined in the crags of holy labo. She climbs out of the pilot module to find Spider stretching fluidly, working out the kinks in his back.

Her servingmate catches sight of her. "So. They weren't kidding about you."

Misery smiles, fuzzy and generous. The floor is uneven and alien under leaden feet. After hours away from her body and conscious mind, reentry into human existence feels like an avalanche. "What about?"

Spider laughs and strikes her over the shoulder. "No one gets into a module for the first time and returns results like that. Even that one"—a tilt of the head toward Ghost's luminous form—"made for order, couldn't touch you. I'll believe it, cap. I didn't before, but I do now. You're blessed."

Misery proceeds as cautiously as she can. "Is that so."

"You don't sound too thrilled about it."

"I'm wiped."

A gentle hand on her upper back. "Come on. We're done for the day. Food, salves, drinks. Doctor's orders. Or would be, if I were a doctor."

Major Reyes watches them file out in sterling, uncontaminated silence. Misery attempts to decode xer icy expression, but its blank resolve resists interpretation. She imagines the major's gaze trailing her like a probe, following her trajectory out of the room.

14

In Angelsteeth tradition, the first dinner after the first day of pilot training is held in the officers' hall, a sacred place that keeps the brass away from the mud and water of the rank and file. An airy dome open to the stars, with a dining floor dipped in buttery light and a plush upper tier sectioned into private booths. The spread prepared for them occupies a long, wide table, a smorgasbord of delicately cultured meats and dirt-grown greens. Each heaping, glistening plate is an illusion, a hologram: as Misery stalks the perimeter of the table she taps the glowing ring beside the dishes she likes the look of. At the end she gets a tray, dispensed from the mouth of a patient render bot, crammed with the slop she's picked. Not much fancier than the regular mess. It's all in the ceremony.

Ono Red-2 has split. Only Misery and Spider are at this lavish party, and the latter is busy with a handsome pilot from Xito Blue-4 (Wolf Siren, they/them), who appears to be enjoying the attention and flattery, at least. Tank and Ghost have gone to eat in the usual place, and who knows where the princess has vanished to. Misery lingers unaccompanied at a cocktail table, picking through food she doesn't quite taste, watching everyone and absorbing nothing. Her mind buzzes, made of static, exhausted from overclocking. A high pitch plays in her ears.

Exhaustion scares her more than other forms of weakness. It makes her feel like a hollow puppet, all clay and brittleness, bait for the nullvoid. And sleep, the only real balm for this exhaustion, is just as dangerous as wakefulness. Misery craves sleep. Misery fears sleep.

It's been a sucking void of a day.

Ruin occupies the other half of the table, and through the force of the void stops others from approaching them. Maybe. Hir smile glitters like shattered glass. "Your mind has been rewritten today," zie says. "It takes time get used to a new normal. But you will. You always do."

Misery swallows a cold mouthful of liquid, citrusy and spiced with carbonic acid. There's a fountain of cremoline, tempting and milky, and the promise of dullness beckons sweetly. But she knows better than to destroy what's left of her internal defenses.

She should go to bed early, but the restlessness won't let her. After being so much out of her flesh, she wants to stay connected to it. She wants to stay close to other bodies. The other pilots gather in loose, gossipy clumps, and from the frequency of furtive glances in her direction she can tell that she's the topic of conversation. Word will get around about her extraordinary performance today. Her feelings on this remain in flux. Being a public figure is new, still, and the gulch of notoriety is patch-worked with opportunity and pitfall. Social clout is a multi-edged blade, which she must wield very carefully. For now, it looks like the General's gamble is paying off from the outside, so her position is safe. It gives her time to gather her strength, to strategize.

Let the servings gossip. Let their imaginations overheat. Let the rumors tenderize the ground for the casting of false belief.

A hand closes around her elbow, unexpected and warm. She stifles the instinct to punch. In her tiredness and introspection, she's failed to notice someone sneaking up on her from behind. It's only her captain, who disappeared somewhere right after training ended, and has just manifested in the dining area. Sunyata Diamond says, "Misery. I hope I didn't startle you."

"Not at all," she lies. "Is something the matter?"

"No, no. I just wanted to speak with you. I—pardon my foolishness. I know this will sound strange, but I must thank you."

"What for?"

Misery asks this already knowing the answer. She can see it in her captain's face. Quiet faith builds in Sunyata Diamond's heart, citadels and minarets dashed by the cruelties of war slowly reassembling block by block. Diamond squeezes her elbow. "I have spent so many nights praying for a sign. I lost my entire crew to Heretics years ago, and since then it's been hard to believe in a just world. Hard to believe in a Demiurge that looked out for us. I thought Zie had turned from me, that Hir ears were closed to my pleas. I almost lost faith. But now, here you are. I was a fool to underestimate Hir Grace."

"You are only human," Misery says, thick and gentle as a cloud. Sermonizing comes so easy to her, and now seems the right time for it. But not the brimstone and fire she summoned back in the Capital. Her captain needs comfort, and she can offer it. "Doubt is the natural state of the human condition. It's how we survive."

"Indeed," Diamond says. "Yet—forgive me all the same. I should not have doubted."

"You have nothing to apologize for." *My child.* Misery zips her lips in time. She hated when Crem said that.

Diamond exits the scene and tension exits Misery through her airways. She's in this for the long run. She needs to keep her stamina up. Can't be caught napping.

Another disturbance. A wave front of mutterings and furtive glances accompanies the passage of a singular figure through the dining hall. Misery recognizes that gait at once, that crown of shining hair. So the General has also given Duke Argan the largesse to come and go as he pleases. The Duke of Apis has on a modest jumpsuit the color of spun grass, slightly reflective and detailed in rich brown, but somber as prison garb by his standards. He makes a beeline for her, and she thinks: void fuck, more trouble my way. But the Duke's expression, although serious, seems more pensive than anxious. He stands next to her, and says, without preamble: "I have been thinking." Then he hesitates, and Misery lets him take his time, because she's interested to know where this conversation will head without interference.

"I have been thinking," he repeats, after several slow breaths. "About what you said before the audience of the Emperor. It has haunted me every day since."

"Indeed? What about it spoke to you?"

"When you chastised the highborn of the Capital for their excesses and carelessness, I too felt the sting of reproach. I know that I . . . I have led a life that is unworthy of salvation. Too often I lost myself in the pursuit of joy. Too many times I neglected my duties to seek comfort. I have claimed a holy mantle, yet I did not lead a holy life. I'm deeply ashamed."

Misery smiles, leaning into generosity. His burden is not hers to bear, and yet here he is, laying it all out for her. If only her problems were as simple as guilt over a lifetime of overindulgence. Still, if he's going to look to her for guidance, if he wants her to tuck him under her wing, who is she to refuse? "Your shame is unnecessary. It's counterproductive. In fact, your repentance means more than your mistakes from the past. You didn't know any better then. But now you do. Your growth is more precious to the Larex Forge than anything else."

There's a power in sermonizing, a poetry that's smoothened a groove in her mind since childhood. Misery hates it here. Misery is comfortable here. She glides along the glossy, frictionless surfaces of devotion and obedience, in the zone, just vibing, leading where she wants her flock to follow.

"Thank you," says the Duke, the second time in the night she's been thanked for doing fuck-all. "I will remember, Misery. I've spent a lifetime acting like a child. It's time to do better."

She smiles, beatific. Her brother might have squeezed a shoulder in kind support at this point, but Misery doesn't want to push it. "I'm sure you will. Tell me, what have you been up to on the station?"

He laughs, the tension of the moment broken. "Not much. I've been given room and board by grace of the General. I think he doesn't know what to do with me either. But we'll figure something out."

"Whatever it is, I'm sure it'll be good. The General is very wise." Misery wonders how well the duchy is doing in the Duke's absence, but she's not curious enough to ask. Things work themselves out, they always do. She can't imagine life on Rootsdown has gotten much better or worse in the weeks since she left.

Without warning, the Duke grabs her hand, and Misery manages to tamp down her reflexes enough to not flinch, draw back, punch him in the face. He says: "I am honored to be here, Misery. For the Larex Forge to have chosen me, among everyone alive today, to play a role in the coming victory—I am blessed. No other word for it, Misery. Blessed."

Well, if you put it like that. "I hope I haven't caused you too many problems, at least."

His joy makes him look like Mother when she was in deepest in the euphoria of her delusions. "None that were not necessary, my dear. None that I regret."

Dinner puts a restlessness in her that will not be calmed by any means. Misery wanders the hallways of Angelsteeth, balancing on feet still yearning for the treacle of Rootsdown's gravity. Everything is alien, and new, and Misery knows she traverses the rim of an endless void; a single misstep will tip her into madness and death, a place where she will no longer be Misery and also not care that she is no longer Misery.

Round and round her mind goes.

"Your life would be happier if you doubted less and accepted more," Ruin says. The delusion floats next to her, golden with satisfaction. Misery briefly wishes the angel were real enough to land a punch on. Instead she just breathes until the impulse passes, and takes another too-light step forward. One foot in front of another.

She's loath to admit how much she fears sleep. Mother's worst dreams came when the nullvoid nipped at her soft tissue like winter frost, and today that same tenderness inflames Misery's mind. Her forced move to Angelsteeth has already manifested one sparkling new delusion, factory-fresh, and she's not thrilled by the prospect of more, birthed from the stress of dislocation and expectation. Fuck sleep. She wishes she could murder sleep.

Unfettered by the threat of nightmares, the rest of Ono Red-2 has gone simply and easily to bed. Tank and Ghost had a good time skipping the pilots' party and retired after exhausting the potential of inane discussion in Ono Red-2's common space, something about crafting musical instruments from industrial scrap. Spider convinced his new pilot friend to join him for the night, and they vanished behind the red-lit rim of a door lock after a brief flash across the length of the common room. And Diamond was already in her private quarters when Misery got back, probably praying or sleeping or deep in contemplation. Her captain has a lot to work through.

The Lady Alodia Lightning, on the other hand, is MIA. Her quarters unoccupied and her presence unaccounted for since they were dismissed from training. As a saint, she can survive off starlight, and can skip eating with the proles if she so chooses. No idea where she went. Misery can pretend she isn't curious. Misery can pretend she doesn't care. But that would be a lie. After lying in bed for an hour getting progressively more itchy and irritable, she sat up with a new goal in mind: find the princess.

She must be somewhere on the station. Maybe high up? Talking to the General, perhaps? Trying to get out of pilot duty, to save herself further humiliation. It's the best guess Misery has. She'll have the best chances of finding her in the highest levels, anyway—something tells her the princess likes spending her time in restricted areas where no one else is allowed. Misery trusts her gut. How does she get there? She thinks of the fight gym she saw on the way to her first meeting with Ono Red-2. A good, accessible starting point. She'll work her way up. Maybe bribe some guards into spilling more information. Can't hurt to try. Misery pings the system now parked in the deep parts of her mind and asks directions.

The friendly system arrow takes her down miles of pale blue carpet, through looping trains of same-ish corridor slotted with the bright, angular features of spacebound living. A lounge pulsing with the shapes of bodies and orange quadrangles of light. Doors of sealed blast steel. Elevator ride. More elevator ride. Awkward silence as she pretends not to notice the other uniformed grunts staring her down, trying to pick apart her existence.

Finally, after the passing of a cosmic age, she reaches her destination. Misery strides between the familiar silhouette of the fighting cages, circular cages of copper strips lined with holy tigereye, and holy tigereye on the base. Misery knows these cages from Rootsdown. Typhoon, one of her many bosses, had one in eir headquarters, cobbled together from stolen blueprints and salvaged mech scrap. Misery had fought a few bouts in it. Maybe a lot. To see a row of them here, deep in the duchy of Canis, sends a fist of homesickness through her chest.

At this hour the gym is deserted except for a single figure sparring with shadow opponents—virtual constructs, blows very real. Gravity on. Misery blinks: through coincidence, or something else, she's found her true target. The Lady Lee Alodia Lightning.

The princess has stripped to a training suit, top and pants, that exposes a broad ribbon of waist. Beneath the finery and/or baggy fatigues, the Lady Alodia Lightning has the physique of a prizefighter, all corded muscle and undiluted anger. The skin of her midsection is a biome of flourishing tatts, its purposeful artistry disrupted by a thick pink scar. The kind of scar you get from a bad knife fight, the kind of scar that forms when you don't get proper doctoring, the kind of scar that Misery is intimately familiar with. She is instantly, irreversibly captivated. Alodia Lightning fights with the viciousness Misery already knows well. Just straight-up brawling, quick and efficient and dirty. Knees and elbows and palms to the nosebridge. Fingers in the eyes. The princess dispatches one shadow in under a minute and pauses to clean sweat from her brow, torso heaving with breath. Then—a small gesture, a half-muttered word— and she summons another four rivals. Misery watches her take them down with a thrill of pleasure: lapel-grab, slamming one into a second, taking out the kneecaps of a third. This princess would have cleaned the floor with half the deadmarbles clatter- ing around Rootsdown. Where did she learn to fight like that? Surely not in the stuffy, tiptoe-through corridors of the Capital.

Alodia Lightning turns and discovers her rapt audience. For a moment she freezes, vulnerable for a second before a curtain of rage falls. "What are you doing here?"

Misery doesn't answer. Instead she steps up to the copper cage and hauls its door open. Silky smooth and weighty, no screech of rust. The princess hisses and arches at the threat. "Fight me," Misery says. "I can give you a better workout than those phantoms."

"Who do you think you are?"

Misery raises a brow. "Afraid of facing someone who's been in a real brawl or two?"

Wrong thing to say. Alodia Lightning's fury intensifies. "You know nothing about me. Leave me the fuck alone." She sidesteps so quickly Misery misses the cue to block her, and she's past and out of the door, unhooking a jacket from the jamb hook and disappearing the evidence of an interesting past life under the drab olive. Misery watches her go in the half-open cage, head tilted, belly full of conflicted feelings. She wants to know more. She wants to know everything.

-¦-

Eventually Misery returns to her quarters, returns to the in- evitability of sleep. She cannot run forever. She is a biological organism, after all, and biological organisms have incontestable needs. Unconsciousness drags her down faster than she expects. One moment she's on the block of memory foam and the next she's wrapped in darkness, the warm velvet of a room, walking toward a piercing light. The transition happened before she was aware of it.

She passes through the meniscus of light and emerges on the other side. It's a doorway she's walked through, and a balcony welcomes her into the radiance of space. Two galaxies collide overhead, a godly explosion of light and color, gas and dust and stars dying. Stars being born. The light show dwarfs the balcony, and if Misery walks off the unprotected edge she will fall forever into the conflagration. The balcony itself is dead stone, pure matter, shaped in ragged angles as though mauled off the skin of a planet. The floor: raw slate, broken and volcanic, interrupted by spikes of unknown crystal. Cracks radiate from under Misery's feet, as though she is the center of a meteor crash, and capillaries of energy thread red and glowing through the glossy stone, which remains cool under her soles. There's a geometry to the layout that speaks of human crafting, yet the whole setup feels undeniably wild.

A figure she recognizes rests at the edge of the balcony, comfortable between the clumps of glacial crystal: Jericho, tall and thin, draped in white cotton splashed with ovals of cyan, magenta, yellow. Hands folded behind him, gazing out at the ineffable wonder of creation. Misery craters with emotion, silently: relief with embarrassment stacked on top at the appearance of a repeat delusion. Having a new one pop up every night would destroy her mentally. Tonight she gets to keep her sanity, whatever's left of it.

Jericho turns, and glances. The soft look on his face is almost a smile. He's pleased to see her, more than Ruin ever was, and she shouldn't be picking favorites among her delusions but Jericho is definitely her favorite delusion. As she walks toward him, the cracks in the balcony follow her feet, as though she is their center of gravity. She breathes. There's the smell of ozone, haunting and familiar. "It's a good view," she says of the intergalactic apocalypse overhead.

"It's an illusion. A projection of a cluster billions of light-years away, with some color added for flavor. A beautiful illusion, though."

How droll, a delusion in a dream talking about things not being real. Misery looks up at the picture of a hundred thousand suns in a death ballet and feels exactly as small as she should. "I like it."

"I'm glad." His expression softens further. "You seem different today. Tired, somehow. Touched by something else."

Misery leans against a crystal cluster, propping her arms up like it's a railing. "Today I learned to pilot a seraph."

"Indeed? How did it go?"

"Very well. Shockingly well. Maddeningly well. Turns out that voidsickness makes you really good at controlling seraphim. Who knew?"

Jericho scratches his chin. "An interesting prospect," he says. "Of course, given the deep connection between holystone and the nullvoid, it makes sense. Humans are very poor pilots of seraphim, physiologically. You seem to have a natural advantage."

"An unnatural advantage," she counters, wagging a finger.

He laughs, and Misery studies the way the skin bunches up around his eyes. It's such a particular feature, delicate and transient. She's surprised her delusion comes with so much detail. The scene sits uneasily in Misery's reckoning: there's a grit to it that seems real, yet it's full of surreal leaps that only exist in dreams. It's a dream, of course. But it wants to trick her into thinking it's not. Half of her wants to leave, head for the green-rimmed exit called waking up. The less advantage she gives to her voidmadness, the better. The other half is fascinated by this particular delusion. In this weird theater of dreams he has a presence that sits on her tongue like melonwater, bitter but in a good way. Jericho fits so perfectly one of the rom-sim archetypes, the soft-spoken intellectual who stays aloof and polite until the end, the one character you can get the best ending with and yet not know how zie really feels about you. She understands that the shape of her delusions betrays something about her, the way Mother's delusions betrayed her wish for her children to be bigger and better than she was. The way her conjuration of Ruin betrays her desire for Mother's prophecies to be true. Her desire to be something other than a failure, an abomination. So what does Jericho represent? Her desire to be loved? To be worthy of gentle want and care?

"Is something wrong?"

She's been quiet for too long. "Give me a break. My brain got turned inside out today. I don't want to think anymore. Let's just fuck."

"Are you sure? I thought maybe you wanted to air your thoughts for a bit."

"Shut up." She seizes him, collar-first, and pulls his lips onto hers. She always plays the aggressive lover in the sims and it works great. Jericho concedes, and she pushes his body to the floor, the wild cracked-slate floor that looks like it's half-broken, looks like it's been through the end of the world. She weighs him down with her hips. "Let's fuck."

"There's a bed back there," he says, gesturing to the doorway she left.

"No." She doubles down, forcing all her weight into her lower body. "Let's fuck here."

She craves it, this unbinding of the flesh under the bleeding stars, her back open to the lashings of the universe. And Jericho assents, letting her take him in while galaxies writhe and flare overhead. Letting himself be used as a distraction, a handy tool, an anchor for the body and mind while the world fractures around Misery. Under the auspices of the Demiurge's Creation she stops worrying about what she wants—Power? Influence? Getting the girl?—and what her next steps should be. She stops trying to piece together an uncertain future as pilot, as Messiah, as hope of the foolish Faithful. Here she is just trashbag moon-rat Misery Nomaki, liar, thief, and murderer, getting her rocks off in a delusion of her own making. She's alive. That's what matters. That's all that matters.

INTERLUDE 5

Thus do two weeks pass on Angelsteeth. Misery Nomaki, shoved headfirst into military life, is forced to adapt. No longer in control of when they sleep, when they eat, or what they are allowed to do. Ono Red-2 is pushed unceremoniously into the flow of Angelsteeth's routines. This is how each day plays out: waking at oh six hundred to shower before breakfast, then a full morning's worth of seraph practice. Lunch, two hours of physical conditioning, then break for curriculum time. They're free to choose the modules they take; Tank does courses on practical machining, Spider does additional combat classes, the Lady Alodia Lightning ignores everything to sleep it off. Misery Nomaki chose classes on history and military tactics, jumping from topic to topic at will. They wanted to learn everything about the new world presenting itself to them.

The regimented structure of Angelsteeth deformed uneasily to accept Ono Red-2's existence. Other servings had their practice time cut to let Ono Red-2 have daily sessions with the seraph simulators. It did not go unremarked upon; whispers filled the halls and corridors of the station. Part resentment, but mostly curiosity. After the dramatic repel of the Heretics, they burned for more miracles. They dealt with a lot in the name of the Faithful; it was only fair that the Larex Forge rewarded them. But the dismal results turned in by Ono Red-2 were disappointing. In the training runs they were regularly trounced by the other servings. Ghost often de-synced with their efforts, Spider often lost patience and surged forward on his own, and the princess was absolutely hopeless. In fact, it was Misery Nomaki, the one pilot not a saint, who was most proficient among them. The servings that faced them and won wondered if they had wild luck on their side, or was the outcome some part of the Demiurge's will? Hir chosen learning the ropes of combat, same as everyone else.

Misery Nomaki studied their new comrades with the same curiosity as one does a new set of tools, keeping track of their natures and proclivities. Tank's enthusiasm; Spider's rough humor; Ghost's strangeness; the charisma of Sunyata Diamond, their captain. The cold distance of the Lady Lee Alodia Lightning. They played out their role as Messiah, smoothing over squabbles and boosting the spirits of their new comrades. At night they slept, plagued by strange dreams that followed repeating paths. There was the dream they first had on the Capital, that of the sad white saint combing her long hair, speaking to the shade of a long-lost lover. A dream they had over and over. And then there were the dynamic dreams populated by the strange, lean creature they recognized as a second delusion. The Messiah deeply preferred the latter: it was one place they considered safe, where they could be raw and confessional with themself. After all, they were merely talking to another delusion, were they not?

Humans are remarkable in their ability to function under strange circumstances. Even when their way of life is upended, even when their truths and realities are turned inside out, they find ways of continuing with the business of existence. It is a peculiarity, I think, of being beholden to a physical incarnation that requires such constant maintenance. One must continue to breathe, to sleep, and to seek sustenance in order to survive. And I think you and I can both agree that Misery Nomaki is very good at survival.

By all means the General is a practical nixen, but patience is not one of their strengths. If it can be done, it must be done as quickly and efficiently as possible. Two weeks after the induction of Ono Red-2, a mere fortnight in the training modules to learn the basics of the system and how not to blow up the precious seraphim, the General decided that Ono Red-2 was ready for their first baby jaunt in the real mech units. They wanted to see the potential of the Messiah for themself. Let the Larex Forge sort it out.

Let us, too, accelerate our storytelling. We don't want the minutiae of every moment of the Messiah's life. How they brushed their teeth and put their hair up before bed, and so on. We want the highlight reel. And so, we come to the juncture before the enlightenment of Misery Nomaki, before the advent of the miracles that live on in the chattering halls of history. Ahead lie the glittering and terrible fields, where there is apotheosis. Where there is destruction.

15

Misery wakes. It's 0430, the system reminds her, even behind closed lids. The blinking numbers smugly vanish from her vision as she lurches upright and shakes off the loose memories of dreams to emerge in the present, in the darkened and cramped confines of her quarters, which have shed the weight of unfamiliarity over the weeks. She runs hands over her face and takes several cooling breaths to steady herself.

Today's the day. It's been two weeks since Ono Red-2 started their journey together, and last evening the General approved them for usage of Angelsteeth's precious seraph units. After training they were pulled into a private room and told the news, away from the other pilots-to-be. Regular servings have to go through three months of learning before being thrown into the gauntlet, a station-wide tournament of rolling virtual matchups where their performance determines their position on the leaderboard. The prize? Top three servings on the leaderboard get called to duty when the Heretics attack. But none of that for Ono Red-2. They get to skip over it all. The General is satisfied with their performance and wants them in the real thing. Never mind that the princess can barely steer the simulation units in a straight line. It's not her the General has interest in. They want to see the Messiah in action.

"Well. Look how far you've come," the major said to Misery last evening, and it wasn't all sarcasm. But the phrase implies progress, implies a direction, implies a starting point of mediocrity from which Misery has journeyed into greatness. But there is no vector to Misery's development. No forward, no backward, no sideways hop. The last two weeks have felt like her mutating in place, trapped while things happen around her. She is not driving herself forward. She is not driving at all. Misery craves directionality. She wants to feel the coordinates change, approaching a distant goal or fleeing a site of disaster. But her life right now feels like neither.

"You have direction," Ruin says. "You are being guided." In the darkness her delusion squats upon her dresser, elbows tacked to knees, wrists dangling, head tilted like a bird's. "You can't ignore all the map markers then complain about being lost."

Misery only smiles. Keeps breathing. Tells herself she's lucky that her delusion hasn't gotten worse, that zie still plays the same tune zie did when zie first appeared. No new eruptions of voidsickness since Jericho, either. By the Grace of the Forge, or some other means, her voidsickness has stabilized. For now.

Time to shower. The one time she has true privacy; even Ruin doesn't disturb her while she's in the stalls. Her mother's amulet hangs heavy around her neck, and Misery gently places it on the counter, reverently drizzling the cord around the unverifiable patterns upon its surface. Stay there. This feels safer than leaving it in the common areas of the bath. She has come to trust her servingmates, but not to that extent.

Over the weeks Ono Red-2 has worked out an unspoken but comfortable morning routine, with an order in which they access the two bath stalls. Misery's sandwiched in the middle, and she runs into Tank as the girl makes her way out, freshly cleaned. Tank, who wakes fresh-eyed at any hour and stays that way till bedtime, pops her fingers in Misery's direction. "It's your day, big shot!"

"It's our day," she corrects, in her gentlest voice.

"You nervous?"

Misery smiles, all saintlike. "I trust in the Forge."

The girl sweeps out, all cheer and promise, and Misery allows her face to fall into its customary scowl.

The frosted door to the second bath cubby softens, and the hand that pushes it aside belongs to Spider. "I see that look," they say.

Misery wrinkles her nose, and they share a knowing chuckle. Tank's boundless positivity dissolves cynicism like water dissolves salt. Others, like their captain and fellow pilots-in-training, chalk Tank's upbeat outlook to her youth. The girl has barely seen life, has never had to struggle, of course she's all sunshine and warm seas. But Tank grew up poor, tucked in a deprived strip of duchy, therefore Misery and Spider understand that her cheer comes not from naïveté but the shape of her personality, which must have been woven from unadulterated gold. Youth is nothing; Misery was a bitter piece of shit long before she hit fourteen. Tank was born with holy opal in her mouth. That's just how she is.

Spider ducks to check his image in the reflection wall, running a palm over his scalp. "Going to be an interesting day."

"You nervous?"

"You'd think, but no. I'm eager to get back in the cockpit. Would never have guessed. But I'm pumped. It's been too long."

"Time to show the doctors they're wrong, huh?"

Spider chuckles with an ease that Misery has worked to draw out of him. "Would be nice. But, you know, dependent on Her Royal Highness not blowing up her unit at some point in the day."

"Come on, she's not that bad."

A snort. "I don't fancy her like you do, so my assessment is automatically more objective."

"Shut up."

Then he's gone and Misery's alone, not even a delusion to harass her. From the sink Misery collects a scoop of water to cool her face with. The reflection wall shows a mirrored image of her pre-shower visage. Cracked lips. Rings around the eyes. Her hair springing outward in every direction, as if trying to escape. She likes to think that her new life isn't as stressful as the old, but her body is saying otherwise. "You look like shit," she tells herself.

By the time she's showered and dressed and out in the common area, some unseen hand has delivered their breakfast in sealed packets, sitting neatly upon the common table. Because their runs are off-record, and because the seraphs of Angelsteeth have their schedules fully booked, the only time Ono Red-2 gets to use them is early, hours before mount time opens to the rest of them. Tank and Spider are sprawled on the foam ring around the table, yukking it up, with Ghost on the side watching with their customary curiosity. Over time Misery has gone from wondering when the white saint ever sleeps, to deciding that they're engineered to not need any. They're always awake whenever Misery looks.

Tank says: "That's why it's always wave dramas for me. You just lose that something-something when you do vods. You need the visuals."

"Pfft." Spider flicks his fingers dismissively. "Some of us had to work fourteen-hour days in a tech suit six days a week. Vods is where it's at. Plus, you know, sometimes people are blind? Sometimes?"

"Fair enough."

Two weeks ago this would have devolved into an argument. Spider spots Misery and opens space between Tank and himself. She slides into position, posture-perfect and casual, and waits to be caught up, which Spider does. "We were betting how badly the princess is going to fare later."

Tank leans forward, bright-eyed and glittering. "I think she's going to make it. I think today we'll be seeing a miracle."

Spider laughs. "I love that backhanded compliment. I'm taking notes."

Misery places her hands on the table. "The miracle is all of us here, together, at this time. We were chosen by an unseen hand and placed upon this path. No matter how it seems on the surface, I believe that the princess is meant to be here."

Spider scoffs. "Well, somebody's got to fill out the bottom of the list, and it's not going to be me."

"I'll put a vote in against the princess," Ghost says. "That will make it even, won't it?"

"Ghost, you don't have to pick a side," Tank says. "I know you have no opinion on this."

"I'd like to have one. I think the Lady Alodia Lightning and I have more in common than not."

"So you're voting against her?"

"I don't think we should vote. So if I even it out, then the votes mean nothing, don't they?"

Diamond shows up, fresh from the showers. Scans the group, notes the glaring absence, and sits among them. "We haven't got much time. Let's eat." Businesslike as ever. A surface of polished stone, hiding an ocean of anxiety underneath. It's the first time since the incident that she's mounting her own soldiers in units. There's no combat here. No risk. But she's still afraid.

Misery lets their captain lead them in prayer. Her invocations are more sincere, and she never seems to tire of it. Sunyata Diamond is disappointed by the Lady Alodia Lightning's no-show. The princess doesn't need to eat, and abuses that fact to skip out of every communal feeding with Ono Red-2, but Diamond had hoped she'd show up for the final meal before their debut. She wanted that solidarity. They have to stand together under the banner of the Forge.

Yet Misery gets the sense, somehow, that the princess's worries extend beyond the cheap psychological hack of team spirit, or at least the facade of team spirit. Like Misery, she struggles with voidbeasts no one else sees. Private battles she refuses to let others witness. Misery doesn't know what the princess fears, or hates, or feels. She's spent two weeks digging but two weeks isn't enough to mine secrets that deeply buried in the core. But the longer she keeps at it, the more she wants to know what lives in the heart of the Lady Alodia Lightning. Forge above, she wants to know.

16

Angelsteeth's most precious resource lives in a massive hangar that glows fat and golden on the station map. Sacred and legendary, it lives in the vernacular of the rank and file as the Butchery. Ono Red-2 walks through the massive steel doors of Bay 3 and emerges on a platform centered against a massive wall. On either side the seraphim hang like corpses, elongated heads fixed to steel hooks meters above, feet dangling over the mesh bottom of the floor, a vertiginous drop away. Fifty feet tall and pure holystone. Despite herself, Misery has to stop for breath.

Seraphim. No longer dreams carried upon the booming voice of evangelical leaders or the bright polish of wave dramas. Seraphim in the flesh, bigger and heavier than Misery imagined. Bodies the size of churchhalls, hands larger than homes, feet that can crush buildings. Brutal, many-limbed forms that promise efficiency: sleek and sharp-edged and aerodynamic. So brilliant they hurt to look at. Weeks in the mock units have tuned Misery to the particular song of holy labradorite, but that was a single, plaintive melody, like a high flute on the wind. In the Butchery the melody punches through her like a siren blast, a sound loud enough to be heard from either end of a planet. The seraphim glitter brilliant gray, and as Misery turns her head they flash glorious stripes in blues and greens and purples and golds. This feeling, it's been so long since it's been wrapped around her throat. As a child Misery used to hike to the dumpgrounds in the middle of the desert, powering through dry heat and burning light to complete her pilgrimage to the graveyard of constructor mechs that built the colony. Decommissioned a hundred years ago and stripped of holystone, the cheap metal was left to rot into the landscape, but in the sterility of Rootsdown's artificial atmosphere they persisted over decades. Misery liked to sit in the foot of one she called Daisy and stare up into the shadows of its shell, and let herself be overwhelmed by the sensation that she was but the tiniest of specks in the universe. Back when she was more sincere about religion it felt like a place where she was in communion with the Forge.

Spider chuckles. "Don't gawk. Wonder is unbecoming of someone so blessed."

Misery laughs. A shot of sarcasm to bring her back to the solid world, the real world. She can't get carried away. She needs control of all her faculties today, because they are going to be taxed like they've never been.

A raft of VIPs has been waiting for their arrival: the General, the captains of the three servings currently assigned to defend Angelsteeth, Major Reyes. And the Duke of Apis, who stands tall but humble among them. The scuttlebutt has it that the Duke has found new purpose in his imprisonment—not imprisonment, making the best of this state of limbo. He stands next to Major Reyes with the casualness that lovers often share. Since coming to Angelsteeth the Duke has forgone the bright colors and flash Misery knew him for, cladding himself in neutrals and monotones. And yet he still knows how to flatter his figure, and carries himself with solid elegance. Asceticism, but make it fashion.

The General looks her in the eye. They've been waiting for this day since Misery's first arrival on the station. They've been very patient through the process of Ono Red-2 finding its feet. Disciplined as only career military folk can be. Today they shall find out if their gamble has paid off.

"So," Major Reyes says, voice dry as bone, "the moment of truth has arrived."

The General grunts. "It's a preliminary run. I am not expecting miracles today."

"But they wouldn't hurt, right?" says Spider.

Diamond shoots him a look that carries withering death. The General, meanwhile, remains unruffled: "All I require today is competence. Nothing more."

Spider mutters. "Well, even that low bar is too much for someone. Maybe she just won't show up."

A disturbance: the massive bay doors are rolling open again. A single rumpled figure stands between their parted lips: the Lady Alodia Lightning. Wrapped in the same fatigues as the rest of the grunts, she looks suddenly human, as if the condition crept up on her without anyone noticing. The top-down lighting of the Butchery carves huge shadows under her eyes and in the hollows of her cheeks. No one says a word as she joins the ranks of Ono Red-2, even though everyone is staring. Did she oversleep? What was she doing? No one knows. Misery glances sideways at her and sees nothing except exhaustion.

A tech comes and assigns tokens to the pilots, holy labradorite with ineffable patterns on the surface. Each one fits in the palm and is encased in hardened gel, with a loop that goes around the neck. "These are the keys that will activate your seraph," Diamond says. "Without them, the units will be useless. Hang on tight to them. You fuck these up, the seraphs will be unusable. For everyone. Permanently."

Misery hefts the stone disc in her palm. She can't help but notice that it's the same size and shape as Mother's amulet. Violet plays under its surface as she rolls it back and forth. Curious. The token taps very lightly against the amulet hidden under her fatigues as she puts it around her neck.

"Let's get started," says General Tsung.

Ono Red-2 splits to their assigned seraphs: Alodia Lightning and Misery to the right, Ghost and Spider to the left, Diamond and Tank to the control center with the rest of them. The princess walks slowly as if through tar, and Misery has no problems keeping up. She observes: jaw clenched, fists held awkwardly, tension running in a column from neck to hip. Misery draws closer, and before Alodia Lightning can step away she says: "Don't worry. You'll do fine. I'm sure of it."

Her tension ratchets up. "I don't need your pity."

"It's not pity I'm offering. You seem really upset."

She turns on Misery so fast they almost collide. "Listen. I'm not like the others. So don't try your chosen-one routine on me. I know you're full of shit. Even if the others believe you."

"I say this as a friend—"

"You're a liar. Everything about you is a lie. Why should I trust you?"

True, but—"I didn't ask for this. It was the prophet of Calister—"

Alodia Lightning reacts as if struck. Grabs Misery by the collar, teeth bared, rage pouring off her. Misery's hands are up, shielding her face; it's instinct. Her heels barely touch the floor. The princess sucks air through her teeth as her nostrils flare. It's fifty-fifty if this will devolve into a fight or not.

Then the tension breaks and she drops Misery. Her expression goes shuttered as she stalks away to her assigned seraph at the far end of the Butchery. Not a word said. Misery tries to control her breathing as the princess walks away, but she blows the air out of her mouth so hard her cheeks pouch. She did not see that outburst of violence coming, and its ferocity has knocked her heart out of place. Her fingers buzz with adrenaline and she closes them around the pilot's token, which feels too much like Mother's amulet.

"Focus," Ruin says. "What happens now will determine the trajectory of your life. It will determine the trajectory of the Faithful."

Ruin is, regrettably, right. Misery has bigger stones to haul than the princess's personal problems. But she can deal with that later. The greatest obstacle is ahead.

Misery closes in on the seraph that will be hers. The nearer she draws, the less it looks like machine and the more it looks like firmament. Like abstract geography that rears over her head, relief and depression in grays and iridescence. The mesh steps that coil around its side look like they could circle a moon. By the time she's climbed up to the mounting platform, stretched across the seraph's central carapace, she's breathing hard. It's not Angelsteeth's watery gravity doing that.

Misery walks to the center of the platform, sharply aware that its mesh floor is the only thing that stands between her and a fifty-foot drop. Heights mean nothing to her, but she's never felt so tiny. She looks up at the surfaces of the seraph. Pure holy-stone. The whole time she's been on the station she's been aware of these lumpen bulks of holy labradorite, a constant background tug. Now it's in her face, its song pounding like seismic surf, or what she imagines surf to be. Misery's soft mortal body stands in juxtaposition against the behemoth she's supposed to take charge of. The sheer power contained within awakens the blood in her heart. She breathes, Saint Agneta's pattern: four in, six hold, seven out. This is holy stuff, reminding her of awe she felt in the churchhall as a child, before the gangrene of cynicism set in.

No. Why the sudden nerves? It's fine. She excelled in all the simulations. Her training has prepared her for this job exactly. She can do this. She can do this.

"You are not prepared," Ruin says. "They had no idea how to prepare you, did not know what they were preparing you for. But that's a good thing. You shall show them what you have come here for."

The delusion will not get to her. Zie will not damage her confidence. She will be fine. Everything will be fine.

"It will be fine. You shall see."

In the center of the seraph's massive, arrow-shaped chest, a circular indentation sits where the ingress to the heart would be. The platform's at the perfect height to access it. Misery squeezes the gel casing around her neck to release the stone token, which fits perfectly. It goes in with an audible click.

Stone folds over stone. Light bleeds from the joints of the

arrow. A low rumble shakes the frame of the platform, and the seraph wakes.

Seized by instinct Misery steps backward as the arrow sublimes like plastic under fire, revealing a pilot capsule exactly like the ones she's practiced in. Familiarity, right? Yet her buzz of anxiety only grows. Steps gleam in the flesh of the seraph, and Misery gingerly climbs their slippery surfaces, trying not to think about falling. Her mother's amulet grows strangely hot against her breastbone.

It's fine. Everything's fine. She's been through worse.

Misery settles into the awkward pilot's cubby like she always does. It's uncomfortable, as usual.

Then the stone starts to move.

Misery spits a startled expletive as the holy labo wakes. It turns liquid and wraps around her calves, her wrists, climbing up her skin like floodwater. She swears again, trying to pull her arms free, but she's stuck. Trapped in stone that's surging up to cocoon her neck and face. Panic surges through her, constricting her chest and throat; she can't even scream for help.

"Don't panic." Ruin's voice in her head. "This is supposed to be happening."

She's not drowning, she's not going to die. Every pilot goes through this. Her mother's amulet is ice against her skin as the stone creeps to her jawline and then over it. She holds her breath as the tide line envelopes her mouth, her nose. Shuts her eyes just before the holystone gets them. The darkness—it's fine—it's just like putting the simulation helmet on, dig? Any moment now she'll see the neon grid of the simulator, telling her what to do and where to go.

Something's wrong.

Misery is machine and the machine is Misery. Zie has no sense of hir body, did zie ever have a body? Who or what is zie? Where are hir limbs, hir wings, hir weapons? Hir visual cortex floods with information. Instead of the simulation's clarity there's a wild cascade, a torrent of data—sensors, pings from hir fellows, feedback from Control—and zie cannot separate them. The data isn't coming in right. It's written backwards on a mirror and zie can't process it. The seraph, Misery, perceives hir surroundings in a wide panorama, front and sides and behind, and the world tilts as articulated arms rise from hangar floor and hoist hir free of hir bonds. Hir fellow seraphim are in line, headed for the slowly opening bay doors.

As the body of the seraph moves, propelled by the machinery in the Butchery, Misery struggles to unite mind and body. Make sense of something. The line of seraphim progresses one unit at a time. But the last one in line is pilotless. This is worse than hir first time in the simulator. Nothing connects. Panic. It's not working. Why isn't it working? There's pain, perhaps, somewhere far off. A mortal thing, pain. But Misery is no longer mortal and—something's gone wrong.

Why can't zie activate the holy labradorite like zie should? Why won't it talk to hir?

The jaws of the hangar door wait for hir. Beyond it lies space, unencumbered by the slim ring of Angelsteeth Base's docks. Just the great unbound, velvet-black and freckled with light. The first seraph in line comes alive, concentric rings on its back bursting blue as the articulated arms retreat. It shoots into the waiting void and its wings unfold, rainbow iridescence sprouting from those rings. It drops out of sight and the next one launches. Misery is propelled to her inevitable doom. The first of her squad—Spider or Ghost?—inscribes enormous loops in the liberty of space, moving with ferocious ease.

Then Alodia Lightning launches in front of her, and it is Misery's turn.

The articulated arms holding hir body detach. The last one gives hir enough momentum to sail through the hangar mouth. Misery floats free; before her the other seraphim dance and weave in the black expanse, overjoyed by freedom. Misery cannot move. Zie hangs in the expectant vacuum, inert, softlocked in the void. Zie does not know where hir limbs are. The holy labradorite of hir body will not heed her commands. Is Control trying to talk to hir? What must they think?

Zie tries to move something, anything, anything would be better than this helplessness— Hir stoneshifting ability has left hir— How— There must be something zie can do— This is holystone— Zie could always connect to holystone—

Something breaks. Deep in the consciousness that is the seraph Misery, something snaps like an appendix bursting. Zie sees the sad organic thing trapped the stone, pathetically fragile. That's her—the human creature Misery. Her chest burns. This stone isn't hers, she realizes. An ugly and sudden epiphany like looking down and seeing your body all meat and all wrong. Not hers, the stone isn't hers, it rejects her as she rejects it, she needs to shuck it off because something in her is calling to something else, to someplace else—

Misery ricochets back into her human body, her soft blood-and-bone body, kicked off the connection entirely. She can't see and there's no air, her lungs scream in her chest and something burns her skin like a laser, she's being crushed on all sides and every joint in her body spasms as her bones twist. This is it, this is death, she's come to the end of her luck and she's paying for it. An avalanche of sparks plays over her vision as the searing pain rears up and swallows her, dragging her into final, blissful unconsciousness.

17

In death, Misery Nomaki dreams.

She's in a cavern so dark she cannot sense her own body. The way the air moves tells Misery of its indescribable size. All of it is holystone, a type she has never encountered and perhaps unknown to all of humanity. She's never been around so much sacred material at once; not even her days on the Capital and Angelsteeth can compare. The presence of the stone feels heavy the way humid air feels heavy.

In the darkness, a light grows. It starts as a pinprick, laser-bright, which swells and swells as Misery watches. First the size of a child, then the width of a room, then greater than the reefs on Rootsdown. By this time it is too much to look at, too hot for thought to process. Still the light expands: now the size of a war-ship, now the size of a jump portal, and Misery is like an atom in its blazing penumbra. Now it dwarfs planets, now it could swallow suns, now it spans all of Creation and still it grows ever brighter, inexorable, inevitable. Misery's heart stills in her chest. Death has come and she is falling into its grasp.

Be not afraid, Misery Nomaki.

She knows this voice. Ruin. Her delusion. The creature that has brought her to where she is now. Zie is here, speaking to her.

She thinks, I am not afraid.

The light is a singular creature, an awestriking thing with no face and a hundred wings. Eight limbs and a nova where a head should be, tied to its shoulders and torso with twisted string. She knows what this is; she's seen this form before. An archangel blazes before her, the highest messenger of the Larex Forge. A being of unimaginable size, made of the fires of Creation. This is Ruin. The first day they met, zie looked like this. But nowhere this intense. Nowhere this beautiful, ineffable, terrible to behold.

Ruin turns hir nuclear gaze toward Misery, and speaks. Every syllable, every vowel every consonant is the sound of a star being born, of galaxies bursting into life.

Long has been our journey together, Misery Nomaki. But you are not far from the destination I was sent to guide you toward. Soon you will see. There is a place you must travel to. Let me show you. Come closer, child.

The archangel develops gravity, and Misery falls toward it. There is no question of resisting. She has no power here. She can only obey her fate.

One of Ruin's jointed arms reaches out. Its six fingers split and flow like latex, the strands forming mycelious nets that shiver and shimmer. They snare Misery in their grasp. The threads pass through her, into her, and become her. Misery is plunged into a stream of screaming and song. A typhoon of sound and image and impression across her consciousness: alien civilizations, branching symmetries, beings made of silicon and silver and gel, ships that resemble fungi. Her thoughts shatter in a million directions. So much to witness. So much to absorb.

Misery. Look at me.

Knowledge comes into Misery, pressed into her like a flame. She has a red-hot awareness of a thing, a *place,* that she has to get to. The sear of this location pin floods every nerve ending and every capillary.

Come to me. I will show you what you were made for.

The light in her dream grows and grows until the angel obliterates everything that Misery is. There is nothing but the Forge. Her mind goes white as the atoms of her body dissipate. Death and rebirth. What is she expected to become?

—⁀—

The first things to return to Misery are touch and feel: her body lying on its back, foam against her neck and spine, cool metal against her arms. Sound from the real world filters in as she emerges from the fog of sleep. Body monitors chirrup, voices converse in tones too low to parse, and somewhere comfortably distant a colossal mechanical heart beats with a low, steady thrum. Misery's fuzzy mind pushes out a thought: I've been here before.

Awareness swamps her in an avalanche-rush. Her life. The station. Her position in the world. Memory sharpens into specifics: The seraphim. The exercise. The helplessness.

The terrifying, unyielding crush.

Misery makes the mistake of opening her eyes too quickly and has to shut them again. Light hurts; the world outside is not a welcoming one. She lets the yellow-pink of her lids normalize before cracking them open. Eases herself into the pain of reawakening.

"Take your time. There's a war, but it can wait."

She knows that voice. Dr. Sower Cabbage. The one who put her implant in. The one with all the stories. Her eyes refuse to focus. Misery struggles to speak through the desert of her mouth and throat and lungs. "Wh—" A wheeze of air.

Water streams into her mouth from an unknown source. Misery swallows. Dr. Cabbage, enormous in Misery's bleary vision, tuts. "Feel better?"

Her voice splutters to life like an electrical engine. "What happened?"

"You died. And the Forge brought you back."

"I died?"

"Don't move. I need to run some scans."

The doctor leaves Misery's field of vision and a series of beeps happen where she can't see. Misery fixates on the ceiling, low and white and inscribed with concentric circles. One of them goes blue, bathing Misery in its glow.

She says: "You can't just say I died and leave it at th—"

"Stop talking. Scan."

"But I died?"

The doctor reappears in her vision, irate. "I'll tell you, if you promise to shut up for the rest of the scan."

"Fine."

Misery stares at the ceiling and counts the beats of her heart. There's a scream embedded in the lining of her throat, in the sacs of her lungs, in the churn of her stomach. She died. She came back to life. She saw unbelievable things, felt indescribable things—was any of that real? Is any of this real? What if she suffocated in the guts of the seraph and this is just one long, drawn-out extinction dream? Stripped of her body, she is nothing more than nullvoid, delusion from end to end.

"There we go." The doctor sounds pleased as the scan completes. The blue lights go off.

"Can I sit up now?"

"You can learn the patience to stay put a bit longer."

Misery seethes, but the doctor keeps talking out of sight. "Remarkable. You're in perfect health. Maybe even better health than you started. Huh."

"You said I died."

"When we cut you out of the seraph you had no pulse and weren't registering. We thought, oh, we've done it. But then you breathed. We didn't have the chance to intervene. Another miracle, huh."

"And I'm fine?"

"More than fine."

Misery lets that information crystallize. She was dead, and now she's alive. The image of the angel in her dream—hallucination?—looms large in her imagination. She picks her next words with great care, yet feels like she's being careless in asking anyway. "What are the chances this is voidsickness?"

"Voidsickness? Is that what you think happened? Well, you're clear. I'd know for sure."

"How? You can't scan for it."

"That's what they want you to think. But you can."

"I don't believe that."

Dr. Sower reappears in her sight, annoyance incarnate. "You don't believe me, the subject matter expert in the room?"

"My brother said—"

"Your brother and his backwater Church doctors don't know everything. All right? If you were voidsick, we would have picked it up the moment you crossed the station boundary."

"Even before?"

"Before what?" Dr. Sower's frown deepens, and suspicion bubbles under the surface of her irritation. Not the outcome Misery wanted, but one she feared. "You mean before any of this happened? No. I would have detected it too."

"So I'm not voidsick?"

"No."

The doctor leaves her. Misery hears, in the background, the beeps of console commands. The low sound of a replicator whirring, packs of matter being shuffled around the guts of some hideously complex machine. She buzzes with an equal amount of fear and possibility. Maybe this is a delusion. An extended dream, a post-death, maybe this is the nullvoid itself and Misery will remain here forever, playing out some extended, overcomplicated hallucination.

Dr. Sower returns with a hypo sting, which she presses against Misery's neck. A burst of coolness and tingling. What is that? Some kind of salve? It's not like she can resist.

A clink, as the doctor turns to deposit something into the recycler. Misery puts her palm over her chest and finds emptiness. "Where's my amulet? My mother's gift to me."

"You mean the necklace? Gimme a sec. Where did I put the damn thing . . . Aha."

She returns with the precious trinket, its cord a messy tangle. Drops it into Misery's waiting palm. Its weight and coolness is a balm. Misery grips it so hard her hand shakes. What would

Mother think, seeing her like this? She would probably say *It's okay, baby, you tried your best.* Mother was always too easy on her.

Dr. Sower seems sorry for her vinegary attitude. With a kinder face and a kinder voice she says: "I know you're worried. You've been through a lot, and it sucks. But you know what? You survived. And that's what counts. The Demiurge hasn't abandoned you. Say a prayer of grace before bed tonight."

Misery stares at the dead ceiling. "Funny you should say that. I mean, I failed, didn't I?"

"Failed? In what way?"

"I was supposed to be a seraph pilot. That's what the General wanted, right? But I failed. Something happened. It resisted me. I don't know why it didn't work."

"Huh. I mean, maybe the General was wrong this time. After all, they're a simple mortal. But you seem as lost as the rest of us. Don't worry, I'm sure it'll come to you eventually." As Misery struggles to understand what the doctor means, she gets poked in the shoulder. "You can sit up now. Try going slowly."

Misery's body is stiff and reluctant to budge from the gelatinous comfort of the bed. But it's not hurt, and it's not broken, and she manages to push herself upright. As she suspected, she's in the glass-and-metal nave of the medical lab where she first met the doctor. Bright and clinical and cool. She scans the room, and her heart drops.

At the nave's periphery, leaning against the glass of the open doorway, is the Lady Lee Alodia Lightning. Brows knit, a plait of shining hair hanging over one shoulder. Waiting for her. Waiting for Misery.

Misery develops instant wariness. Her fingers hurt where they clench around the edges of Mother's amulet. The princess's expression is tightly wound, and purple shadows park under her eyes. "What are you doing here?"

"Someone had to make sure you were okay."

"Isn't that the doctor's job?"

"Shut up. You were dead when we brought you out of the seraph."

"So she said. Does that mean I'm in trouble?"

The princess detaches from the glass frame she's been using for support. "I think we are all in trouble."

Her heart skips across a star system every minute. "What kind of trouble? What happened?"

Dr. Sower says, "I don't think our dear Misery is up to speed with what's happened to the seraph. They don't seem to have much recollection of anything. I might even say they're confused."

"Can they walk?"

The doctor shrugs. "They're standing, aren't they? You: Can you walk?"

Misery nods numbly. The princess studies her standing form, and her appraisal scours Misery's skin like a solar flare. "Good. Because I want to show you what you've done."

-+-

Misery trails Alodia Lightning through the chattering labyrinth of Angelsteeth Base. The brightness of the implant overlay hurts her head, but she can feel the beginning creep of salve-muting: that detached, floating feeling that seeks to dull her mind and blunt the force of her emotions. So the good doctor's hypo was loaded with salves after all. She hopes they wear off soon. Doctors developed salves as a last resort to curb the violent mindscapes of the voidsick, but they have never made Misery feel any better. Mother hated them too, and would often hide and toss her pills when Crem wasn't looking. A vast distance develops between Misery and the physical world, as though her head lingers a hundred klicks above firmament, her feet barely touching the ground.

Ahead of her the princess walks in silence. The Lady Alodia Lightning: an enigma, the shiniest mystery in the temple of interlocking mysteries that now comprises Misery's life. Misery hasn't forgotten their last conversation, nor the princess's brutal snap of anger. Together they've endured so much since the violence of their first meeting, yet Misery remains shut outside the thick metal hull that Alodia Lightning has placed around herself. "You must be glad," she says, another futile attempt to crack that shell.

Alodia Lightning spares a brief glance over her shoulder. "Glad for what?"

"Well, you won. You fared okay in the real test. I failed."

Alodia Lightning's gaze returns to the path ahead. "Wasn't a competition. Don't know why you thought it was."

Silence reigns. Around them, other soldiers are busy; they're barely spared a passing glance. It's nice to think that the Imperial princess and the Holy Messiah—two high-profile criminals condemned to execution—blend in so easily on Angelsteeth. As if they are ordinary humans like everyone else. Misery walks, the Lady Alodia Lightning walks. The steel-boned elevator that will take them to the Butchery is unguarded, unutilized, and the doors open automatically as Alodia Lightning approaches. They board. Misery positions herself where she can look the Lady Alodia Lightning in the face. The princess stares back, undaunted.

Buoyed by the lightness of her salve haze, Misery asks: "Why do you hate me?"

"I don't. I don't know why you think I do."

"You literally called me a liar and a fraud before we boarded the seraphs."

She looks away. "I had my reasons."

"What reasons?"

The elevator reaches its destination and its metal doors grind open, sparing Alodia Lightning the ordeal of giving Misery an honest answer. Misery tails after her silent form while pushing her sluggish mind to find new angles of attack. This deep in the restricted zone the floors aren't coated with padding, and their boots clatter against bare metal. The rhythm of the noise is hypnotic.

Misery asks: "Where's the General? I haven't heard from them. I haven't heard from anyone." Since waking up she's talked to two people, the good doctor and the princess, and neither are in her direct chain of command. Where's her captain, where's the debrief? These dreamlike, illogical events lend themselves to her post-death delusion theory. Why else would it be Alodia Lightning who waited for her as she lay near death, as if she cared about Misery?

The princess says: "The General is in a crisis meeting. Presumably enacting emergency plans to deal with what happened to your seraph."

They've stopped in front of the Butchery's double doors, big enough to swallow ships, big enough to hold destinies. The fully armed guards on either side are unreadable under their opaque faceplates, and Misery imagines they're not really human at all. Just statues. Or overlays on her implant. Hallucinations.

She says: "What happened to the seraph?"

Alodia Lightning frowns, all action in suspension. Misery watches her breathe slowly and deliberately for a few seconds, a pattern she recognizes. Finally she says: "You're about to see."

--+--

Her seraph has changed. Her seraph is blue.

Misery paces the length of the Butchery's viewing balcony, sick. She tilts her head to make sure it isn't a trick of the light. But there's no denying it. Among the regular seraphs, with their pale golden flesh that she's used to, hangs a singular creature made out in terrifyingly dense blue. A twilight-sky blue. Gold flecks glitter in its depths.

A handful of soldiers are on duty inside the Butchery and Alodia Lightning sends them to patiently wait outside the doors, leaving Misery and the princess alone in the cavernous space.

The princess stands by the railing, arms folded, a deliberately sketched picture of calm and rationality. "It's holy bluestone. You've had some experience with it, haven't you? It lines the insides of jump portals. We use it for transport pads."

Misery grounds her feet. Forces herself to breathe, deliberately. "That's the seraph I was in?"

"It was."

"It's transformed."

"Very astute observation. It's no longer a seraph. It's a storehouse of holy blue in the shape of a seraph."

"That's a rare stone. Isn't it?"

"Holy bluestone has never been found in the wild. Nowhere else outside the jump portals the Larex Forge put down for Hir Faithful. All the transport pads come from the one jump gate we found broken and torn apart. Now you've gone and made five hundred tons of it."

Misery stops pacing, tries to think about what this means, and starts pacing again. She wants to vomit. "Did I do this?"

"You tell me. Did you?"

Here's the thing. It's almost certain she did. She's fucked with holystone all her life—it's always been her thing. Holy labradorite, flesh of the seraph: this is what happens when it touches the mind of the voidmad. The first time they put her in a seraph, she fucked it up permanently. She's really blown the bag here. She's screwed.

"It was I who did it."

The voice startles Misery into near-panic. Ruin has been missing since Misery woke, but under the grip of the salves she hasn't noticed. Right now the angel—the delusion—resolves hirself in the dark space between Misery and the seraphs. Zie shines in the odd light of the Butchery, more radiant and ineffable than before.

"You saw my true form after you touched that seraph, didn't you? I am showing you the way, Misery Nomaki. I am showing you the path to your destiny. To our destiny."

Misery doubles over, head throbbing. The salves are trying to fight this delusion, trying to beat back the nullvoid. But the voidmadness has won. Misery's body heaves as it struggles with the weight of the Great Destroyer, humanity's bane. It's going to come through her soon. It's going to boil her marrow and shatter her teeth.

"That is no longer a seraph," Ruin says, triumphant and golden. "It is an invitation. Will you answer?"

Someone catches her as she falls to her knees. It's the princess, the Lady Alodia Lightning. Arms all strong and supportive, pulling Misery upright before her chin hits the floor. "What's wrong?"

The query comes from very far away. Misery hears it perfectly fine, but she can't find her jaw or tongue in her body. She's too dizzy to answer and the world grows more insubstantial every minute. Or maybe it's Misery that's vaporizing. Phasing out of existence. The nullvoid clipping though her. Is this how Mother felt when she died?

High abovehead, and everywhere at once, Ruin says, "Come find me."

Then zie's gone, and the vacuum zie leaves behind sucks Misery in. Her dizzy mind whirls, trapped in a shrinking radius of thought and coherence, and at the center of that maelstrom is the blue seraph. She will die if she doesn't touch it. The agony she feels is fire in her bones.

Cool hands on her cheeks. A face before her that she mildly registers as Alodia Lightning's, but she can't condense the various features into a cohesive whole. "Let's get you back to the doctor's," she's saying. "Something's gone wrong."

18

Misery is dreaming. Misery is falling. Her mind is a bottomless pit, a primordial cave, an endless night without relief. It is the great empty that stands in opposition to the hereness of all the universe. It is the nullvoid.

Connection: light and sound, a boy blinking in the vastness of the not-cosmos. Jericho. Her other delusion. Most nights, they meet in vistas strange to Misery's eyes, but pleasant to look at, like a walk through a meditative sim. On the left, you will see the twin suns breaking over the horizon of Yerven-4, their yellow light symphonious over the purple waters. Breathe in. Hold. Breathe out. But today there is nothing but void. Whirling, screaming void, and they're plunging through it like they're skydiving. Wind whips hair into Jericho's eyes and mouth. "What's going on?" he shouts over the howling. "What have you done?"

"It's over," she says. "The void won. Your side won."

"We're not enemies, Misery."

It occurs to her that she's never heard Jericho shout like this. "Yeah, we are."

"I don't want to be."

She doesn't care what he says. Why should she trust what a delusion says?

He thrusts a hand across the wild void, trying to reach her as they fall. "Give me your hand," he says. "Please."

But she won't. He thinks he can stop her from falling, but he can't. No one can save her.

Jericho is gone, and in his place something else, also familiar. A dark room lined with red carpet, full of bronzed furniture, which Misery falls infinitely through while it stays static. She's been here before. She recognizes this dream. There's the mysterious saint, gender unknown, combing a shining curtain of hair, leaning over the rectangle of light where hir lover lives. Misery first had this dream on the Capital, and it's repeated a dozen times since, but her dreams of Jericho have choked them out. Now it's back. Now she's back. Why? Who is this saint? She falls, she cries out. She reaches for that still, elegant figure as if zie would turn around to help her.

The saint turns. Misery catches hir eyes, pale and wide like Pyrex Imogen's. And then zie's gone, the room is gone, and Misery is falling through void, alone. Flailing.

Then she's not alone in the void. Here is Ruin, the angelic terror: eight limbs, obsidian skin, rows of sensors glistening pale in hir elongated head. Even through the medium of dreams she feels the sear of hir impatience, hot as a thousand exploding suns. What a terrible thing is an angel enraged! Misery's soul melts under that pressure; she cannot look away from the nova that is Ruin.

Come to me, Misery. You know what to do. Your life until now has led up to this.

Come.

Misery wakes with the taste of vomit in her mouth. She gains control of her soft mortal body, limbs thrashing in a damp darkness she doesn't fully comprehend. She falls off a bed, landing hard on her hands and knees. The pain grounds her in the waking world, this horrific reality where force and gravity exert a hold. A mad impulse screams at her to *get up*. To *go*.

This is the medical bay, powered down, its confines outlined in the soft glow of auxiliary lighting. Misery doesn't remember being brought here. Already the nullvoid is fracturing what she recalls and what she knows. She is no longer a person. She is merely a vessel for the nullvoid and its demands. The agonizing gravity of Ruin's demand pulls at her from across the galaxy like a quasar of divine wrath. *Come,* the voice says in her mind. *Come.* She has to go.

Misery stumbles to her feet and fights to stay upright as the world tilts. Angelsteeth's system and its indomitable directional arrows have primed her to accept this inexorable force pushing her forward. Her life will end when she gets to the transformed seraph and she knows that, but she can't refuse. There is no way to keep living while feeling like this. And she's always known the nullvoid would claim her someday. Better there than here.

She slouches toward the glass doors, turning will into strength, forcing her body to stay upright. She can make it to the Butchery. She will see to it.

Sudden, unexpected warmth. Hands close around her arms and a body presses against hers, blocking her path. "What are you doing?"

It's the Lady Alodia Lightning, coming out of nowhere. Not nowhere. She's been sleeping in the medical bay too. Watching over Misery. Making sure she gets up to no mischief. Like now. Misery finds her tongue and the air in her lungs. "Let me go."

"Where are you going?"

Misery tries to pull free, but the princess has an overpowering grip. "Leave me alone."

"Do you think you can run? On this station? Where to?"

"I'm not running." She gives up struggling, letting her weight rest against the princess's slender bulk. She has to keep her strength up—for something. She's not sure what. "I have to go. It's calling me."

"What is?" Alodia Lightning still won't let her go. "That seraph? The one you transformed?"

Her skin is cold from the sweat lifting off it. "Holy bluestone," she says. "It's the transporter stone, isn't it? It sends you somewhere when it's activated."

"Only if it's programmed. What are you trying to say?"

"It's an invitation," Misery intones, clearly and slowly. Repeating what Ruin told her in the Butchery. As the syllables form in her mouth she knows them to be real and true.

"An invitation? From whom? To where?"

"The nullvoid." Misery doesn't know how else to explain it. The tangle of her life, the lies she's told, the things she's hidden. Mother's death, the black hole in the center of her life, around which she whirls in a rapidly shrinking orbit. That event horizon will claim her soon. It's better if the princess lets her go.

She says: "You heard the conversation I had with Dr. Sower?"

"I did. You think it's voidsickness, what happened here."

"Because it is."

"The doctor says it isn't. If anyone knows about voidsickness and its manifestations, it would be her. It's her life's work and very personal."

Misery starts to laugh, and each jolt of her diaphragm sends pain through her chest, yet she can't stop. "Why can't you believe I'm voidmad? You're the one who said I was full of shit."

"Forget that. I was pissed, and—it doesn't matter. You need to get back to bed."

"No." Her energy renewed, she starts pulling from the princess's grasp again. "You were right. This whole time, this entire Messiah gig? It's a lie. I fucking lied out my ass the whole time, Princess. That's my nature. I lie, I steal, I cheat. That's how I was back home. I homebrewed salves. I shifted goods. All under the nose of my brother, the man of the Church. But he was a liar too. He hid my mother's sickness, and mine. I guess it runs in the family."

"None of us here are free from sin," says Alodia Lightning.

Why is she being so voidfucked stubborn? "No. You really don't understand. My mother was voidmad. She had me when she was voidmad. I was born with the nullvoid in my flesh. It took her. I watched her die. And now it's going to take me, too."

She doesn't know when she started crying, but she is, and the princess just stands there and listens to her sobbing in the dark. Everything is upside down and awful. Her chest hurts.

The princess asks: "So it's all a lie, everything you said about messages from the Demiurge?"

"No. Yes. I don't know. I mean, there's a messenger, but zie's a delusion. It's the voidmadness speaking, you know? There's this creature that calls hirself Ruin, that claims to be an angel, a messenger from the Larex Forge."

"So. There *is* a messenger."

"A delusion," Misery repeats.

The princess doesn't respond to that. Alodia Lightning's thoughts are opaque at the best of times, and now—in the dark, with her head a wound and her heart a storm—it's absolutely impossible to know what she wants. She says to Misery, after a pause: "You said you want to go to the seraph?"

"I have to. It's calling for me."

"All right. I'll take you. I'll go with you."

"Really?" Misery's heart is so loud in her chest, her temples shake with the beat. "I don't know why—"

"I'll tell you later. Let's go."

"All right. Wait. No—wait." Her hand goes to her chest to check for Mother's amulet. It's there. They haven't taken it. Good. She won't be separated from it again. "Okay. You take the lead."

Past the miles of corridors and clusters of guards the Butchery awaits, dimmed by the sallow pinpricks of late-night lighting, enough to make out the shapes of the seraphim hanging from their hooks, but not enough to trigger their iridescence. Misery and Alodia Lightning approach the transformed seraph, pitch-black in the low yellow light. Past the viewing platform, past the control station, up and up the winding steps until they're on the pilot's boarding platform. The long journey from medical bay to station's bowels has given Misery time to find her feet, and she's largely vertical and self-supporting as they stand in the great shadow of the seraph. She looks up at the wound bisecting its chest, the gouge left behind when they cut her out of its core.

Alodia Lightning says: "You're going in, aren't you?"

Misery nods. She's all dizzy and she can't blame the salves this time. They've worn off. This is where it happens. Her life ends and the void takes her. She's strangely okay with that fact. She's come to peace with it.

The princess says: "I'll go with you."

"What?" The declaration catches her off guard. "You can't. It's dangerous."

"I'm not afraid of danger. Who do you think I am? I'm coming with you."

Misery pulls air into her lungs, slowly. The princess is as voidmad as she is. She's followed Misery into the realm of delusion. It's the only explanation. "You think there's something to this prophecy thing, don't you?"

Alodia Lightning's eyes are reflective in the dim hangar, gleaming with emotion Misery cannot read. Studying the shape of the blue seraph like a lover. "If you asked me a month ago, fuck, a week ago . . . I would have punched you. But now? I don't know." She turns the same impossible gaze upon Misery. "I have to see it for myself. Your miracles. Whatever happens, I have to know."

"You could die," Misery says. "You'll probably die. I'm dead too. You sure about this?"

"I'm sure."

"Okay. All right." Misery can't even laugh. All emotions have been crushed out of her.

They climb in. Even the creamy insides of the seraph have turned to glistening bluestone, striped with pale veins of gold. Misery slides over the frictionless surface, easing into the wound where she once lay. The princess follows behind, sometimes using her shoulder or arm for grip.

The hollow that used to be the pilot's seat retains her vague form, even with all the stone that's been cut away. Alodia Lightning slips on an awkward incline and Misery lunges to catch her. The princess's panicked hands latch on—one around her neck, one around her waist. She swears quietly, then calms, like a bird.

The hollow wasn't built for the two of them. Alodia Lightning's body presses against Misery's, and within that pressure is her heartbeat, like a small creature struggling to break free. Lightning's breath whispers across the back of Misery's neck. "Okay, now what?"

Now what? She's here. She shuts her eyes and sinks into the well of her body, the pathetic flesh sack with all its weaknesses and limitations and needs. The song of this alien chunk of holy-stone has been so loud, so anywhere and everywhere, that Misery's mind is numb to it. It's background radiation, black noise, a baseline of fatigue. But here, wrapped in its embrace, Misery feels sensation in the core of her being again. At the base of her spine. She presses deep into the glassy stone. There it is. That angry jolt of connection. The stone is eager, so deeply hungry to fulfill its purpose. One push and she'll be over the edge.

"Don't let go," she whispers with her mouth, hoping that it reaches Alodia Lightning in the world of flesh. Then she pushes.

Stone wakes around them. Cold ultramarine keens and glows reactor-blue. It hits them with the force of a thousand gales, a choir of planetary crusts splitting, a hundred thousand stars bursting to life. The stone roars, then flings them into the void.

Misery shatters. The universe forces itself through her, every atom and iota of energy that comprises the cosmos rushing through the fontanelle of the speck she calls a body. In an instant her consciousness spreads across the firmament, a range of infinite light-years from alpha to omega, covering the chasm between galaxies in a blink. To be infinite is to be nothing. To be everywhere is to be nowhere. For an infinitesimal fragment of time Misery is the great void, her humanity vanishing against the vastness of Creation. She is all there is, and this is all she is.

Another light, another presence: the Lady Lee Alodia Lightning. Not supposed to be here. In this infinity space their forms overlap and phase in and out of one another, simultaneously each other's inverse and also the very composition of the universe. They are a wave, they are particles, they are energy and nothing but, they are two soft bodies and two disparate minds become something else. A unity. Misery-and-Lightning can only cling to each other, become one another, and ride it out.

19

The journey ends the way ash settles over a landscape: a long, slow coming down, a few flickers of light that grow thick and fast. Misery's awareness of her boundaries returns cumulatively. First the concept of physical matter, then the idea of time, then a realization that space and time are fixed. She first senses that she is a person, a discrete individual, and that individual has a body curled on its side against some cool, dark and flat thing. Blood pulses in that body, and she feels it coursing through her chest, worrying the hollows of her neck, twitching down the insides of her legs. Her lungs fill and empty themselves of air. She has a face, a mouth with parted lips, a pair of eyes that lie shut.

Someone moans, a sound somewhere below her. Misery registers the sensations against her left hip and her chest as pressure, weight. Not hers: another body, prone against her still form, cold and trembling strangely. The Lady Lee Alodia Lightning. The Imperial princess.

Something is deeply wrong. Alodia Lightning isn't breathing right. Misery finds awareness of her own hand in the dark—a small useful thing of bone and tendon and knuckle—and forces it to move. The hand responds, remembering that it is part of a body. She needs to find her eyes, her limbs, the rest of her flesh and gristle, she needs to get up and do something. See what's wrong. She's fighting, swimming up a long tunnel of inertia toward consciousness, glimmering over the surface she just has to reach.

Misery breaks through. Her surroundings snap into focus:

she's in a huge, dim cavern full of chilled air. Her body is intact and free of pain, almost like it's been numbed.

Beside her, crumpled into an inert comma, Alodia Lightning is dying.

Misery forces her body into action. She gets to her knees. Takes Alodia Lightning by the shoulder, tries to roll her over. Not good. The soft flesh of her has been irreparably broken in transit, whatever divine protection that kept Misery whole not extended to her. Breath sloshes through lungs full of liquid. Blood pools dark and sticky around her mouth, her face. "Hey," she says. "Princess. Lady Alodia."

Her eyelids flutter, vaguely, and her lips move. "Sorry, I— guess I wasn't supposed to—"

"Hey." Misery squeezes Alodia Lightning's shoulder as she fades. "Don't do this—you said." But what did she say? Misery isn't clear. The words simply tumble from her mouth.

No response. The princess falls deathly still, and the liquid rattle of her breaths stops. A loud, high ringing fills Misery's head. This isn't happening. The void was supposed to take her—to take *Misery*—not this bystander. Is she being punished? What has she done wrong? *Ruin, help.* She's reaching for the delusion, for the angel, the way she used to reach for prayer and Hir Grace as a child, hoping that Mother could be saved. Stupid and desperate and yearning.

Bring her to me.

That voice. That command in her head. Ruin. She's done as zie asked—she's come to the place zie told her to. She's given in to delusion, to void. Please—let her have this much. Let the princess live.

Mind and body in shambles, Misery scoops Alodia Lightning's body into her arms, adrenaline feeding her strength as she hobbles forward. Darkness surrounds her, but not completely. Ahead and above a glacial light shines from a distant and unknown source. As Misery fights to make a straight line forward she realizes she knows this place. This is the cavern she

saw when she died, where Ruin revealed hirself to be an apocalyptic force. Is she dead again? Will Dr. Sower come to rescue
her this time? Misery's blood pounds in her veins, thickened by
the weight of all the holystone around her.

She makes pilgrimage to the place Ruin stood in her dream,
feet guided by instinct rather than knowing. The distant smear
of light swells in brightness and summons greater attention with
every step she takes. Something comes slowly into focus. Something huge. An enormous plinth, size of a building. All white,
paler than the palest bone. The single light source pours cold
illumination over the top of scalloped stone. The patterned lines
appear abstract at first, but coalesce into understandable form as
Misery's vision adjusts to the gloom.

Enormous stone wings, folded into a sarcophagus.

Awe drowns her. There are no words. None formed by human tongues are adequate to praise the thing before her. The
sarcophagus has not been put together by human hands, has
never before been touched by humanity. In front of that colossal
construct she is desperately and beautifully insignificant, a wisp
of an idea, a tiny candle flickering beside the suns of creation.

Come here.

Driven by want and the command in that voice, Misery
walks the interminable distance to the foot of the building-sized
monolith. The tower of white stone expands until it envelops her
horizon and there is nothing but Misery, the sarcophagus, and
the dead weight of Alodia Lightning in her arms.

Put her down.

Misery places Alodia Lightning at Ruin's feet, a silent heap of
limp flesh and gray skin. If there were ever a time for a miracle,
that time is now.

The sarcophagus begins to hum; its white stone cladding
glows. Misery scrambles backward. Her blighted survival instinct. She falls and continues her retreat on heel and palm, skin
torn bloody by the stone. She can't take her eyes off the sarcophagus, nor the piteous jumble of limbs at its base.

The strange white stone flows like lava, stretching and mar-
bling over Alodia Lightning's still form. Misery shivers. Her
throat closes as bile plumes in her stomach. She can't watch.
She can't think. Eyes shut, on her knees, she does the one thing
that was drilled into her the moment she learned language. She
prays. She prays to the Larex Forge, resister of the darkness, the
dam that holds back the nullvoid, the hand that leads the lost
from the darkness to the light. She prays to a Demiurge she had
long given up on, who yet still extended Hir Grace to this stupid, insignificant moonrat, this nobody nothing really; she prays
to be saved, for the one she brought here to be saved.

The cocoon of stone that contains Alodia Lightning rises
from the ground and melts into the surface of the sarcophagus.
It vanishes. A gong sounds. Misery collapses, nauseated, ears
ringing. Silence descends upon the chamber once more, and
it's just Misery and the deathless stone, which has consumed
the Imperial princess. She vomits, but nothing comes out of her
wretched body.

Stone rumbles. A low noise ramping, avalanche, death approaching at speed, inescapable, coming to swallow Misery in
its embrace.

The sarcophagus wakes.

The cavern shudders as the colossal outcropping of stone expands. Cracks open on its surface, following the outlines of the
feathers, and light pours from them. The ground under Misery
glows in concentric patterns: intersecting lines like the map to an
unknown solar system. Like the patterns on her mother's amulet.

The wings of the sarcophagus unfold.

The sarcophagus had appeared as a single massive pair of
wings, one pulled over the other, forming a closed vessel. Now
those wings unfurl and stretch outward, revealing more layers
underneath: six wings, eight wings, eighteen, an avalanche chorus of shifting planes. Their gray stone surfaces melt and recede
in scaly patches, revealing hidden iridescence. Wings of silver,
wings of gold, wings of rainbow green. Glittering black opal

wings. Wings shimmering and refractive as crystal. Luminescence, nova-bright, burning Misery's eyes as she stares.

The wings are attached to something. An alien figure, floating, wrapped in a fetal curl. As the cocoon wings keep opening it too starts to unfold. Long, cool limbs of stone ripple and stretch out. Four arms: two long, two short. A tetrad of lower limbs, curved and sloping and strangely articulated. Hands with six fingers, feet with four toes. A pelvis tethered to a bisected torso by the suggestion of stone ribbons. A striated oval where a head should be, burning with terrible light.

Archangel. A being the size of a building, skin shining like the moon. Beautiful, ineffable, terrible to behold.

Yet as Misery's vision clears, she realizes it is no *creature*. Its soft edges take on resolution. Precise, engineered lines. A fighter, a mech. A seraph.

The thing before her is an archangel mech.

Archangel: Eater of Sorrows, Eighth Form of the Divine. The existence of archangel mechs has only been guessed at, gleaned from sacred murals where other war machines were discovered—seraphim and warships and jump portals. In the history and breadth of the Empire, a real unit has never been found. Until now.

Misery's skull sings. Her blood is aflame. This is no delusion. The nullvoid cannot thrive in the presence of such holiness. This here is the touch of the Forge Hirself. She stumbles forward, hands clasped to her chest, soul filled with unutterable light. The archangel calls to her.

It's hers, isn't it? This is what she had been sent to pilot. An archangel. A glorious machine to turn the tide of war.

The mech descends to the floor, coming to rest in a hollow that surrounds its form perfectly. The remnants of the sarcophagus it slept in for void knows how long. On either side of the hollow's opening, stone walls branch outward in thin filaments, light as ice. In front of it hovers the pod that contains Alodia Lightning's body.

The archangel mech waits for her in its glacial thicket. Compelled by awe, Misery goes to the husk of the sarcophagus. It's not a long journey, but it seems to take forever. Every footfall is sacred. Holy books will write of this precise path she's walking in ages to come. Misery reaches the bottom of the cocoon, where the first strut of the stone filaments bars her at chest height. The feet of the archangel are enormous, each splayed toe larger than Misery is. She looks up. The heart of the archangel—where the pilot's pod must be—seems impossibly far away.

She grips the bottom strut of the ladder formed by the sarcophagus stone. Pushes herself off the floor and finds that it holds weight.

Misery climbs.

It's a long way up, but this is demanded of her. She must. The filaments are perfectly spaced for the scale of Misery's dismal human body. Her muscles start burning as she crosses the threshold of the archangel's many knees. She keeps climbing. Past the waist of the mech. Past the hovering specter of Alodia Lightning's stone cocoon. Her breath burns her airways and chest.

Still she continues. Her limbs shake with near-collapse by the time she draws level with the archangel's heart. A deep, wide slit bisects the mech's chest between its set of arms. Misery slides along the length of the rungs until she's positioned above the center of the archangel mech.

Now what? Misery wraps her arms around the stone filaments and spends a couple of moments just breathing. Exhaustion has slowed her thoughts to a crawl. Before her is the slit, an inward turning of the pale holystone big enough to swallow her.

She gazes upward. On one lip of the slit, almost invisible in the dim glow, sits a shallow indentation that matches the ones seraphim mechs have. A small circle, waiting for a token to be placed in it.

The stone is the same color, has the same translucent quality as her mother's amulet.

Misery's arms tighten around the filaments of stone that are her only support. If she lets go, if she allows the dizziness to overtake her, she will die.

Mother's amulet. Mother's voice, telling her how she found it on a distant airless rock. Mother recounting how an angel came in her sleep and told her the amulet belonged to the unborn child she carried. Mother saying the angel proclaimed that the child—that's *you,* my pickle!—would be the savior of the Faithful, and would one day lead the armies of the Faithful to victory over the Heretics.

The same amulet now hangs around Misery's neck with a weight of its own. The amulet that has been Misery's before Misery was Misery. It is a key. It is a key that will unlock this archangel. It is the key that will unlock her destiny.

It's clear what she must do.

Now you understand, sounds the voice of Ruin. *Now you see what your life has been building up to.*

Mother was right. Mother was right all along.

Misery knows what she must do. She needs to board the archangel.

A spun nest of stone filament surrounds the pilot's module: the husk of the archangel's sarcophagus growing vasculature for Misery's sake. She ducks between the rungs of the ladder she's climbed and shuffles across the latticework until she's flush against the cool stone of the archangel. Now she's next to this thing that has never been touched by human hands. Gingerly she reaches out and presses her fingers to its smooth skin. A faint buzz travels up her wrist and arm. She shivers.

Misery carefully detaches her mother's amulet from around her neck. With one hand gripping stone filament she tiptoes and slots the amulet into the shallow dip that waits for it.

It clicks into place, just as she knew it would.

The amulet blinks and comes to life. Its carved lines glow and start to move like gearwork. After untold millennia, it has found its way home.

The archangel awakens.

Music splits the cavern. Sacred chorus resonates through the fine atoms of Misery's body. Soft light flares hard white, furnace-bright, too brilliant to look at. Misery's eyes snap shut but still light comes through her eyelids, and sparks flash against the veiny pink of her vision. Stone moves around her and the timbre of the archangel's song changes along with it.

With her eyes still closed Misery senses that the slit in the archangel's chest has scissored open into a foramen. How does she know this? Inconsequential. Within this gap is a pilot's hollow just like that of a seraph's. But this hollow stands nearly three meters tall, with space for eight limbs and a horned head.

In Scripture the writings tell of similar findings in virgin seraphim. No human pilot has come for this archangel mech. It bears only the marks of the divine creatures who have made it.

If this is real, if this is no delusion-through-death, then truly she is in the presence of a holy artifact.

Come home now, Misery Nomaki.

Time to go. Time to fulfill her destiny.

Misery leans forward and puts her palm against the pearlescent insides of the archangel. The gap between the stone lattice and the pilot's hollow is just narrow enough for her to climb over.

This is what she is meant to do. Misery clambers into the hollow on her hands and knees. The archangel's skin welcomes her with friction enough to keep her from falling to her death. The hollow is too big and too many-limbed to suit her. The mech's hum shifts in key and the stone begins to move, rippling like jelly around her soles. Then it begins the climb that Misery now knows too well. Up to her waist, past her elbows, creeping over her shoulders. She finds herself eager for this sequence of events.

All's well, all's well, and all will be well.

The stone closes over Misery's head.

Silence.

Then a whisper. Then a song.

Misery Nomaki the human vessel, the small creature made of flesh and bone and limited will, the mortal tool that will lead the crusade against the Heretics, that Misery Nomaki, chosen of the Larex Forge, becomes infinite. Becomes archangel. Becomes a being that knows no boundaries, in touch with the breadth and depth of the whole of the universe, one with the core of Creation that humanity calls the Larex Forge. The Demiurge. God. This is a homecoming: from the stars we are born, to the stars we return. Zie is archangel and the archangel is zie. The archangel Misery looks out upon the world with new eyes-that-are-not-eyes. Zie is aware of so many things at once: the geography of hir new body. The force of omnipotence that is Ruin, truly now part of hir consciousness, one and the same. The place in the universe zie must travel to, where the beginnings of hir destiny await hir. The station, Angelsteeth. Systems and systems away now, but not for much longer. At hir feet is the cocoon that holds the body of the princess Alodia Lightning, whose life shall be restored by Hir Grace, the will of the Larex Forge. Zie must deliver her back to her people.

The human vessel Misery Nomaki had felt a fraction of this holy power when they stood upon the platform in the Capital, in sight of the Emperor and all the Faithful. Then, they had moved stone in the name of the Larex Forge, a tiny gesture to bring Hir loving wrath upon those who had strayed far from Hir guidance. That display was a pittance, a terrible first skim of the potential and power that the Messiah could wield. Now, as the archangel Misery, zie has a far greater mission to carry out. Zie must destroy the Heretics.

The archangel Misery breaks free of the fragile stone that has protected hir until now, its usefulness at an end. The archangel Misery scoops the white stone containing the human Alodia Lightning to hir chest, precious as an egg. The archangel Misery sees Angelsteeth Base as a pinprick in a soft galaxy that can be folded upon itself like fabric, no more than a breath away.

The archangel Misery is ready. The archangel Misery is coming home.

INTERLUDE 6

And so it was that Misery Nomaki returned to Angelsteeth in hir final form, archangel, the promise made before hir birth finally fulfilled. Hir new form was all angles, all limbs, and zie knew every part of it intimately as though zie was made like this. The universe spread like a glittering blanket before hir, dancing with potential like the heart of a burning star. Zie pulled open the fabric of space-time and emerged into the lands of flesh in sight of Angelsteeth Base.

Imagine yourself a soldier on Angelsteeth. Part of the rank and file, unremarkable as the hundreds of others who also serve under captains and lieutenants. Techs and maintainers and ships' gunners. Exhausted from months of living on a base housing a secret that burns like a nuclear core: shore leave banned, every communiqué screened, curbs on who you can see and what you can do. You don't know when you will next hold your mother's hand. Rumors swirl, from both inside and outside, about a Chosen One of the Forge, who lives among you and is the reason for the secrecy. You have seen them once or twice, you think, in the vastness of the dining hall. When you started serving you delighted in the idea of being on the front lines, of fighting these evasive Heretics yourself. Finally you would be contributing to the war effort. But the attack from weeks ago still unnerves you. The truth of how close you came to destruction is something you think the higher-ups keep from you. Every thought you think, every action you perform, is dogged by a haze of uncertainty and low-grade anxiety. About your fate, and the fate of the greater world, things you have no control over.

Then space tears open, the way it does when the Heretics come for you, and what emerges is the shape of an alien monster, something you do not recognize. Imagine what you would feel. Imagine the reactions on the ground. The defense systems waking and alarms crying out. The night-shifters and their captains running to wake the guns and aegis. Imagine the fear. Imagine the thought that the Heretics have come to retaliate for their losses, and only doom awaits.

And then the message that broadcasts from the unknown mech, white and blazing in its glory. It says *I am Misery Nomaki. Nullvoidsbane, chosen of the Larex Forge, the Ninth Messiah. I have come to lead you in glorious victory against the Heretics.* Then the order to stand down, to allow this unknown mech to board the station. The General, guided by their own convictions, deciding to take the risk and believe the words of Misery Nomaki. Deciding to trust that, despite all appearances, this is not a trick.

Angelsteeth took in the archangel Misery Nomaki, and what happened next changed the path of humanity's future.

Humans are strange creatures. They hang their identity on their sense of self, but so much of it comes from external sources. There are very few whose self-conception is whole and complete within themselves, inalterable by the thoughts and actions and accepted norms of those around them. What rare, extraordinary creatures who cannot be swayed by the desires of their peers and loved ones. There are various names for them. Psychopath, narcissist. Sometimes they are even called *Messiah.* Let us return to the mind of our dear Misery. I'm sure what you find there will fascinate you.

20

They interrogate Misery upon her return to the gravity-bound, metal-sealed spaces of Angelsteeth, upon her return to the bone-bound, flesh-sealed body she has existed in for twenty years. She's not surprised by this. In fact, she would be disappointed if they just took Misery for her word. Divinity must be proven, it must be made real, it must be demonstrated in the realm of salt and iron. She's taken from the archangel mech, separated from the cocoon that contains the Lady Alodia Lightning, and taken to an interrogation room in the deep bowels of the station, where she sits patiently on a backless stool, metal bolted to a steel floor in a room with steel walls, her hands clasped lightly and patiently in her lap. They've taken her fatigues and put her in a one-piece gown that drapes to mid-calf and leaves her arms bare. Blue as the hearts of ice. That's fine. Misery sits up tall; her spine has never been this straight her entire life. If only her brother could see her now.

The room is bisected by a stern yellow aegis. On the other side of it is a long table attended by those who think they are in charge here: Captain Diamond Sunyata. Major Reyes Photon. The Duke of Apis. And General Tsung themself, quiet and craggy, standing behind with one hand on their chin. Not sitting, not questioning. Just listening. Misery has taken the panel through the happenings of the past hours, a bone-dry recollection of this mesmerizing pivot in her life. The call, unavoidable. The journey, ineffable. The truth revealed, undeniable. Her return, triumphant.

Her panel of interrogators don't see her story that way. Instead they see a string of threatening occurrences they cannot explain or understand. They see danger in the alien white mech that entered their radar zone without warning, much like Heretics do. They see the changed shape of someone they have taken in, vouched for, and believed in, and they're not sure what that shape means. What it means for their faith. She sees the fears telegraphed on their faces, shining like lead.

But there is light. Under the tectonic plates of stress and anxiety burns a core of molten hope. That same fiery belief that led Duke Argan to champion her cause and led General Tsung to organize sedition against the Throne. She sees trust in her captain's expression. There's exhaustion in the low tones of her words, but there's also luminescent faith. For the first time in many years, she sees a way out of the despair she lives in.

Everything is laid out before Misery like a map. The once-dark and messy void of her past, present, and future have been illuminated by legend, scale, and objective. Scatters of dust have been grouped into constellation, the broken points of her life joined into a meaningful route. She no longer drifts through a cold and hostile universe, but floats above it all, seeing the truth of what things are. Before, in the muddle of her doubts, she considered the people before her tools that she could use for her means. With the clarity of enlightenment, she sees that they *are* tools she must use for her means. But not for personal, selfish purposes. They are the chips and stone of the Demiurge's great plan for humanity, and she must move them and use them as Zie sees fit. She must break them and make them anew, just as she has been broken and made anew.

Duke Argan slouches in his chair, consumed by thought, hands folded in a wiry ball over his stomach. He says, abruptly: "The Lady Alodia Lightning. Why did she come with you?"

"You could ask her that when she wakes up. I didn't make her come with me. She chose to."

"When she wakes up?" The Duke laughs. "*If* she wakes up."

She can read nobles like Duke Argan so much better since she's accepted the Demiurge into her life. He's worried about the princess, of course, but more importantly he wouldn't know what to say to Pyrex Imogen. They entrusted the girl to him. He was supposed to protect her in any way he could. He failed.

"All will be well," Misery says, to comfort him. "Her fate lies in the hands of the Larex Forge." And Zie will not let her fall, she's sure of it. Her hands, loose in her lap, close into fists.

"You should have come to us first," Diamond says.

"I was compelled to act by a higher power."

Misery sees the battle being fought in her captain's soul, her military training on one side and her faith on the other. Angels-teeth has a chain of command, a fiber-clad set of protocols, and she took an oath on her life to honor them both. But her faith is an older and stronger credo and it has been part of her life since memory started forming. The miracles she witnessed in the past week exert a stellar pull on her grief-worn soul. Misery wants to tell her, come to me, come as you are. It is so much easier in the cradle of belief. She feels incredibly light, the anxiety washed from her being, and replaced by the Grace of the All-Seer, All-Maker, All-Knower. Mother was right. Mother was right all along. Her death was not for nothing. The nullvoid hasn't won. Her captain is the closest to this glorious embrace. The Duke isn't far behind. Misery will not push them, will not give them ultimatums, yet. They must take the final steps themselves.

"So," says Major Reyes. "Now what?" Ever the skeptic. Still clinging to xer stubbornness. The lines between xer brows a testimony to the depths of xer doubts.

The General strides forward and comes between Diamond and Major Reyes. Now the quiet takes on the weight of expectation. On the table, housed in the yellow bell of another aegis, Misery's amulet floats over a disc of holy tigereye. The General taps the apex of the bell and the aegis hums. "This token," they say. "It's yours?"

"Given to me when I was born. My mother found it. A messenger told her she would bear a holy child . . ."

"You've had it all this time? It's never been registered."

"It's always been on me. You can ask my captain. Or the Duke." A light gesture in their direction. "It was a sentimental object for me. A reminder of home. They took it from me when I was arrested on the Capital, but Pyrex Imogen recovered it for me. Possibly in secret."

"And you did not know its purpose?"

"Not until now. Not until it was revealed to me."

The General nods, thinking their slow and deliberate thoughts, armored by heavy caution. A nixen who bears the weight of responsibility and bears it as well as one can. They already know what they believe, but are they willing to drag all under their command along with their folly? Their decisions will change the course of the Faithful's future.

Finally, he says: "What happened here was a blessing. A holy miracle. It cannot be denied. I do not know what the next steps will be, or should be, but I do know that you are not dangerous. You were sent to us for a reason."

Air gusts through the interrogation room. As the stars move the trajectories of the comets that pass them by, so too do the opinions of the powerful pull others in their wake. Misery watches the faces of the interview panel change. Relief that the General is giving them permission to stop fighting their skepticism. To give in to the sweetness of faith.

Over the General's shoulder, brilliant and gleaming like the future, is the creature known as Ruin, strutting in the form she has always known, triumph in hir golden face, a fierce joy in hir inhuman eyes. Zie has been there all this while, watching as she takes her first stumbling steps toward her destiny. Now zie's telling her she knows what must be done.

And she does. "Divinity must be proven, not just taken at its word. The Heretics that have plagued this station for so long—

let me take care of them. The next time they come, they will see. They will see, and you will know."

Lady Lee Alodia Lightning looks for her the moment she wakes. Misery follows the system's supportive red arrow through the byways of Angelsteeth Base. Beside her Ruin floats, triumphant and silent. Since she's returned with the archangel mech, the creature has appeared more spectral in her vision, yet feels more present in her life, like a pressure in her soul that never leaves.

The arrow leads Misery through the tangle of the med and research lobe. Deep in some duodenal twist is the highly secured unit in which Alodia Lightning has been recuperating, blastproof doors guarded by a stern pair of soldiers. The one on the left makes the sign of the Forge before opening the door. A shiver ripples through her; this is the first time she's been saluted this way. An honor reserved for generals and emperors and archbishops. What did General Tsung tell them? What had they entered into the system, and what floats invisibly over her head now?

Inside: a room so white she can't tell its true size or shape. It appears curved, a glittering bank of controls sat in its far vicinity. In the middle, a bed, or in other circumstances an examination pallet. Perhaps even an autopsy table. On it, Alodia Lightning sits upright, draped in a fine slip, hair loose and shimmering over her back. She's halfway through a conversation with Dr. Sower, who turns as Misery comes in. Alodia Lightning follows suit and her face brightens like a switch has been thrown.

Dr. Sower tucks her hands into the pockets of her coat. "I'll leave you two to it, then." Full of hidden meaning. When she nods to Misery, it's almost a wink. "Call me when you're done. I have more tests to run." And then she's out of the door the way Misery came.

Misery and the princess gaze at one another for a silent moment that stretches like gel. The princess studies Misery like she's sizing up a stranger. Her eyes, Misery notices, have gold flecks in them, tiny and bold against the darkness. Like holy bluestone, as though she'd been tainted before birth.

She finds the request for a chair in one of the system's many menus. It brings a sculpted white thing out of the floor, its seat shaped like a flower blossom. Misery sits. Its surface looks hard and plastic but it's foam, and molds to her form as she settles in.

Alodia Lightning breaks the silence. "So you lived. You survived it."

"I did. And so did you." She puts her hands in her lap to keep them from wandering. "I wasn't sure that you would. You were dead, at some point, while we were in that chamber."

"The doctor filled me in on what happened. You found an archangel mech."

"I did. I flew it too. Almost as if it was made for me, specifically." Even though she knows it isn't. The archangel is a generous gift she is fortunate to borrow. She taps the amulet strung around her neck. "My mother's amulet . . . her gift to me when I was born? That was the token to activate the mech."

The princess shifts in her bed, absolutely rapt, her entire being leaning toward Misery. "So it's true."

"What is?"

Her dark eyes never leave Misery's face. "So the General believes you. They're letting you take on the Heretics, next time they come."

"They are. You don't approve?"

"No. I do," says Alodia Lightning, leaning forward so close Misery can smell the antiseptic they've washed her skin with. Her hand crosses the border of the bed's territory and closes over Misery's, knuckle on knuckle. "I never wanted to believe it, the prophecy surrounding you. But I have to now."

"The first time we met you tried to kill me."

"I thought you deserved death. You were a fraudster, dabbling in things you had no knowledge about. I was appalled by it. Offended. Such gall."

"Why did you think that? After all, I woke the Tear of Assan. Could I have if I were a fraud?"

The princess withdraws to the shelter of her bed, coy now, curling her knees toward her face. "How much do you truly know about the prophet of Calister?"

"As much as any child would, from what I heard and saw on the waves. The news. The bulls. Why?"

Alodia Lightning lurches forward once again. A strange glitter in her eyes—a madness, almost. "I was the prophet of Calister."

Silence for a long, stunned moment. Then laughter bursts out of Misery like a boil lanced. "You? Come on. You're my age. And the Imperial princess. How—"

"I was a child," she says. "And the Church kept an airlock seal on my identity. Do you want to hear the story, or not?"

"Please." Misery presses her knees together and shuts up. Starts to listen.

"My father died when I was a child," Alodia Lightning says, curling back upon herself. "We were very close. I was his favorite. When he died I was devastated. Inconsolable. They tried to distract me. Tried to pacify me. But I was broken inside. No salve or kind word or pretty trinket was going to fill the chasm where he had been. He was gone, he wasn't coming back."

"That must have been hard," Misery says. Using the sympathetic tones she learned from her brother as he ministered others on Rootsdown.

A shrug. It was a long time ago. "The Throne feared I would go mad, that the nullvoid would claim me, as it was already beginning to claim my mother. So they brought out a new salve. An experimental drug, which they administered to me." She tilts her head up, gazing into the lights of the ceiling. "It worked. I felt better, I had more energy, I wasn't in bed constantly embarrassing the family. The drugs shut a mains in my head. My emotions were gone. I felt nothing. I was *free*. The drug was like magic, a miracle. I didn't have to feel anything anymore."

"But?"

"But there was a price. One that I didn't recognize back then. I started having dreams, powerful ones, frightening ones. Sometimes they came true." She rests her hands on her knees and her chin on top of them. "More often than not, they came true. Or some version of it, anyway. If someone was going to betray the Throne, I would dream of it before it happened. I could predict Heretic attacks. Troop movements. I would have dreams where I'd be in the commanders' minds."

"The Heretic commanders?"

"Yes. My abilities did not differentiate by fealty."

"And what did you think about all this?"

"I was a child. What did I think? I don't know. The grown-ups seemed to like what I was saying. I just went along with the flow. Wherever they took me, there I went.

"Back then, I was Grandmother's favorite. I was latched to her hip. She asked my opinion on court proceedings, individual nobles, minister supplicants. I was her oracle. Her little silver child. And I was so serious about my pronouncements, so *calm* so *collected,* nothing like they thought a child should be, that everyone believed that I had been divinely inspired."

She stops herself short, wets her lips. "The Church, too, wanted me. Gave me a name for public consumption: the prophet of Calister. Named after the hall of residence my brother and I had been sent to after Father's death. All the predictions I made— the Tear of Assan, everything, I made in this state. It was all very secret. I suspect that back then, just as much as now, the Throne and the Church did not get along well. And they didn't want it known that a member of the royal family had been bestowed this divine gift, or whatever." She shrugs. "As I said, I was little. People asked my opinion and I answered. Grandmother doted on me. I liked it. I stopped missing my father."

"And what happened?"

"Everything has a price, you know. The salves were killing me. I got sick. I almost died. So they stopped the doses." Alodia Lightning snorts, a sardonic noise. "And you know what? When they took the drugs away, they took the visions away. They hadn't come from some divine source. They were the product of a drug-addled mind."

"That's what you told yourself afterward," Misery says.

The princess leans back, almost dreamy now. "So it ended. My grandmother was so embarrassed, she stopped talking to me. It killed my mother, you know. The shock of it all. My brother became Emperor. My darling older brother Abiel. He loathed me. He had been so jealous when I was the chosen one, and now that I had fallen out of favor he never let me forget it. Ever."

"Not very kingly of him," Misery murmurs.

"It gets worse," Alodia Lightning says. "Those drugs fucked me up for life. My body never recovered. I can't take normal salves anymore. My brain no longer makes half the chemicals it should. I take a dozen pills each day to keep my nervous system functioning. So you know. It was all worth it."

"You were bitter about it."

A volley of dry laughs shakes her narrow frame. "I ran away. I tried to be someone else, in places no one knew me. I ran salve lines. Made a name cooking tripsalves. But they caught me eventually. Dragged me home like a whelp. Pyrex Imogen was supposed to be my guardian, you know. Because Grandmother couldn't handle me. Couldn't stand the sight of me."

Misery puts a hand on her shoulder, the barest touch of skin against shielded flesh. Alodia Lightning makes no move to flinch away. "I know what it's like to be hated by family," she says. "To want to run away. That's my story too." More than the princess knows. The self-hatred, the thought of being irreparably broken—those things live in Misery's marrow too.

A fierce smile crosses the princess's face, more teeth than

necessary. "When I first met you," she says. "When I was angry at you. I knew that you were a lie, that you were lying on top of lies. I know how all the prophecies happened. I had a theory, see. My theory was, the salves let me read other people. In dreams, when I was awake. That's a thing they can do, you know? Telepathy. There's a huge branch of research, here and on the Capital. It's very rudimentary. Doesn't work on normal people. But I thought I had it, you know? I was picking up all these clues about people's inner lives, and together with the knowledge I had as Imperial princess, in the center of all that power . . . My salve-muddied brain wasn't predicting the future. It was synthesizing probabilities from points of data. Like a human AI."

Misery pulls her hand away. "So telepathy was more plausible to you than prophecy?"

"It was," Alodia Lightning says. Eyes wild, teeth glinting. "I refused to believe in a Larex Forge. Stupid stories that people made up because they're chickenshit in a scary universe. But I refused to believe in a god that cruel."

"And then I came along."

Her lips widen. "And then you came along. And you were a liar too. Another purveyor of bullshit. I thought I knew you. And you thought you knew too." She reaches out, crosses the gulf again. One oval nail taps the gleaming surface of her amulet. "But this. How did I predict this? You, a thousand galaxies away, already living your life. Already set in motion. You, coming to me. You, making what I had said real."

"Almost like it was preordained," Misery says.

"Almost like it was preordained." Alodia Lightning's voice drops to a whisper. She ducks her head forward. "So. I believe. I believe it now. Do you?"

Misery stares at her. Princess. Prophet. A dear comrade, a tender, living thing. A miracle before her. There are threads in Misery's life story only now being made whole, the missing pieces stitched into the gaps one by one. But these days have been a revelation for Alodia Lightning, a straightening of the tangle of her life. Suddenly, it all makes sense. The two of them are mirrored, in tandem, one of them explaining the other. Almost like it was preordained.

"Yes," Misery says at last. The conviction hardens as the syllables leave her mouth. "I believe. I do."

21

In sleep, Misery Nomaki dreams.

She stands in a desert she knows too well. Home. The crags of old mines in the distance, the faces of inhospitable bluffs casting deep shadows across the blasted land, around her the struts of ancient metal as monuments to human industry. The familiarity of the environs wakes the nostalgia in her marrow. That ache. A loneliness. She turns, thinking of finding the town and its twisty alleyways reeking of sewage water. She longs for the reef she grew up in, where Mother and her warm arms wait. Misery has barely dreamed of Mother since she died, a situation she's grateful for—why torture herself with things that can never be? But right now she wants Mother. Wants to tell her she was right all this time. Let her see what her little pickle has become.

But dream-Rootsdown is not like the Rootsdown she remembers, and there is no way out of the desert. She walks in the direction of her hometown, only to find herself back where she started. So that's how it is. Ozone on her tongue, in the back of her throat: this isn't a dreaming where she's in control. Her worldmap is locked and she has an objective to head to. And she already knows what—or who—she will find.

She crosses the burning gulch, letting that acrid taste guide her forward. Her destination lies deep in the mech graveyard. The sand eats her footsteps as she walks. Strangely she feels no apprehension, no anxiety. Her mind has been armored by the Grace of the Larex Forge, and she has nothing to fear. Not void, not delusion.

A figure stands in the shelter of the constructor mech she

named Daisy in the real world. She recognizes that shape: slender, loose-robed, sandy hair billowing in the ersatz wind. Jericho. She falls toward him as though he has developed gravity.

He's fixated upon the shape of the dead mech and doesn't turn when she steps into the radius of his body heat. "This is where you grew up, isn't it? It's a harsh land."

"Shit's hard in the boonies," she says. "It is what it is."

"You're a survivor. You've fought every step of your way here."

"I'm glad for it. It made me what I am."

Jericho turns. Studies her with hooded eyes. "You seem different," he says. "You've been gone for a while. Did something happen?"

Of course he would know; he lives in her head, after all. "My eyes were opened," she says. "I've learned the truth about myself. About who I'm supposed to be."

"The seraph test went well, then."

He folds his hands before him, a paragon of peace and calm. No wonder she likes being here. A false sense of refuge from the sharp edges of the world. She says: "I found it, the archangel mech I'm supposed to pilot. The reason I was brought here all along."

"I see."

Misery scrutinizes Jericho. Now that her mind has been enlightened she sees him clearly for what he is: the true nullvoid that has lived within her all these years. Her mother's dark gift to her. She shouldn't allow herself to linger in the embrace of her delusions. But her dreams keep drawing her here, and that has to be a sign. All her life she has feared the taint of her mother's legacy. She ran from the specter of voidsickness that lives in her blood. She watched delusions shred her mother's mind until there was nothing left of her, and thought she would prefer death if the voidsickness came for her. Misery's life has orbited this phobia for as long as she's had memory and the architecture of her soul was shaped by its gravity, an accretion disk surrounding this singular terror.

But things have changed. Held in the protective grip of the Larex Forge, she knows she can no longer be hurt by the nullvoid. This gentle delusion can do her no harm. How soft it is here, how perfectly beautiful. She has no fear. As long as she acknowledges the hallucinatory nature of her dreams, she has control over what they can do to her. And what they can't. She holds all the power. The Demiurge is showing her the way, breaking down the rock and ice of her and releasing her from dread, shaping her into the mighty shield she can be.

"I know what you are," she says to Jericho. "It's all right. You don't have to pretend."

The delusion's brows crinkle. "And what, precisely, do you think I am?"

"A mirage. The nullvoid working through me, sucking up my wants and spitting out something that can lead me astray. Something to whiteout my focus and motivation, to drive me to madness and distraction."

"A distraction, you say?"

"It won't work, though. I can see through you. And you're a nice delusion. But I know my mission and my duty."

Jericho looks slightly baffled for a moment. Then he bursts into laughter. "That's sweet, Misery. You think I'm the man of your dreams."

She likes the way his face crinkles with joy. "You're not too bad. I could do worse."

He shakes his head. "Why are you still here, then? If you know that I am a delusion, would it not be easier to simply walk away? To resist the temptation?"

A good question. She understands now that Jericho was born from a deep well of loneliness, a need for companionship and understanding that she has been denied her whole life. She has that now in the real world, the waking world. Does she need the delusion any longer?

"I like it here," she says. "And I enjoy the challenge."

"Very well. I shall then do my utmost best to be a good challenge. Perhaps I can still charm my way into your heart."

He's cute. He's got that going for him. Misery doesn't mind. As long as she knows what the deal is—as long as she keeps her thoughts strong and clear as water—she'll be in control. She can't lose.

She smiles. To the delusion, she beckons. "Come here. There's plenty left to the night."

22

Of course they won't pitch the archangel into battle with the Heretics while it's untested. The General may be working off faith, but they are no dithering fool. As soon as humanly possible they put Misery back in her archangel mech. They want to see what this miracle can do. They want a glimpse into their glorious, triumphant future.

Misery welcomes this decision ecstatically. There is nowhere in the universe that suits her more than the womb of the archangel she was destined to pilot before the clay of her was formed. In that holy seat archangel and Messiah become inseparable parts of one whole, seed buried in fruit, the universe melting before them, becoming as a song to a musician. Space and time, the great auteurs circumscribing and limiting the existence of the mortal Misery, are mere notes in that orchestration, not but a simple thread of melody and harmony in a greater arrangement. Human language, designed to describe human senses, has no words to describe Misery's perception of the cosmos when zie is transformed, when zie is weapon. When the archangel Misery swings the blades in hir hands and feet, that movement does not come about or register in the way a mortal body speaks to its mind. It is wavelength. It is mathematical function. It is a state of being.

Facing the archangel Misery are the three seraphim controlled by the remaining pilots of Ono Red-2. A cynical calculation: if something disastrous happens, the disaster would at least be contained to one serving. Ono Red-2 is still the General's dirty secret, hidden from sight and knowledge of Throne and

Emperor. Why should other, legitimate servings suffer if something goes wrong? Sunyata Diamond accepts the General's suggestion and bears the brunt of her pilots' responses. Spider, with his mix of insecurity and anxiety. Ghost's intense curiosity. And Alodia Lightning, having recovered from her ordeal, brimming with strange confidence.

And yet none of them can match the abilities of the archangel Misery Nomaki. These poor creatures are tied to the feeble directions of their human pilots. Still bound by force and mass and acceleration, constrained by the shortcomings of human mind and flesh. Easy to block. Trivial to evade. When Diamond gives the signal to begin their assault, Misery bats them away like mosquitoes. When they come forward, swinging their blades, the archangel Misery blocks them with the aegis borne on hir legs. When they coordinate their attacks, the archangel Misery has more than enough limbs and more than enough speed to counter them. Zie dances between these puppets on strings, reveling in hir dexterity and strength. How can they hope to face hir when they are shackled by their mortal limitations?

One of the seraphs is different. The archangel Misery spies it on the edge of formations commanded by Diamond Sunyata, shunted into a support role: the mech piloted by the Lady Lee Alodia Lightning. She glows like a star at the heart of her assigned unit, and the archangel Misery knows they underestimate her potential. The princess of the Faithful plays her role with perfect fidelity, but her changed nature cannot escape Misery's keen omnipotence. A little too much fluidity in her motion. A bit too much freedom. She, like Misery, has been freed from her limitations.

Fierce joy burns through the archangel Misery. Not the weak human filaments of biochemical signaling, but real joy, the purity of celebration, an abstract and universal concept. Zie loves this. It is what zie was born to do. Hir blades hunger for the destruction of battle, real battle. And hunger is thought of as a human thing, a mortal thing, a need driven by the myriad requirements of a soft organic body unable to power its own engines of existence. But it is also a universal want, a fundamental force. A free radical hungers for an electron pair. A negative hungers for a positive. The archangel Misery wants to fight. The archangel Misery hungers to destroy.

When Misery comes back in, when the archangel is returned to its spot in the middle of the Butchery and she detaches from it, when she is fully human again and beholden to gravity and the laws of physics, she stands on the pilot's landing between the door and the command center and looks up. The lights of the Butchery, enormous bright-white strips of holy opal suspended from the ceiling, turn her vision purple and green when she shuts her eyes. This human body, which she has inhabited for some twenty years, seems so peculiar all of a sudden. You don't notice the quirks until you're shown something else. Something superior.

The other pilots shuffle behind her, silent, each cloaked in a mantle of private thoughts. Even with their inexperience they know the battles they fought were abnormal. Nothing like the simulations. They were absolutely outclassed.

Diamond comes to meet them, accompanied by Dr. Sower. Her captain is radiant in her exhaustion. Shining with pride at her defeat. "I've never faced an adversary like you," she says. "I've never seen a unit that could move as fast and react as fluidly."

"If I didn't know better, I'd say I was looking at a Heretic unit," chirps Dr. Sower.

Silence falls. Misery says nothing, but she can feel the heat radiating off Alodia Lightning, who has come to stand beside her. Diamond smooths over the doctor's faux pas by saying, "This is divine will. When next the Heretics come, they will not be prepared for what they will find."

"Of course not," says the doctor.

"We have held them off for long enough," Misery says. Who's

we? She's been here for less than two months. It doesn't matter. "The next time they come, we destroy them."

Dinner is awkward. It's bound to be: after touching the apex of the universe, Misery's expected to sit and eat slop in a long hall with the rest of the rank and file in their multitudes. And Ono Red-2 is expected to treat her the same as before, when her supposed powers were unproven and the bounds of her favor extended only to General Tsung. Still, mortal bodies require mortal food, and even the pilot-saints still sit and eat with the techs and other uniformed grunts every evening. It's considered bad form to fuck off and starbathe, segregating themselves from those who can't. A grave insult to the esprit de corps. So Ono Red-2 has to partake in this ritual of eating dinner with the rest. They're stared at as they make their way to their assigned table. The slight turn of a thousand heads, all thinking they're too coy to be noticed, trying to catch a glimpse of the Messiah among them. The banquet of Angelsteeth had watched Ono Red-2's sparring exercise out of acrylglass in defiance of orders handed down by captains who also joined them in breaking those orders. They saw the archangel mech take on three seraphim and dance circles around them all. In the reverence and awe upon the faces turned in her direction Misery knows that the truth of what she has done and what she can do cannot be contained on Angelsteeth Base for long. In the inevitable way of these things, word will spread to the Capital whether the General wills it or not. Whispers will reach the halls where the sulky Emperor lounges on velvet chaises, ignoring the long-simmering war between the Heretics and the Faithful. Things will come to a head, one way or another. The day when Misery leads an army into battle is not far off; it's so close she can almost taste the metallic tang of war. She will bring destruction as she skims the void between stars in archangel form. Her fate was sealed the moment she answered Ruin's call.

How the shape of her life has changed. No matter how high Misery pushed herself up the rungs of Faithful society, she would always have been small. An insignificant creature, working for herself. Now she answers to a higher power. Her wants are not her own, but that of a greater being. She performs the will of the Demiurge: the will of an aspect of the universe. When she fights to get her way, she is fighting for Creation itself.

That her calling is now duty scares her—she is not a dutiful person and has never been. But this is the lot that was cast in her name. Growing up, her brother often extolled the virtue of duty, but he had no idea what that word meant. She'll show him how it's done, that sorry piece of shit.

Ono Red-2 eats quietly. Even Tank's motormouth has been silenced by the weight of the past day. The serving has been gripped by a stiffness, an alertness, ever since Misery returned with the archangel mech. Once they were comrades, but now her fellow soldiers sense a gulf between them, the mere mortals, and Misery, chosen of the Larex Forge. Diamond looks at her differently now. The balance of power in their serving is different now.

Alodia Lightning's silence, on the other hand, sets her apart and catches Misery's attention. She's quiet in a way that tells Misery she has something important bottled up. A secret, only to be shared with Misery. As Ono Red-2 is leaving the dining hall, she makes use of their newfound closeness to press into her personal space. "You seem upset. Is something wrong?"

Alodia Lightning stiffens. Her gaze scans their surroundings furtively—the clamor of Angelsteeth's greater banquet, the chatter of their servingmates. Her voice drops. "Not here. Come to my room later."

—⊦—

When all has fallen still and the lights have dimmed in Ono Red-2's quarters Misery slithers through the dark and taps twice on the princess's door. Alodia Lightning has been holed up in there since they got back, marinating in her secrets. The door slides open for her.

Alodia Lightning's room surprises Misery with its spareness. With the other pilots, chaos set in after weeks of habitation: the trappings of hobbies, trinkets ordered off the waves on impulse, hints of personality. Spider's floor carpeted with unrecycled cast-offs, a miniature diorama of his home city sprouting on a shambled-together table, lights glinting from the tiny floating trains. Tank's room choked with tubing and plastic and the half-finished shells of musical instruments she's building. Even Ghost has accrued a modest display of things they've found they like. But Alodia Lightning's room is bare. Dresser empty, her clothes all tucked into the wardrobe away from sight. Exactly like Misery's. She prickles with delight: a kindred soul, untethered to a life of small, fussy things.

Alodia Lightning sits hands-clasped on the edge of the bed. Her eyes shine with a queer light as she looks at Misery. "When you're in your archangel, what does it feel like?"

Misery knows where this is going. "I can't describe that. It's like being absorbed into something else, something bigger. I'm not Misery when I'm in there. I'm the archangel."

"Is it like dancing? Do you feel like you could dance?"

"I do. I dance." It's a poor descriptor for the beauty of combat in the archangel mech, but it will have to do. "Did something happen to you?"

"Did something happen to me." Alodia Lightning rises from the bed, flush with nervous energy. Tight as wire she paces the length of the bed, fingers laced together, knuckles pink. "You know how I barely passed training? How I could barely respond to anyone's commands in time? The first time I was out in the seraph, it felt exactly like that. I could barely control the unit. It was like a sack of powder, dead weight, I could drag it forward or throw it one length away, nothing in between. Like fighting a gravity well. But not this time." She lurches in Misery's direction, as if throwing herself into her grasp. "You saw how well I fought, didn't you? It was like ballet. I was perfect. I performed better than anyone."

"You did fight very well. I noticed that."

"But there's more." She starts pacing again, but this time so close Misery can smell the faint salt of her skin, feel the heat off her chest. "I was just following instructions, but I didn't have to. I could have broken out. I could have danced. Could have wrestled you, if I wanted to."

"So you can move the seraph freely? The way I do? The way the Heretic units do?"

She reacts as if stung. "The Heretics? Are you saying—no. It's nothing like them. I mean, I don't know— But this felt holy to me. Ordained. Like I've been granted sacred power."

Misery takes her hands to calm her, draw the princess back into her orbit. "The Heretics would replace the Larex Forge, themselves," she explains. "Everything they do they call a miracle. They try to ape the sacred triumphs of the Demiurge. But their achievements are holy only in appearance. Beneath it is the nullvoid."

Alodia Lightning nods slowly. "I'm nothing like that. I have control of my unit, the way you have control of yours."

Misery already knows this. She pretends she did not. "Why didn't you say anything? I'm sure Diamond would like to know. And the General."

Her gaze is feverish. "I didn't. I wanted to keep it secret. I—I thought it was your time. They should focus on you." She pulls away and starts pacing again.

"So something's changed about you. You've been transformed." Misery thinks of that white cocoon Ruin put Alodia Lightning in. How long she spent in there.

The princess worries at her knuckles. "You said that I died in that cavern."

"I thought you were dead. You looked dead." And she was dead. Her heart had stopped. Misery remembers precisely the feeling of carrying Alodia Lightning to Ruin, that horrible meat-weight, devoid of movement, slowly leaching warmth.

"Your archangel brought me back. The Larex Forge. I was dead, and now I live."

Alodia Lightning is so terribly close, and her breath shakes as she sucks in air. Fear or excitement? It could be both. "You think you've been reborn."

"It's the only explanation. I was made whole. Made new. All my shortcomings, corrected. The Larex Forge needs me as a seraph pilot, and now I can pilot seraphs. And this! Look—"

With a sudden motion Alodia Lightning pulls off her shirt to expose the topography of her back, its ridges and valleys verdant with tatts rendered almost black by the diffuse lighting. That dense cover has been cleared in a neat, wide path that runs from mid-vertebra to left hip, a miners' road of pale, untouched skin. "You see it?" she asks, over her shoulder.

"Shit." Misery leans and presses two fingers into the blank space, into the yield of her flesh. She understands the signs. "This was a scar."

"And now it's gone. The tissue dissolved, remade. Zie fixed it all."

"Remade you as a tool." A tool to serve Misery's needs. Blood pulses in her mouth, but she's not sure if it's her heartbeat she's feeling, or Alodia Lightning's. The princess has always aroused a depth of feeling in Misery that she could not articulate, but now it feels entirely different. Her fingers absently trace the patterns across Alodia Lightning's skin. The angular blocks of it, pregnant with meaning. Big and beautiful.

The princess's breath quickens. "The first time I saw you, I wanted to kill you. I didn't understand it myself. I was angry, but it was more than that—I wanted to absorb you. But I think I had it backward. The Larex Forge took me into Hir hands and released me again. Pushed me in the right direction."

Her voice is almost soundless by the time she stops speaking. Misery feels the same desperate emptiness. One hand wraps itself around the princess's hip bone and grips it. Their eyes meet, and then she's peeling off Alodia Lightning's clothes like the skin of a fruit. Their bodies collide as Misery pushes her toward the bed, then Alodia Lightning is sinking into the obedient foam of the mattress, sighing, her knees falling apart, the battle over before it even began. Misery untangles herself from her clothes as her mouth finds the lines of Alodia Lightning's neck, the shape of her clavicles, the textured bump of a nipple. Her body is a solid, breathing form under Misery's, remarkably dependable and yet a surprising delight, the way it moves and ripples as Misery sinks into her. This too is holiness, a pulse in the throat and between the fingers, the soft rush of skin against skin. Coming undone is only half of it. The other side of the journey—the two of them knitting together, the synchronization of their bodies, of cause and effect—is where word incarnates into form. The joining of their flesh is the consummation of their fates. Misery rides high and watches as Alodia Lightning is resculpted by pleasure, novel feelings being shaped on her face.

Afterward they lie together in silence. Misery studies the languid rhythm of her partner's breaths, the intimate geography of her veins and tendons. A calm settles over her like the heaviness of air after a windstorm. Is this contentment? Happiness? She doesn't know. She feels comfortable, that is all. She is so rarely comfortable.

The princess stirs with sleep-laced determination. "I have a request."

"What is it?"

"Call me Lightning," she says, voice muffled by their proximity.

"Your personal name? Are you sure? No one here calls you that, not even the Duke."

"I'm giving you permission," she says.

Misery mouths the word carefully and slowly: "Lightning."

Testing how it fits on her tongue, against her teeth. It's delicious, like a vine-fresh fruit, packed with sweet juices. "Lightning."

A smile curves across Lightning's face. "There. It's yours now."

Misery runs a fingertip under the curve of her lower lip. "It is." That the princess belongs to her now in this intimate way delights her. She lets that thought carry her into sleep.

INTERLUDE 7

Thus did life on Angelsteeth Base enter its next phase. As it discovered a new center of faith, so too had its Messiah. The station found its footing the way a human child learns to walk, stumbling through confused first steps, foolish and eager for more. The commanders and captains of Angelsteeth had, in aggregate, a hundred years of battle experience, but they had never seen a mech like the archangel. They had never seen anyone fight the way Misery Nomaki did. Even the most cynical soldier was moved to imagine a lucent and victorious future, envisioning the end of war and a united Empire, the descendants of Earth's children once again family as intended. The barren wastes of practical, war-worn cynicism could yet yield a bountiful crop of wonder, naïve and sheened with the promise of fairy tales.

This is the way of humans. Your mortal bodies are beholden to millions of years of evolutionary pressures. Your minds seek patterns in the noise, trying to make sense out of entropy. Your love for pareidolia and your search for meaning lead you to see cause and effect where there is none. Not one of you is exempt from these weaknesses of the flesh. No matter how blessed. No matter how exalted. No matter how wise. Misery Nomaki knew this in the core of their bones, and they used it to their advantage. They intoxicated those around them with the promise of a leading role in the story of how the Empire of the Faithful was saved. The promise of being somebody important. There is no sweeter nectar to the human psyche than the thought of being indispensable, and Misery Nomaki forced no one to drink that poison. All they had to do was offer it. When you humans choose a belief for yourself, you hold on to that belief tighter than anything that was simply handed to you. Isn't that true? It was true of Misery Nomaki, too. As you will see. As you should know.

PART THREE

THE SIEGE OF MONKGLASS

23

The Heretics come at night. The alarm song rouses Misery from sleep. An image of her last dream lingers: the long-haired saint in a dark room, speaking inaudibly to her lover. The dream comes by once every few days, regular as an orbit. Her mortal brain has been through a lot, it needs its soft comforts and this dream is a passive fantasy, nowhere near as dangerous as Jericho. Unimportant. She unmoors from Lightning's warm limbs as the latter struggles with her blanket of sleep. Her meds do that to her. Emblazoned across Misery's vision is the stark red of the General's summon. The time has come. Blood sings in her veins. She punches her partner in the shoulder. "We've got to move."

Sealed into the appropriate fatigues Ono Red-2 spills out of the barracks and into corridors frantic with bodies and panic. Angelsteeth Base is on the move. Misery squeezes Lightning's hand once before breaking the connection so they won't impede the flood. The air heaves with electricity; every face they pass is tight-lipped and grim. Yet Misery sees determination in all the small signs: in the lines of Spider's back, in the length of Tank's stride, in the smooth silence from Ghost. It has been a week since Misery returned with the archangel mech; a week since she awakened to the truth. The time has come. Finally they will meet their destined foes through the medium of metal and aegis. It is not fear that governs them. It is hope.

They come to the fork in the path where they will have to split: the pilots to the Butchery, their captain and tech to the command center. Diamond squeezes Misery's shoulder. "Let the Grace of the Forge go with you." Tank is less prosaic: the girl pops her fingers and makes a crude, anatomically impossible suggestion that earns her an impatient knock on the clavicle from their captain. But it delights Misery. "Go with the Forge," she says. The two peel from the pack and vanish in the human tides of emergency.

The system directs the pilots to the Butchery by the cleanest way it knows, avoiding logjams and long go-arounds. Ono Red-2 breaks into a sprint as the lanes clear up. In the cold bosom of the void their enemy approaches on burning thrusters, and every second wasted is a second closer to their arrival. The system parks a battle grid in their collective vision: there's the Heretic triplet of Beggar, Tinker, and Sailor, a triangle of doom shuddering forward on the map. Behind them is something else, an enormous red dot, marked as an unknown by the system, but next to it a lozenge feeds in what the station exterior sees, and there, magnificent and terrible, is the shimmering black wedge of a Heretic destroyer. Bigger than the last one they sent. Was that incident only two months ago? Back when Misery first arrived on the station. Time is fake and elastic. Several lifetimes have passed since then. Her marrow sings with purpose: that destroyer is hers to take out. It has come to finish the job its smaller sibling failed, but it shall meet the same fate.

Then they're in the Butchery, already, and the pilots split to their respective units. "Good luck out there," Spider says. Misery and Lightning exchange one last look. They've talked about this moment. They know what to do.

A flash, and a video plaza beams into their collective skulls: the broad face of General Tsung, waxy with tension. Behind them the lights of the command center blink. "That warship is of a new configuration," they say, straight to the point. "We don't know what its capabilities are. It's likely to have some surprises. Take caution, but use as much force as necessary, as fast as possible. There can be no losses today. Is that understood?" And while Misery returns an affirmation to the system, they continue: "What happens here, today, will define the direction of the war, and the future of the Faithful. Go with the Forge, and make good history."

In the present, her mind a tornado and her body a weapon, Misery cares little about the shape of her life or the trajectory of its arc in future history books. What she cares about, what's driving the engine of her heart, is the thought of her blades cutting through Heretic flesh. Adrenaline blurs the present into a series of snapshots. The archangel, a blaze of white in her vision, nova-bright in her consciousness. Getting closer. Then she's climbing in, being swallowed, stone moving up her legs. The system's heads-up display goes under, sucked in by the archangel. Misery dissolves into the ecstasy of connection. The delight of once again being one with the universe.

The archangel Misery Nomaki slices through the void, limbs fervid with power and the desire to tear into hir foes. The mortal human Misery might be subject to doubts and anxiety, but the archangel Misery Nomaki perceives the universe with absolute clarity. Zie has a single task to complete, and zie will see it done.

Ahead is the Heretic destroyer, a massive wedge of ultraviolet energy in hir awareness. A strange confection, working stone twisted and warped by human hands for human purpose. The archangel Misery can ignore the seraphim that accompany it— mere gnats, irritants better left to the pilots of Angelsteeth and their feeble human biology. The units swarm before hir: four from Xito Green-2, four from Jota Red-4, and the three from Ono Red-2. Among the last group is a brilliant, joyous core of destruction. The seraph controlled by Lee Alodia Lightning, liberated from its mortal limitations. The rest of the serving, the rest of Angelsteeth, does not know what the free seraph can do. The humans Lightning and Misery agreed this would be their backup plan, their great surprise, should things go wrong.

Instructions come from the control room. Xito Green-2 and Jota Red-4 latch onto their targets and begin the tedious, ungainly wrestling they trade in. Ono Red-2 has its instructions as well. But that is of no interest to the archangel Misery Nomaki. Zie rises on thruster engines and locks onto the Heretic warship, hir true enemy. Despite hir omniscience the warship remains frustratingly opaque, defying the will and laws of the Forge. Its shell of black holystone resists knowledge, and the archangel Misery Nomaki cannot elucidate its anatomy. But zie understands that a human ship will have human occupants, and human occupants require the webbed infrastructure in each of these bastardized vessels to stay alive. A human ship will have a human interior. Such things are easily destroyed.

Zie sails forward. Hir blades cannot be denied. Zie will cut the ship open as one cuts open a sacrificial pod, spilling gut and gelatin into the universe. The Heretic warship corkscrews into greater speed, their respective trajectories headed for collision. They share an understanding, then. Their meeting is fated. It's one or the other.

In the background, chaos. Ono Red-2, one seraph short, struggles against Sailor, all their learned patterns inadequate. A serving hobbled before the battle starts. Sailor's bladestrike clips a seraph mech in the shoulder, the one belonging to the manufactured pilot Ghost, which spins out of control, deeply wounded.

The free seraph has seen enough. It has held back in training, exercising patience to keep its secret safe. But now its fellows are in danger, and it can hide its prowess no longer. It stops listening to its captain. Thrusters flare and it shoots straight up before diving at an impossible angle, spinning like a moon past the enemy's attacks. Its blade finds Sailor's golden heart. Sailor did not expect it. Could not have expected it. Did not and could not block the blade. The free seraph has cut right into its pilot's module: the beating heart of any mech, Heretic or Faithful.

Things go to shit. It's like bullet hell. The commlines between seraph and station erupt in confusion and dismay while the battle explodes in a dozen unexpected directions, too much for mortal minds to take in simultaneously.

—The archangel Misery Nomaki catapults toward hir target—

—Light bleeds from Sailor, erupting into solar blaze as its borders shred—

—Laser batteries rake the archangel Misery Nomaki, but energy is matter and matter is energy, and the stone that comprises hir body is more than mere matter, existing on more planes than the physical—

—The free seraph peels away from Sailor's explosion and surges left, toward Xito Green-2—

—Held down by Xito Green-2, Tinker struggles for purchase as the free seraph comes barreling toward it—

—The archangel Misery Nomaki evades the Heretic ship's defenses and lands on its obsidian skin—

—Aegis-yellow blooms from the Heretic ship, hot and desperate, and the archangel Misery Nomaki lets it slide past and over hir like a soap bubble—

—The free seraph, power-drunk, takes off Tinker's head and slices both blades lengthwise—

—The archangel Misery Nomaki turns one arm into a shear of pure energy and plunges it into the black skin of the Heretic ship—

—Beggar, the last enemy seraph, comes loose from Jota Red-4 and hurtles toward the free seraph, incorrectly identifying it as the biggest threat on the battlefield.

This is it. This is how it should be. This is how it was always going to go.

Beggar and the free seraph tangle. Blades spark in combat, close to overload. With both units unfettered, their true potential unlocked, they should be equals, but one of them is soft, too used to drones with limited movesets, while the other is a born fighter, hungry with ambition and the desire to prove itself. The Heretics doomed themselves witsh their complacency. Limb pushes against limb, blade catches against blade.

Then, a slip, and Beggar breaks loose a blade arm to hew into the front leg of its enemy. The free seraph recoils, wound-struck, and Beggar has an opening to deal a finishing blow. But fresh arms seize its limbs: the other units from Ono Red-2, on standby, under their captain's watchful eye. The free seraph does not hesitate. It sends its blade directly into Beggar's heart.

Perched on the Heretic destroyer, the archangel Misery No-maki pushes its arm-blade deeper into the coated skin. But zie's not carving through it. Zie's decided on something better. This blade is a conduit.

Holystone defies the pulpy understanding of human minds, trapped in the Newtonian constraints of their mortal realm. They do not understand that matter is merely a front for other things, and the faces shown to them by holystone are not per-manent, that holystone by its nature is multipotent. Some facets more than others. The archangel Misery Nomaki is right now turning, turning, and turning those faces, disrupting the ecosys-tem of the Heretic warship, pushing its guts inside out, deacti-vating all the functional slices of its machines. Imagine, if you will, a human body, its liver transformed into bone and blood into keratin, and you will understand the particular nature of the destruction that spreads through the Heretic ship. The ship bucks, desperate to shake off its executioner, an animal scream-ing as the butcher's blade opens its spine. But it cannot stop what is happening.

Underneath the archangel Misery Nomaki the Heretic war-ship crests into agony. The corruption of its innards has reached the vicinity of energy lines that feed its stonecores. Turn, turn, turn, and a slab of holy pearl transforms into holy tigereye, and the sudden surge of energy rips those lines apart, one thing leads to another, then the stonecores are out of control, energy spiraling from them like the hearts of suns, then there is no Heretic warship, only a furiously expanding ball of heat and light, visible from every portal on Angelsteeth, so bright it obliterates the shape of every combatant on the battlefield.

When the light clears only twelve slender figures hang in the velvet of the void: the three servings, and the archangel Misery Nomaki. They are victorious. They have prevailed.

"What I don't understand," says the General, "is why you said nothing."

They're not in the interrogation room. This is where Misery first met Ono Red-2, the large and long conference room at the top of the station. It feels like an interrogation, however. The same layout erected, with Lightning and Misery on one side. The princess has a hand—long, cool, hard—latched around hers. On the other side, the same panel of stakeholders: Diamond, the Duke, Major Tsung. And the General, leading the charge. Misery can read them so much better now: the threads of unease and dismay, the echoes of the shock they felt still rattling around, surfacing on their expressions as little bursts of anxiety. They don't understand why they were lied to. They thought they kept enough secrets that no fresh ones might ambush them. They're suspicious of what else they don't know. What other truths are concealed from them in places they can't see, in places they can't reach, in places they wield no power. Foolish. Misery has nothing but contempt for their worries. After all that's been done, after all that's been achieved, they still worry? They need to be set straight.

Lightning sits tall, spine a steel beam, eyes bright with fervor. "I said nothing because the truth was not mine to tell. It was not time for me to reveal it. I would have been told so otherwise."

The General's frown deepens. Unused to being on the wrong end of need-to-know. Their words come out sharper than usual, syllabled hard enough to cut fruit. "You are soldiers under my command. Your first duty is to report such things."

"Our first duty," Lightning says, "is to a higher power. The seraphs and the archangel are under Hir jurisdiction. Or have you forgotten that they are gifts from the Larex Forge? Have you started to take them for granted?"

She slips into this mode so easily, her path oiled by her memories of prophecy as a child. It pleases Misery how well their respective upbringings have prepared them for their roles. Their destinies so clear in hindsight. In truth, they kept their secret between them because they liked it. The intimacy of their shared deviancy. But it feels right to explain it like this. An explanation truer than truth.

Misery says: "The Larex Forge has dominion over everything, but most of all over these gifts Zie has bestowed upon us. We beckon to Hir call, and no one else's. This," she says, leveling her gaze directly at the General, "is something you should understand. Are we not all servants to the same cause?"

Silence descends upon the room. The two accused, absolutely unapologetic. And why shouldn't they be? Have they not secured the greatest victory Angelsteeth has seen in all its years? Instead they're being reprimanded like children with their milk teeth still attached. This sensation is familiar to Misery, but this time she will not stand for it. This time she has the force and fury of cosmic righteousness on her side.

Finally, the Duke sighs. "She's right, Wolf. This has gone beyond military jurisdiction. I think you know what needs to be done. You've resisted bringing Imogen on for a week, but I think it's time. The Church has to get involved."

The General folds their arms, paces, struggles with their warring instincts. It is true that they started the ball rolling down the hill. Now that it has gained so much momentum they can no longer control it, they are uneasy. The nature of the military soul is one that prizes discipline and known outcomes above all.

Deeply at odds with what faith commands. And yet they are two sides of the same coin.

Finally, a deep sigh. "I cannot deny what has happened today. Nor can I hide it for long. Our long-term enemies have been vanquished. A new enemy, one we should have feared, was instead destroyed. Not only should the Church get involved, so should the Throne."

"What we saw today will change this war for good," says the Duke. "This is a good thing. A blessed thing. We should be glad."

Lightning tightens her grip on Misery's hand. The General says, "We are grateful." Half to themself, half to those listening.

Across the span of the room, visible only to Misery, the angel Ruin sits cross-legged in the air, a recalcitrant swirl of mirth. "No more direct guidance will come from the Larex Forge," zie says. "You were called, and now you are in the place Zie needs you to be. Left to do as your heart directs you. It does not worry you, does it, Misery Nomaki? Do you fear that your heart will guide you wrong?"

Still the angel tests her. Zie is wrong. There is no fear in her heart. Has she not already proven her worth and her power? The Larex Forge chose correctly. This is what must be.

24

Angelsteeth parties hard. Under the shell of austerity and military discipline its guts have always been swollen with distraction and vice, as such things tend to be. From inside closets and under metal plating emerge the paraphernalia of illicit joy, free to exist in the light at last. Boxes of juice and the pink bottles of tripsalves. Dizziness riots through the corridors and bright places of the station, equal to the euphoria in the shadows and behind closed doors. The enforcers don't look the other way. They too down their glasses, leaving them sparkling and empty. The enemy is vanquished. The prophecy has come true. For once, there is nothing to hide from the sight of the Larex Forge.

Ono Red-2 heads to the big party, organized for those whose celebrations must end in a haze of forgetting and chemical re-crimination. The location: Blacklights, the upscale bar that Misery has never gotten the chance to visit. Partygoers spill out into the corridor in a loud, messy whorl. Misery knows too well this flavor of abandon: pupils blown on tripsalves, smiles sloppy with cremoline. Hands everywhere and greedy. Their serving is recognized at the door and let in, despite the crowd.

Blacklights is a double-tiered affair, walls darkened metal and lights radiation-blue. The bottom half is largely dance floor, bodies churning mad with song, jostling against one another. Sweat and alcohol sublime into a thick soup. Ono Red-2 trickles through the crush, elbows in ribs and breaths caught in the cups of their ears, until a pink flasklight swivels and directs its cherry beam into Misery's face. Recognition hits and a roar goes up from the crowd. The dancing stops, even though the music continues, pulsating and blood-hot. The waters of the dance floor part for Ono Red-2, and a wave of adoration follows Misery as they cut through the room. A sea of supplicants yearns for contact with their Messiah; fingers grasp furtively across the gap and fragments of prayer split the air. Misery recalls her brother, hands filled with holystone—was it a lump of holy ruby or holy sapphire they kept in that chest?—threading the pews on feast days, the sway of the congregation as they reached to brush hands across that luminous surface. She never cared for that kind of reverence, but now she sees the raw animal power it bestows upon the one who wields it. But she has to be careful. This fire could go wild at any moment, lashing out like a tongue of holy obsidian.

"Let's get upstairs," Diamond says. "Less of a ruckus there."

Upstairs is for officers only and Tank isn't interested in its stuffy bounds. She convinces Ghost to stay with her on the dance floor. They split: Diamond, Spider, Lightning, and Misery ascend. It's quieter above, the music subtly baffled, the thin ring of byway packed with small clusters of people, drinking and talking but not dancing. They find space in half of a dim-lit alcove, vaulted ceiling high enough it doesn't feel intimate. Diamond gets them canisters of peach-laced cremoline, which Misery downs in two gulps, spilling froth down her chin. The alcohol hits hard and fast; around her the room fuzzes into pleasant noise and light. Touch and sound grate less. While Lightning wanders over to talk to Spider, Diamond settles next to Misery on the circular foam of the couch. "You look better," she observes.

"Better than what?"

Diamond laughs softly, but there's no real mirth in it. "You've looked like death for most of the day. The fight took a lot out of you."

"I am death," Misery intones, "destroyer of worlds." An old story from an old story, quoted over the millennia. Misery feels particularly apocalyptic now; every time she shuts her eyes, every time her attention drifts, her mind turns alien again. She tastes life as an archangel, bright and blessed and terrible. A being for whom the galaxy is a plaything. When she clenches her fist she remembers the sensation of her blade in the flesh of the Heretic warship, the electric surge of holystone transforming under her.

Diamond takes a sip of cremoline and stares at a spot between her feet. The carpeting here is velvet, plush, a galaxy of luminescent pinpricks adorning the fibers. They're in civvies for the party, and the golden mesh of her captain's overshirt drapes over the tension in her shoulders and core as she leans forward. Misery sits very still to listen, waiting for Diamond to let loose the troubles lodged in her psyche and held there for years.

"I have to thank you," her captain finally says. "But I don't know how."

"You don't have to thank me." Her patience draws from ministerial wells. "We are all vessels of a greater will. All of us have a part to play."

"Many of us are called, but not all of us answer." Guilt plays over Diamond's face. "I— You know, I've lingered on this station so long. Failing every psych test they threw at me. I could tell that they were eager to have me back into the fray. The Church, for certain. The Throne, too, strangely; I think they thought I would be a good tool in the negotiations. But I didn't want to return to active duty. I was glad, each time I failed." She looks at Misery, despondent, waiting to be chastised. "Isn't that awful? Such a cowardly thought?"

"But you were active. You helped with the raids."

"That was nothing. I think they expected more of a war hero."

She downs another quarter of the canister; Misery watches her throat bob, fascinated. "It's not nothing to those who live here. You've probably saved them more times than they can count. Whether they know it or not."

Diamond meets her gaze, finally, and in the knit of her brows is the great conflict that plays out in her: the desire to be forgiven, versus the desire to be punished. She's lived in guilt so long she's forgotten how not to. "The psychs kept saying my talents would be of better use elsewhere. And you know, they weren't wrong. But I was—I'm weak. I couldn't go back to the battlefield, not after what had happened."

Misery presses upon that tenderness. "What did happen? It was never made clear to us."

"You . . . I suppose myths travel differently through the duchies. What did you hear, from the outskirts? Indulge my curiosity."

In the pit below, Tank has won control of the music box, fiddling with color and temperature, squaring waves and pushing envelopes. The music turns deep and throaty, edged with sinister intention. Sunyata Diamond is a figure of legend across the Empire, in the vague way one becomes a legend through headlines and two-minute blurbs, all nuance and context stripped away. A few bare-bones lines of verb, object, and consequence, the spaces in between subsequently filled by the febrile human imagination and its propensity for tale-telling. An accidental collision becomes a herald of fate, a strangely shaped birthmark a harbinger of doom. Misery first knew of Diamond as a beacon of great brilliance, one of the youngest in Faithful history to captain a destroyer. The reams of holos and picture waves of that ceremony, the woman in her twenties with her crisp uniform and shorn hair and fierce expression. A few months of silence, and then she's in the news again: as a victor, a survivor, of a vicious attack by the Heretics. A creature named Esse Temple had commandeered her loathsome fleet and attacked Diamond's ship during a routine patrol. The stories about this Esse Temple were wild too: a Heretic who had inhaled the nullvoid whole, who could turn her body to stone, who could turn herself the size of a mountain, an asteroid, a sun, who had obliterated a deep space station with one blow from her godlike fist.

What Misery knows concretely, for sure, the part that isn't made up, is this: "You fought a Heretic fleet that attacked you.

There were ships that we'd never seen before. Somehow you survived and defeated them. It was a miracle, you were a hero. Who knows what would have happened if you didn't stop them. That patrol was in a straight line to the Capital itself. We guessed that was the fleet's final destination. It was a clear violation of the terms of the Truce of Logan. Unprecedented and unprovoked. The incident nearly destroyed the truce."

"I see." Diamond swallows the rest of the cremoline and puts the canister on the floor. "So that's what everyone believes."

"Is it not what happened?"

Diamond's gaze seeks something else parsecs away. "It's . . ." A long exhale. "It's close to the truth, but it's not all that happened."

Misery says nothing, just tilts her head to show she's listening.

A geological sigh. "This was five years ago. There was, in fact, a fair amount of tension across duchy lines. The place I was sent to patrol—on the edge of Duchy Taurus—saw a handful of sorties every day. Meaningless engagements, shots off the bow, tactical retreats, that sort of thing. Lots of saber-rattling on both sides, trying to push the balance of power one way or the other. Political stuff, but it was our lives on the line. It was a balancing act. I had a ship, *The Gloaming*. Cherub-class destroyer. Twelve servings, forty-eight pilots. I—no, we met Esse Temple and her three ships. New models. Something we'd never seen before. She . . ." Here Diamond pauses to take a breath, as if the memory burns her still. "Her ships could jump, the way their seraphs can, and she jumped into the core of *The Gloaming*. Tore it apart." She shivers. "I still dream of it, the sound it made, that unholy screech . . ."

"But you survived. Spider survived."

"I don't know why we did. There were a couple of others, but . . ." One thumb makes a line across the knuckles of the other hand, back and forth. "I could never understand why I had been spared. Every priest I spoke to said it was preordained, said it meant the Demiurge had plans for me, and I wanted to deck every single one of them, right there." Her fist goes white-tipped as she tightens it, bone straining against skin. "My crew were good people. Upstanding. Brilliant. So many of them kept the faith better than me. If they weren't good enough for the Larex Forge . . . I kept asking, why me? I never got an answer."

"You doubted," Misery says gently.

The shame on her face could blister skin. "I—could not think of a reason that satisfied me. And I began to think, maybe it's because there is no reason. None at all. There's no reason because it's all random. Just chance. And the Larex Forge—"

Her words falter. Misery touches the back of her hand, gently, and she reacts like it's heated metal. After all this, she still does not believe she is worthy of grace.

"I'm sorry," Diamond says. "I don't know why I'm saying all this."

"You are in pain," Misery says. "There's a wound in your soul and it hasn't closed."

Diamond shuts her eyes, and Misery knows that sensation too well. She knows the weight carried by the eyelids, the heat and inflammation swelling along its edges, collecting in the ducts. In the background, in the corner of her vision, Lightning has glued herself to Spider's hip. Misery understands the shape of that interaction at once, the creep of a hand around the waist, the soft lowering of eyelids. Something for later.

To Diamond she says: "Do you know the Parable of the Stonehunter?"

Diamond sits up, looks up. She knows it, of course. Anyone raised under the canopy of the Church would. "A stonehunter, working alone, was exploring an asteroid zie landed on."

She pauses, looking for guidance, and Misery reels a thread forward: "Zie explored, but the surface was harsh and jagged, its dust as barren as the void. All zie found . . ."

"All zie found was a series of scattered outcroppings. Silver and covered in carvings. Zie thought they were important, but could not make out what they were for. They seemed entirely random. Meaningless."

Misery says, encouragingly: "Zie climbed up and down the mysterious pillars, scanned them, even tried explosives to take pieces of them. Still they eluded hir. Until . . ."

"Until zie sat down," Diamond says. "Exhausted and despondent, zie sat upon a rock outcropping high over the asteroid's surface. And zie saw that the outcroppings made a pattern. Up close, zie had only seen strange pillars, and zie thought the pillars were the whole story. Fooled by the size and shape of the stone, zie thought they were hir reward. But they were not. Zie could not see the pattern, until zie had stopped hir questing and simply . . . looked from afar. From that lofty vantage point, the pillars formed an arrow. A gesture, a direction. Zie followed the guidance of the pillars and found a cavern full of treasure. A crown of holy ruby. Engines for a ship. And hir faith in the Larex Forge."

Misery nods. "Do you understand?"

Diamond folds her hands together, her expression softening. "The Larex Forge always has a plan, a reason for things happening. Even if we can't see it for ourselves. From above, from Hir vantage over us, there is a pattern."

"That's right. So it doesn't matter if you don't understand why you were saved. You were, and that's the important part. The Larex Forge has a plan for you, even if you cannot see it."

"No. You're wrong."

"I'm listening." She enjoys the steel that has crept into her captain's voice. And she does listen, even though Diamond telegraphs her thoughts clearly on her face. She knows what's coming.

"I can see the Forge's plan for me. I see it clearly now. The last few months . . . I doubted, at first. But not anymore. I know I was saved to fight, and I know that together we will deal the fatal blow that will destroy the Heretics. The reason I told you all this—the reason I started speaking in the first place—is I simply wanted to tell you. I wanted you to know the sins of my past. So that—so that you'd know. So that you could absolve me. Then I could stand by your side bright as a star, banishing the void."

"It's not for me to grant you pardon," Misery says. "But in speaking your sins, alone, the Larex Forge has already exculpated your mistakes. You are forgiven, Diamond."

Her captain exhales, and the shudder that runs through her is part relief, part epiphany. Misery feels it in her own chest. She touches Diamond's hand again, the lightest contact, and her captain nods.

"You know," she says, "one of the greatest lies of that story, and the one I hate the most? We didn't defeat the Heretics. After destroying my ship, Esse Temple fled. She jumped away. So she's still out there, biding her time. Roaming the void between the stars. That thought has haunted me every night since." Under Misery's fingers, Diamond's hand clenches into a fist. "But her time will come. I am sure of it. One day we will destroy her. I shall see to it myself."

Sometime in the hazy length of the party, Lightning has convinced Spider to stay the night. They meet in the bare sanctuary that is Lightning's room, him leaning against the wardrobe, arms barred across his chest, hips canted at a perfect angle and held still. Lightning, parked next to the bed, carefully scans Misery's face for hints of approval.

"Why do you want to do this?" Misery asks of Spider.

He prickles defensively. "We beat the bad guys, I'm horny, do I need more reasons?"

Lightning frowns in her direction. "Just say no if you're not into it."

"I am. I just wanted to make sure we're clear about what's happening here. That we're all on the same wavelength."

"Well. I've put my frequency out there. We gonna fuck, or what?"

Then they're getting undressed, exposing skin for exploration, navigating the angles and interactions between their bodies. The air grows heated, thickens with breath. Misery splits her attention between Lightning and Spider, but it's the latter who draws the most of it. The long confessional from Diamond has opened a thick seam of questions about Spider that she wants answered. Misery tucks Spider's hips between the points of her knees and studies the spill of his tattoos across his arms and chest.

He says, "It's rude to stare," but there's laughter in it.

"Rudeness," Misery says, "is a function of distance. You can only be rude to ones you're not close to. Isn't that true?"

"Speak for yourself," he grunts, but he's shed his carapace of humor and underneath it is something tender, something curious. Misery leans forward and kisses him, catching that expression and locking it in place. Lightning watches closely as Misery eases herself over and onto him and settles her weight right. Rocks back and forth as Spider puts his hands on her hips.

"You're looking at me," he says.

"I could shut my eyes if you want."

He laughs. "It doesn't matter. You'll still be thinking loud enough for me to hear it."

"Oh? You can read minds now? What am I thinking? Go on."

They're moving slow enough to keep their voices calm. Spider says: "I saw you talking with Diamond earlier. So you know everything that happened. Is this just a pity fuck?"

There's no anger in it, just a wryness. A resignation. Misery tilts her hips further back. "Pity? Only if you think that way. I thought we were having a good time."

He thrums, and Lightning envelopes Misery in her arms, from behind. They both watch him as his movements gain momentum. "Your markings," Lightning says. "What do they mean?"

"My shipmates," Spider says, his voice venturing into breathier territory. "One for every person who died. Something that reminds me of them."

Misery rocks on the base of her spine and says, over the tightening of his calves and thighs, "Tell me about them. What were they like?

A moment's reluctance, a slowing in his response to her rhythm, and then it's gone, melting away as he gets into it. Spider begins to talk. About the three hotshots he served with. Twins, Ivory and Fox Quilling, who sometimes completed each other's sentences. Arbiter Milon, whom he was in love with. The camaraderie in the mess hall, the rivalry between teams, the league table they pretended they didn't keep. His unit, Blue-1, always jockeying for pole with Yellow-1. The daily red alerts. The parties to stave off the despair. And the sex. Oh, the sex, wild and happy and unconditional, the boys and girls and nixens he slept with, singly or in pairs or in groups. An infinite number of combinations, an infinite amount of joy. Arbiter had this one trick e did, just like this, and there was one kid from Red-4, Leonardo Friday, who had the most intense climaxes, shaking and shouting like the Forge Hirself possessed them.

The more spills from him the faster they go until his words comes in laser bursts, short and forceful. It was all sex, all the time on those ships, on the frontline, where even salves weren't strong enough to keep them in joy. Not just the pilots, the crew too, even the captain. She came into their multitudes of congress like a comet, like a wandering bird, dipping in and out as she pleased. She was the most beautiful of them all, the most passionate. The way she burned like a sun. The brightest star in their sky.

As he shudders Misery leans over to kiss him and finds his face wet. Lightning's breath is silk against her skin, fingers clawing into her shoulder and back. Misery, at that moment, is one with the canopy of the universe, infinitely generous and expansive.

Afterward they lie tangled and still, cooling skin against

cooling skin. Spider says to the air: "I used to wonder, you know. Why I survived when everyone else didn't."

"You were the only pilot who lived," Misery says, a fact harvested from her chat with Diamond.

A low chuckle, electric in the darkness. "Diamond didn't save me. In the week before I was in trouble, picking stupid fights left and right. Just being an asshole to everyone around. The night before, Diamond took me off duty. Said I wasn't stable. We had a bust-up, she threw me in the brig. Had one of the backup pilots take my place. Radish, their name was. A ship's tech. Next thing I know, things went dark and when I woke up everyone was dead, and I wasn't. That Heretic ship jumped right into us. Smashed every seraph, cut our ship in half. Fucking monsters. Not one of the pilots made it. Most of the tech crew didn't. That jail cell saved me. Double-reinforced and all. I don't know why I was spared. Rewarded for being a piece of shit?"

"Diamond saved your life."

"Kind of wish she didn't."

"That's bleak," Lightning says, mumbling into Misery's shoulder.

Spider's laugh rumbles through their joined frames like thruster bass. "Listen. I haven't spent the last five years failing every psych test for nothing."

"And yet." Misery drums her fingers on the warmth of his skin. "Imagine if you'd passed. Imagine if you'd been released into duty, reassigned somewhere else. We wouldn't have met. Eh?"

"Don't. I know where that's headed. This is preordained, the Demiurge moves in mysterious ways, you were saved for a reason. Blah blah. I've heard that shit. Sat through the sermons. Recited the parables. It doesn't help."

"And what does?" Misery pushes, gently. She has an inkling where his answer lies, but she wants to hear him say it.

Spider is silent, but the tension builds in his body, stiffening his spine. "Revenge." A hand curls into a fist, hard upon her thigh. "The Heretics . . . those murderers . . . I will enjoy crushing them. I don't care about being saved. I want to end them. The Demiurge? Put me in the right place at the right time. I will fucking destroy them."

"That's what I like to hear," Lightning says. The hunger radiating from them is delicious. Misery luxuriates in it as she drifts into sleep.

25

Misery rolls upright into a new dream. She's in the courtyard of a cross-shaped building, two polished black oblongs stacked atop one another, the cantilevered edges gleaming with light from a distant and unknown sun. Trees float over the smooth stone of the yard in large, clear bubbles. The only sounds come from the sheet of water pouring off the side of one block into a huge pool below. Unusual architecture, this: both sleek and impractical. This is a Jericho dream. Beautiful, concise, otherworldly.

She shouldn't be here. She's allowed herself these luxuries on the thinnest of justifications, testing her resolve with these morsels of honey. But she knows, she damn well knows, that if she turns this indulgence over she will find greed pimpled across its underbelly. She wants the emotional comfort of these dreams without the consequences. She is the Messiah, chosen of the Larex Forge. Can she afford to be selfish? She should rid herself of distractions. The Larex Forge has given her the strength to purge the blight upon her soul. She doesn't need this.

She does not need this.

Jericho stands in the shadow of the strange glassy building, gazing wistfully at the ripples in the pool. He looks strangely tired, and the air around him feels sour. There's a hunch to his thin shoulders she isn't used to seeing. Maybe it's her doing, the knot of recrimination that clogs her ventricles pumping poison into the atmosphere of this dream-place. She lets the delusion speak first. Let him show his hand first.

He says, not looking up: "We used to swim here on the temper days, especially when I was younger and we had one every week or so. The water kept warm for a long time. Highest heat capacity and all. Me and Ally, we'd spend the whole day with our chins below the meniscus, blowing bubbles and growing more wrinkly until the pool reached thermal equilibrium. That's what Father used to say. The pool didn't get cold, it reached thermal equilibrium."

She has no idea what he's talking about. "What does any of that mean?"

"You mean the physics? I guess it's hard to explain if you weren't taught. I—"

"Fuck the physics. I'm not stupid. You don't have a father."

Jericho laughs, but it's the laugh of a wounded creature. The laugh of a man stabbed through the chest but refusing to admit that the fight is over. He looks at Misery carefully, top to toe. "Something big happened on the station today."

"It did."

"Were you at the center of it?"

"I was."

"You did something that upset things on the station. Upset people. Everything's very tense."

She laughs. He couldn't be further from the truth. "I destroyed a Heretic ship today."

Jericho goes stiff and pales, his features tightening. The delusion's never been this way and anxiety looks alien on him. "A Heretic ship? What ship?"

"Just like the last time, a warship came with the three units that keep attacking Rootsdown. You know them. Beggar, Tinker, and Sailor. And just like the last time, we destroyed the ship."

"So a ship came with them? What kind of ship?"

"What? Who knows? Who cares? It was a Heretic ship. You think I know what Heretics call their ships? They're roaches to me. I destroyed it. We got the mechs, too. Good riddance."

Jericho turns from her, paces in tight turns, digs his fingers into the flesh of his arms. The delusion has always pretended to be more human than he is, but this wide-eyed toddler act is working her last nerve. "Why are you so upset?"

"There were people on that ship. You murdered them."

"It's war. What is it you think soldiers do?"

He inhales and exhales deliberately, not looking at her. "I didn't think—the war hasn't been that way in ages, I thought—" He runs thin hands through his sandy hair. "So. I see."

In her dreams Misery has never brought up the scores of nobility she sacrificed before the Larex Forge. She's been the bladesaw of the Demiurge, only she's doubly unapologetic about it now. It needed to be done. The masses of the Faithful needed the wake-up call. And yet—why should she confess any of this to a mere delusion? Jericho only serves to entertain her; he has no will independent of her own.

Or does he? Misery presses him again: "Why are you so upset about Heretic deaths?"

"Because they're people, Misery. Heretics are people. I know the Church of the Faithful teaches otherwise, but I didn't think you really bought into that rhetoric."

"Well, you thought wrong." There it is. Misery understands: the nullvoid is trying to seed doubt in her soul. Make her feel bad for what she's done. But she won't. "Haven't you realized? I'm chosen of the Larex Forge. My mother was right about me. What I did today was absolute proof."

"You don't care about killing people?"

"I do care. I care very much about killing voidtouched assholes. I saw my mother ripped to pieces by the nullvoid. Right in front of me, when I was a kid. I'll never stop having nightmares. And the Heretics want us to be friends with the void? Worship the void? They're evil. They're delusional. They want humanity destroyed, is what they want. So I do care. It's my life's goal to end their existence. I won't stop until they're all dead. Every last one of them."

Jericho starts to laugh. Not an arrogant laugh or a joyful

laugh but a broken one, the kind of laugh that's come loose from the rails and gathers pitch and momentum as it ricochets from dirty corner to dirty corner of the psyche. Jericho laughs like a man who wakes in a hospital bed and learns everyone he loves is dead. He laughs like a child who has to watch her mother die and can't do anything because she isn't all-powerful, she can't turn back time and she can't undo the sickness rending the flesh. Misery hates that laugh. She wants to push Jericho into the thermally stable water and hold his head under until he stops moving. Shut the fuck up.

Jericho looks at her, eyes rheumy from laughter. "You really—no, I don't know why I didn't think—"

He starts to laugh again and Misery snaps. She shoves him and he staggers, enough to lose his footing but not enough to fall into the water. Should have shoved harder.

He looks up at her from the ground. "You want to kill every Heretic? All of them? You should start with me, then."

She kicks him in the shoulder and he flops, landing with a thud. No resistance. Misery plants a foot on his chest and wonders what would happen if she stomped on him, just crushed his throat with her foot arch or smashed his skull in. Would his flesh split like a normal person's? Would it be blood that comes out of him, or just ichor? Or—maybe—this is a dream, who knows what could happen? Could be butterflies instead.

Jericho says, "Go on. Do it. I'm a Heretic, you have to kill me."

"You're not a Heretic. You're the voidsickness that I got from Mother. You're a delusion. But you're not stronger than me."

He looks at her, sad. "But I'm not, Misery. I'm a real person. I'm a Heretic, a prisoner like you, except they keep me locked in a cage at the bottom of Angelsteeth."

"You fucking liar."

"I know, I know. I let you think I wasn't real. Like I was one of your delusions. It was wrong of me. I'm sorry. I've been here for a long time. You were the first person I got to talk to like a friend. I was so lonely, and you found me through your dreams. Your abilities, whatever they are, let you connect with my mind. In my sleep."

"Don't be stupid."

"You don't believe me? Look around you. This is where I grew up. You've never seen it before, have you? Where would it have come from? All these places we meet and you don't recognize, they're from Zone Alpha. Where I used to live. Misery—"

She steps on his throat. The bob of his larynx comes through the rubber of her sole as he swallows. She peels her lips back. "Shut up. Shut the fuck up. You're a lying piece of the void and I fed you when I should have killed you." Why did she indulge these dreams? She knew something was wrong but just kept quiet about it. Didn't report it. Didn't tell anyone and let the dreams continue, night after night. Selfish. Stupid.

Jericho speaks in quick, halting sentences: "Just ask anyone. Ask your superiors. Ask Dr. Sower. I'm real, they can tell you the truth—"

She stomps on his throat. Just raises her foot and drives it down with all the weight in her body. Goes through the cartilage with a crunch and a wet sound, and—

Misery wakes into the dark of her quarters, limbs tangled around Lightning and Spider. Heart in overdrive like it's hooked up to holy ruby. The sensation of flesh and bone collapsing still fresh in her mind. She breathes calm into her lungs, letting the tension drain from her muscles. The anger she feels isn't real. It doesn't matter. It was only a stupid dream.

Too late. She's got Lightning awake, warm and worried in the dark. "Bad dream? What's wrong?"

Misery digs her nails into the foam of the mattress. Her chest hurts and sweat prickles along the length of her spine. Fuck. She doesn't have to say anything. Doesn't have to explain what happened. Yeah. Just a bad dream. Nothing to it. No one needs to know about the hold the void still has on her.

Ruin sits on her dresser, well haloed and nuclear-eyed in the gloom. "Dumping your problems out of the airlock again, are we? I thought you'd learned better by now, Misery Nomaki."

She shuts her eyes and clamps her teeth together. Suppresses her first thought, which is that she would absolutely toss Ruin out of an airlock if she could.

"Hey," Lightning says. "What's wrong?"

Now Spider is stirring from sleep too, his soldier's instinct alerting him to a developing situation in the room. Misery can't wipe the memory of her foot going through Jericho's windpipe. The way he looked at her, all resigned and pathetic, before she did it.

She breathes. Saint Agneta's pattern, four in, six hold, seven out. Buries all thought of Jericho deep in the landfill of her heart. They don't need to be brought into this. They don't need their faith in their Messiah shaken. Right now, both their visions are clear; she doesn't need to muddy it with confessions of voidsickness and delusions. Jericho is her burden to bear, and hers alone.

"It's nothing," she says. "A bad dream. Go back to sleep."

Spider obediently settles down, unruffled by the brief interruption to his sleep, but concern gleams in Lightning's eyes. "Are you sure?"

Misery frowns. "Do you think I don't know my own mind?"

"No, I just—you're right. I was just concerned."

Misery closes her hands over Lightning's. In the waking world, away from the weaknesses of her mind, she has control of how things go. "It's nothing to be concerned about. Rest. Tomorrow's a big day." Radiating concern of her own, smothering the princess's worries with softness.

Ruin hovers, verdant with amusement. The angel offers no

judgment; hir duty done, zie merely watches the chosen of the Forge upon their path. "You make the most interesting choices, Misery Nomaki," zie says. Teeth shining like bones at the bottom of a lake bed.

26

In the morning the silver blade of a holy ship arrives under the arches of the station. As promised, *I Will,* class-A diplomatic transport, personal vessel of the Archbishop of Remus, comes in like an asteroid, streaking light across the sky. In her quarters, muscles sore from exertion and neck stiff from interrupted sleep, Misery is greeted first thing by the red bleat of a system message. The Archbishop wishes to see her.

The summons are not evenly distributed; of Ono-Red 2, only Lightning, Diamond, and Misery make their way to the command ring. They're headed to the fanciest meeting room this time. Silence reigns in the long elevator ride to the top. The shadows under their eyes speak for themselves, and the distance between each of their bodies feels deliberate. Exhaustion gleams in Diamond's expression, flecked with uncertainty. So much has happened. So much is yet to come.

In a long room with a long table slotted with holy opal, Misery meets the Archbishop of Remus again. Tall and slender and draped in deep red that interrogates their milky skin, Pyrex Imogen looks exactly the same as they did when Misery last saw them. Framed by starlight and holding court over the vast room, the gravitational center for all the attention in the room. But it's not the same. In the Capital, they had been the adult and Misery the child; those roles no longer apply. The Archbishop regards Misery like someone expecting a long-awaited present. The yearning takes years off their face. Next to them is the Duke of Apis, shining with rapture, and on the other side are General Tsung and Major Reyes. The troupe of sedition, now complete.

"It's good to see you," says the Archbishop, quiet as quick-sand. "Much has changed since we last met."

"It has," Misery says.

"Argan filled me in on the details. What you have done is extraordinary. It seems the prophecy has come to pass."

"It *will* come to pass," she says, a mild correction. She has barely begun her journey; the hardest work is ahead.

Some grunts bring them breakfast, officers' food served on silver trays. Pot-grown roast on buttered grains, thick mugs of milk tea. As the circ network thins the savory fumes Misery studies the expressions of those around her. She's gotten good at reading people, saint or no. The blend of hope and terror in this room is peat-rich and full of potential. Such orchards she could plant in this fertile ground.

"I have come," Pyrex Imogen says, "to ask a favor. Or perhaps I should not call it such. I have come to encourage you upon a course of action."

"It's a good course of action," says the Duke. "The only rea-sonable one, really."

They've talked about this beforehand, the two of them alone. General Tsung and the major know just as little as Misery does. Secrets and machinations. She nods to show she's listening.

"I have been monitoring closely the actions of the Throne. While they remain unaware of the many miracles that have transpired on this station, there is a growing sense of their im-patience with the Church. The Emperor remains spooked by his last brush with divinity, and has chosen to withdraw further into the shells that protect him. He will not entertain audiences, nor will he appear in public. He has, to all appearances, vanished."

"Coward," Lightning hisses.

"We would expect nothing less of him, and the apparatus of the Throne," General Tsung says. "What are you truly asking, Imogen?"

The Archbishop folds their hands, calm as ice and just as

bright. Their food glistens cold and untouched before them. "Word from the inner circles is that the Throne is close to a deal with the Heretics. A refreshing of the Truce of Logan, or perhaps even a cessation of hostilities. An end to the war, but in the worst possible way." They fix their gaze upon the General. "You are, I presume, entirely unsurprised by this."

General Tsung leans back in the silver of their chair, brows heavy. "No. I am not."

"A surrender to the nullvoid," Major Reyes mutters, shaking xer head.

The Archbishop continues: "What I am *saying* is that the miracles here may not be enough to sway the Throne from its foolishness."

Major Reyes slaps the table with a fist, the sound bouncing off the walls like a shot. "We vanquished enemies that have plagued us for cycles. We destroyed a Heretic ship. Will they deny that?"

Pyrex Imogen remains unmoved, still and resolute. "I am telling you what I know. The Throne values making peace with the Heretics. I fear that our achievements here will not sway them. Church analysts think they will take our archangel and present it to the Heretics, whose curiosity over these sacred artifacts is both profane and insatiable."

"Surely not," says Major Reyes. Under the steel-boned exterior xe conceals quiet embers of belief in institutions and faith that logic and good sense will always prevail. Surely the Throne can be persuaded by the undeniability of the miracles xe has witnessed.

"After the injury suffered to their fleet—the loss of the ships and the mechs—they are sure to ask for something in compensation," says the Archbishop. "And the Throne will appease them."

Lightning sets her fork down, grim with knowledge and pessimism. "The Archbishop is right. I know my brother, and I know my grandmother. They would do it." A shake of the head, disgust. "They want to make nice with the Heretics. It's their life goal. You've noticed, haven't you?"

Unease swells like saltwater. The princess is right. A lifetime of appeasement to the Heretics—and therefore the nullvoid—is the common thread that has drawn all of them here, today, in a little knot of sedition. Misery cuts to the quick: "What favor do you wish to ask, Archbishop?"

Pyrex Imogen's face remains impassive, but there's a sigh in their eyes, a slight lowering of the lids like the air's been let out. "We must strike directly at the Heretics. Score a victory so immense, and of such military import, that it cannot be denied. And no, the destruction of a single Heretic ship is insufficient. We must achieve something on a scale never before seen."

The General stiffens. "Are you suggesting invasion? The banquet of Angelsteeth is insufficient. Even with the archangel at our head. To do so would be suicide."

"Nothing quite so bold," says the Archbishop, although the idea fills them with a bright frission. "The Heretics, on the contrary, have had no qualms in entering our spaces. Encroaching upon our territory. Perhaps this is something we could address."

"You mean the siege," Diamond says. "You want to break the siege."

The siege. Her captain can only mean one thing. The siege of Monkglass, which the Heretics have held for nearly a year. Misery has heard of it. Misery hasn't thought much of it. But it makes perfect sense. Now that it's laid before her—of course— this is the biggest incursion into Faithful space—the biggest insult to them—and yet it has been treated like nothing more than a diplomatic standoff.

"I do mean the siege of Monkglass," Pyrex Imogen says.

A sigh ghosts through the room. The siege of Monkglass has stretched for unhappy months. In the grand schema Monkglass Station isn't so important, a vestigial organ on the edge of the

Empire, an old trading post between two smaller duchies that has been eclipsed by newer, faster jump routes. Yet it still bears the crest and colors of the Faithful, and the pride that comes along with it. When the siege first burst over the station, outrage and disbelief flooded the waves, top lede, every development followed second by second by the breathless masses. A hundred Heretic ships, a net around the trading outpost, a toothless Throne that held back on retaliation. And then days turned to weeks, and weeks turned to months, and the nerve circuits electrified by the adrenaline of fresh hostilities went tired and numb. A siege is a siege, a long waiting game, and with no change of status on the horizon the attention of the Faithful eventually lurched elsewhere. Updates slowed and shrank to eight-point at the bottom of bulletins. Misery was aware of the siege in the same dim way she knew of happenings in the Capital. Summarized and distant, filtered of all color and interest. Unless the siege disrupted major supply lines, it had no real bearing on her life. On Angelsteeth, this military installation where the threat of deployment swings merrily overhead, people pay more attention. But there isn't much to see. It provides a blanket of white noise, nothing more.

The Archbishop folds their hands on the table before them. "To break the siege would be to score an unprecedented victory against the Heretics. A gesture grand enough the Throne cannot lock it away or suppress its existence. It will be undeniable. A nova that can be seen from one end of the Empire to the other. A blow that will puncture the nullvoid."

"Enough of this bombast," General Tsung says. "You want us to carry out a major engagement without backup, risking the lives of all the troops who serve here. That's unacceptable to me."

"Or to me," says Major Reyes. "I see why you called it a favor. Dress it up all you want, Imogen, but we all know why you're asking."

"Photon," says Duke Argan, sharply. Tension ices the atmosphere; the Archbishop remains silent but anger gleams off their expression.

"Enough," Misery says. There's too much to parse simultaneously: the senior officers' hard-baked resentment toward civilians, the Archbishop's deeply held knot of pain, the Duke's anger and torn loyalties. Diamond's ambivalence. And the way Lightning brushes her ankle against Misery's, a gesture that seeks assurance as much as it provides it. She doesn't know what is going on exactly. But she does know that the molten moments of these conflicts are perfect places to act. When no one knows what is going on, the loudest voices always win.

She stands, and the room's center of gravity shifts, the weight of all their expectations tilting toward her. Misery spreads her hands, welcoming light into her arms. "The archangel mech was not presented to us as a gift. It is a tool, made to carry out the Forge's will. We are not to use it to settle human vendettas. We follow Hir guidance and none other."

The Archbishop frowns, unsettled. "What, then, is the Demiurge's guidance?"

At the far end of the room Ruin pendulums across the vast, curved viewport, a shining blade drifting among the stars. Zie shrugs as Misery silently casts hir a questing look. "You were chosen, were you not? I am merely an observer. My message has been delivered; now you act upon your own instincts. It is as it is."

Her first instinct is anger. She lets it wash through her and fade away unseen. The archangel tests her. She cannot allow base emotion to dictate what she does. She's better than that. "All will be revealed in time. You insist on a timeline that suits your human sensibility. But the universe existed for billions of years before we did, and will continue to exist for billions of years after we have gone. Patience. Nothing revolves around us."

Unease seeps into their expressions; these are people not used to thinking that they are not, in fact, at the center of it all.

She leans forward. "This is a test of faith," she says. "Will you wait? Or will you plunge forward to satisfy your impatience?"

Murmured uncertainty. The General folds their arms. "Of course not. No, these decisions should not be made rashly. Not over the course of breakfast. Let's look at the situation surrounding Monkglass in depth. Tactically. And perhaps a briefing about the situation on the Capital. What does the Throne know? How long can we hold them off?"

Pyrex Imogen nods. They can't afford to be squabbling at this point; it benefits no one. They look almost grateful to Misery for stepping in and reminding them of the fact. "Those sound like prudent steps to take. Without doubt, the will of the Larex Forge will make itself known soon enough."

Triumphant, Misery says: "For now we eat. Afterward, I should like to speak to the Archbishop, alone."

⊹

Misery lied about that last part; it's not just the Archbishop she wants to see, but the princess also. Lightning trails behind as Misery walks elbow to elbow with Pyrex Imogen through the hallways of the command module. The floors here swallow their footsteps with carpet. The placid blue stretches before and behind them, flecked with gold; on the left acrylglass forms a curved wall, open to the soft light of space. Despite her exalted status, Misery has spent little to no time in this officers' domain, and its silence surprises her.

"I appreciate this gesture of yours," says the Archbishop. Their strides long and fluid, their demeanor cleansed of the upset that had plagued it earlier. "I had hoped that your General would be more receptive to my ideas, but it was good to be reminded of the picture. Forgive me, Misery. I must not ever forget my place."

A strange chill in her liver, being asked forgiveness by an

archbishop. But yet she would offer it when begged for. "Why did Major Reyes say your request was a personal favor?"

"Do you not know?"

"I would not ask if I did."

Pyrex Imogen casts a wary glance backward, directed at Lightning: Did you not tell them? But they answer Misery's pointed question. "The commander in charge of Monkglass . . . its administrator and chief, is my sibling. The Lady Storm Mirelle."

The Lady Storm Mirelle. Instant recognition, recall, recalibration: a name that has scrolled past on a feed more times than Misery can pinpoint, a set of syllables that has knitted itself into the tapestry of white noise surrounding news from the centers of power. Misery has never made the connection. Of course. Shit. "I'm sorry to hear. Are you close?"

The Archbishop draws a long, cold breath. "Mirelle and I are twins," Pyrex Imogen says. "Born of the same place, at the same time. Growing up, Mirelle and I were inseparable. We shared everything: clothes, interests, secrets. We completed one another's sentences. We lived in a world that was divided into halves: us, and everyone else. Everything else."

Their voice has turned membranous, web-thin. Misery is asking them to cut themself open and expose viscera, soft and messy. "Mirelle and I were called to very different vocations. Such are the vicissitudes of life. My sister was drawn to serve the Throne of the Faithful, and I to the ranks of the Church. Even so, we have always kept in contact, through the distance between us, in between the demands of faith and duty." Their expression turns difficult. "The months of the siege have been the longest we've not spoken."

"I am sorry," Misery says.

A laugh. "Do not feel sorry for me, child. I am lucky, in many respects. There are so many ways an engagement with the Heretics can end badly. Mirelle is safe for now, and every day I thank the Forge that the situation remains the same."

"It seems to me," Misery says, "that a diplomatic resolution to the siege would in fact be in your interests."

"Yes." Their steps slow and they bow their head. "I understand why the two esteemed officers think the way they do, but attacking Monkglass directly would put Mirelle in a great deal of danger. I would not have suggested it if I did not think it would do greater good."

Their words are sincere, at least. Still, Misery says, "I would err on the side of caution, especially if it would place your dear sister in danger. If the Forge wants us to act, Zie will send a clear sign."

From behind them, Lightning asks: "Have you told Diamond what you told me?"

"I have not. Emotions are running high enough; we would only make it worse."

"You're probably right."

"What—" Misery begins to ask, but the princess silences her with a hand to the wrist. A question for later, for private quarters.

Ahead of them, Ruin floats, observing but saying little as usual. "You should ask the princess. There are some fascinating things to be discovered."

They take the elevators downward to the metal and bone of the lower decks, where Angelsteeth hides all its secrets and treasure. The Archbishop wants to behold the Larex Forge's gift with their own eyes. Misery squares herself with breath, letting her fevered mind cool across the length of the journey. Targeting the siege of Monkglass *feels* right, and she knows she can push the General into it. *Should* push the General into it. Commit Angelsteeth to military action, bring new miracle to life beyond the bounds of Angelsteeth where the rest of the Faithful can witness it.

But can she? Is this what the Larex Forge desires of her? Does she feel the certainty within her, clear as the pull of gravity?

Past the fortified, heavily guarded doors of the Butchery they go. The cold, harsh light welcomes them. The rows of seraphs on either side; the transformed blue one with its mortal gash bisecting its chest. Not yet carved for transport pads. The white mech pulls the attention like a sun. Larger than a seraph. Uncannier. More limbs, longer ones, head a fan of bone. Against the stark environs of the Butchery it gleams like a pool of white blood. Misery dizzies with joy at the sight of it, hungering to be one with the mech again, to feel all its eight limbs as her own, to be something beyond human, beyond definition.

The Archbishop exhales and lowers their head in prayer, voice choked with emotion. Their devotion rolls through the room like a tide. Misery, eyes fixed upon the shining figure of the archangel standing among its lessers, allows her heart to be lifted up and swept into the arms of ecstasy.

In the silence that follows, Pyrex Imogen stands in quiet contemplation. "For years, the only evidence we've had of archangel mechs were the murals at the Kalanchov Pass and the writings of the Eight Messiahs. We searched every planet, every asteroid where stonetraces were found, in hope that we might uncover one of these legendary artifacts. Something that could change our fortunes. Now one has come to us." Their expression is beatific. "Not in my lifetime, or in the lifetimes of anyone living, have we been thus blessed. You are right, Misery. We can do no more than await guidance from the Larex Forge."

Misery gazes at the crown of the archangel mech and imagines it ablaze with light. Her bones ache for that sense of unity, one with the mech and one with the universe. The gestures of the Larex Forge are not subtle; Zie makes it known what Zie wants. That's what Misery needs from a sign: the absolute fucking certainty that she's doing what is right. None of this uncertainty. None of this insinuation and machination. She needs a sign that flares across the cosmos like a supernova.

Ruin perches on the glorious head of the archangel mech.

"Do not wait for the sign to come to you," zie says. "The will of the Forge is not a child that comes when called. It is treasure that rewards the dedicated. Seek it, and you will find what you need."

The question of Diamond's connection to the siege stays lodged in Misery's chest all day, a smoldering lump pumping out acidic fumes. Misery bears that discomfort in silence, having learned patience. While she shows off the archangel's moves to Pyrex Imogen, the Church contingent and the General's office prepare their briefings on Monkglass and the Throne's movements respectively. In the afternoon, the General recaps their battles against the Heretics for the Archbishop, a light show with sound, letting them witness the glory of the Demiurge's will in full technicolor.

She bides her time. She waits with her question throughout dinner, the extra-fancy shit now that the Archbishop is here. Tamps it down in the after, when Ono Red-2 chills in the common room of their quarters, breaking into the cremoline with lips and limbs getting looser and looser. Holds it in until she and Lighting are in the sanctuary of her quarters, balanced on the edge of the bed, breaths mingling. Still clothed, but on the precipice of shedding that encumbrance.

"What was the thing about Diamond?"

Lightning's features, muddied by the low light, grow heavy and somber as she turns away from Misery. The mood in the room shifts. Misery lets the chill seep through her body and becalm her soul. She will not allow the truth to escape her this time.

Lightning's gaze is pinned to the floor as she speaks. "We know who the commander of the Heretic siege is. There's solid intelligence and I believe it. Kept from the public for a reason, the reason being that it would cause panic if it were known. And my family is allergic to panic. As you are well aware."

Misery studies the lines of her profile as she dances around the truth, circling the matter of a name without touching it. "Who is it?"

An inward draw of air, a long and slow release. "Esse Temple. The commander of the Heretic siege is Esse Temple."

Murderer of Spider's compatriots. Haunter of Diamond's dreams. Misery's pulse quickens against her bones. "You never told me."

"It's not important—"

Misery catches Lightning's wrist as she tries to pull away. "I decide if things are important or not. This was important. You should have told me."

A spark of irritation; the princess gets up, crosses the room. Misery half expects her to find the door. But she sulks by the wall, arms folded. "What good would it do? I tell you, you tell Diamond, we don't do anything anyway, everyone's just upset for no reason."

"That's not the point." Misery rises from the bed. Saint Agneta's pattern keeps her breathing even. "You can't be keeping secrets from me. Any information you have, I need to know. Lightning, I have to look for signs. What if this was the sign from the Larex Forge and I missed it?"

She stiffens. "Is it? That's the sign?"

Blood rushes through Misery's body, in her veins and in the hollows of her head. It clouds her thoughts; she cannot hear her own voice, much less that of the Forge. Ruin is notably absent, watching silently. "It could be." It could be! Why else would the Forge have brought her into Diamond's orbit, and rolled the greatest of her foes into their path? What other reason could there be?

Her guts heat with impatience. Misery summons a screen into the air of her quarters. Demands it tell her all it knows about the siege at Monkglass. Screw the General's presentation tomorrow, she wants to know now. Information fountains across the bright rectangle, too fast for her to read. Headlines, essays, classified briefs. She taps on one lozenge after another before they are swept away in the scroll-by. This is all information she knows, there must be something else, something she's missed—

That. What's that?

Her finger lights on an image whizzing by, its pixels smeared into vague form by speed. The top embed in a longer profile. Singled out by her will, the photo freezes and coalesces into human form. Misery's breath stops in the gap between her lungs.

A saint with heavy eyes and a silver waterfall of hair. Glorious in her melancholy and elegance. It is a picture of the commander of Monkglass Station, the Lady Storm Mirelle. Misery recognizes her immediately. She knows that face from other quarters. The dream of the dark room, the long brushstrokes through glittering hair, the grief and slow acceptance.

The bottom falls out of her stomach. She had this dream on her first night on the Capital, right after meeting Pyrex Imogen. The dream kept returning to her, and she kept ignoring the signs. Thinking it wasn't important. Thinking it was some quirk of the nullvoid. After all, she's had repeating dreams all her life, and nothing about these changed very much. It felt like the same dream, over and over.

She missed it. She missed what was right under her nose, nestled in her mind, coming to her in her sleep. The clues have been in front of her all this time. She knew the name of Monkglass's commander. She could have looked for a picture anytime she wanted. But she did not.

Lightning picks up on her stillness and shock. "What is it? What have you found?"

"This is it," Misery says, tongue thick in her mouth. The bone-bright certainty she has been looking for. "This is the sign."

—¦—

"A dream? I don't understand."

Strain cracks Major Reyes's voice as xe speaks, exposing a vein of frustration that borders on exhaustion. The decision-makers on Angelsteeth have been hauled into a meeting room at a voidtouched hour; sleep dep and weeks of extraordinary stress have demolished every psychological wall that keeps their minds intact. Before Misery's eyes they are being torn down and remade by the Larex Forge. Let their tempers flare here, in this sealed room—silver-lined, top of the station, fenced by guards and holy obsidian, all of them clumped around a long table and still scrabbling toward the light. Let them struggle with the scale of revelation in the way that mortals do. When they leave the room, they will be firmly set upon the path that has been opened to them. Of this Misery will make sure.

She explains, again: "Since my time on the Capital, I have had a recurring dream of a saint I did not recognize. I thought little of it, as there was much else to worry about. I couldn't have guessed I dreamed of a real person. After the previous meeting, I looked deeper into the siege of Monkglass. When I saw a capture of the Lady Storm Mirelle, I recognized her immediately. She was the one who was haunting my dreams."

Major Reyes drags thumbs across xer eyelids. "And you never thought to say anything?"

Misery decides on generosity. "I understand, Major. It's not that you're skeptical, you're simply tired of surprises. You did not expect that being called to serve the Forge would come with so much uncertainty. But we are all on this path together. A shared journey. The Larex Forge reveals Hir hand to us when Zie wills so."

Lightning ducks her head as Misery says her piece. Yes. Good. Let her contemplate her role in the way these events have played out.

In the ensuing silence, the Duke of Apis leans forward. "Misery, did you really not know what the Lady Storm Mirelle looked like? The siege started months before this. She was on the waves quite a lot."

Misery glances evenly at him. He should know better, do better than this. "Lord Argan. You have not spent much time outside of the duchy's capital, have you?"

The guilt that shines through is all the confirmation she needs. General Tsung, who like Misery grew up in an area of neglect, says: "I believe their testimony." The cut of their gravelly voice silences the rest of the room.

Diamond is not here, by Misery's choice. She doesn't need to be here. Ono Red-2's captain still doesn't know about Esse Temple, still doesn't know about her great foe's involvement in the siege. A volatile mix, waiting to go off; Misery would prefer she learn these facts in a controlled environment. After all, Diamond's already convinced of the cause. She would follow Misery to Monkglass with no reservations. She does not, in fact, need to be here.

"Child," says Pyrex Imogen, the words trembling like jelly, "when you dreamed of her . . . when you dreamed of Mirelle. Tell me. What was she like? Was she all right?"

"She was . . ." Misery wonders how to articulate the granularity of her dreams, their simultaneous bleakness and blandness. The suffocating nothingness of being within them. It's a state of waiting, she realizes. Waiting with no end in sight. A state of besiegement. "She was all right. She seemed sad. Tired."

"Oh." Pyrex Imogen's exclamation is quiet and matted with grief. They lower their head, trapped in private agony. Misery wishes she understood. Her longing for home has dulled to a soft ache that no longer bothers her. In a way she was blessed by the Larex Forge, growing up in a broken house that broke her also. It leaves her with few attachments, no psychic tangle messing her up, no homesickness to catch her by the ankles. She can get where she needs to go.

"So this discovery," the General says, breaking the silence. "Is the sign that you were looking for?"

"It is indeed." Now that she is sure, now that she has decided, the anxiety has left her like a swamp drained. She will not rest until the will of the Larex Forge be done.

"Then it is decided," says the General. "We shall move upon the siege of Monkglass."

27

The command center is packed with the forty-eight captains of the seraph servings, and the commanders of the other divisions. The whole banquet of Angelsteeth will be involved. A buffet of data sprawls across the length of the table, captures and images and charts. Ono Red-2 has scattered across the breadth of the room, obtrusive in their baggy number twos beside the pressed, heavyweight uniforms of the upper brass. Major Reyes resisted the serving's inclusion in this meeting, but Misery said: "We are a team and we attend together, or not at all," and the General agreed with her, so that was the end to that. Ghost hangs on the periphery with birdlike alertness; Tank leans over the smorgasbord of information, features blanched by light, glasses rimmed with yellow reflection. And then there's Spider and Diamond, hip to hip, huddling as though for warmth.

Between that midnight gathering and now, Diamond has been told about Esse Temple. General Tsung did the dirty work, hedging on their long shared history to cushion the blow. From Diamond the news trickled down to Spider. Their faces shine with the light of their new knowledge. Spider is easy to read, aglow with the simple fires of rage. Primitive and uncompromising emotion. Diamond's renewed resolve is a little more complex. Joy, gratitude, but also a measure of sadness. Still unsure of her worthiness in her role. Doesn't matter. Misery has what she needs.

"This is what we know of the situation at Monkglass."

Major Reyes makes a wide gesture and the diagram of the besieged station expands, a knot of holystone and metal with a loose shell of purple netting, surrounded by an asteroid scatter of yellow dots. An overlay of tabs and infoboxes blink on and off in concert with the movement of Misery's head. It would be distracting, if she were susceptible to distraction.

"It has been over two dozen years since the last major siege," the major says. "This model is scraped from the old data and current drone skims. It's a guess, but the best one we can make." Pointing to the dense lilac parked around the station like an orbital shell: "Here, the primary siege mechanism. Approximately two dozen Heretic ships project a baffling sphere that blocks all transmissions, both ways. Don't know how they do it. Communications with Monkglass have been cut off for the past two months. Every scout flight has come into contact with this." Finger stabbing at the yellow pinpricks. "Seraphim. Estimate at least a dozen. Too dangerous to handle. We lost six scouts before the Throne pulled back on sending them. Since then, nothing. Blackout."

General Tsung stands with their arms crossed; the heft of a dozen contradictory joys and worries weighing upon them. "We are tasked to raise the siege upon this station, but we cannot launch an attack with this little information. I cannot simply send troops into a situation where we know neither the numbers nor the nature of the enemy."

"But we've done that twice now—and won," Tank says, with all the fearlessness of youth. "Surely, if we all pitch in, we could—"

"Luck," Major Reyes growls. "We got lucky. Two times. Third time, maybe not so lucky. Don't overestimate our abilities."

"Or underestimate theirs," Diamond says. Heat fissures the vowels of her words. "The commander of this siege is a war criminal. A monster. Mortal decency is not something she knows. She cares nothing for the cost of human lives."

"Esse Temple is an enemy unlike any we've faced," the General says. The table's light ages them, highlighting the weight gathered under their eyes. "Her actions are unpredictable. We cannot model for that."

Tank slaps both hands on the table. All of fourteen and unfazed by her elders. "If we can't model for that, then we don't have to plan. If she's that unpredictable, then all the planning in the cosmos will be useless. We have might with us. We have the Faithful's brightest with us." Finger flung out, tip angled at Diamond. "Most of all we have the mandate of the Larex Forge with us. Isn't that enough?"

The room goes extremely quiet in the wake of her outburst. Then the General laughs, a belly-deep sound that shakes their frame. In the wash of that sound the tension in the room drops, and some even join in with laughter. Isn't it absurd? It is absurd. They've been placed in an unbelievable situation. Who would have guessed that they would see a Messiah? Who would have guessed that they would be deep in conspiracy against the Throne, plotting a major operation behind the backs of the Emperor and his grandmother? It is madness, they've all gone mad.

"Tank is right," Misery says. "We have all the tools we need. We can plan an all-out assault." In truth she knows nothing about military tactics and her month on this station has taught her next to nothing. But does that matter? She swells with restlessness, her veins thick with the need to get into action. Prove to the world she is truly as blessed as she says she is. Her journey here started with a pack of lies, and now the time has come for truth to reveal itself. "Esse Temple has the blood of far too many on her hands. For too long she has escaped justice. The Larex Forge has spoken and shown us the way. I have my orders, and they come from a power greater than anything the filth of the Heretics can rustle up. We have our weapon, let's march."

A collective intake of air around her, a confectioner's scatter of reactions to her pronouncement. Boldness, anger, confusion, epiphany. Faith. Joy. Misery seeks out the gazes of each of her servingmates and is rewarded with concession, approval, delight, and from Spider in particular a fierce bloodthirst. Righteousness rushes through her body like warm water.

General Tsung holds their hand up, summoning their attention, recalibrating the mood in the room. "Be that as it may. We cannot run an operation without a plan. There is a difference between faith and foolishness." A patrician air to their speech, which Misery understands but still resents them for. "And a plan can only be as good as the information we possess. We know too little about Heretic operations and technology to—"

"But we have a source."

Lightning cuts through the General's protestations and heads turn in her direction. General Tsung frowns, suddenly wary. "What do you mean?"

"The Heretic prisoner," she replies. Syllables crisp and snappy.

"I'm going to stop you right there," the General says, but the damage is done. Gasps burst from the assembled captains, a surfbreak of surprise and alarm: this is news to plenty of them. It's news to Misery, too. A band of anxiety tightens across her chest. "There are Heretic prisoners on board?"

The General's expression tightens further. Speaking fast, as though ashamed. They *are* ashamed. "It's an ongoing situation. We were tasked to retain a Heretic on board. It's not ideal, but we have so far complied—"

A ball of ice sinks slowly though Misery's guts. She cannot put away the flood of memories: his eyes, the give of his flesh, the way he looked at her before her foot came down. "What's his name?"

Beside her, Lightning's shoulders tense. She turns her head, deliberately. "*His* name? No pronouns were mentioned."

They're all looking at her. They're all hoping the same thing. They pray the divine touch has already reached her, showing their Messiah the shame tucked so deep within the lightless folds of Angelsteeth, an abomination known only to those in closest orbit of the Throne. There lies gleaming desire for miraculous pathfinding that will solve their immediate quandaries, a tool put into their waiting hands. They don't know the truth of Misery's dreams, that maelstrom of carnal desire, and the weaknesses they carved into her. They won't understand the well of hate that has sprung open in Misery's chest, unless she explains it to them. She doesn't want to explain it to them.

Her mouth has dried out. She has to ask. "Is he Jericho? Is that his name? What he calls himself."

The General doesn't answer her directly. These things cannot be discussed before the serving heads—they don't have the right kind of gold to their name. "Meeting dismissed," they say, directed at the gathered and gawking captains. "We'll continue later." They point at Misery, Lightning, Diamond. "In my office. Now." But the anxiety in their eyes tells Misery all she needs to know. Jericho is real. He had not lied to her about being a Heretic prisoner. And right now, at that very moment, he is somewhere in the depths of Angelsteeth, away from Misery's sight and perception. Alive. Breathing. A witness to her shame.

"This is a lot to take in."

Major Reyes presses xer fingers against the bridge of xer nose, half-slumped in a chair. The General's private office is a long oval that accommodates a dozen, located in one of the tips of Angelsteeth. The floor is ivory carpet and the walls are real wood, bisected by acrylplate that extends to the ceiling. The cosmos overhead blesses the meeting suite with cold light. A glass partition keeps them segregated in a corner of the office: there's the General, stoic as usual; the major with xer bone-deep exhaustion; the Duke, underslept; Diamond and Lightning, holding it together; Dr. Sower, summoned for her expertise; and then there's Pyrex Imogen. Caught between dismay and hope.

Over their collective heads looms a data lozenge, bright and unavoidable, plastered with a photo of the man imprisoned in the deep guts of Angelsteeth. The mug shot exposure blows out the finer features of his face—the lines under his eyes, the hollows of his cheeks—but Misery cannot deny his identity.

That's him.

Until Dr. Sower pulled up the picture she had clung to the mad hope of prophetic coincidence. The promise of the creature in her dreams bearing no resemblance to the prisoner held in secret on the base. But Jericho was telling the truth that one time.

Her stomach cramps. He's been in her *head*. She could throw up thinking of it. How he showed up, loose-limbed with a gentle smile, and disarmed her with his smooth words. She, who should have known better. She, who prided herself on seeing through people. What a joke. A disgrace. She is furious. She should be ashamed.

The Heretics are dangerous. She's never met one before and now she has. They're dangerous and cannot be left alive. She will destroy them if it breaks every bone in her body.

"His name is Jericho Malturin," says the doctor. For Misery's benefit. For the benefit of the major and the Duke and Diamond, who had no knowledge of this buried explosive. "He's been under my care for years. My dirty little secret. Or should I say, the Empire's dirty little secret. Seems like a lot of them wind up on Angelsteeth. We might have a monopoly on them."

The major breathes slowly and deeply, a saint's pattern. Xe seems to be taking this hardest of all. Blindsided by this wrecking ball of information about Angelsteeth, which xe thought xe knew everything about. But the happenings in the research wing have always been invisible to xer—xe commands the seraph servings, what need would xe have of the day-to-day of the scientists and doctors and saints learning the miracles of the Larex Forge? Of course the science wing has its secrets. Of course it does.

Still, Misery hungers to know more. "What's he doing on Angelsteeth?"

Dr. Sower blinks flatly and impatiently at her. Deliberately misconstruing her question. "Being a prisoner. Unlike you, he doesn't get to run around and pilot mechs. He's in a cage. We got bored of poking him a while ago."

"Jericho Malturin is a prisoner of convenience," says the General. "By which I mean it is convenient for the Throne to have him imprisoned here. He was captured four years ago trying to infiltrate the Capital. He claims to have been rescuing his father, whom he believed a prisoner of the Empire. However, the venerable Elden Manifest is a defector, and has been working for the Throne for the past decade. The prisoner either misunderstands, or refuses to understand this fact. Unfortunately, since his capture, he has become a political bargaining chip between the Throne and the Heretics. So we must suffer his presence upon this station, and repel the Heretic attacks when they come."

"And you, Misery. You've been dreaming of him?"

The question comes from the Duke. The scheming, duplicitous, innocent Duke. He imagines visions of Jericho popping into Misery's head the same way as her dreams of the Lady Storm, passive and beautiful. He doesn't know the truth. Should Misery tell him the truth?

"Does it matter what they know?" asks Ruin. The angel is propped on a locked silver cabinet, full of the General's personal secrets. "As long as you get what you want, does it matter to you?"

The angel baits her with barbed questions. Misery's jaw tightens. She knows what true prophetic dreams are like, and she knew that her dreams with Jericho were not that, and yet— She will never let anyone else know the content of these dreams. "He came into my mind while I lay asleep," she says. "He concealed his identity from me. Pretended to be a friend. But his true nature was revealed to me and I banished him from the arches of my mind."

"He came to you?" Dr. Sower blows air through her lips. "Well, shit."

"You sound surprised by this."

"We tested him for telepathy," the doctor says. "That's the research his dad is doing in the Capital. Got some idea that it's the way to communicate better with the Larex Forge. I think he's kind of a whackjob, but whatever. We did all kinds of tests. The conclusion: he can't read minds, exactly. Maybe some mild empathy, able to perceive emotions, even subconscious ones. We thought we had him worked out. But invading people's dreams. Is that a thing? Guess it is. Shit."

"A voidtouched ability," Lightning says. "As expected of a Heretic."

"Fuck that," Dr. Sower says. "Should have salved him into the void. You bet both asses that we're going to do that now. Stuff that could knock an entire banquet out. Make sure he doesn't have another conscious moment until, you know. Y'all come to a decision, one way or another."

Dr. Sower thinks they might execute him for his transgressions, and she has the right idea. She's dealt with Jericho personally, she knows the danger that lurks under his soft exterior. But it's too late for Misery. They should have done him in a long time ago. "He is too dangerous to keep alive," she says.

Dr. Sower taps fingers against her pensive chin. "Is that why you asked about voidsickness? Why you thought you might be voidmad?"

Clever. Sharp. She remembers that conversation from before Misery's enlightenment. "Yes," she says. Let her think that. Let her blame Jericho, who should have no sympathy afforded to him. "I knew those dreams weren't normal. I thought they might be the work of the nullvoid."

"So what does this mean?" The Duke is perplexed, he continues to be perplexed, he struggles with the amount of information he has had to digest. "Is this not a sign, then? Is this the work of the nullvoid, thwarting us from the Forge's intended path?"

No, no. That cannot be it. Jericho cannot destroy things for her this way. She won't let him. Misery breathes, Saint Agneta's pattern, four in, six hold, seven out. The Larex Forge—Zie has done everything with a purpose—everyone she's met, everyone who has come into her life, for better or for worse, has had a role to play.

She was put on Angelsteeth for a reason. She was introduced to Ono Red-2 for a reason. She was given the visions of the Lady Storm for a reason.

Could the Larex Forge, so wise and deliberate in Hir doings, be thrown out of orbit by a single Heretic so low, so worthless? Could a single voidtouched piece of filth destroy Hir ineffable plans like that?

No. Of course not. Even someone as sunken and unholy as Jericho has a role to play. Can be made useful in the hands of the exalted, those who are blessed as Misery is. The banquet of Angelsteeth was lost, unable to see a way forward with the siege of Monkglass, ready to admit defeat because they knew nothing of Heretic technology or how to surmount it. But the Larex Forge had already served the solution to them. To *her,* specifically. Who knows better how a Heretic siege worked, than a Heretic himself?

Misery lets out a long, slow breath. With it goes all her anxiety, all her self-hatred, all of her doubts. She is blameless in this. She is doing what she is meant to do. "The Heretic prisoner was sent to Angelsteeth for a reason. Divinity works in its own way, on its own schedule. It is no coincidence that the one Heretic prisoner held by the Faithful was held *here.* Jericho is merely another stone in the fortress of righteousness the Larex Forge has built for us. He will tell us what we need to know. He will tell us how to break the siege."

Pyrex Imogen has been silent until now, wrapped in the

chains of their own thought. They speak now, low and sono-
rous: "Misery is right. I can think of no better source for the
information that we need."

There: she has the backing of the Church, she has an authoritative weight behind her that can stoneroll over any protestation.
"Let me speak to the prisoner," she says. "I will extract the
information we need from him."

28

For the first time Misery enters the lower bowels of Angelsteeth, where the brig sits jowl to jowl with the research center. She has chosen Diamond and Lightning to follow her into the maw of this confrontation; the rest of them will watch from a secure room, safe in the steel heart of the station. The Archbishop. Duke Argan. Major Reyes and the General. A limited audience. Misery does not care to expose the wound that is Jericho to anyone else. Ruin strolls next to her, fluid as time, luminescent with grace. Zie seems particularly invested in this excursion, for reasons opaque to Misery. But she doesn't mind. She needs the backup in case the Heretic tries anything. The full might of the Demiurge shall be her shield.

Their escort is a full detail of armored guards, faceless and bristling with weaponry. Dr. Sower, flanked by two assistants, leads the group with her concerted gait and omnipotent pass-card. Beyond a door painted arsenic yellow and labeled AUTHO-RIZED PERSONNEL ONLY lies a labyrinth of clinical minimalism: walkways and steps distilled to metal bones, walls and ceilings piped with ducts and vents. Flat discs of holy opal bloom from the ends of wires, flooding the spaces with harsh light. Their path takes them on unguarded walkways over open-plan labo-ratories and workshops. In one, two engineers conduct an or-chestra of drones over the rubble of their vanquished enemy, the Heretic warship, spitting fire and cutting loose small chunks of the unknown holystone. In another, a bubble of sleekly robed scientists floats in a wide circuit over a group of white saints, each sealed in a featureless cubby with a desk and scratchpad.

Ghost's siblings, perhaps? One of the bubble-scientists looks up and briefly catches Misery's eye as their little contingent marches through the upper bounds of the room. Eyes widen, but zie says nothing.

In the next room over the walkway cuts across an enormous pool, clear and copper-blue, wide and long enough to be a lake. Massive spheres stud its crystalline depths, green-striped and smooth, each inscribed with a complex network of golden lines. Misery has never encountered this kind of holystone; the melody they play in her head is unfamiliar, yet alluring. Lightning seems unfazed by the size and scale of the room, but Diamond tenses, frightened and offput. "These are childstones," Ruin says coolly, by way of explanation.

Misery frowns. Childstones? An urban legend, picked up from tall tales native to the unsourced wilds of online fora. There was a whole series of books, a fantasy epic centered around the idea of childstones, that Misery had inhaled while growing up. A pretty solid wave adaptation that she never watched. She was too old by then. She could not have imagined they were real.

There are a lot of things about her life now she could not have imagined, yet here she is.

It takes time to cross the breadth of the lake, and through the slog of those seconds the submerged nubs of melon-green stare dolefully up at them. Misery imagines the surface of the lake breathing like a thin, blue amniotic skin. Eventually the horizon turns blank and silver, a single door cut into its flank. An exit, marked red and angry in the system HUD. "We're nearly there," Dr. Sower says.

Through the door, down two flights of steps that ring with angry footsteps, and then along a narrow corridor with flat walls on each side. Drones circulate in the silent, watchful air, bristling with glass and stone. This is the prison segment of Angelsteeth, which would have been her home here, if not for the intervention of the Forge. It's cold here, cold enough to purple the tits. By the Grace of the Demiurge she was spared.

Sixty measures from their destination they're stopped by a ring of plate-faced guards. Ahead of them, at the limit of Misery's vision, a doubly armored door waits for them, drenched in blue light. At Dr. Sower's insistence, they part for the contingent. And then step by step, moment by moment, they draw closer to the thick holy jade holding the prisoner, and Misery can no longer pretend the pressure building in her chest is not fear. If the door opens to reveal a waiting maw of tooth-studded void she would welcome it. Anything better than facing the creature that has humiliated her so.

Dr. Sower pauses in front of the door, face harshened by the flickering light of its aegis. "Here we are."

The room beyond the holystone door is smaller than Misery expected. Not a cell—an interrogation room. Clean and hard-walled and lined with helmeted guards. The deep guts of Angelsteeth hold so many surprises for Misery, like this endless parade of security goons. The air: even colder, and poorly illuminated. The brightest thing in the room is an aegis, a blinding yellow ring spanning floor to ceiling.

Within the narrow, hot circle of the aegis, hands locked and head bowed, kneels Jericho.

Misery's flesh burns with dull anger. It hurts to breathe. Jericho looks exactly like his self-conception in her dreams. It's surreal, like a holo stepping from wave drama into reality. But no. Look closer—the man kneeling before her is thinner, the shadows carved by the harsh lightning starker. His signature glasses gone. When he looks up, blinking and confused, his eyes are wide and enormous, startlingly so. Like a prey animal's. Hair sandy brown and dull, so not a saint—but what does that mean for Heretics? Scripture teaches that they fell from grace daring to harness the void for stonebending.

Heat scours Misery's cheeks. She tightens her fists as though that might ease the fire in her chest and in her teeth. This scoundrel, who came into her mind, who acted under false pretenses so she'd fuck him, this absolute, spineless piece of shit—

She hates him. She hates him. She hates him.

The aegis surrounding Jericho snaps off, leaving a sonic void in its wake. Dr. Sower stands before the prisoner, fists propped on hips. "Now, Jericho. You remember our Messiah, don't you? Of course you do. They have some questions for you that we want answered. Answer them properly, and all will be well. Fuck around, and . . ." She raises a hand curled around the telescoping length of a shock stick, an instrument of less-than-gentle persuasion. "You're going to find out."

Jericho's eyes flick in her direction. There's no fear in his expression, only weariness. It's not his first go with the stick; he's been here a long time. Done this dance more times than he wanted. "Now," says the doctor, in her sing-song voice: "You'll be a good boy, won't you?"

His only response is to look away. The doctor tuts, and jabs the stick into his left shoulder. He cries out as voltage snaps through skin and flesh. "It's a yes or no question, Jericho."

"Yes," he gasps. Voice smaller and higher-pitched than in the dreams.

"Good."

Dr. Sower hands the stick to Misery and withdraws. Pressure around her upper arm, warm and steadying: Lightning, giving her a quick squeeze for comfort. Misery realizes she's shaking. It's not from fear, though. She's not afraid. She faces the creature who lied to her, who used her and violated her. He seems so much smaller in real life; a couple of swift kicks to the gut and throat would end him. She could end him.

"Jericho," Misery says. "It's me. Do you remember?"

"Do I remember you?" A soft laugh. "You're pretty hard to forget." He looks up, finally, and their eyes meet. "What now, Misery Nomaki? What do you want from me?"

"You know the answer."

"I don't."

"You're a fucking telepath. Don't lie to me."

"I'm not a telepath. I told you. I didn't come to you, you came to me."

Misery kicks him. Drives the toe of her boot into the soft cartilage of his knee as he kneels. A sound of bone dislodging and he cries out, doubling over in pain.

From behind, Dr. Sower laughs. "Forge, I like your style."

Jericho looks up at her. Eyes rheumy, skin blue in the thin hollows around the bone. "Misery, you really have no idea . . . Do you?"

"Stop playing games. You think you can trick me a second time?"

Jericho shakes his head. "I'm telling you. My telepathy is relatively weak, and its range is limited. I could not have reached out to you on my own."

"The Forge directed me to you. So I could see what I'm dealing with. I understand it now." To her the Heretics have always been abstract figures, creatures of myth, as distant from her lived reality as the Eight Messiahs from generations ago. The snarling mechs she fought might as well be robots to her, cold and impartial. But in Jericho she has a human figure, a beast of warm flesh and desire that manipulated her and hurt her. Humiliated her. Now she knows what they're like. Now she has a reason to fight.

"No. You really don't understand. I see."

"What don't I understand?"

"Has it never occurred to you?"

Misery jabs the shock stick forward and he flinches, but she doesn't discharge it. She slides it under his chin and tilts his face up, into the glare of the light. "Stop talking in circles before I split."

He's shaking so hard even his lips tremble. "Misery. Have you never considered that you're a telepath?"

He's trying to distract her. She sees that. She knows that. But she can't let him get away with this. She presses the tip of the shock stick against his voice box, hard. "You really think I'm an idiot, don't you?"

"I'm telling you what I see. You came to me. Your insights into people—what you told me—that's not normal. It's telepathy—"

She lets him have it. The spit gurgles in his throat, choking his screams as she electrocutes him. Good. Let him suffer. When she jerks the shock stick away he doubles over and vomits, throwing up a glut of watery bile, translucent and gummy. They've been starving him. The room fills with a sour stench.

Jericho slowly uncrumples as Misery watches dispassionately. He looks at her again, a thin string of spittle suspended between lip and chin. His breath comes in spurts. "You're not chosen— Everything I've heard— I know what you are. Your abilities— You're like us—"

She jams the stick into his throat and turns it on. Full power. Jericho screams and arcs backward, convulsing. Serves him right. Little fucker. He falls to the ground and she follows, the shock stick vibrating against the bones of her hand. Misery wants to fry his eyes out of his head, fry him until his skin peels blackened from his bones—

Cool stone closes over her wrist. Dr. Sower's mechanical hand, gentle enough not to twist her arm. "All right, that's enough. I think he's learned his lesson."

Misery jerks away, freeing her hand from the doctor's grip. Stalks the room as Dr. Sower goes to check if the Heretic is still alive. Swings the shock stick to expel the anger from her limbs. Blood boils merrily in her veins.

"Misery." Lightning's hands close around hers, soft and warm. Holding her still until she calms down. Misery meets her gaze and sees no judgment there, no fear. Only a desire for them to succeed. "Chill," she says, squeezing her hands.

Misery breathes. Saint Agneta's pattern. Four in, six hold, seven out. It's fine. It's fine. She has to focus. The Siege of Monkglass. He must know how to break it.

Jericho lives. Dr. Sower pulls him upright, where he remains, head bowed and swaying. He's soiled his pants from the shock. "No more of your nonsense," she tells him, sternly.

To Misery she says: "Try not to kill him, hm? I don't need more messes to clean up."

Misery circles Jericho, this pathetic, broken shape still knelt on the floor. He draws shaky breaths through scoured lungs and won't look at her this time. Misery flicks her wrist and pulls a file out of the system. Light coalesces into shape. A diagram. Major Reyes's schematic of the siege of Monkglass. "Tell me how to break this siege."

He glances at it. "I don't know where that is, or what—"

She strikes him across the brow with the stick; all force, no electricity. He doesn't cry out this time. "Please," he says. "I really don't. I don't know what you want from me. I've been here for years. I don't know of any siege."

"You're a Heretic. You know the technology." She expands the diagram, shoves it in his direction. "Look up. *Look*. How do you break the siege?"

He glances up, frail and desperate, and studies the pinpricks of light. "It's . . ." He points, with one shaking finger. "You see this formation of rec ships?"

"I don't care what they're called."

"The way they're arranged, they're projecting a dampening shield." He pushes the words out with difficulty. "It blocks electromagnetic radiation. Nothing . . . in or out."

"How do you break it?"

"I—" His face crumples in pain, and Misery gives him a few seconds to compose himself. "There may be . . . I know what this is. It's a Schroedinger shield, it's fully blind. Both ways. The siegers can't see the inside either. If you can jump . . ."

"If we can jump units inside the shield," Diamond says, "we can take it out from the inside without being detected. Is that what you're saying?"

No wonder they call her a genius. Faster than anyone else her captain has picked up what Jericho put down. The Heretic shuts his eyes, still in agony. "It shouldn't be hard. If you know. You have to collapse the pillars—they're built on KD principles . . . if you calculate the ratio. It's probably one plus six."

Misery frowns. "What the fuck does that mean?"

"It's okay," Diamond says. "I got it. The reso engineers can figure it out."

"So we got what we needed?"

Her captain nods. The stiffness in her spine telegraphs wariness; Diamond was surprised by the force and swiftness of Misery's violence. She doesn't know what it's like. Must be nice, growing up in a place where you didn't have to watch yourself, where you weren't always aware of the potential for violence curled up in any moment, waiting for the slightest trigger to lash out.

She leans forward and lifts Jericho's chin one last time. Looks into the bruised face, the mismatched eyes with one sclera half-red. Burst vessel. "You got off easy," she says. "You can thank the Larex Forge that you made it out alive. Think on that in your cell, Heretic. Maybe you'll finally wake up."

29

"You're upset," Lightning says.

Misery unclenches her cramped fists in the middle of the wide circuit she's been making. "Oh? I hadn't noticed."

After the interrogation they came to rest in one of the observation modules, she and the princess, tumbling from the bright flare of that confrontation into the cool, wide quiet of this contemplative space, acrylplate dome open to the velvet fabric of space, a place where the light of the Forge can touch the soul. The saints who come here to starbathe often congregate during the times non-saints eat, as though the routine would impart them some sense of normalcy. A relatability. Right now they're alone, just Lightning and Misery and her elevated blood pressure. Misery turns away from her lover and toward the patient carpet of stars, who offer no judgment, only light. The acrylplate catches her reflection and displays her as other people see her: this short, squat nixen, with their freckled skin and springy hair, deep bags around the eyes and the scar bisecting a swatch of their face. Just some regular schmuck, a dozen of them on every backwater moon and settlement. Nothing worth taking notice of.

Ruin stands to her left, hands latched behind slender back, contemplating the stars also. "The chosen one could have been anyone. But it was you. That means something, doesn't it?"

The Larex Forge chooses Hir tools in ways that only Zie understands. Human logic cannot be applied to it. The nullvoid—the great unknowable, entropy itself—preys on the weaknesses of humans and their gelatinous mortality. The Demiurge, in all

Hir infinite wisdom and compassion, took it upon Hirself to protect them, in the ways Zie saw fit. To claim understanding of those reasons would be the height of hubris. It's something a Heretic would do.

A sudden bout of sensation: arms around her waist, a head upon her shoulder. Lightning would never be caught dead in a moment of tenderness like this, yet here she is, all gentle and vulnerable in front of the great theater of the stars. "You let him upset you," she says, voice tinted with reproach.

Misery shrugs her off; that tone won't work with her. She didn't let Jericho upset her, he was deliberately trying to upset her. He's a demon of manipulation, it's what he does. Framing it that way is disgusting. Lightning sighs as Misery returns to pacing. "You don't believe him, do you?"

She turns to Lightning, head tilted. "Do you?" That's what she's interested in.

Lighting sweeps forward and gathers Misery's hands in the heat of her own, pressing the palms together. "You know I trust you. The ravings of a Heretic can't change that."

Lightning is desperate to believe, and be believed. Her broken idea of herself has just been mended, and it's too soon for it to be shattered again. Jericho's words were a knife in her side too, and Misery twists that blade further. "Maybe I'm just a voidmad telepath, like the Heretics are," she says.

Lightning looks at her. "Then tell me what I'm thinking right now. If you're a telepath, why don't you read my mind?"

In all honesty, she's too easy to read. When they first met, the princess was absolutely opaque, but Misery now knows her, inside and out, and doesn't need telepathy to figure out what she's thinking. The burst of slyness in her expression, the way she scans the outlines of Misery's body—it's too obvious. "Calm your tits," she says. "Now's not the time."

"Sorry. I thought you'd appreciate the levity."

Misery hooks her by the loops of her belt and pulls her close. Studies her expression at close range. Love and lust and longing, the last of which is the most potent, and carries the most potential. Misery could drink of her longing all day.

Ruin is right, and Jericho is full of shit. She's been chosen for her path and made extraordinary by the gifts of the Forge. Whether or not her instincts, that ability to read people—which is not telepathy, that's nonsense—are born-with or Forge-given matters not. The important thing is that it makes her perfect for her role. She sees the hearts of people. She knows how to guide them. She stands on the cusp of greatness and will guide the Faithful into the blessed star fields of tomorrow.

Fucking Jericho thought he could bust something in her mental architecture, make her distrust herself. But the one thing— the only fucking thing—she's ever been sure of is her trust in herself. All her life she's been her only ally. Jericho thought he could use her insights against her, turning her uncanny ability to read other people's cues into something sinister. He thought that with one revelation he could upend her understanding of herself, the world, and her place in it. Wrong. Wrong. She will prove him wrong. Just you wait. Just you see.

INTERLUDE 8

How fickle the human psyche can be, how quick to react when it is injured. Love turns to hate with the spin of a wheel, and the tincture of events changes from blue to red in hindsight. It's uncomfortable, is it not, to watch something dearly familiar change shape and form into something you can no longer claim to know? Is it not true, however, that the beauty of the human condition is its unconditional capacity for change? It is fascinating to watch, at least. Perhaps what is mourned is your loss of right to claim ownership of something so changed.

Still, the changeability of the mortal mind never fails to amaze me. How much of history is written by those with wounded hearts? The ugly truth of the matter is that Misery Nomaki may have behaved abominably at various points in this tale, but they were not alone in their disgrace. For sure, they lied and manipulated others, over and over. For sure, they made choices that were selfish and ill-judged, then blamed others for those choices when they became embarrassed by them. But what of the greater injustices around them? The Heretic, held in secret in the catacombs of Angelsteeth, denied light and the warmth of human touch, taking advantage of the Messiah's confusion, pretending to be innocent and harmless. The Throne and Emperor, who turned his existence into a dirty secret by concealing it from the rest of the Faithful—the media, their loyal subjects, the heaving syrup of the peasantry—and yet readily used that same existence as a tool in their negotiations with the Heretics. A hostage. A little political pawn. Then there's the Church, who were not above using the young and vulnerable as means to achieve their ends, in their eternal power struggle against the Throne. The Archbishop of Remus, who connived to undermine the tenuous peace between Heretic and the Faithful. Not to mention all the bit players, each one carrying private gems of motivations and desires. The Duke. The General. More who haven't come into the story yet. Who was right? Who was wrong? Who comes up top on the exalted list of the morally superior, and who is the scum of the universe that comprises the bottom? I cannot make that judgment. Can you? Or will it fall to those who shall write the record of what happened here? Perhaps it will be you. I suspect it will not be me. That is the way of these things.

30

Several people on Angelsteeth know what KD principles are, and the phrase incites a great froth of excitement. Engineers swarm through rooms, chattering in language Misery cannot understand and cannot follow. Large and complicated diagrams blossom across the displays of the station's command centers, packed with esoteric formulations and figures, quantum shit way above Misery's reading grade. Lightning tries to translate, but it's still too much. All Misery can do is listen, head empty and palms idle.

"You don't understand," Tank says. "Key-Demeter principles have been mere theory up till this point. No one's ever got them to work. This is a huge deal. You have no *idea* how huge. Forge, I can't believe I'm alive to witness this."

Diamond is similarly impressed, despite herself. "The Heretics have somehow achieved this with their technology. It's quite the achievement."

"Unless that Heretic was lying," Lightning says. Still piquantly bitter about Jericho, about what he is and what he's done.

"No," Diamond says. "The math works out. Empirically, we can explain a lot of things we've observed about the Heretic siege using KD ratios. He's closed the circuit for us."

The brains on the station take the shabby mumblings of a Heretic and spin them to gold. The Schroedinger shield cuts information from inside and out, but the ships themselves make an information network, crucial for keeping them in formation. Should the six or so ships that comprise the net pillars be taken out, the shield would be shattered, ending the siege, and leaving the other thirty ships floating in discombobulation, easy pickings for the banquet of Angelsteeth.

Tank gets to present the engineers' findings to the higher brass. "Based on the models and our simulations, and what we know of the architecture of Monkglass, we've picked out these ships as the likely net pillars."

They're in the command nerve center again. An outsize graphic of the siege lords over the central display with its suffocating wrap of Heretics. Purple overlays specific nodes in the nets, and as the graphic cycles under Tank's guidance, a constellation of potential attack strategies waxes and wanes around them, written in chunky military shorthand. Tank explains the strategies they could employ for the external assaults, the success and failure rates, the backup strategies should the pillars be instead one of the other three possibilities—

"Stop," says the General, interrupting her stream of technobabble. "How sure are you that these six are the pillar-carriers?"

"About eighty percent. There's a bunch of higher math behind it, but—"

"It's closer to ninety-five percent," Diamond says, cutting in. "Based on context, we're pretty sure these are the ones."

"That's a five percent chance we're wrong. Those odds are too big for me." They pinch their chin. "We only have one shot at disabling this shield and taking out the Heretic lead ship. If we fail, the banquet could be destroyed."

There has to be some way for them to know for sure. Misery fixes her gaze upon the angel who scouts the room like a curious hawk. Are they on the right track? If there was a time for divine guidance, that time would be now.

"Guidance has already been given to you," Ruin says. "The Heretic did not mention jumping within the siege net idly."

Emotion punches her in the stomach. She hates being reminded of Jericho, hates thinking that something out of his cursed mouth might be of use. She has tried to forget everything about that last encounter: the evil that he tried to enact, the dark feelings he drew out of her. She is not proud. Curse that Heretic, the void take him, let his marrow rot and his mind be torn asunder.

And yet—can she argue with Ruin? Her mission has to be more important than her ego. The Larex Forge was born of the nullvoid. Blessings can come from corruption.

Fine. She says to the room: "The Heretic said the shield is blind from the inside. What if we jumped inside the net, and took it out from there?"

The major is instantly skeptical. "Yours is the only unit that can jump freely. Are you saying you want to take out six ships by yourself? And again if it turns out we were wrong?"

Yes, she wants to say. Yes. She will destroy an entire Heretic fleet by herself, just give her the chance. She will cut them open one by one and she will revel in it. But Diamond says, "Wait—there's another thing. Monkglass. We can use the station. Their scanners could confirm which of the models is correct."

Tank slaps the display table, incandescent with excitement. "Shit. That's fucking genius. You could jump in, make contact with the station, get the confirmation, and get back out."

Her childish enthusiasm balances the muted response from the rest of the room, weighed down by years of anxieties. The fears of carrying out such a complicated operation. The memories of failed sorties past, ghosts of the many dead lodged under the skin.

Major Reyes cannot contain the force of xer objections. "This is stupidity. This is shit-tank stupidity. We know nothing about the conditions within the siege ring. To jump inside without any intel—to hinge the entire operation on jumping inside without any intel—that's madness."

Misery seethes with nuclear heat. "We have intel. The Larex Forge guides us."

"And does the Larex Forge tell you exactly what to expect inside the siege shield?"

No. But yes. "After everything you've seen, you still doubt? How long did Angelsteeth suffer repeated insults from the Heretics before Zie reached forth Hir hand and crushed them?" *Through me,* she wants to add. Zie worked through me.

"Are you certain you can pull it off?" asks the General.

Finally, someone with some faith. "I am."

"We still have to work out the logistics," bleats the Major.

General Tsung grunts. "We can work them out."

Pyrex Imogen, who has attended in silence, knowing the technicality of the details are beyond their station, says: "Can this be done without alerting the Heretics?"

"Absolutely," Tank says. "Like, you don't even have to touch them. The beauty of knowing the KD principles is that you can just scan the patterns, visually, and run the data against your predictions. It's, like, really basic stuff. We can pull it off, for sure, no problem."

The other attending engineers seem equally confident, in expression if not in speech. Misery folds her arms, thinking. Getting to Monkglass and getting inside will not be a problem. Not for her. Not for the archangel. Yet— "Will the crew on Monkglass understand what we're planning? How much explaining will I have to do?"

Tank and Diamond exchange glances, a moment of uncertainty as they each weigh the question and all the factors that make an answer. But Lightning says: "Don't worry. I'll go with you."

A buzz of confusion—the knowledge of what the princess can do has not been widely disseminated. Lightning sighs. "Look. Since I was returned from the dead—well. Since I was returned from the cave where we found the archangel, I've been able to control the seraph freely. I was touched by divine Grace, and the tools of the Larex Forge now do my bidding, as though an extension of my body."

A hush descends over the command room as the meaning

of her words sinks in. Veins of disbelief and bewilderment run through the other captains, who weren't fully briefed on this new ability of Lightning's. Captain Crystal Martin's face wrinkles with uncertainty. "You can control it the way Heretics do?"

"I can move it with my will. The Forge's will." The last part said with concentrated acid; Lightning chose her words carefully, and she does not appreciate the captain's spin on it. "As I was in slumber, healing from my long journey, I heard the voice of the Forge call out to me. Zie said that I had been chosen as companion for the Messiah upon their journey. I was the first to herald their coming. I was present at their enlightenment and awakening. So let me accompany them. Let me be there as they deliver the most glorious of victories into our hands."

She has a speechmaking instinct that would make Crem proud. Misery expects nothing less of the Imperial princess, fed the milk of power and influence from birth. "I need her by my side," Misery says. "She will ease our path when we reach Monkglass."

"Yes," murmurs the General. "After all, they have been cut off from our networks for months. They would not know of her . . . fall from grace, shall we say. They would recognize her as a figure of authority."

Silence falls again, contemplative and unsure. Misery scans the room trying to average out some kind of mean, gauge the overall mood of Angelsteeth's decisionmakers. They're afraid of commitment, afraid of saying yes to the big risk. She understands. Commitment is a scary thing. But that's what faith is.

"So," the major says, breaking the silence, "it's decided, then?" Xe's not thrilled about it. But the General believes, the Archbishop believes, who is xe to object? That no-nonsense character of xers, tending toward impatience. Xe desires quick resolution, aching for a path forward, a next step that requires action, even if xe does not agree with the principle of the action. A good soldier.

A collective breath held. The General nods once, finally. "It is decided. The two of you shall go. Let's get to planning."

"What you said at the command center. What was that about?"

The day has stretched into exhaustion territory, gill-stuffed with meetings and obsessive strategizing down to the position of each ship and soldier, and the transition protocol between each scenario depending on what Misery finds out at Monkglass. Contingencies running from "Monkglass is crawling with Heretics" to "everyone on Monkglass is dead," Forge preserve. It's an ugly scenario, and it upsets the Archbishop to be even thought of, but it has to be prepared for. Tomorrow Misery and Lightning will practice their jumps while the rest of the station gets their garters in gear. The day after that, they move out. There isn't much time; the threat of being discovered hangs ever over them. But for now they must attend to mortal needs: food, sleep, silence. Misery and Lightning have come to rest in the warm cubby of the shower stall, a routine that Ono Red-2 has learned to give them space for. Skin glides against skin, agreeable in the mist and pulses of the sonic cleanser. It smells like clementines in here. Their own slice of paradise.

Lightning blinks sleepily at Misery's question, as if she doesn't remember what Misery is referring to. "What was what about?"

Misery presses the weight of her hands into the princess's hips. "The Larex Forge spoke to you in your slumber?" She's not accusing the princess of lying. She's just curious why she's never heard of it before this. It would have been nice to know, if it wasn't something she just made up for the benefit of the upper brass.

"That." Guilt suffuses her expression and she looks away.

"I— Did I dream it, or did I dream I dreamed it? I haven't spoken of it before, have I?"

"You haven't."

"It's not— I wasn't keeping it from you, or making it up. I promise. It's just . . ." She pulls away for a second, creating a void between them, air rushing to fill the space. Lightning presses the knuckles of her thumbs into her eye sockets, as if as if she could crush the uncertainty out of her mind. "I have the memory of it, so it must mean it happened, right? The Larex Forge speaking to me, in my mind. Just as Zie used to when I was a child."

"It's all right to doubt."

"I don't doubt it. I don't! It's just—I don't remember when it happened, exactly, that's all. The whole stretch of time between going with you and coming back, waking up on Angelsteeth . . . It's just a big mess. I think it happened then. I think. But if I try to grasp the memory for more than a few seconds, if I try to place it precisely in the sequence of events in my life, then it slips away. And I start to doubt everything I recall."

Misery takes Lightning's petulant fists in her own and massages them, working the tension out of bone and tendon. "If you remember it, then it happened."

She turns to Misery, shining with gratitude. "It did, didn't it? I was the one Zie told of your existence. I was the one Zie placed right beside you as you answered your calling. All this while, I've resented the path my existence has taken. I resented you, even. But I understand now. Why things had to happen the way they did . . . I'm grateful."

Lightning leans her full weight upon Misery's hips. She's close enough their clavicles are almost touching. Misery can see in her expression that the thoughts in her head are hardening, her convictions setting like stone, becoming part of her architecture. "The Larex Forge told me I was to be your handmaiden," she says. "The one to be by your side, always. And when Zie said that it was like thunder going off in my head. Suddenly my life made sense. Everything I do, I do for you."

Misery slips her fingers downward, curling the tips into the thicket of hair between Lightning's thighs. "Good," she whispers. "Give yourself to me, then. Give me everything that you are."

Lightning pushes her face into the side of Misery's neck; her breath tickles Misery's ears. "Gladly," she whispers in between breaths. "It was all yours anyway."

31

Misery spends the day as archangel, in that body of stone that sees all and does all, practicing jumping into the space between the stars. Some call it the great unknown, but that's mortal-speak, with their limited vision and limited bodies that fear things greater than they are. There is no unknowability in the great cosmos, only boundless potential, and the archangel Misery stands before the banquet of stars like one looking to dine. Zie likes hirself better like this, all arms and feet and a core of power that hums the melody and bassline of the universe's song, unafraid of anything and ready for action. All her life the mortal Misery resisted being told what to do, resisted the hand of her brother and the wisdom of the Larex Forge, thinking that she would lose the greater part of herself trying to obey. Resenting the idea that she would have to cut herself down to size. But how wrong she was! How misguided. Her brother, he was misguided too. There is no smallness in service of the Demiurge. Now that zie has accepted hir duty, now that zie has accepted hir role, Misery discovers hirself more vast than zie has ever been. Having found obedience, zie has been rewarded with the infinite. Zie sails from star to star, free as zie wishes. In fearing the null-void, humans learned to fear the vastness of space, leading lives suffused with paranoia, afraid of every small thing that might disturb their minds and let in corruption. But there is no fear when one is cradled in the arms of the Larex Forge.

All this the archangel Misery now understands. So does the princess, hir companion and hir handmaiden, the two of them made for one another, fitting together like tongue and groove.

She, too, has spent a lifetime running from the destiny presented to her, until Misery brought her back and set her upon the right path. Both of them have suffered pain as a result of their divine fates, but that pain did not come from the Larex Forge. It was the result of human fallibility. Misery and Lightning understand one another like no one else can. They are each other's mirrors, after all. Indivisible until the end of time. Together, they— archangel and liberated seraph—learn to take measured leaps away from Angelsteeth, first the hesitant step of half a parsec, followed by a full parsec. Then two, four, eight, sixteen. Each time they gain more confidence in their movements. More joy. Misery remembers the first time they jumped together through the vastness of space, when they were only mortal and so tiny, so fragile and foolish. Awe had ripped them asunder as they were transported toward the archangel. Now they are that awe incarnate, with their colossal and tireless bodies, whose forms inspire ineffable emotions in the human mind. They have become death, destroyers of worlds. They have become life, the origins of species. Both are aspects of the Forge.

The evening before the great operation, Ono Red-2 dines in private by request of Diamond, who wants space from the wide-eyed clamor of the greater banquet of Angelsteeth. Time to think in silence, unobserved and unjudged by the swathes of rank and file who have yoked their hopes and existences to what plays out tomorrow. Oven-hot trays are brought to their quarters. It's a plain meal, quiet: rice and slot-grown veg in mild gravy, slivers of fish protein. To eat extravagantly before a major operation is bad luck. Puts one in a last-meal mindset. Invites the nullvoid.

"You weren't there when the General made their speech to the masses," Spider says. "I thought they'd want their Messiah there, say some pretty Forge-touched words for the soul."

"What did they say?"

"Oh, nothing important. Rabble-rousing speech, talk about sacrifice and gratitude and faith that we've been put here to do the right thing. You know, the usual."

"You think it would have gone better if I was there."

"Frankly? No. It's all bluster. Hollow words. Wouldn't have made a difference."

"Words make all the difference," Lightning says quietly. "They always do."

In the lull after, as food makes heavy the bellies of those who eat, Misery drifts to Ghost's side. Ono Red-2's quietest member sits by themself, observing the rest with a fevered expression. Gravy gleams at the bottom of their tray. "What are you thinking?" she asks them.

"Not much," they say.

Misery knows this to be a lie: thoughts brim over in their mind, loud as a stonecore's melody. She sinks into the foam beside them. "I've been meaning to ask a question," she says, which is true. She has always wondered this about Ghost, a background hum to their every interaction, and Jericho's lies have only darkened her curiosity. "You said you weren't a telepath."

"I'm not."

"Is that why you were taken out of the saints' program?"

"I don't know what you mean."

They seem genuinely perplexed. "I met a lot of your kind on the Capital. Clones, right? In service of the Emperor and the Throne. They're telepaths, aren't they?"

"No, they're not. Why do you have the impression that they are?"

Good question; she admires that. "It's a rumor. They don't speak, they take orders and communicate through unseen methods. Is it not telepathy?"

"No." Ghost lifts their heels onto the chair, boots and all, to tuck their knees under their chin. "They don't speak because we were disciplined for speaking in the program. Their communication—I assume they have a system, the way we do here."

Such things did not exist in the constellations of her understanding when she was first on the Capital. She presses on, moving smoothly over the hump of embarrassment in her way. "So you weren't raised to be telepaths, then."

"No. It's as Dr. Sower said. We've tried, but it doesn't work. The Heretics have managed to breed telepaths, but we don't know how."

She leans forward. "Because it's not possible. Because it's a cavity of the nullvoid." Triumph blossoms in her chest. She's right, again, about Jericho being full of shit. She's getting confirmation everywhere she looks. "The pure reject the stings of nothingness. There's no reason the Faithful have any need for telepaths." But of course, the Throne would fund and encourage these sorts of research. She likes Dr. Sower well enough, but that will not be allowed to stand. She shall see to it.

Ghost rests their chin between the points of their knees. What's troubling them is slowly bubbling to the surface. "Do you think I'm impure, Misery?"

"No. I didn't say that. When did I say that?"

"You didn't. But I've read a lot of holy writing lately." They fold their arms around themself. "In Scripture it says creating in the image of humanity is a sin. Only that made by the Forge is pure. The Demiurge alone can cut from the cloth of the universe, beyond the taint of the void. Humanity must refrain from creating intelligent life by unnatural means."

Misery issues a gentle correction. "That's talking about artificial intelligence. Like ALISS, you know. It's forbidden to make an AI. For good reason."

Ghost squints, unwilling to accept this wisdom. "Do not presume to emulate the labors of the Forge," they intone, quoting the words of Saint Jota. "An artificial being shall ever be contaminated with the radiation of the nullvoid."

They're being stubborn in a way Misery particularly understands. They've thought about this a long time; those words have sunk into their marrow and a forest of doubt has sprouted there. They crave both the sting of rejection and the salve of exoneration, and they don't know which one they deserve more. Right now, they're asking Misery to decide.

She puts her hand on Ghost's arm. Warmth rises beneath the synthetic layer of their clothes. The nixen blinks, surprised by the contact. "Hey. Listen. I know what you're thinking. For the longest time I was also told I was tainted and broken, an abomination to be shunned and hidden away. I believed those voices. I thought my abilities were conferred by voidmadness. But you know? They were wrong."

Ghost listens intently, their appraisal bright and untouchable as the surface of a sun. Misery continues: "The Larex Forge moves with absolute purpose. Everything and everyone Zie has put in place, Zie has done so deliberately. Even that Heretic, Jericho. The Heretics are Hir children too, even as they reject Hir teachings. The Larex Forge takes care of all." She squeezes the wiry muscle of her servingmate's arm. "If you're here, then you're meant to be here. That's all there is to it."

They smile. A rare and dazzling event. Spider comes by, all noise and flash, draping arms over them both. "All right, enough gloom, I don't believe in all that being po-faced before missions shit. Let's make some merry. Let's dance."

So they dance. Music rills through the room, courtesy of Tank. Cremoline flows. No undertable salves: Diamond and Misery are in vocal agreement about that. Their performance tomorrow cannot be compromised. Misery sways to the slow thunder of the beat, lines of sweat gravitating to the dips in her skin. She presses herself against the flesh of her servingmates, absorbing their stickiness and warmth. The flesh is a gift from the Forge, fragile yet precious. She revels in it, basks in the sensations that wash through her.

Somehow, she ends up next to her captain, their hips bumping bone to bone. Diamond's eyes are dark with cremoline and a childlike energy blazes from her. She burns with more hope and ecstasy than she's felt since the incident. Tomorrow she gets to close the loop of her tragedy, and she knows that it is only through the Grace of the Forge that she has been given a second chance to take out her foe. She will not waste it. Diamond spins on a heel and seizes Misery's hands in hers. "Thank you for all this. Know that no matter what happens, you will always have my gratitude."

Misery grins, baring her teeth to the void. Hunger boils in her veins. "To destiny," she says.

Diamond roars back. "To destiny!"

Pyrex Imogen leaves before the banquet sets out the next morning. It can't be helped: their unexplained absence is already noticed upon the Capital, and a simple search would expose the trail leading them to Angelsteeth in a minute. They cannot stay to watch the triumph to come; they must return to the orbit of Emperor and Throne to provide cover for their holy sedition. Misery goes to see them in the slumber hours, meeting them in the exit bays before they leave. In the cold strength of the bay lights the Archbishop looks paler and more washed-out than ever. Sounds echo, bouncing off the huge dark walls of the bay, the metal struts and harsh surfaces. "Oh, child," Pyrex Imogen says, at Misery's approach. "You should be resting for the fight."

"I don't need rest," she says, and it's true: Hir Grace gives her all the verve she needs. "I wanted to see you before you left."

The Archbishop smiles and the lines around their eyes deepen. "If it's my blessing you seek, you hardly need it. You have all the gifts you require from the Forge."

"I was not seeking benediction." The idea is absurd: what could the Archbishop offer her that she does not already have? "I wanted to tell you that I will do everything in my power to make sure your sister makes it out safely."

"Oh, child." Pyrex Imogen clasps her hands, holding them tightly as though in prayer. Their knuckles shine as they lower their head, brow heavy with curious thought. Misery is patient. She waits. Something weighs upon the Archbishop's conscience, and it will dislodge itself soon enough.

Finally, Pyrex Imogen says, "Forgive me, Misery. I had my doubts, you know. Not when you came to us at first. But in the amphitheater, watching the wrath you brought down upon the nobility, the ones who just happened to be watching . . . I knew people in the stands who died. Most people on the Capital did, friends of friends . . . It's not such a large place that it can easily absorb the impact of such a tragedy. And my faith faltered in that moment, and I began to doubt. I even thought, this must be some kind of evil, for why would the Larex Forge rain such destruction upon Hir own Faithful? Forgive my weakness in that moment. I know I was seen by the Demiurge and I will be accordingly judged."

The amphitheater. Her confrontation with the boy Emperor. It seems so long ago now. Misery was a different creature back then, still darkened by doubt and her core of ego. Still unhumbled and saddled by hubris. But the Larex Forge was working through her even then. "You are already forgiven," she says. For if even she—the liar, the cheater, and unwilling Messiah—can be absolved of her crimes and granted the Grace of the Larex Forge, why shouldn't the Archbishop? "The compassion of the Demiurge is infinite, and far outstrips the foibles of our weak human natures. Nothing you do can turn Hir love away from you."

"This I believe. This I know." The Archbishop raises their head, their head and heart already lighter. "And you were right, in the end—the Larex Forge was right. Zie guided your hand toward a truth I was unwilling to see. Sometimes things have to be sacrificed in order to save something greater. Those deaths were necessary, a wake-up call that would otherwise have never come."

She nods. "Sometimes a small sacrifice saves the greater whole."

"I wish you luck," says Pyrex Imogen. "Do it for me. Do it for my sister. Most of all, do it for those who still do not believe. Perhaps this way we can save their souls."

INTERLUDE 9

Thus the banquet of Angelsteeth set out on the mission that would place them in the annals of history. Four courses of thirty-two dishes, each with four servings, hundreds of personnel of all ranks and ages. A hundred sleek black ships, with hearts of live holystone, surrounded by the iridescent silhouettes of seraphim. A sight for the poets and playwrights and propagandists, enough grace and majesty to fill the hearts of billions scattered across the wide, starry voids. Yet no more than a swarm of fleas, mere specks, a sea of microorganisms, when juxtaposed against the scope and width of the universe. A bare flicker of existence in a firmament billions of years old.

Angelsteeth has prepared as well as it could, the last twenty-four hours consumed by a maelstrom of activity. The major briefed the commanders of the operationally ready courses, the commanders briefed their captains, and so on. No time for drills. Protocols put into action, systems tested and checked, supplies stocked and countdowns started. In their private quarters, in slivers of downtime, soldiers writing last letters to loved ones. Just in case things don't work out. Just in case things go south. Hope carries them aloft like a divine gale, but below them, ever present, is a bottomless ocean of fear, whose acid-blue waters would swallow them without mercy or remorse. These are unprecedented times within unprecedented times. There's only so much a human person can do.

On the edge of the duchy of Canis they quietly ride a jump slot with a convoy booked by Marquis Wayhire, whose long history with Pyrex Imogen has accrued significant personal debt. The ships exit in the mouth of the duchy of Suidae, home of

Monkglass, whose Duke had arranged passage to the besieged station. There they will wait, half a light-year away from their destination, while the archangel Misery and the freed seraph take a prayer and leap, driven by faith, into the heart of the siege of Monkglass, where they hope to make contact with its crew, dismantle the siege mechanism, and wake the jump portal that serves the station. A plan that sounded shaky even in line-by-line bullets; the potential for failure lurking at every point. It was unwise, and some would even say madness, to jump into an engagement that was a black box from the outside. Despite their meticulous planning, despite the intel from the Heretic prisoner, none of them knew what was truly waiting for the Messiah when they arrived on Monkglass, assuming they made it through in the first place.

But then again, that's what faith entails, doesn't it?

The banquet of Angelsteeth takes up positions by the jump gate assigned to them. The archangel and the free seraph make preparations to leave. Their captain goes over the plan with them one last time, just to be sure: a precisely calculated leap into the innermost cavity of the siege, proof of life and visual contact with the commander of Monkglass, confirmation of the siege net's configuration. And then the riskiest part by their current calculations: exiting the shield, taking out the six network pillars, and activating the jump portal for the banquet to come sweeping in. It's the part of the plan the Messiah is most confident about.

Signoff. All stations go. The banquet of Angelsteeth begins its long, tense wait. The archangel Misery Nomaki takes company of the liberated seraph, fires up hir engines, and takes a leap forward into the waiting arms of destiny.

32

Something isn't right.

The archangel Misery knows this the moment zie tears through the fabric of space and emerges within the borders of the siege mechanism. The stars coalesce around hir as though emerging from water, and overhead the net of Heretic ships looms like a great glass ceiling. A human eye would see nothing—thirty-six ships scattered over the surface equivalent of a small moon would be lost in the blanket of the cosmos, the billions and billions of pinpricks set against the cold, each one a sun too far away to touch. Hard to find something as small as a ship in all of that. But the archangel Misery is more than human, and each of those stars is but a waypoint, a marker in the map of the universe. The Heretic ships blaze with malicious will in hir sight. Thirty-six darts tilting the entropy of the nullvoid in their direction, sinks of possibility that map onto the human Misery's neurology as a jolt of tartness, increasing in acidity as time moves forward in material space.

And then, there—lording over them, cutting an enormous orbit around the siege net, is their leader. Outside of the shield, but in command. The archangel Misery instantly recognizes the blade for what it is. A sibling to the ship zie cut open in defense of Angelsteeth Base, which seems an age ago. Here is another for them to destroy. Esse Temple lurks within, wicked and bloodthirsty, a foul blossom on the nullvoid. Hunger rises: zie aches to do it again. The archangel Misery could split that ship's skin and spill its profane contents like so much seed pulp. But no—zie must be patient. That is not the agreed-upon plan. And the human Faithful, the captain Sunyata Diamond—she has been given the honor of dealing the final blow. As she should.

Before them, at the center of it all, lies Monkglass Station. The subject of their labors, waiting for liberation. On the left are the jaws of the jump portal, its gums rendered gray and inactive by the siege mechanism. On the right is the sparkling top that is Monkglass Station, fat in the middle and tapering to spike points above and below. Acrylplate shines in generous swathes, making up most of the upper dome, and beneath that clear layer lives a canopy of lights and metal architecture. A pretty bauble floating in space. In happier times Monkglass was a thriving spaceport, a center of commerce, a waypoint between the duchies Taurus and Canis. Thousands called it their home. And there are thousands still, even in these days of decline. Those same thousands have been trapped under its gleaming facade for months. Now the renegades of the holy have come to rescue them from their long confinement.

Yet something is wrong. As the archangel Misery sails toward the glittering cabochon of Monkglass, the free seraph by hir side, the sense of something being off-kilter grows and grows. The archangel Misery understands situations by means inexplicable to human minds and human bodies; zie sees the truth in patterns and possibilities. The patterns here say alarming things. In the shape of the Heretic dragnet, in the flickering of Monkglass's lights, there's a lack of tension zie expects of a siege. It's more than a visual cue, of course. There are layers and layers beneath what can be seen and perceived by mortal eyes. But the archangel Misery knows something is wrong.

The Heretics continue on their trajectories, unaware of their presence. The Schroedinger shield appears to hold. Monkglass, stuporous from long inactivity, has not yet noticed their presence. But it lights up all prickly and alarmed when the free seraph opens a channel, every needlepoint sensor going alert at the appearance of these intruders. The princess Lee Alodia Lightning speaks to the comms grunt on the other side. Tells hir who they are, what they've come to do. Asks permission to board. To speak to the commander, the Lady Storm Mirelle. It's a calculated risk, taking the time to see her in person, but that risk was calculated by the best strategists in the army, so it has passed muster. Even in these days of faith, nothing substitutes for face-to-face contact, for physical proof of life. The miraculous must be witnessed in the flesh.

A crackle. A long pause. The uncertainty and suspicion that permeates the wait is palpable. They don't recognize the archangel mech, they don't know if the intruders are friendly or not. But surely the voice of the Imperial princess is enough? Surely her signing code is all the authority they need?

The voice returns. Permission granted. Yet Monkglass doesn't let its guard down. Distrust follows the two holy units as they sail toward the port opening in the station's underside. Should they not be grateful? Should they not be overflowing in joy at the possibility of their salvation? It's more suspicion than is trained on the net of Heretics abovehead.

Metal jaws open to reveal more metal jaws, and the two mechs are sucked down the gullet of Monkglass into a vast dry dock that at one time roared with merchant ships emptying or filling their bellies. In these days of siege it stands hollow and empty, except for the ominous ranks of security filing in to greet their visitors. There are no mech hooks—Monkglass isn't military, it has no mechs—so the archangel Misery gingerly places hir four feet on the ground. Next to hir the free seraph does the same. The structure of the station shudders as their enormous bulk comes to rest.

Every soldier on Monkglass has assembled to meet them. There's less than a tenth of a full banquet assigned to the station, but that's enough to line every sharktooth deck and observation tier with severe faces, flanked by the muzzles of weapons ranging from palm phasers to near-range thermal bazookas. A ragtag mess, but teeth are still teeth.

A voice booms in the recycled air beyond the archangel's stone shell. "Exit the units immediately."

It feels like a mistake, exposing the soft vessel that is the mortal Misery Nomaki to their guns and their naked hostility. But perhaps the denizens of Monkglass will be appeased by their human forms. Surely the Lady Storm just wants to make sure they are who they say they are. So the separation occurs. Misery Nomaki detaches from the womb of the archangel mech and her consciousness withdraws into her fleshbound body with its inadequate senses. The loss is keenly felt. As stone recedes from her torso and legs, as cold light and cold air seep into the crack widening over the pilot module, Misery's fingers seek out her mother's amulet. Of course, it's not there. It's embedded in the teeth of the archangel mech.

Misery's implant connects immediately with Monkglass's system. Superimposed letter and light flood her visual cortex as she steps onto the lip of the pilot's module. This is the visitors' index, bright and fulfilling and meant to instill comfort. A singular data lozenge appears over the figure that scowls on a floating platform a rock's throw away from the two mechs: Commander Ashe, they/them, second-in-command to the Lady Storm. Small and ropy, hard-jawed, with light eyes and hair flat and copper. As Misery crawls up to pry her mother's amulet from its keyhole, they bark: "Keep your hands where I can see them!"

Misery scowls. "I need this with me."

"Hands in the air!"

Misery keeps at it, inching the disc out of its receptacle. It comes loose and she slips the amulet's cord over her head, taking her sweet time. Commander Ashe is not a saint, and neither are the soldiers trembling upon the metal rails of the drydock. They aren't going to shoot. No one will dare. Monkglass is one of a dozen trading posts, absolutely unremarkable before the siege thrust it into the spotlight. Built and staffed for mediocrity. Its personnel came into their assignments knowing that they were the second pull, the midlist of their cohorts, those assigned after the star pupils have been sent to the exciting, dangerous, challenging parts of space. They expected a life of ease and quiet: placid days spent supplemented with cremoline and sex and other harmless endorphin jolts. If they want to strike fear into Misery, they'll need to try harder.

On the other side of the gulf between their units, Lightning perches on the edge of her seraph, crackling with indignation. "Is this how you welcome a member of the Imperial family?"

To their credit, Commander Ashe doesn't buckle. Maybe their voice trembles a little, but beneath it lies commitment and loyalty to their superior officer. "Your Highness. The Lady Storm asks an audience of you."

"*We* sought an audience with *her*," says the princess, reminding this simple grunt of the hierarchy at work.

Commander Ashe shifts uncomfortably. "Yes, of course. You are right." They fear an eruption of violence within the station, after so many months of carefully balanced peace.

"Well, don't keep us waiting," Lightning says. "Can you not see this is an emergency?"

"Yes. Your Highness. At once."

A floating platform comes up to each mech, nuzzling against the lips of the pilot module, and as Misery steps onto its scuffed surface an aegis snaps across its open edges. Intellectually, she knows it's a cargo platform. Psychologically, she feels imprisoned.

Ruin manifests next to the platform as it slides forward. "Be careful, Misery Nomaki," zie says. "Things are not as they seem."

She already knows this, and the angel's confirmation bolsters her spirit. She's right to be suspicious. With her guard up and her spine clad with steel she lets the platform take her where Commander Ashe and the Lady Storm want her.

The platforms snap to the edge of a loading dock, one after another, depositing them into the grasp of armed escorts. As Lightning steps onto the ringing metal, the last to disembark, the ring of faceplated soldiers closes around them, Commander

Ashe at their pole. Now that they are on a level surface Misery can see that Ashe is barely taller than she is, with the same kind of stocky build from a supergrav upbringing. Their data lozenge calls them a citizen of Tabonis Outpost, in the duchy of Canis. Wasn't there a wave drama set there? Mining colony, ice moon, higher than average number of murders? Misery can see Ashe's life story now, written clear in the tilt of their chin, the narrowing of their eyes. Grew up scrappy and dustpoor, first in the family to make the Imperial Academy, now full commander of a good-sized station, rubbing shoulders with nobility and all that. Once they were small, now they are big, and nothing intimidates them anymore. They glint with the untamed hubris of the traded-up. This might have been the path of Misery's life if the Demiurge hadn't decided otherwise.

In the end, it doesn't matter. Commander Ashe is irrelevant to the plan; they have no role to play here. Misery falls in step with Lightning as the commander leads them down reinforced walkways to the dock exits. The princess seethes quietly, fists tight. "Wasn't the welcome I was expecting," she says to Misery.

"Be on your guard," Misery says, low enough to escape Commander Ashe's attention. "Something here's not right."

Lightning thinks the same thing Misery suspects. There are contingency plans for Heretic infiltration and the ruins of genocide. But they seem to have landed in the best-case scenario, Monkglass firmly under righteous control. Yet Misery's skin crawls with urgency. The Demiurge warns her to keep her guard up. Caution, caution. Misery's already thinking of escape routes, ways to carve through security and bulkhead if things go sideways. Monkglass vibrates with stonesong, holy obsidian and holy jade at her fingertips at every turn. If they test her, if they decide to fuck around, they're going to find out.

They trail after Commander Ashe, sandwiched between nervous wedges of the rank and file. The personnel on Angelsteeth have become acclimatized to Lightning's presence, but these simple soldiers are nervous around someone whose name, whose family name they have only heard as whisper in prayer, whose visage they have only seen in archival newsreels. To them the Imperial princess is a mythic figure on level with the Eight Saints and Benthen of Korth. Yet here she is. Elegant, shoulders held straight, face crimped with a heavy mix of suspicion and disdain.

The soldiers surrounding them spike with adrenaline, stressed out by this disruption to the diurnal sameness of the siege. They've gotten used to porridgy days melting into featureless nights, nothing happening and nothing changing. Misery senses their willingness to continue living this gray limbo and their dismay at the disruption that is ongoing. The siege hasn't been bad for them.

It's a long march. No teleport pads here, for sure. The station's corridors are narrower and barer than on Angelsteeth, but that's by design. It's a smaller, humbler place than a hub of research and a seraph training base. Monkglass's system feed betrays an outpost chugging along at optimal capacity. Refreshing squares of information live-update its denizens on stockpile levels of everything from stonecharge to meal napkins. What's being rationed and what's not. What's on the waves, which R&R areas are open today. A scroll of uplifting pap at the bottom to boost the spirits. "The hands that shaped you will be the hands that save you." Whoever comes up with these aphorisms should be strangled.

Things are definitely off. Everyone's watched at least one entry from the glut of wave dramas about the Siege of the Vine, which come in a wide variety of grimness and self-importance, but even the creamiest, frothiest of these offerings agree on the hallmarks of a long siege. Finger-numbing temperatures, unbearable dimness, flashing yellow marking sectors where gravity has been shut off. Monkglass bears none of these wounds, somehow. Stonecharge is the first thing to dwindle in a station siege, yet Monkglass seems to have an unlimited supply of it. In the living areas the station hums warm and bright and unblemished. Their path cuts through the upper level of a forum, a glass-and-metal pathway over a park that reminds Misery of her time on the Capital. The station's public areas have been emptied, everyone sent back to their rooms at the appearance of the strange intruding mechs. But even this emptiness has an aura of peace. Meditative and considered.

Ruin floats next to Misery, unseen to all but her. "We seem to be interrupting a good time," zie muses.

As emissary from the Demiurge, it would be really helpful if the angel could shed some light on what's happening here.

"I shall have a look," zie says, and vanishes.

The padding of the civilian sectors gives way to the stark metal of the operational zones. Commander Ashe takes them through back door after back door, heavily armored and yellow-striped, their passageways bare metal and open vents and noise. Lots of aux stairways. They're headed upward in the most circuitous way, keeping them away from elevators and other personnel. Misery can summon a map of the station on her system HUD, but the areas they're traversing through are gray blanks. She's been set up with visitor's access, which might be the most insulting part of it all.

Then the door before Commander Ashe slides open and light rushes in. Beyond the stark frame lies a vista of glass and gleaming chrome, pulsing with the energy of a nerve center. On aesthetics alone Misery knows where they are. Monkglass's command hub coruscates with screens in a selection of aggressive colors. Personnel weave from station to station with the jitter and pitch of cheap salves. The orb of a room isn't built for a parade, it's barely larger than Ono Red-2's quarters, and their contingent—Ashe, guards, and all—takes up most of the space as they pass through. Techs stare. Misery tastes their confusion and anxiety. A common refrain: *You're not supposed to be here.* But it's not for them to decide.

The terminus of their pilgrimage lies ahead. A kidney of mirrored glass lords over the command hub, held aloft by holy tigereye, its contents concealed, its surroundings stretched and distorted over its bright surface. A sense of watchfulness emanates from it, as though a thousand burning eyes lie under the silver skin. In her gut Misery knows that the truth of her long, strange journey waits within. Adrenaline, her old friend, pools under the arch of her sternum.

A door carves itself open in the gleaming pod. Commander Ashe leads them up the crystalline ramp and into the cool darkness within. Inside, the silver walls are upholstered by display screens, turning the office into a view pod with a live feed of the outside. Stars glisten in velvet. Monkglass's circulatory systems hum. A lavish cone of flowers sits on the touchdesk.

In the middle of it all, standing upon a disc of holy opal, is a figure all too familiar. She's in conversation with something, or someone, via a white-bright screen obscured by her silhouette. It snaps off the moment she hears them come in, but not before Misery registers that she was having a conversation with someone. A conversation she does not want anyone else to see. Her senses go electric. Secrets, hiding in plain sight. No. She will not stand for this.

The Lady Storm Mirelle. Outside of Misery's dreams her beauty hurts: dark eyes, sharp cheeks, fine lips slanted in controlled disapproval. Ivory tuille layers a gracile figure, granting her a crystalline silhouette. Unlike Pyrex Imogen, there is color to her skin, startling against the pale scrim of her hair and dress.

Through the medium of her dreams, Misery had glimpsed someone gentle but sad. The woman before them is something else: a blade, cunning and sharp-edged, absolutely glacial with fury. She registers Misery's presence through narrowed eyes, but pulls on a cloak of deference as she addresses Lightning. "Your Highness. I was not expecting you." A slight bow.

Lightning does not return the courtesy. "Quite the welcome you prepared for us."

"Quite the surprise you've sprung on us," counters the Lady

Storm. "We are under siege. You can understand why we don't take well to strange mechs showing up in our airspace. How did you get past the siege mechanism?"

"Through the Grace of the Larex Forge," Lightning says.

Which is the truth, but it's not what the Lady Storm wants to hear. She wants details, she wants plans of action and chains of command. She wants explanations that will place Lightning and Misery's appearance safely in a matrix of cause and effect. "That white mech that came with you. What is it? I've never seen anything like it."

Does she think this a Heretic trick? Her thoughts don't taste that way, somehow. Her fear and suspicion stem from different sources. "The archangel mech is also a gift from the Larex Forge," Misery says.

The Lady Storm's cold regard fixates back on Misery. She does not recognize this strange, stocky nixen, and why should she? Her ordeal began months before Misery was raised up by the Larex Forge. She has not heard. She does not know. Her query cuts to the point: "You are that mech's pilot, I assume?"

"I am." Misery lifts her chin, absorbing the chill in that gaze. Welcoming it, even. There must be pathways to the center of the Lady Storm's being where trust resides, and Misery intends to push her way in. She knows her sibling, the Archbishop, and there must be some shared thread of faith between them. As she swayed Pyrex Imogen to her side, so too will she sway the Lady Storm. "The hand of the Larex Forge guided me to it, just as Zie guided me to Monkglass in its hour of need."

"In the hour of our need." The Lady Storm's echo is laced with pure distilled skepticism.

Lightning says: "Misery is the Ninth Messiah, chosen of the Larex Forge, the one I saw in my visions as a child. They were led to the archangel mech. I went with them. I watched that miracle unfold. And they had dreams of you, even though they did not know who you were. It was a sign. Now we come to liberate Monkglass from the clutches of the Heretics."

"So the Throne sent you? They ordered that the siege be ended, by force?"

How skillfully she cuts to the center of it! Lightning hesitates. She knows her brother would never. She knows the weaknesses of the Throne. Yet she does not want to lie to the Lady Storm. Shouldn't the truth be sufficient?

Misery cuts in. "The Larex Forge sent us. What more authority do you need?"

"Your twin sent us," Lightning adds, loud and bold. A truth balanced on the edge of a lie. The perfect tool, angled just so. "They are worried about you."

Breath bursts out of the Lady Storm. She turns away, face twisted with emotion she cannot hold down. Misery latches onto that fount of information—there, there! Something she can use. A way past the glacial walls of the Lady Storm Mirelle. A pungent, caustic fear lives in the heart of her and if Misery could strike at it, the commander of Monkglass might come undone, her resistance broken. The Lady Storm harbors secrets of her own, and she's afraid of them coming to light. Falsehood lives in the heart of the siege. Misery sensed it the moment she stepped outside the archangel. She draws closer and closer to its shape.

The Lady Storm composes herself, looking a dozen years older as she addresses them. "Well. Imogen is strong-willed and they always have been. They have their ideas about the best way to end this war. But they shouldn't have done this." She takes in another breath and drops it. "They should have left this alone."

Lightning said: "Are you implying you don't want the siege ended?"

The Lady Storm speaks through her teeth. "I will not have it ended through violence."

There it is. The ugly thing the Lady Storm wanted to hide. Here stands someone whose loyalties lie with the Heretics. But why? And how?

"Not through violence?" Exasperation bursts forth from Lightning. "Do you think they'll just withdraw if we ask nicely?"

"Don't try that on me. Someone of your station should be well aware how close we are to a formal truce. This endless, pointless war could be over in a few years. One senseless act of aggression could derail the peace process."

"Aggression? They made the first move."

"Please. Stop. I have not asked for this help. Tell Imogen—"

"You wish for the Heretics to triumph," Misery says. She is absolutely sure of this now. The betrayal is familiar, but cuts deep.

"I wish for the war to be over," says the Lady Storm.

"You're just like my brother," Lightning spits. "And Grandmother. You don't see that to compromise is to lose."

"And you are a foolish child. I see now. You've decided to defy your brother's wishes and have used the resources of the Church—somehow—to pull this off. I don't know how you put Imogen to this, but you've placed us all in grave danger."

Lightning's teeth are fully bared. "You don't even know what you're talking about. You're going to see how wrong you are."

The clues are all around Misery. Commander Ashe is an open book, terrified of disrupting their friendly equilibrium with the Heretics. There's the abnormal ease with which Monkglass has adapted to its months of siege. And the Lady Storm herself? The Larex Forge has been showing Misery the truth all along. Her dreams were the message. The dreams have always been the message.

The realization strikes Misery like a live lead. She recalls the now-forgettable details of her prophetic dreams, the bits she has buried thinking they were embarrassing or unimportant. In her first vision of the Lady Storm, an age ago on the Capital, near the start of the story, the saint had appeared while speaking to an onscreen lover. *A soldier-type butch, handsome-jawed, summer-straw hair shorn in hedgerows.* The lover, Misery thought, was a red herring: a distraction from the Larex Forge's greater message. A private moment she was not supposed to see, that she had stumbled upon by accident. But the lover was the dream's center of gravity. She interpreted the signs wrong.

The call that the Lady Storm was taking. Who was she speaking to? How is Monkglass, ostensibly under siege, getting calls from ships on the outside? The answer, self-evident, reveals itself to Misery almost at once. Of course. It's the only logical conclusion. As she realizes the truth of what's been happening on Monkglass all this while, her cheeks heat with righteous fury. "You were speaking to someone before we came in. Who was it?"

The Lady Storm's expression hardens. "You have no authority to ask those questions of me."

"But I do," says Lightning, cutting in with vigor, ready to abuse her station at the drop of a nail. "As Imperial princess I demand you answer the question. Who were you speaking to?"

"You—" The Lady Storm addresses the princess with the air of an angry aunt. "Standing here, telling me what to do, while you act in the shadows against your brother's interests. The Emperor. I know he didn't send you. To think you could order me—that's rich—"

Ruin appears in the office, haloed with light, eyes the color of a sun. "Some interesting things I have discovered," zie says. "Would you like to see, Misery Nomaki? Would you like to see the truth surrounding Monkglass yourself?"

If there's anyone who can override the Lady Storm's stubbornness, it should be the angel. Surely zie can do something? Surely zie can answer the call?

A smile cants Ruin's lips in the right direction. "As you wish."

The air hums. Light shimmers, and a call screen sharpens into being, projected from the top of the office. As the room reacts with dismay to this unasked-for development, a human face resolves in the vid plaza. Sharp-jawed. Brown-skinned. Scar across the face, just like Misery's. Hair almost luminescent, but not quite—a hint of gray amid the white, a matte quality to the brisk waves that cover the crown of hir head. Shaved sides and back, with an indecipherable pattern buzzed into it.

The Lady Storm blanches beyond her complexion. "How did you—what?"

Lightning, drawing from wells of information better fed than Misery's, recognizes the intruder at once. "Esse Temple."

The face from her dream. The answer she's been looking for all this while. Esse Temple is the woman the Lady Storm was speaking to in Misery's dreams. A Heretic. She's been talking to the enemy.

Commander Temple has no courtesy. She does not wait for the alarm and confusion in the room to calm. She jumps straight into it: "So what is going on? Who are these people?"

Her voice is deep and smoky, crackling like plastic on fire. "Esse," the Lady Storm says, pale and angry, "I'm not done. I—"

"Did the Throne send them? What was that mech?"

Esse Temple, demanding answers from the confines of her screen. Behind her the walls undulate at random angles, dark and gleaming, glass and mica embedded in the surfaces. It's Misery's first glance at a Heretic ship and it makes her ill.

"I'm sorry," says the Lady Storm. Misery's hackles raise further. Apologizing to a Heretic—apologizing to *the* monstrous Heretic Esse Temple. In all the calculations on Angelsteeth, they never considered this: What if the Lady Storm, beloved sister of the Archbishop of Remus, has herself fallen to the nullvoid? "They're renegades, I'm trying to deal with them. Please—"

"We're renegades?" Lightning's voice goes up a pitch. She's vibrating with disbelief and indignation. "Look at you, pleading for supplication from a Heretic. Is this my brother's will? Or was this just you, with your history—"

"Shut up," snaps the Lady Storm, and Misery knows that flavor of anger. The initial eruption of rage, the sting of a slap that follows soon after, fury that turns its wielder into a beast. She clenches her fists, fight-or-flight activating, as the station's commander turns on Lightning. The princess bristles, but she shuts

up, struck by the ferocity of the Lady Storm's wrath. She knows
when not to fuck around.

"You can't control them," says Esse Temple. "I have to protect my fleet."

"No," says the Lady Storm. "I have it under control. We have
both their mechs, and they're both here, if we can get a message
through to the Throne, we can sort it out—"

"They're selling us out," Lightning whispers.

She's a traitor. The Lady Storm is a traitor. All this time Pyrex
Imogen has been worrying themself skeletal about their sister's
fate, and here she's been, cozying up to the enemy, whispering
sweet nothings to a monster, letting the nullvoid in. Misery fills
with righteous disgust. There will be a reckoning.

"Cut the feed," she says to the angel. She's seen enough. She's
seen all she needs to know.

Ruin tilts hir head and Esse Temple vanishes in the middle
of an angry sentence about broken trust. Broken trust, as if
Heretics could be trusted with anything, as if they were good
for anything except extermination.

Misery flashes her teeth. The rot at the heart of Monkglass is
finally laid bare. Was there even a siege in the first place? Were
the Heretic ships for show? All the news stories, all the hand-
wringing, that entire pathetic narrative, had it been a lie? The
station is not asking to be saved. It has never been.

The Lady Storm gestures to Ashe. "Arrest them." She will
hold these two interlopers in custody. Keep them imprisoned
where they can't do any harm. Their existence here is a wound,
tearing into the fragile body of the truces both political and personal. She will staunch the flow of blood, heal the unexpected
rift opening before her. She will maintain the status quo.

But Ashe freezes in fear: Arresting the Imperial princess?
Is that allowed? That moment of hesitation costs them. It's all
Misery needs. Do something, she thinks, and the angel sent to
her by the Forge grins, bright-eyed in hir triumph. Mere human
folly cannot thwart the will of the Demiurge.

In the flash of a human eye, Monkglass falls into divine hands. Ruin controls the station as easily as zie extracted secrets from its core. Power fails across the nerve center. Stonecharge fails. Darkness descends. Before anyone else in the office can react, Misery grabs Lightning by the wrist, and runs.

33

Misery and Lightning crash through the maze Monkglass has become, lit only by yellow strips of battery-run emergency lights, a gloaming just enough to wayfind without hitting architecture. Monkglass exerts a heavy pull, and Misery has dismissed it as part of the station's wrongness, the taint of the nullvoid manifesting as physical discomfort. But in this state of flight, lungs burning and limbs burning, she realizes it's gravity. Where Angelsteeth was a subgrav station, Monkglass's settings tend toward supergrav, possibly at its commander's vanity. It's just like home, except that Misery's body has forgotten what home is like. But at least she's built for this, her bones solid and her calves thick. Lightning, raised in the weak gravity of the Capital, is not having a good time. Breath scours her airways and acid stings each thudding footstep. The princess isn't complaining, and she won't stop: driven by need and adrenaline she will run until her body gives out. But Misery can't have that. Needs her whole and at her peak when she steps back into that cockpit.

So she pulls them sideways into a narrow service corridor. A moment to breathe and collect themselves. Panicked bootfall makes a surround-sound orchestra, some sections more distant than others. Monkglass seethes, trying to locate its intruders. The veil afforded by Ruin won't last forever. But they can afford this brief moment. They must.

Lightning's eyes gleam, pet-like, in the dark. "What just happened? You did this?"

"No. That was the angel. Ruin. My messenger. Zie cleared the path."

Understanding washes over Lightning. Of course. Saved by
the Grace of the Demiurge, they have been granted a tiny window to regroup. To plan their next moves. "I can't believe what
I saw. What I heard. The Lady Storm . . . she betrayed us."

"Collusion," says Misery. "All this time we thought Monkglass
was in danger. But they weren't. Maybe they got supplies in—or
someone was keeping them fed." At some level, Pyrex Imogen
must have known what was happening, the Church must have
known. Even if they stayed drunken in their denial. The Throne
was complicit in this betrayal, using Monkglass as a point of con-
tention with the Heretics as they edged toward a truce: the siege
an insult to them, a point of leverage in the endless back and
forth. *Negotiating* with Heretics. Misery grinds her teeth. "In my
visions of the Lady Storm . . . I saw her speak to Esse Temple.
But I didn't recognize the Heretic at all. I didn't think it was
important. I missed the signs. My dreams weren't meant to be
guidance. They were a warning from the Larex Forge."

"You couldn't have known." Icy fingers close around Misery's arm, pinched bloodless by adrenaline. "Even I didn't an-
ticipate this. My brother must have known, but it was kept so
hushed, I—" She shakes her head hard enough Misery sees her
braid flicking in the dark. "No, this was on me. I see it now. I
was supposed to teach you the ways of the Throne. I did not."

"None of that now." Reflection and recrimination can wait
their turn. Pressing matters are at hand. "We need to go."

Lightning tenses. "What's the plan?"

Misery unsheathes her teeth. She knows what she wants
done. She knows what she must do. Esse Temple, the woman
they've parleyed with, is a murderer. Her palms crusted with the
blood of innocents. Forget the war, forget the truce, forget the
petty shape of political ambition. Fuck what the Throne wants.
Fuck what anyone wants. There is evil here and she cannot suffer it to live. Misery has not forgotten her promise to Diamond
and Spider. They will get their vengeance. "We get back in the
mechs," she says. "We destroy the Heretics by our own hand."

The princess frowns. "We didn't get the information we sought."

The config of the Heretic siege. Does it even matter? "Fuck that, we don't need it. The moment power comes back, that traitor will rat us out to Esse Temple." She cracks her knuckles. In the main corridor, an unseen soldier barrels by, a dopplering shout of "T-minus two" that fades into muffled syllables. Time is running out. "We'll never take the Heretics by surprise; we have to subdue them by force. Fuck the siege net. It's for show. We have a bigger target."

"Esse Temple," Lightning says.

"She deserves no less than death," Misery says. "And the Demiurge granted us the tools for victory." Conviction fills the cage of her sternum. Today is the last day of Esse Temple's life. She will see to it. "Let's get to the units. Where we're going we don't need a map."

"It's a long way down."

"They can't stop us." Of that, Misery is sure. She has spent her life eluding the grasp of her enemies, going places she isn't supposed to. "Do you remember when we first met? Do you remember how hard I was to stop, even back then?"

Lightning grins, her face close enough to share breath with Misery. There! There she is, that flame-haired whip of danger Misery first encountered in the hot bowels of the Capital. Hungering for fat and thirsting for blood. She wets her lips. "You were a worthy match then. Now you're invincible. Destroyer of obstacles. I remember what you did at the arena."

"And I'll do it again," Misery says. Her blood and bone vibrate with the need for action. "Let's go."

Back down the corridor, hand in clenched hand, navigating the unfamiliar dark again. But Misery doesn't need light to see. All she needs in the song in her veins. Like all space-fed settlements, Monkglass runs on holystone, layers upon layers of sacred material, but the call of her archangel is louder and clearer than any of that weakwater melody. Misery runs in its direction.

Bobbing alongside them, luminescent in the dark, Ruin says: "For what it's worth, your engineers were correct about the composition of the Heretic shield. Not that it matters now. You're just going to destroy the lead ship, aren't you?"

Destroy the lead ship, and they destroy Esse Temple. Forget the six-dimensional plans and DK ratios or whatever the fuck they're called. Sometimes the easiest solutions are the simplest. The archangel Misery will chew up the Heretics and spit out the bones, littering them across the stars like beacons, like flags of victory, proving to the Faithful that the nullvoid shall not prosper while the hand of the Demiurge moves.

Around them, Monkglass shudders to life. The lights come up, the station's lungs breathe again, and the HUD stutters back into existence. All around them a faint cheer goes up at the restoration of power. An expletive escapes the princess. They both have implants that Monkglass's system can track down in a heartbeat. "How far are we from the hangar?"

"Too far," Misery says. The archangel burns in her awareness like a supergiant, and that nova is several floors beneath their feet.

"So how fucked are we?"

Misery smiles. She shouldn't, but that emotion bursts from her anyway, that wicked curve like a blade. Layers and layers of holystone lie between them, pregnant with ability, just waiting to be awakened. "The real question is, how fucked are they?"

Lightning glows with a similar hunger. "Do it, then. Cut us through Monkglass. Show them the mistake they've made. Do it."

So Misery does. Down the corridor, a safe sprint away, stands a door bright-fenced by an aegis. Holy obsidian bracketing its frame. Misery reaches in. Wakes the stone. Pulls at the aegis until it expands and breaks, lashing out, dissolving wall and structure, lancing into the panels on the floor, which crumble like clay leached of all moisture. Through the gaping wound, sparking and hissing fluid, Misery sees more doors, more walls, more targets to eat through. She reaches out, the borders of her awareness growing, and pillows of holy obsidian light up across Monkglass's structure. Hers to manipulate. Hers to command. Again and again she bursts the bubbles of aegises and carves wormholes through the guts of Monkglass. Screams, destruction, the acrid punch of ozone. Just blips in the limitless velvet of her consciousness. She expands like a sun's corona, like a supernova's shock wave, and the more she cuts into Monkglass the more of it she feels and sees, until the station is a mere trinket in her grasp, a pearl against the oyster-flesh of her tongue. She closes her teeth as she wins access to the hangar where the other half of her lies imprisoned. A long way down for the frail human body, but nothing to an avatar of God, and Monkglass's gravity is stone-made and stone-maintained.

Lightning walks to the edge of the pit she's carved and peers down. "Long fucking fall," she says.

"I'm good at those." She strides toward her lover, the might of the cosmos in her every step. Opens her palm. "Hold on to me."

She sees in Lightning a blossoming of ecstasy, a lotus flower unfurling. Then they're plunging, hand in hand, off the serrated edge she's made, the gravity around them failing as Misery shuts it off. They're falling, and then they're floating, and below them their units wait for them, mouths open like baby birds.

Here's how the battle breaks down:

The archangel Misery bursts from the pulp of Monkglass into a universe in action, consumed by chaos. The Heretic siege-ships, alerted to the threat of the violent intruders, are on the move. A mortal observer might see nothing, just points of light arcing faster than usual across the vast distances of space, but the archangel Misery knows better. Zie perceives the cosmos with the clarity of the Forge, a distributed omnipotence that works in force and pattern, without thought and without language. The siegeships have broken their net, and all of them

sluice, piscine, toward a focal point. Their determination eluci-
dates their purpose. They are forming a shield.

At the center of their efforts, an unfamiliar shape lurks in
the folds of an inverse aegis. An enormous cabochon of synthetic holystone, finned and white like the legend of Leviathan
from Old Earth, hunted by the great demon Ahab. The *Edgeless
Blade,* Esse Temple's ship. The thing they have come to destroy.

The archangel Misery speaks to hir companion seraph
through the connection they share. Instructions given without
the use of words. The seraph will bait the Heretics while the
archangel Misery wakes the jump gate. No longer shackled by
the vise of the siegeships, the confection of carbon fiber and
holy bluestone is once again free to admit vessels of the Faithful.
Perhaps even an entire banquet.

The two units split, their paths diverging. The seraph
surges toward the slowly forming knot of siegeships, drawing
its blades as the enemy brightens with alarm. The archangel
Misery pulls a cloak around hirself, hiding from the *Edgeless
Blade*'s view the same way the *Edgeless Blade* is trying to hide
from hir view. But the archangel Misery is better at it. Zie will
not be detected.

The seraph's blade slices through the belly of one Heretic
ship as it sails past. A single touch, surgically applied over hidden points by a knowing hand. By the time the Heretic ship
realizes what happened it's already splitting apart, stonecores
melting, heat and light bursting through the incision. Then
there's no ship but a ball of furiously expanding holystone
shrapnel, a light in the void. But the seraph has long moved on.
It seeks out a second target, a third. It is more powerful than its
pilot can imagine.

The archangel Misery comes into the vicinity of the jump
gate, parked at the periphery of Monkglass's jurisdiction. Even
at top speed the journey has taken too long. The archangel longs
to join the fight. To wet its blades with the bile of the Heretics.

But no—backup is needed. After all, there are thirty-six enemy siegeships, and only two of them. Plus, zie wants to save the finishing blow for Ono Red-2. The archangel Misery wakes the ring of holy bluestone with the lightest touch, and hir soul shivers in resonance with the jump point as it inserts itself back into the universe-spanning network. Home at last, proud and glowing and blue. The archangel Misery sends a message through the portal, directed at the jump gate by Angelsteeth. *Come now. We are discovered; the Throne and the Lady Storm have betrayed us. We must destroy them all.*

Hir job done, the archangel plunges joyously into the fray. The seraph is swarmed by the siegeships, more than its hungry blades can deal with. The archangel Misery rolls, dives, swoops through the mighty freedom of space, weapons out, blades unseaming the siegeships with a touch. The vast nothingness fills with light and ozone and stone debris. And yet for every ship zie destroys, four more appear to harangue hir. They've gotten smart, too, dodging and rolling away from hir attacks. Firing their turrets. One such bolt crosses the skin of the archangel Misery's left hind leg, leaving a long, angry scar. A mere scratch from a moment of carelessness, but those shots can do real damage. The Heretics are merciless in their drive to destroy the sacred, after all.

They are struggling. A dozen of the siegeships have formed a net around their foul leader, the *Edgeless Blade,* leaving the rest of them free to hound the knights of the holy. The seraph is struggling: one of its legs is wounded and useless, and as the archangel Misery rolls to avoid another beam, zie watches two of those ships corral the seraph so a third can take aim. The bolt clips through its upper left arm. The pain it feels, the archangel Misery also feels, and the rage that blazes through hir should rip apart solar systems. But all it does is blind hir to the approach of another enemy. The archangel Misery dodges, but barely, and zie is spared not a second before another attack charges up, from another vector. These Heretics will not stop. They will not give their foes a chance.

The battle trembles upon a pivot of chaotic entropy, yawing back and forth, desperation cut with confusion. If the archangel Misery were human zie would be filled with rage and frustration, but hir elevated, sacred form knows no such fleshly weakness. Zie sees that it would be fruitless to eradicate the siegeships before taking on the *Edgeless Blade*. It would destroy them, and for what? They must hold on until the banquet of Angelsteeth arrives. Only then will the tides be turned—

The jump portal wakes, a shiver running through the cosmos, holystone connecting to holystone. Help is coming at last. They took their sweet time, the battle could have fallen the wrong way in the time it took to get them here.

Something's off. An imbalance of mass, a sense of something vaporous, a pulse of wrongness through hir systems. Whatever's coming through the portal isn't big enough to constitute a banquet, eight courses of eight dishes with four servings each. Something else is happening. Something else is coming through.

A series of blips shoot from the portal, dwarfed by that curving mouth. Three seraphs. A single, Cherub-class commanding ship. It's Dish Ono Red-2, and only Dish Ono Red-2.

Where is the rest of the banquet? As the archangel Misery rolls to avoid another bolt, zie considers that they have been betrayed. After everything, after all the promises made, after all the rallying and recruiting, the banquet of Angelsteeth has not come to hir aid. Has abandoned the fight against the Heretics. Has let hir down, at the most crucial moment.

So. The archangel Misery is alone, except for hir closest allies. Vastly outnumbered by the enemy. Betrayed by those in hir closest confidence, yet again. A lesser being—a mortal—might fall into rage and despair, and be distracted from their mission. Not so the archangel Misery, blessed with divine purpose. Zie has come to destroy the *Edgeless Blade,* and nothing can thwart hir purpose. There is a narrow opening where zie can strike at the Heretic leviathan, and zie must use it, even if it means sacrificing other things in hir path.

Zie transmits hir intentions to the seraph. An answering surge of understanding, determination. The seraph is committed to their shared goal. Even if it means death. Even if it means losing everything.

First, a feint. The two units shoot away from the hidden warship, sword arms blazing, as though in retreat or in pursuit of another objective. The siegeships, sensing victory, sensing the tide of the battle turning their way, surge forward, even the ones protecting the *Edgeless Blade*. They will destroy these strange, otherworldly mechs before dealing with the half serving that has just materialized. As a finale. As dessert.

Just as planned. When they've drawn the siegeships far enough, when the gap in the *Edgeless Blade*'s shield is big enough, the archangel Misery jumps. A micro-jump, a momentary shifting of the space-time continuum that displaces hir infinitesimally. Zie reemerges over the rear of the *Edgeless Blade,* straddling its spine, and it is here, over the beating generation core that powers the *Edgeless Blade,* that zie plunges the length of hir blades. Just like zie had before. The archangel Misery is no stranger to destroying Heretic ships. Now victory is certain.

Except the *Edgeless Blade* will not accept its doom. As the archangel Misery turns its spine to jelly, its guts shift. The ship writhes, slippery, and the stone of its skin pulses with powerful light. The blast catches the archangel and throws it backward, wrenching its blade free of the Heretic ship. What was that? Zie can't move. The consciousness of the archangel has been separated from its body, the two cleaved so thoroughly it's as if a galaxy lies between them, unnavigable and impassable. What void devilry is this?

The *Edgeless Blade* turns sideways and pops out of Newtonian existence. It too can micro-jump, reemerging a short blink away. It lists to one side, gravely wounded: the archangel Misery has left hir mark, at least. But now zie floats helpless, all eight limbs inert. Unforgiveable, what these Heretics have done. They must pay. But zie can't move. Hir rage is indescribable.

In another sector of the battle, something moves with great deliberation. The Cherub-class destroyer, under the command of Captain Sunyata Diamond, cuts through space at full speed, its destination fully clear. At its helm is the woman whose life was destroyed years ago, whose existence had lurched forward on featureless gray tracks until the Messiah Misery Nomaki had come and showed her grace and light. She once again had found hope. Once again had a direction charted on the map of her life. A reason to be, a purpose for existence. And Captain Diamond Sunyata has sacrificed enough to get here. Crossed so many boundaries she didn't think were breakable. She's conspired against the Throne. Lied and participated in sedition. Abetted those condemned to death by law, admired them even. And at last, when she least expected it, she betrayed the direct orders of a general—the order to hold back, to abort the mission they had planned together, the path she had affixed her entire soul to. Captain Sunyata Diamond is prepared to give her entire being to the fight led by Misery Nomaki. She has pledged it. Her crew has pledged it. And it will be done, no matter the cost.

Captain Diamond Sunyata sees that her archnemesis is wounded. She knows she stands no chance against this ship. She does not have the weapons to fight it one-on-one.

She also knows this is the only chance she'll get. If she wants to avenge her crew, if she wants to right the wrong that has darkened her life for the past five years, she has to act now.

The destroyer angles itself toward the gaping wound in the side of the *Edgeless Blade,* as though moved by the hand of the Larex Forge Hirself. This is a gift, the captain knows, this vulnerability in their inhuman and merciless enemy. She will do what needs to be done.

The hand of the Larex Forge cannot be denied.

Sunyata Diamond's ship plows nose-first into the side of the *Edgeless Blade,* destroying matter, igniting lines of stonecharge.

The generative core in Heretic ships is unlike anything known to the Empire of the Faithful. Unlike anything known in the shallow pools of human history. It does not simply explode. Thermal combustion could never dream of expressing the breadth and depth of what is lost when a generative core is destroyed. The *Edgeless Blade* folds inward, inverting reality, and for an infinitesimal moment a supermassive black hole hangs where the ship used to be. Pin-sized, a thousand angels dancing upon its surface. Then the charge reverses, and matter spews outward in a glorious ball of heat, a plasma soup resembling the expansion of possibility that birthed the universe.

The light fades, and in its wake: a haze of vapor and fragments of stone. The fate of survivors unknown. But the arc of Sunyata Diamond's life that spanned the hopeless stretch of time since her calamitous first encounter with Esse Temple has come to an end. In that cataclysm, in that bright flare, the archangel Misery saw the map of the cosmos, from its first seconds to its last, all of history and its infinite branching possibilities laid out before hir. Zie saw the face of God.

INTERLUDE 10

Thus it came to pass that the Messiah, Misery Nomaki, was taken into custody once again by the Faithful. The Siege of Monkglass was ended, but at what cost? Hundreds dead on the station itself, courtesy of the Messiah's fine carving. Several ships destroyed, including a flagship of the Heretics. One of the finest minds in the Empire of the Faithful, dead. The sedition exposed, the whole of the Empire's military and bureaucracy thrown into disarray.

How did this come to be? Despite the lashings of fate that held them together, despite the tool they had in their Heretic prisoner, the outcome of the siege was something they did not predict. Could not have predicted. Such is the way of the universe. The best-laid plans of gods and geniuses defeated by the unknown on the regular. Chaos rules over order. In the Siege of Monkglass, the Messiah and their seditious band worked off bad intel. The Heretic, it seems, provided outdated information—no? Even if what he said was truth to him, wasn't it? As far as he knew, siege mechanisms were supposed to be double-blind. Schroedinger shields are double-blind. It's how the technology works. It's why sieges were so rare even during the days of active war, hot and seething. Would you risk the maneuver knowing that you could not look in, just as they could not look out? I did not think so.

Things, however, are no longer that way. The Heretics, with their disregard for the sanctity of holystone and other artifacts, make new toys of them every so often. In the five years the Heretic spent in the lightless suffocation of Faithful custody, the Heretics found a way to tunnel through the siege shield. This was the technology deployed at Monkglass. The Lady Storm and Esse Temple had been in contact all this time. The Lady Storm and the Throne had been in contact all this time. All this time, all this time. All this time . . . the tense political maneuvering behind the siege—all that saber-rattling, all that plumage-puffing—had been transparent to Monkglass, the station at the center of it. They were not crying out for help. They never were.

No, it was no mere coincidence that led Misery Nomaki to Monkglass. You might already have guessed the answer. The ansible bond between the Lady Storm and her sibling, the Archbishop of Remus—those early childstone experiments resulted in their being linked across any separation of space and time. I do not think they were aware of this connection, themselves. Misery Nomaki's abilities allowed them to access this link after they met the Archbishop. Pyrex Imogen did not even realize they were being used as a conduit.

So, was this ordained? You tell me. You do not believe in these things, do you?

You can only imagine the problems caused by the lifting of the Siege of Monkglass. The fragile balance of power between Heretic and Faithful flipped on its head, the tenuous acceptance between them shattered in an instant. The Faithful blamed for not keeping one of their own in check, for plotting to end the siege even though agreements had been thumbprinted between the two sides. A stew of accusation and recrimination thick as golden syrup. The Church and Throne equally afraid of losing control of the narrative within the Empire. The coils of an enormous, glittering and slippery mess lay before them, and none of the sides involved wanted responsibility for it. Wouldn't it be better if they just averted their eyes? Wouldn't it be easier to simply push the problem out of the airlock, and pretend that none of the transgressions happened?

And that is how the mess fell into your lap. Your problem to tease apart now. To do whatever you so desire with. As a form of curiosity. As a form of restitution.

Am I wrong?

34

There is a cell, cold and dimly washed in blue light. There is a door, fortified by plastic and metal instead of an aegis, things Misery can't yet bend to her will. A wide scoop of Monkglass has been excised of its holy obsidian, the gravity within an echo of the pull from other floors, and in the middle of it is Misery Nomaki, prisoner of the Faithful. A ring of brushed aluminium circles her ankle, tethering her to the ground. She floats in a bitter haze, furious and alone. Imprisoned. Hungry. Unsure of her future. In these cowardly actions she can taste the fear of her captors, afraid that she might once again casually gut the station to escape their grasp.

They should be. If she could, she would.

In its final blow the *Edgeless Blade* disabled her archangel mech with its dark magic, locking Misery from the unit's controls. She, the bearer of the Larex Forge's greatest gift, was reduced to a mere spectator as her captain's ship met its fiery end. Could only watch, helpless, as the remaining siegeships aided the scattered servings assigned to Monkglass in rounding them up. Dragged them back to the hangar and pulled them from their units at gunpoint. All the pilots survived: she, Lightning, Spider, Ghost. She remembers watching rage boil in the princess, furious and violent, as she was shackled. The disbelief and despair rising in Spider, as though a pipe had burst. They were pumped full of salves to keep them docile, enough brain-fuzzing chemicals she can't feel her hands and feet. They marched her to her cell that way, she a synth model in a video plaza, someone rigging her arms and legs, correcting the unsteadiness in her walk cycle.

Misery replays these memories over and over, hoping that divine insight will come to her and show her the seams where things went wrong, where the treacheries of the void seeped in and cracked the foundations of their plan. Over and over she has been betrayed by those whose loyalties should have lain with the Larex Forge, but had turned away from Hir light and embraced the chaos of the nullvoid. She catalogues them, picking at the edges of each wound:

—The Emperor and the Throne, mealy-mouthed cowards with their desire for reconciliation;

—Jericho, full of sweet lies and a heart of deceit, whom she trusted too easily, who used her weaknesses to fool her over and over again;

—The Lady Storm, repaying her sibling's love and devotion with slick treachery;

—General Tsung, who had seemed so receptive to her message, whom she had thought the most reliable ally in this fight against evil, who had abandoned her at the most critical juncture, and she doesn't even know why.

The cosmos itself works against her. The forces of entropy and madness twist the shape of events against the will of the Larex Forge, thwarting Hir hand and disrupting her path. She understands now the lengths to which the servants of the nullvoid will go in this war of theirs. She was complacent; she will be no longer.

At least she's alive. Her mission is not over. She has accepted, fully and truly, her role as Messiah. Chosen of the Demiurge. An honor that she was chosen for before she was born, when she was no more than a glimmer in the eye of the universe. As long as she lives, she will continue to fight for Hir. For the Larex Forge.

They've taken her mother's amulet from her. She was not al-lowed to retrieve it from the flesh of the archangel mech. There's a hollowness in her where the negative weight of its absence resides. She doesn't know how she's going to get it back. She must get it back. Among the many other things she needs to do.

Movement at the periphery of her vision: the angel Ruin flickering into existence at the edges of her cell. There's something ephemeral about hir glowing form, a kind of translucence or lack of solidity, as though zie were merely a projection. What's different this time? Misery wonders if the angel's appearance is a hallucination, another trick played by the Heretics or an artifact of the salves they've tried to dull her mind with. But Ruin tilts hir head, birdlike, and Misery knows that this is the same creature that has guided her throughout her journey. So insufferable she thought hir a manifestation of voidmadness. But her journey has taught her humility. Taught her tolerance and magnanimity. And Ruin's appearance here is a welcome one, although she senses there's something different about this meeting.

"You guess correctly," Ruin says. "I suspect that we will soon come to be parted. But it is no matter. My job here is done, and I am satisfied. What path unfolds beyond this will be entirely up to you."

Is it the doing of the Heretics? Or the will of the Forge? What unfolds will be entirely up to her, zie says. Misery considers the slender figure of the archangel, the crossed arms and the shapely calves, the eyes glowing triumphant in that sculpted face. She has grown almost fond of the angel in their time together. Hir help, which she rejected at first, turned out to have led Misery right at every juncture. Even as she sits locked in a cell, she's grateful for that, a fact that surprises her. But Ruin is right. Hir job was to show Misery the way, lead this wayward child of the Demiurge back to the destiny she forsook. Having guided her from the path of voidmadness and toward the light, hir job is done. Misery has grown her wings. Now she must find the wind on her own.

Ruin laughs one more time, teeth shining like glass chips. "You have a heart of diamond, Misery Nomaki. I have no doubt you will set out to accomplish whatever it is you desire."

—+—

Sometime later—a thousand, two hundred and sixty-two breath cycles later—the cell door opens. Framed in the white light is Commander Ashe's unmistakable figure, flanked by several guards in faceplates, untagged and unlabeled, names and genders a mystery. "The Lady Storm has asked for you," the commander says.

Floating in her cold prison, Misery says: "Is she not afraid of what I might do?" She gestures widely to encompass her surroundings, the station scalped and neutered so she can't turn it against them.

Ashe's lips tighten, and Misery hears the echoes of the arguments they've had with their boss. They think this is a stupid idea too. But the Lady Storm insisted. "She thinks you can be reasoned with," they say, and the emphasis in their sentence makes clear that they don't. But Commander Ashe has little choice. An order is an order. If they defy it because they think they know better, they'll be no different from the traitors they've imprisoned, will they?

Misery smiles slyly. "I'll be good," she says. "I promise." She's curious about the Lady Storm's desires. And she craves exit from this dismal shell of nothingness, where she can do nothing but marinate in her fury.

Commander Ashe stares dead at her. "Your promises mean nothing to me." But they escort her out of the cell anyway.

On the outside, Monkglass is a station riven by disaster: lights at half strength, constructor drones busy at some distant site, their presence known through the staccato noise of their labors. Misery has been cut off from Monkglass's system, but she

imagines that overlay of pop-up hell, with its chipper determination and uplifting tat, readjusted for a much different tone. The
armored guards form a box with Commander Ashe in the rear
and Misery in the center. As they march, the muzzles of their
weapons make a hungry cage around her. If Misery breathes the
wrong way, she's dead. They barely need an excuse: the rage that
emanates from them has the clog and volume of boiling steam.
Misery welcomes this danger. She has always thrived in it.

She is not afraid.

Her path is shorter than her previous journey between hangar and command center. The simple corridors melt into a
bright, wide space: a multi-floor conjugation of steel forms and
pale stone. A medical center. Chlorine laces the air. The convoy marches across the polished, markless floors with Misery
embedded within, and with every step she feels the Grace and
will of the Forge within her. Between the examination rooms
and the clear box of a surgical nave stands a series of salvation
tubes filled with nanocrit plasma and the suspended shadow
of a human patient. Their trajectory heads toward the singular
figure that stands before it, clad in a generous sheath of mourn-
ing white. The Lady Storm Mirelle, head bowed in grief and
contemplation. A ghostly veil spills from her crown. As they get
closer the shapes in the cloudy liquid begin to resolve, and Misery's chest squeezes as she recognizes the one in the tank she
holds vigil at. That crop of hair, with the patterns in it. Esse
Temple somehow survived the collision and explosion, and now
hangs loosely in the tube, an exchanger clamped over the lower
half of her face. She's been burned: raw pink extends over her
skin in wide swatches. And there's deeper damage: bites of flesh
replaced by molds of viscous gel, the protective stone ribs of a
regenerator closed over half her torso. Her left leg ends at the
knee.

It's not fair that Esse Temple survived after all she's done.
Why is she here, when Diamond isn't, or any of the people she's

murdered? The cruelty of the universe astounds Misery sometimes. She tried her best to enact justice, and still she failed.

No—she's lying to herself. She spent so much time rejecting
the role she was chosen for. Didn't commit to the role until far
too late. She lacked in faith. Who's to say things might not have
gone better if she'd wised up earlier?

She knows better now. She won't be so callous next time.

"They're here," Commander Ashe says, quite unnecessarily.
The Lady Storm has been brightly aware of their approach. She
turns to face Misery as the convoy of guards dissolves to take
up watchful positions on the periphery. Her face is hollower
and colder than Misery last saw, the skin around the eyes faintly
bruised. Silence follows as she studies Misery, glancing over the
lines of her face and form with the intensity of a scientist exam-
ining a specimen. The events of the past day deeply punctured
her, draining all the rage from her being. All that's left is a sad,
empty shell.

She says: "I learned what you did on the Capital. All those
people you killed. You are a dangerous creature, Misery Nomaki. If I had known, I would have been more cautious."

Misery tilts her head. It's not the main point, but: "You've
been in contact with the Capital?"

"I have. We were never out of contact, so to speak, but I suppose the pretense is over." A laugh dry as pure acid. "The siege
is over. I suppose you did what you came to do after all. In a
fashion."

Not at all. Misery came to Monkglass to annihilate the Heretics. That did not happen. Still she says, "You've been in contact with the outside world all this while. The siege was a lie
concocted by the Throne."

An alarmed look. "Of course not. The siege was a real siege,
if you must know. Even if we were allowed contact with the
Capital, it was very limited. No more than a few minutes a day.
No supplies in or out either. But I was in contact with Esse, and
she in turn in contact with her superiors. So I knew the tenor of

the negotiations that were happening between both our sides. It was a tense period. The negotiations were extremely delicate. The last thing we wanted was for it to end in violence."

Misery huffs air. "You judge me, when you were consorting with the enemy? You wouldn't know hypocrisy if it nailed you in the ass."

The Lady Storm looks at her with both pity and sadness, which Misery didn't ask for and doesn't want or need. She came peaceably because of her curiosity, and because she thought she might sugar-talk her way out of this. But now she knows that's impossible. There is no negotiating with someone so compromised with the nullvoid.

Eventually, the woman turns away to contemplate, once again, the tube holding Esse Temple. When she next speaks it's wistful. "We met twenty years ago, Esse and I. During the Truce of Logan. I was an ambassador's attaché, she was a cadet in their diplomatic program. We were instantly drawn to one another: same odd family background, same sense of humor, both of us transwomen. It was a strange time, a hopeful time. Peace seemed almost within reach. And we were both young, and foolish . . ." A moment of quiet. "Separating at the end of the summit was the hardest thing I've ever done. Since then I have never loved anyone as much."

Lost in her recollections. Who benefits from this? Misery gets a sharp impression of the Lady Storm's memories—the nights spent together, the jokes shared, the hope in their impressionable young minds. Tales as old as time. She cares nothing for these details, filled in by her imagination. So Esse Temple seduced her at some point. So what? A monster is a monster no matter what sweet face it puts on.

Still the Lady Storm goes on. "When her fleet arrived, when she hailed me, when I saw her again, after so many years—I too thought it was a sign. Relationships between our two sides had deteriorated so much since the truce. She'd even become a major villain in our telling of things. Yet hope persisted. Rumors

that the Throne had been working hard to secure peace with the
Heretics. When Esse arrived—when I was told not to engage,
to let the siege continue in peace—I genuinely believed it was a
sign from the Larex Forge. I had so much hope, so much joy that
I had been denied for the past twenty years . . ." Her narrative
runs dry, and she looks at Misery sadly. "If only you knew what
you destroyed."

"I know," Misery says. "My only regret is that I didn't destroy
enough."

A sigh, a giving in to the inevitable. "Come with me," the
Lady Storm says, beckoning with a finger. She walks and Misery
follows. The circle of guards tracks with her position. Their destination is a tube several columns downwind. Misery blinks in
surprise: she also recognizes the person suspended in the nano-
plasma. The diminutive frame, the cottony shock of hair, the
pixie-ish features. Tank.

"We found your colleague in the wreckage of the ships," says
the Lady Storm. "By some miracle, she's still alive."

Misery wants to close her fists in anger, but forces herself to
stay still. The Lady Storm's actions seem like a threat: *We have
something precious to you, vulnerable in our hands.* "Why are you
showing me this? What do you want from me?"

"I thought you would be glad to know she's alive."

The Lady Storm radiates sincerity, but still Misery peels her
lips back from her teeth. "Your attempts at emotional manipulation are pathetic. Do you understand why Diamond did what
she did? The Heretics aren't our friends."

She sighs, heavy with a great and unnameable sadness. "It
was an accident, you know."

"Oh, I'm sure."

"It's the truth, like it or not. What happened to your captain's crew, years ago . . . Esse's ship was new, they didn't quite
understand its mechanics yet. She was trying to leave. The ship
was giving her problems, technical problems, she didn't want to

engage in battle. But the jump didn't work right. She dropped
in the middle of the seraph cluster. An accident. She never intended to do it." A shake of the head. "Her superiors . . . They
made her a hero. She kept saying it was an accident but they
didn't want to hear it. Didn't want to believe it. Propaganda is a
terrible, soul-consuming beast. It haunts her, those deaths. She
kept bringing it up, over and over. I could not get her to stop."
She looks at Misery, full of sorrow. "Believe what you wish. You
never knew the real Esse, the person behind the name on all the
waves." Pensiveness overtakes her. "Your captain . . . I wonder.
If they had met, if they could have talked, would she have
forgiven her?"

"She would never." Flames shoot through Misery's veins at
the very thought. "You never knew her either. Some things are
not forgivable."

In the Lady Storm's face she sees the closing of a door. She
too has realized that there is no compromise to be had here, no
portal that can cross the warped gulfs that lie between them.
Whatever closure or reconciliation she wanted, she will not get.
She bows her head. "To be honest, I have forgiven you for what
you did to my station, Misery Nomaki. I know I will be better at
peace not holding a grudge. In truth it is not my place to pardon
you. That will be up to the Emperor and the Throne. Tomorrow
a ship comes to take you and the Imperial princess back to the
Capital for judgment."

Misery's fingers vibrate. "And what's your purpose in telling
me this? To emphasize that if I'd rolled over for you, you would
have put in a nice word with those shitbirds?"

She folds her hands over her belly and turns away. "I thought
perhaps talking to you might shed some light on why things
happened the way they did. I thought I might find some answers. But I've clearly wasted both our time."

And that's it. Misery won't get anything useful out of this
meeting. Except this: she's out of the cell. She's surrounded by

holystone. It's now or never, if she's making a break for it. She curls her hands as she reaches outward, seeking the closest disc of holy obsidian she can find—

The Lady Storm twists around, face drained of all color, as if she's just read Misery's mind. "Stop her!"

How—? Taken by surprise at being caught, Misery doesn't break into a lunge until it's too late. Something fires, something hits her in the back of her neck, a small sharp snap like an angry finger flicked. Misery stumbles, and then the floor is rising toward her. Impact on her chin and her vision bursting into black nebulas. Her legs, she can't move her legs, and in fact her whole body is deadweight. She can't draw breath, can't turn her head. Poison? A paralytic? What have they done to her?

Boots surround her and block her whole field of vision. Someone wrenches her arms behind her back and cold envelops her wrists, locking them in place. Not that it's needed. She can't move, she can't do anything. The world is muted, muffled. This is some ultrasalve they use on the dangerous condemned, something experimental that's dulling her mind so much she can't even stonebend.

"It didn't have to come to this," says the Lady Storm from somewhere above her. She sounds less angry than sad. "I'd hoped to understand you, Misery Nomaki. But there's no reasoning with this kind of hate."

If Misery could answer, she'd say: *You don't understand. You don't know what the nullvoid does. One day you'll find out why you're wrong. One day you'll be sorry.*

A ship comes to take them to the Capital as promised. Misery, heavy and sickened with salves, lets a flock of soldiers drag her from cell to hangar, where a boxy shuttle in Imperial red waits to transfer her to a ship. She can't fight them. Time has melted. Has it been days or weeks since she failed her mission? She doesn't know and has no way of telling. After that meeting with the Lady Storm, she's been repeatedly filled with drugs that slow her down and dull her mind until she can barely hold a thought in that fog. Walker jeans keep her moving from the waist down, without which she would crumple like a pile of cotton.

She can't hear the song of holystone any longer. For as long as she's had memory, she has nurtured their soaring melodies in her breast. Now those voices have fallen silent and that absence rings without cease, a tinnitus of the soul. It's like the organs have been plucked from her body, leaving a weak-walled flesh husk behind. This is the work of Heretics, carried out by those who call themselves Faithful. She will never forgive this betrayal.

There's another prisoner bound for the ship, tall and slender and spitting fire as they tug her in directions she doesn't like. The Lady Alodia Lightning hasn't been given the VIP salve treatment like Misery has, possibly because she's been better behaved. Misery's heart kicks up in joy: even in this low moment, she is not alone.

Across the field of harsh white light the princess catches sight of her. Instant joy on her face, and fresh determination: she's found a reason to fight again. She elbows a guard and makes a sprint forward. "Misery!"

The muzzles of a dozen weapons snap upward to block her way. An armored hand pulls her back by the shoulder as its owner barks, "No talking! March forward!"

Lightning slings her shoulder free, defiant and angry. No one tells her what to do. She takes another step and the closest soldier raises hir gun, ready to fire.

The princess narrows her eyes. "You wouldn't dare." She's been treated relatively well since capture, and she's maintained that core of arrogance, without which she wouldn't be Lightning.

Even here, even in these circumstances, her family name protects her.

Standing at the door to the waiting shuttle, Commander Ashe says, "You may not be disposable, but your friend is. Bear that in mind."

Lightning hesitates. Maybe she can call their bluff. But is it worth the risk? If she's wrong, Misery's dead. Is she sure enough to take another step? She isn't. The potential cost is too high to bear.

She locks eyes with Misery across the space that separates them. Even from afar she can tell something's amiss in Misery's deflated posture and dull eyes. She knows the bastards running this station have done something to her. After all, she's had plenty of experience with being unwillingly slugged to void depth on salves. Plenty.

If only Jericho's lies about telepathy were real. If only Misery could read minds and project thoughts like he said. Then she could shed the cruel distance between her and Lightning and let her know that she's sorry things happened this way. She's sorry things didn't go as planned. But she's not giving up. Not now, not ever. Her crusade against the Heretics has only just begun.

Lightning's eyes widen as though she heard, as though she understood what Misery thought. As though the telepathy thing worked, the way Jericho said it did. But instead of questioning it, on her face descends a fierce tenderness, a promise that she feels the same. What she said, back in the healing chamber, about their lives being tied from start to end. She meant it. Wherever Misery goes, there she will be. She has dedicated her entire life to their shared cause. Nothing will come between them, nothing is strong enough. Her brother can try. He will fail.

Then their moment of respite ends and the furious guards wrench Lightning away, hauling her back onto trajectory and shoving her forward. Misery knows they will be kept away from each other during the long journey back to the Capital. As they are marched into the gums of the shuttle she realizes she doesn't even care if Jericho had been right. She's not alone. There is hope in the future. That's what matters.

CODA

Stories repeat themselves over and over, the curl of narrative finding familiar patterns to fall into. We end the way we started: with Misery Nomaki imprisoned in the Capital, a raft of offenses to their name, and a clash of opinion on what to do with them. Locked in a dull saint-proofed room and stripped of all their possessions, even their mother's amulet, Misery Nomaki had no access to the rolling avalanche of events shaping the world around them. The lifting of the siege had undone the delicate balance between Heretic and Faithful, putting under threat the ongoing peace negotiations and tilting the balance heavily in favor of the Heretics, who, after all, saw the destruction at Monkglass as an affront, a breach of the agreement they had clandestinely struck. These dynamics, I am sure, are well known to you. You were privy to the arguments that occurred between the Emperor and his grandmother and their generals and the Church, and envoys from the Heretics, patched in from afar, played a five-sided game of tug over the fate of this so-called Messiah. You likely know how Major Reyes, in exchange for protecting xer lover the Duke, testified against General Tsung, pinning the blame of sedition upon them. You have probably heard that Pyrex Imogen escaped blame, for no one could get an accusation to stick to them. They were not present when the Messiah launched toward Monkglass, after all. And I am sure you know how it all played out. The Throne, eager to rid themselves of embarrassment, wary of the narrative power contained in the archangel mech, agreed to hand it, and its pilot, over to the Heretics. Other compromises were extracted from them as well. But you would be more suited to tell those stories than I.

Of course, I cannot know for sure what the Messiah said or thought while they were incarcerated. But I have spent long enough time with them that I can extrapolate the workings of their mind and perhaps muddle to an approximation of what happened. Indulge me my fancies, if you will. I imagine Misery Nomaki, in their cell, dissecting every moment of their life in the past few months, shattering memory into the finest shards and turning every glittering incident over and over in the light, seeking fault and meaning that they could make a lesson out of. I imagine they spent long hours in prayer, sorting through gospel and psalm from childhood, trying to glean from it guidance, meaning, clarity. Perhaps they succeeded, and found their heart filled with light and resolution. Or perhaps they did not, and they continue their search still.

But oh, allow me one more indulgence. Let me imagine what happened the day after, when the Faithful finally had the Messiah delivered to the enemy. This is beyond the scope of my knowledge, I know. This is pure speculation. But in my time with the Messiah they have become dear to me; I have grown so fond of them. And so have you, I imagine. Let me put myself in their shoes as they are woken by the Imperial guards and taken down the shining, twisted silver corridors of the Capital. The Ninth Messiah Misery Nomaki walks without a spring in their step, despite the subgravity; in their heart they wonder what fate they are being led to. Has the Throne decided upon execution? Does a cold metal chair await them at the end of this journey, flanked by the unfeeling faces of doctors? Perhaps they are to be subjected to a lifetime of experimentation, like Sower Cabbage, like others they met on Angelsteeth. Or perhaps they are to be pardoned. They cannot know, and so they keep moving forward as they are wont to do. Here, they are brought to the lower decks of the Capital. Here, they are being led into a hangar where waits for them the strangest ship they have ever seen, an angular, rough-hewn rock with no windows, streaked through with red translucence like ruby. A Heretic ship. The Imperial guards hand custody of the Messiah over to a pair of Heretic guards in their birdskull masks. Misery Nomaki, cuffed in plastic, is brought up the ramp of the ship and into the maw of the first Heretic ship they have ever boarded. It is as dark and sloping and ineffably strange as they have imagined, and it looks just like the glimpse they had of Esse Temple's ship. The ship, if even possible, seems bigger on the inside, comprising slanted corridors that seem to fold upon themselves. Misery Nomaki is sure they have walked two lengths of the hangar when they finally arrive at the cell that is to be their new home. And there, in the depths of the alien visage that is to be their new normal, they stop, heart hammering, half-bewildered and half-amazed. For in front of them stands the man they were sure they would never see again in the flesh. Jericho Malturin smiles at them, and it is clear he is in charge here. How the tables have turned. In his hand is the amulet Misery Nomaki's mother found on a distant asteroid in the months before they were born. In the moment before they are shepherded into the cell, in the moment before the red-stone of the ship closes over the hole where a door should be, Jericho Malturin says: "Hello again, Misery. I think this time we should get to know one another properly."

EPILOGUE

And so we come to the end in the same place we started, in the desert that has no name, an arena where time has no meaning, a place where a story has been told. It hangs between our two figures like the ribs of a divine beast, and in its wake they reckon with the path that they have chosen. The roles that they have played. The wind has fallen silent as though it too has been listening, and is now part of the narrative, woven into place.

The smaller of the two figures steps back from hir companion. "There," zie says. "That is all you wanted to know. Were your questions answered? Are you satisfied?"

The tall man, thin as a rail, doesn't answer immediately. He sinks onto the weathered nacelle of an old constructor mech, and sighs. Thoughts and events cloud his mind. "Yes to the first," he says, "and no to the second."

The smaller figure—who at one time called hirself an angel, a messenger, an emissary of the Larex Forge—merely tilts hir head, content to let hir companion take all the time he needs.

"For every question answered, I have five new ones in their place," says the tall man. "I thought it strange, too coincidental, the way events played out. I even thought, from the cold of the cell on Rootsdown, that there might have been some truth to Misery's claim she was being guided by divine insight, but that was mostly you—wasn't it, Ruin? As well as other convergences. There's a psychic bridge between the Archbishop and their sibling, isn't there? One which she got sucked into."

The creature called Ruin simply says: "If that is what you believe, then that is what you believe."

Jericho shakes his head and laughs. "Ah. To think I imagined

you would give me a straight answer." Another moment of contemplation. "I wonder if Misery believed me about the telepathy, in the end? I tried to tell her, you know. But she's a stubborn
one, isn't she? No one can convince her of a truth she doesn't
sell herself."

"All that you've seen is all that I know," Ruin says. "With that,
do you think they did?"

"Hmm. In my hearts of hearts, I do think so." He gazes into
the distance and allows himself a brief flare of hope, which dims
like a candle. "I suppose I'll find out."

"They are a difficult one," Ruin says. "Hard to sway when their
mind has been made up."

"And yet you directed her very well." Jericho hefts a disc
of stone in his hand, the facsimile of a real object that forms
the heart of an archangel mech that a woman once found on a
stone-scrimmed asteroid. "You judge me for the lies I told, but
why didn't you tell her the truth? About what you are. About
what you did to her."

"They found their own truth. Is that not more valuable than
one simply given to them?" The creature named Ruin folds hir
arms behind hir back. "My only desire was to reunite with the
mech I was made for. Everything else I simply observed."

"You lie even to yourself." Jericho laughs softly. "I think I am
beginning to understand why our ancestors were afraid of artificial intelligence. All these things which happened because of
your curiosity."

Ruin looks toward the horizon of the desert, where the wind
is once again starting up. The Heretics' programming simulates
weather quite admirably. "Is there one among us who has not
behaved badly in this tale?"

"Touché."

Silence once again settles between them. Jericho tosses the
pretend-amulet in his hand. The real thing sits several rooms
away under glass and aegis, a locus of intense interest, both
precious and terrifying. His mind is swamped in thought, which

would drag him from the clear waters of clarity and into the depths where no logic can penetrate. He mustn't get ahead of himself; much work remains to be done. His gaze traces the patterns inscribed over the amulet. "It's strange," he muses. "All these years we have struggled to make this alien tech more amenable to human biology. But we went about it the wrong way, didn't we? It's us that needed to change." He smiles, and allows anticipation to fill him once more. "I think we will learn a great deal from studying the genesis of Misery. I quite look forward to it."

ACKNOWLEDGMENTS

The process of writing this book was a long, long slog that spanned many years, a global pandemic, and deep troughs of despair. Many accompanied me on this journey, and I am grateful that you did.

This book would not be what it is without my editor, Lindsey, whose insight, support, and unbridled enthusiasm for the project kept me afloat. My agent, DongWon, spent years patiently guiding me through the process of revising this book, with multiple complete restarts. Devi Pillai saw the potential in the submission draft and took it on despite how much more work it needed. Thank you for believing in me.

Sing Lit Station provided me time and space to write during the Jalan Besar residency in 2018 and, subsequently, a co-working space. The National Centre for Writing in Norwich, UK, provided a rest point between drafts.

Most of all I owe a debt to the many queer and BIPOC writers who are my community. Because of you, I feel less alone and more empowered to weather the challenges that come with bringing a book into the world. Your presence, encouragement, and successes are everything to me. Particular thanks go to Miri Baker, Nino Cipri, Emma Suyenaga Candon, Kate Dollarhyde, Athar Fikry, Grace Fong, Nilah Magruder, Nicasio Reed, Nibedita Sen, Kellan Szpara, Suzanne Walker, and Alyssa Wong—thank you for being there as I kept rolling that boulder up the hill, day after day after day.